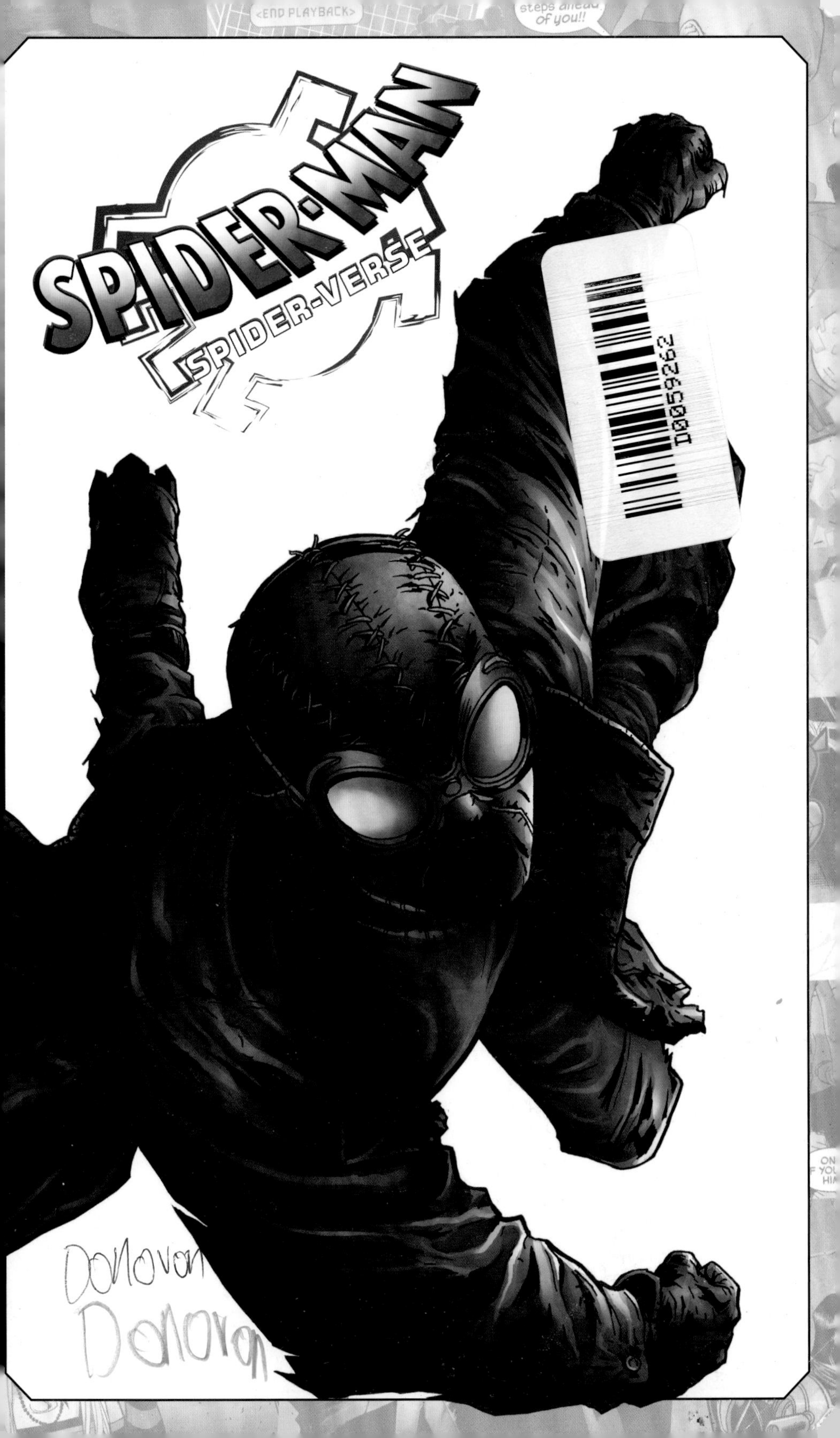
SPIDER-MAN
SPIDER-VERSE

SPIDER-MAN
SPIDER-VERSE

SPIDER-MEN

SPIDER-MEN #4-5

WRITER: **BRIAN MICHAEL BENDIS**
ARTIST: **SARA PICHELLI**
COLOR ARTIST: **JUSTIN PONSOR**
LETTERER: **VC'S CORY PETIT**
COVER ART: **JIM CHEUNG
& JUSTIN PONSOR**
ASSISTANT EDITOR: **JON MOISAN**
ASSOCIATE EDITOR: **SANA AMANAT**
EDITOR: **MARK PANICCIA**
SPECIAL THANKS TO DAN SLOTT

EDGE OF SPIDER-VERSE #1

WRITERS: **DAVID HINE**
WITH **FABRICE SAPOLSKY**
ARTIST: **RICHARD ISANOVE**
LETTERER: **VC'S CLAYTON COWLES**
ASSOCIATE EDITOR: **ELLIE PYLE**
EDITOR: **NICK LOWE**

SPIDER-HAM 25TH ANNIVERSARY SPECIAL #1

"PETER PORKER, THE SPECTACTULAR SPIDER-HAM MUST FACE THE MENACE OF... THE SWINESTER SIX!"

WRITER: **TOM DeFALCO**

ARTIST: **JACOB CABOT**

COLOR ARTIST: **EMILY WARREN**

"WHY NOT HAVE SPIDER-HAM BE A HUMAN?"

WRITER: **TOM PEYER**

ARTIST: **AGNES GARBOWSKA**

LETTERER: **JARED K. FLETCHER**

COVER ART: **JOE JUSKO**

EDITOR: **TOM BRENNAN**

SUPERVISING EDITOR: **STEPHEN WACKER**

EXECUTIVE EDITOR: **TOM BREVOORT**

EDGE OF SPIDER-VERSE #5

WRITER: **GERARD WAY**

ARTIST: **JAKE WYATT**

COLOR ARTIST: **IAN HERRING**

LETTERER: **VC'S CLAYTON COWLES**

COVER ART: **JAKE WYATT**

ASSOCIATE EDITOR: **ELLIE PYLE**

EDITOR: **NICK LOWE**

SPIDER-MAN CREATED BY STAN LEE & STEVE DITKO

COLLECTION EDITOR: **JENNIFER GRÜNWALD** ASSISTANT EDITOR: **CAITLIN O'CONNELL**

ASSOCIATE MANAGING EDITOR: **KATERI WOODY** EDITOR, SPECIAL PROJECTS: **MARK D. BEAZLEY**

VP PRODUCTION & SPECIAL PROJECTS: **JEFF YOUNGQUIST** SVP PRINT, SALES & MARKETING: **DAVID GABRIEL**

BOOK DESIGNER: **JAY BOWEN**

EDITOR IN CHIEF: **C.B. CEBULSKI** CHIEF CREATIVE OFFICER: **JOE QUESADA**

PRESIDENT: **DAN BUCKLEY** EXECUTIVE PRODUCER: **ALAN FINE**

SPIDER-MAN: SPIDER-VERSE — SPIDER-MEN. Contains material originally published in magazine form as SPIDER-MEN #4-5, EDGE OF SPIDER-VERSE #1 and #5, and SPIDER-HAM 25TH ANNIVERSARY SPECIAL. Fifth printing 2019. ISBN 978-1-302-91418-9. Published by MARVEL WORLDWIDE, INC., a subsidiary of MARVEL ENTERTAINMENT, LLC. OFFICE OF PUBLICATION: 135 West 50th Street, New York, NY 10020. © 2018 MARVEL No similarity between any of the names, characters, persons, and/or institutions in this magazine with those of any living or dead person or institution is intended, and any such similarity which may exist is purely coincidental. **Printed in Canada.** DAN BUCKLEY, President, Marvel Entertainment; JOHN NEE, Publisher; JOE QUESADA, Chief Creative Officer; TOM BREVOORT, SVP of Publishing; DAVID BOGART, Associate Publisher & SVP of Talent Affairs; Publishing & Partnership; DAVID GABRIEL, SVP of Sales & Marketing, Publishing; JEFF YOUNGQUIST, VP of Production & Special Projects; DAN CARR, Executive Director of Publishing Technology; ALEX MORALES, Director of Publishing Operations; DAN EDINGTON, Managing Editor; SUSAN CRESPI, Production Manager; STAN LEE, Chairman Emeritus. For information regarding advertising in Marvel Comics or on Marvel.com, please contact Vit DeBellis, Custom Solutions & Integrated Advertising Manager, at vdebellis@marvel.com. For Marvel subscription inquiries, please call 888-511-5480. **Manufactured between 6/26/2019 and 7/23/2019 by SOLISCO PRINTERS, SCOTT, QC, CANADA.**

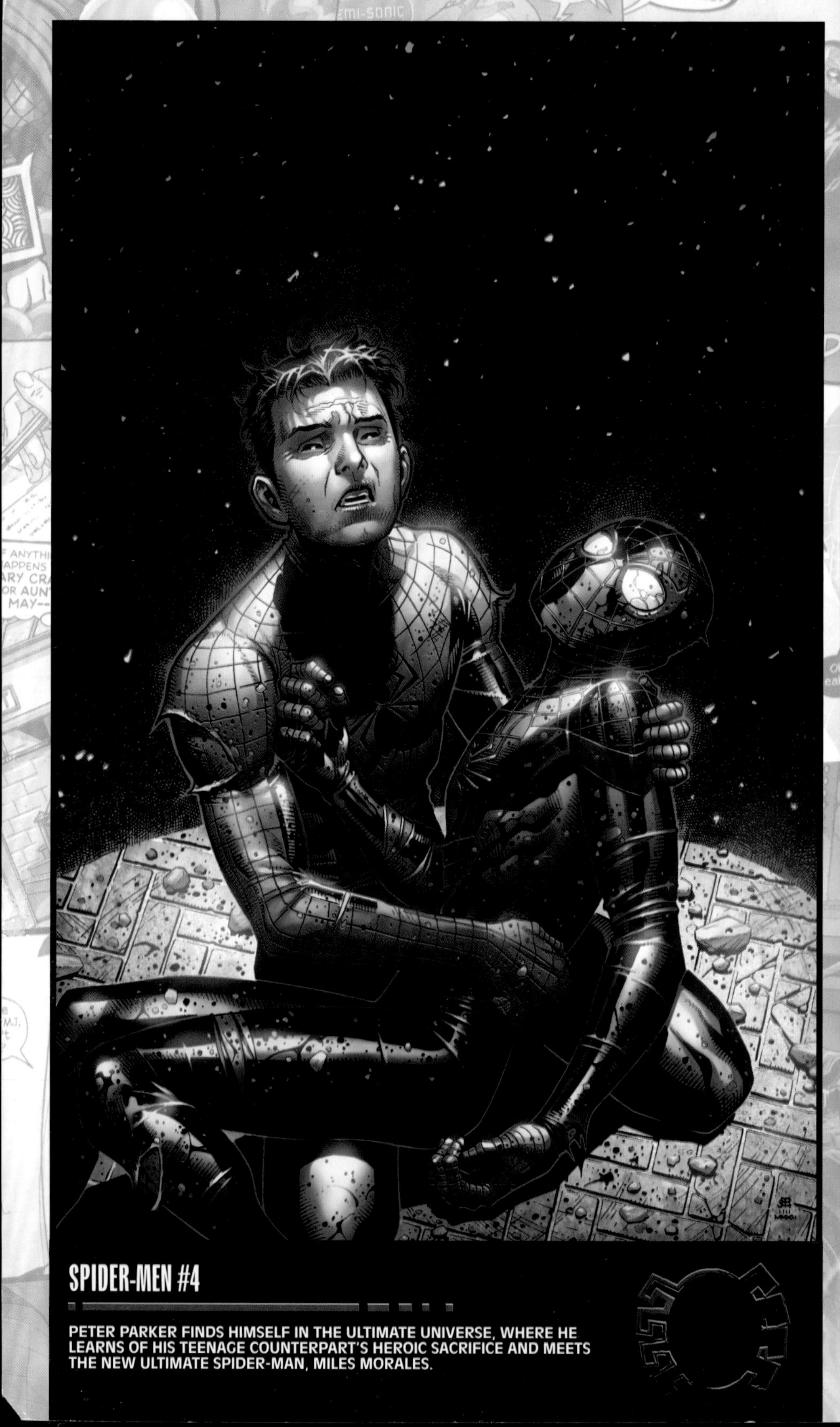

SPIDER-MEN #4

PETER PARKER FINDS HIMSELF IN THE ULTIMATE UNIVERSE, WHERE HE LEARNS OF HIS TEENAGE COUNTERPART'S HEROIC SACRIFICE AND MEETS THE NEW ULTIMATE SPIDER-MAN, MILES MORALES.

EBIPEDIA
VEB-BASED ENCYCLOPEDIA

LEVANT ARTICLES

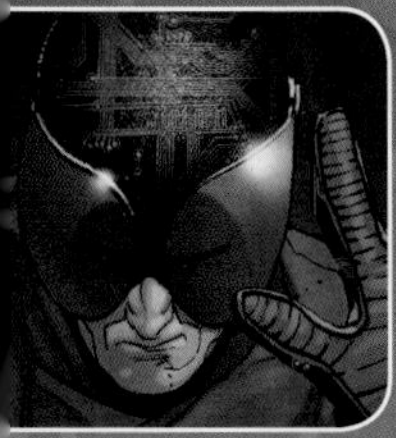

MYSTERIO

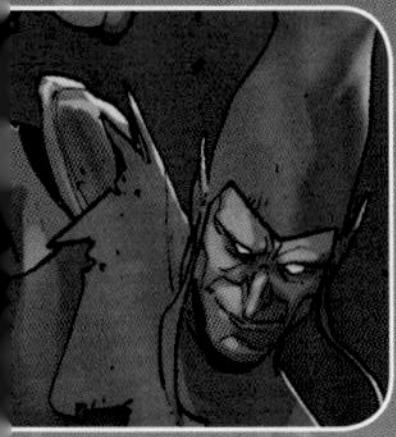

ALLUCINATIONS

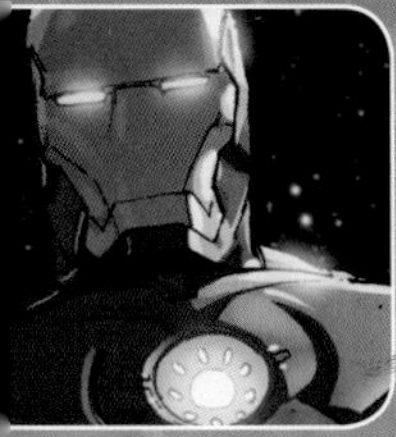

IRON MAN

ARTICLE | TIMELINE | ARCHIVE | SPIDER-MEN

THE AMAZING SPIDER-MAN

From Webipedia, the web-based encyclopedia.
"Peter Parker," "Avenging Spider-Man" and "616 Spider-Man" redirect here.

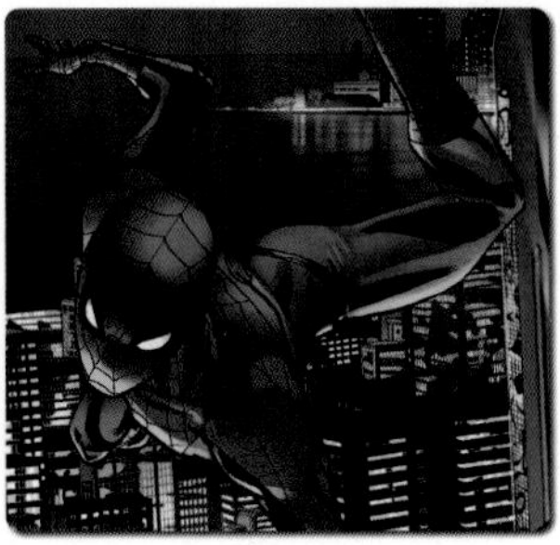

While attending a demonstration in radiology, high school student Peter Parker was bitten by a spider which had accidentally been exposed to radioactive rays. Through a miracle of science, Peter soon found that he had gained the spider's powers and had, in effect, become a human spider! From that day on he was...

the AMAZING SPIDER-MAN

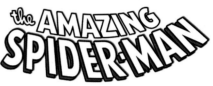

THE ULTIMATE SPIDER-MAN

From Webipedia, the web-based encyclopedia.
"Miles Morales," "All-New Spider-Man" and "1610 Spider-Man" redirect here.

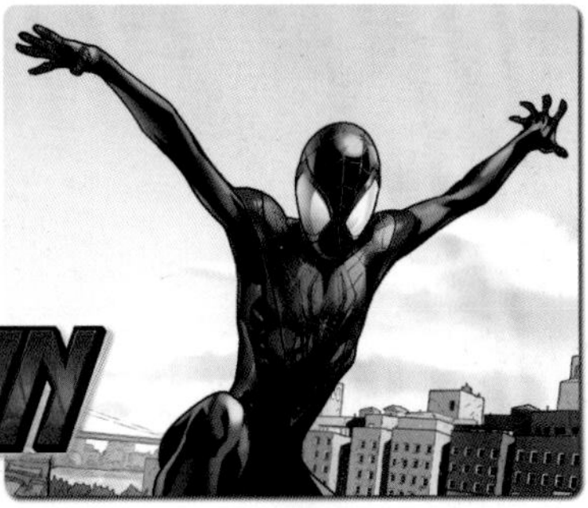

In a world where Peter Parker is dead, grade schooler Miles Morales is bitten by a stolen, genetically altered spider that grants him incredible arachnid-like powers.

He has chosen to dedicate his life to the legacy of Spider-Man. He is...

ULTIMATE SPIDER-MAN

PREVIOUSLY

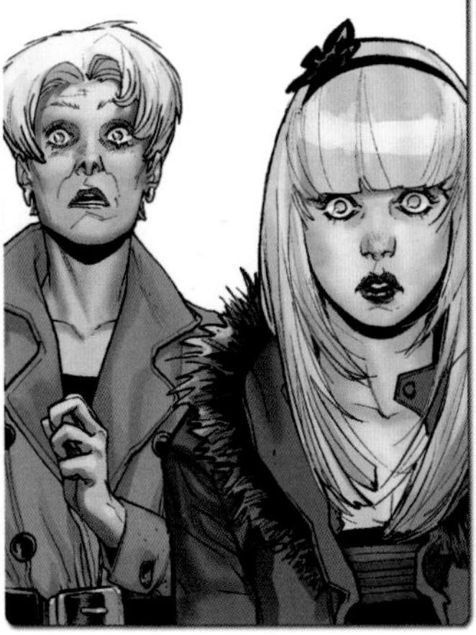

Peter Parker, the Amazing Spider-Man, stumbled upon arch nemesis Mysterio's hideout and discovered the villain was manipulating a dimensional portal. With the use of an avatar, Mysterio was building a criminal empire in a different dimension. The two enemies fought and Spider-Man was accidently transported to the other universe.

On this parallel Earth, Peter Parker was a teenage Spider-Man and had been killed in a vicious battle against a group of super villains. Inspired by this heroism, a young boy named Miles Morales took the mantle of Spider-Man.

Mysterio attempted to kill them both, but the Spider-Men defeated him. The avatar is now in the custody of Nick Fury and the Ultimates. While they try to figure out how to get Peter back to his home dimension, Peter explores this world and ends up on the front lawn of a stunned Aunt May—the woman who raised...him.

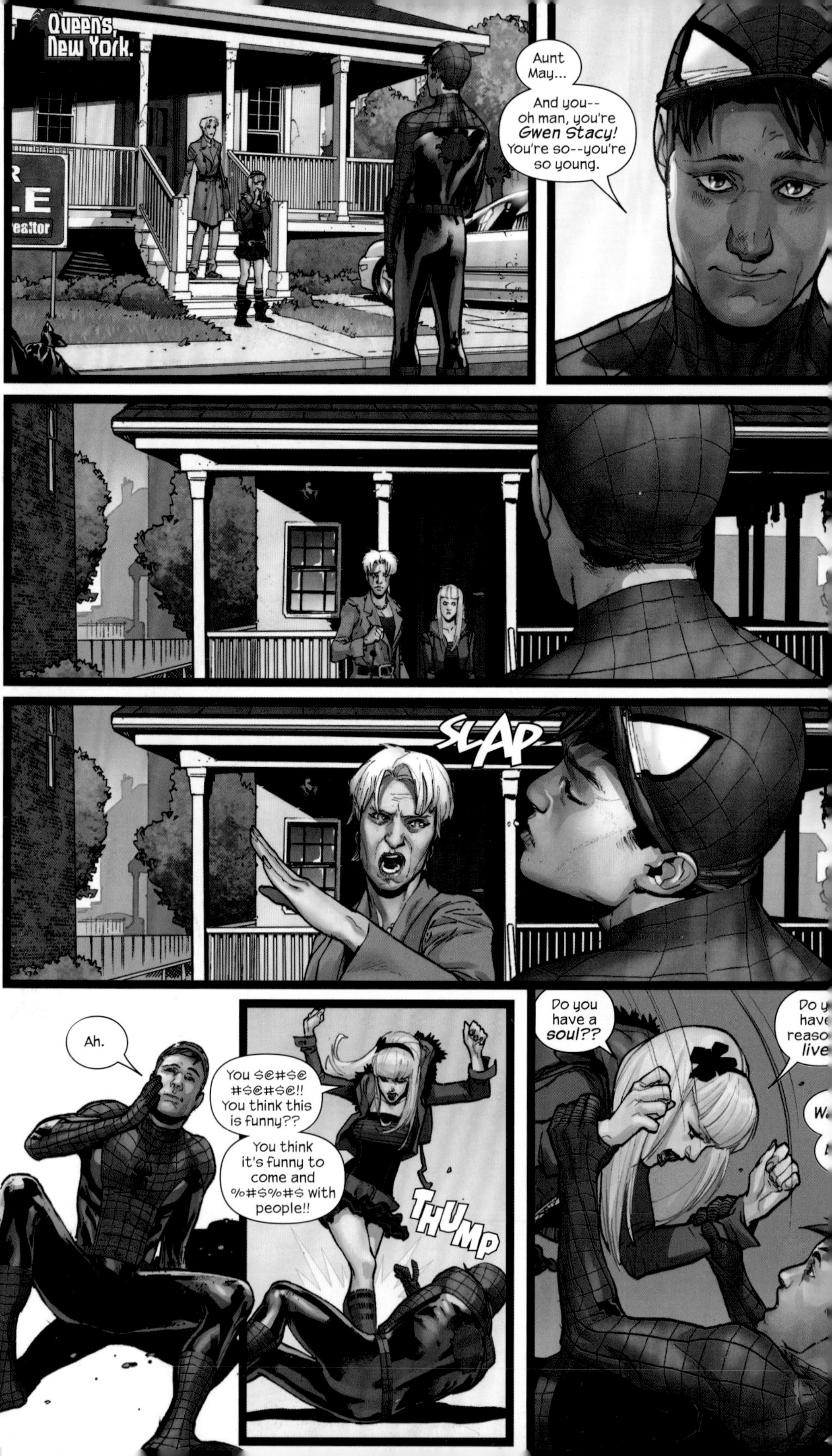
Queens, New York.
Aunt May...
And you-- oh man, you're Gwen Stacy! You're so--you're so young.
SLAP
Ah.
You $@#$@ #$@#$@!! You think this is funny??
You think it's funny to come and %#$%#$ with people!!
THUMP
Do you have a soul??

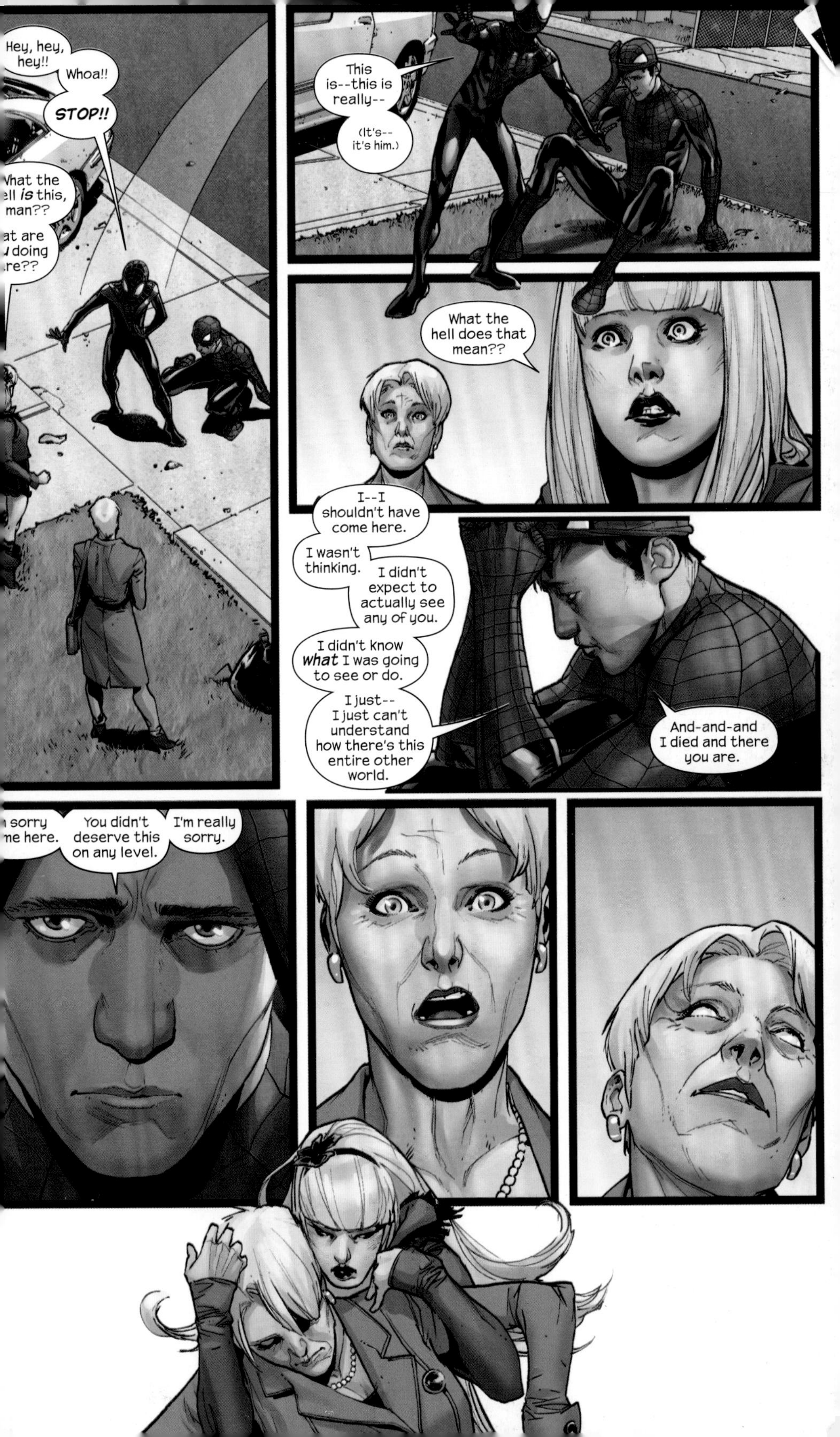
Hey, hey, hey!!
Whoa!!
STOP!!
What the hell *is* this, man??
What are you doing here??
This is--this is really--
(It's--it's him.)
What the hell does that mean??
I--I shouldn't have come here.
I wasn't thinking.
I didn't expect to actually see any of you.
I didn't know *what* I was going to see or do.
I just--I just can't understand how there's this entire other world.
And-and-and I died and there you are.
I'm sorry I came here.
You didn't deserve this on any level.
I'm really sorry.

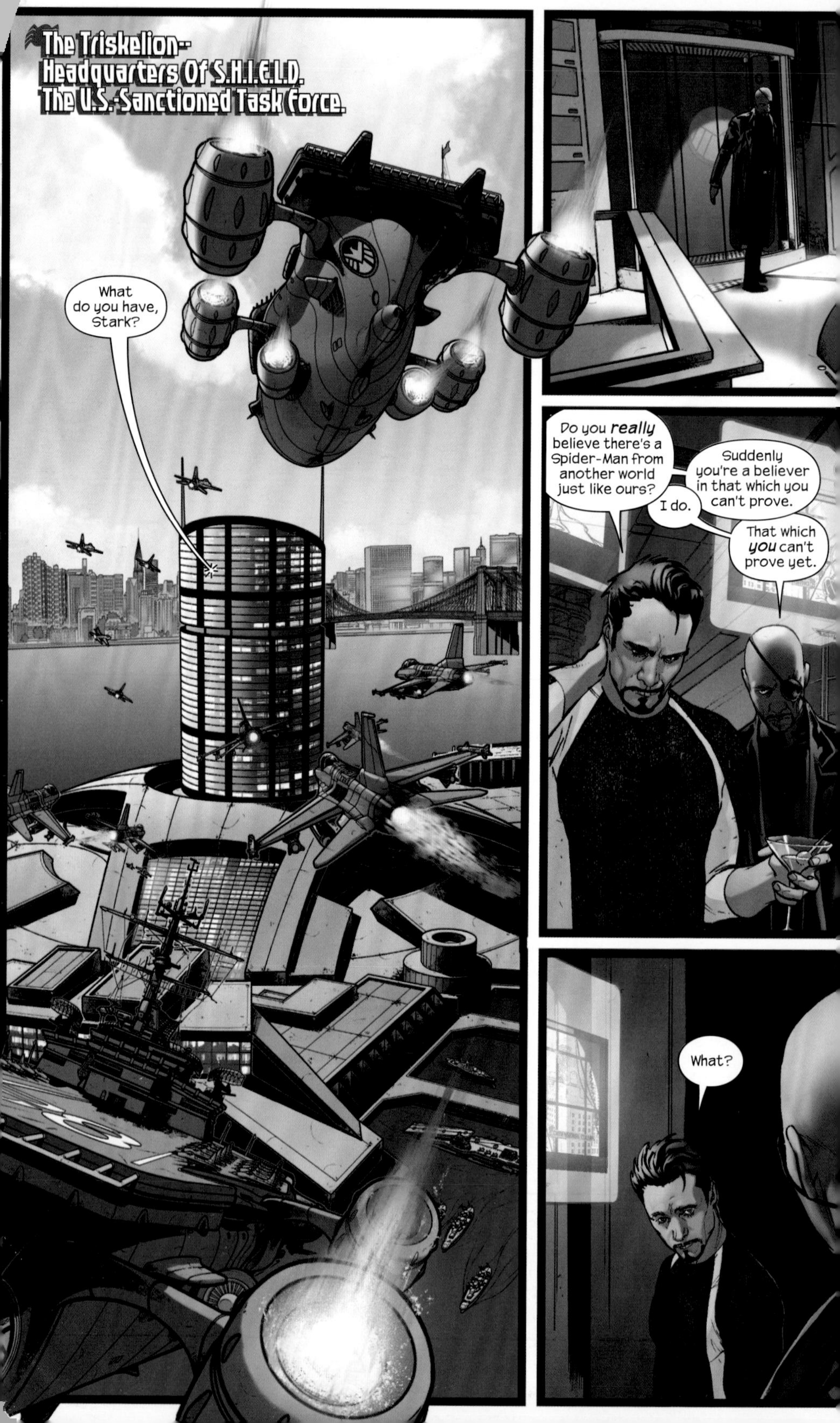
The Triskelion--
Headquarters Of S.H.I.E.L.D.
The U.S.-Sanctioned Task Force.
What do you have, Stark?
Do you really believe there's a Spider-Man from another world just like ours?
I do.
Suddenly you're a believer in that which you can't prove.
That which you can't prove yet.
What?

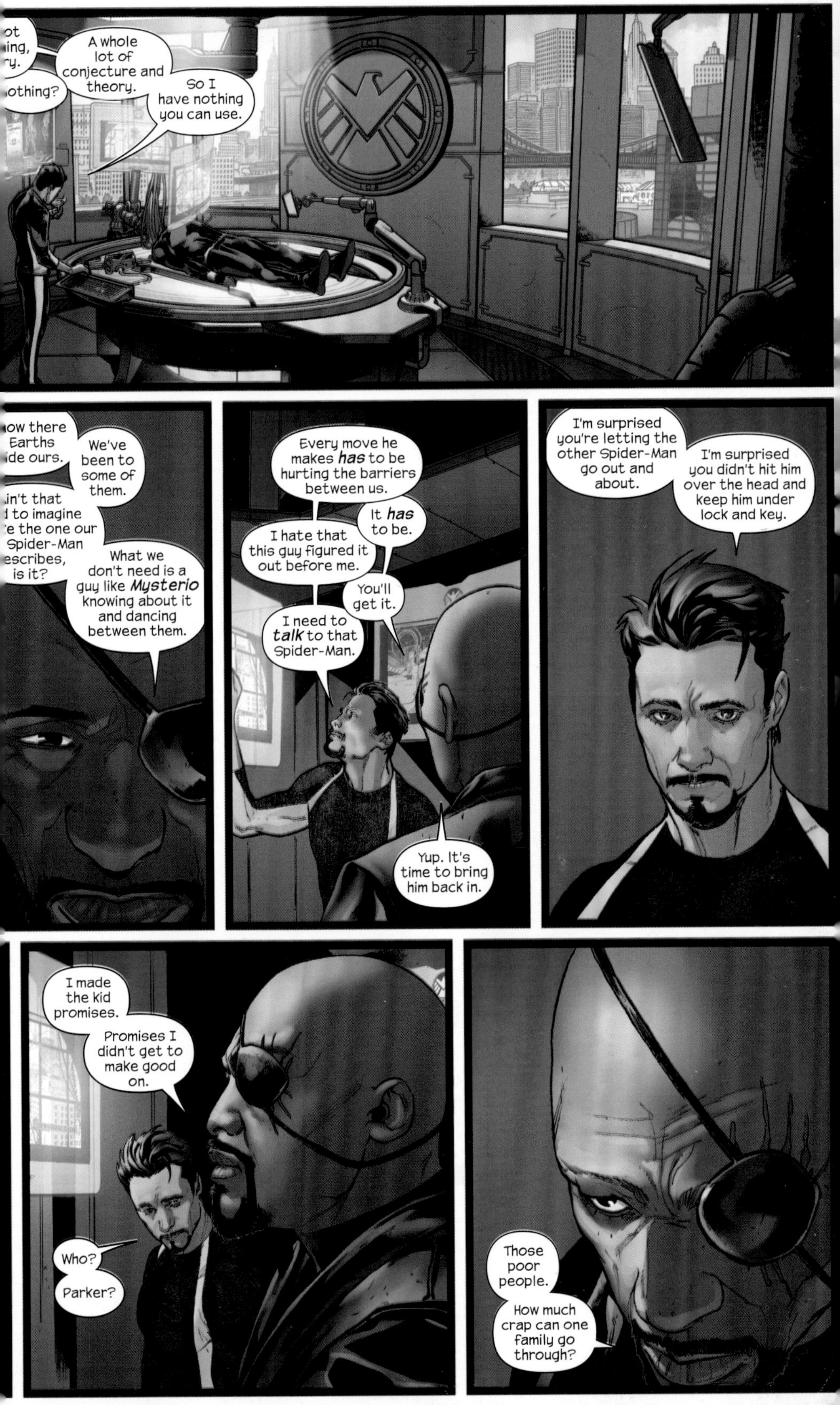

ot
ing,
ry.
othing?
A whole lot of conjecture and theory.
So I have nothing you can use.
ow there Earths ide ours.
We've been to some of them.
in't that d to imagine e the one our Spider-Man escribes, is it?
What we don't need is a guy like *Mysterio* knowing about it and dancing between them.
Every move he makes *has* to be hurting the barriers between us.
It *has* to be.
I hate that this guy figured it out before me.
You'll get it.
I need to *talk* to that Spider-Man.
Yup. It's time to bring him back in.
I'm surprised you're letting the other Spider-Man go out and about.
I'm surprised you didn't hit him over the head and keep him under lock and key.
I made the kid promises.
Promises I didn't get to make good on.
Who?
Parker?
Those poor people.
How much crap can one family go through?

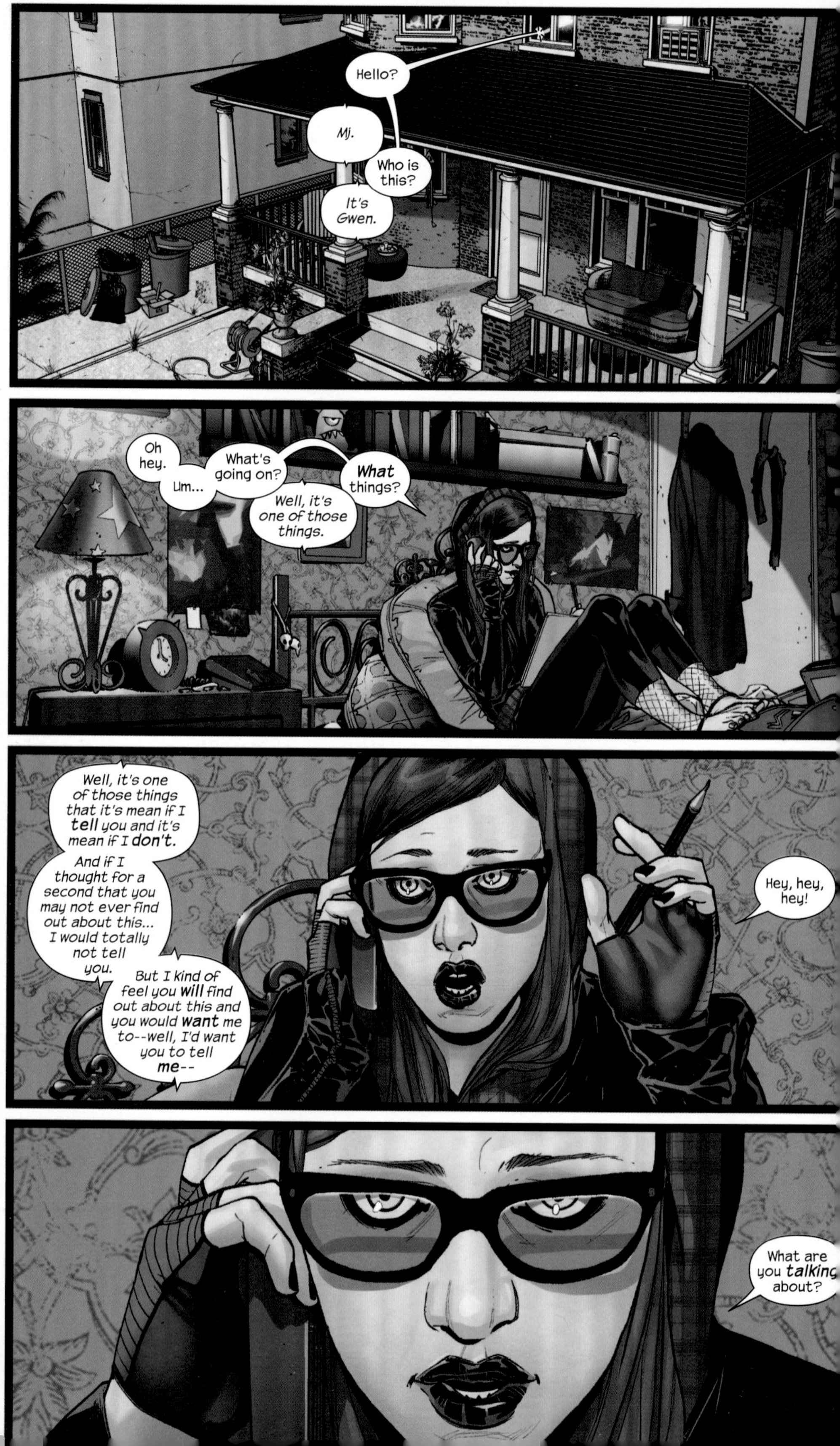

Hello?
Mj.
Who is this?
It's Gwen.
Oh hey.
Um...
What's going on?
Well, it's one of those things.
What things?
Well, it's one of those things that it's mean if I tell you and it's mean if I don't.
And if I thought for a second that you may not ever find out about this... I would totally not tell you.
But I kind of feel you will find out about this and you would want me to--well, I'd want you to tell me--
Hey, hey, hey!
What are you talking about?

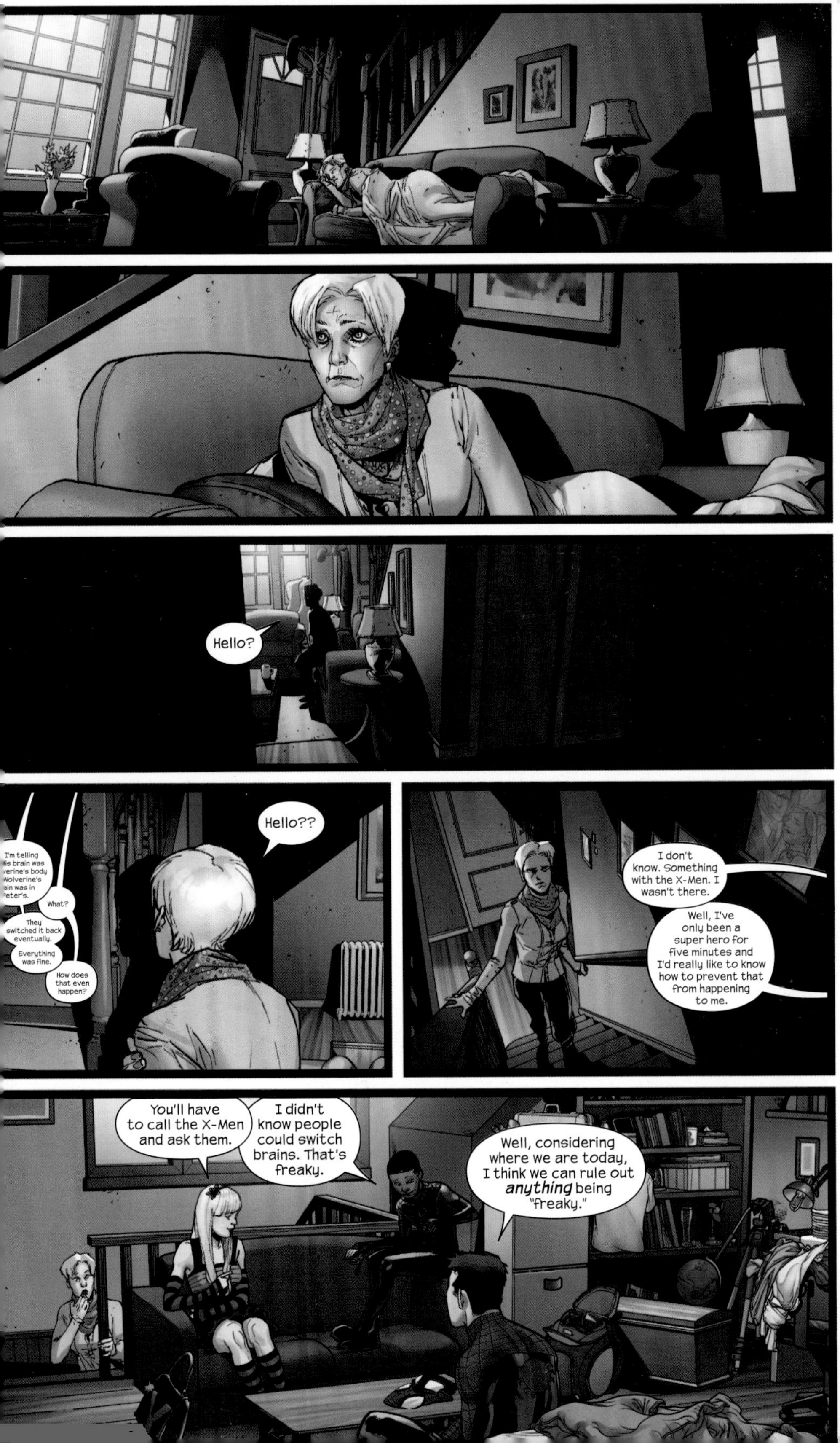

Hello?
Hello??
I'm telling is brain was erine's body Wolverine's ain was in eter's.
What?
They switched it back eventually.
Everything was fine.
How does that even happen?
I don't know. Something with the X-Men. I wasn't there.
Well, I've only been a super hero for five minutes and I'd really like to know how to prevent that from happening to me.
You'll have to call the X-Men and ask them.
I didn't know people could switch brains. That's freaky.
Well, considering where we are today, I think we can rule out *anything* being "freaky."

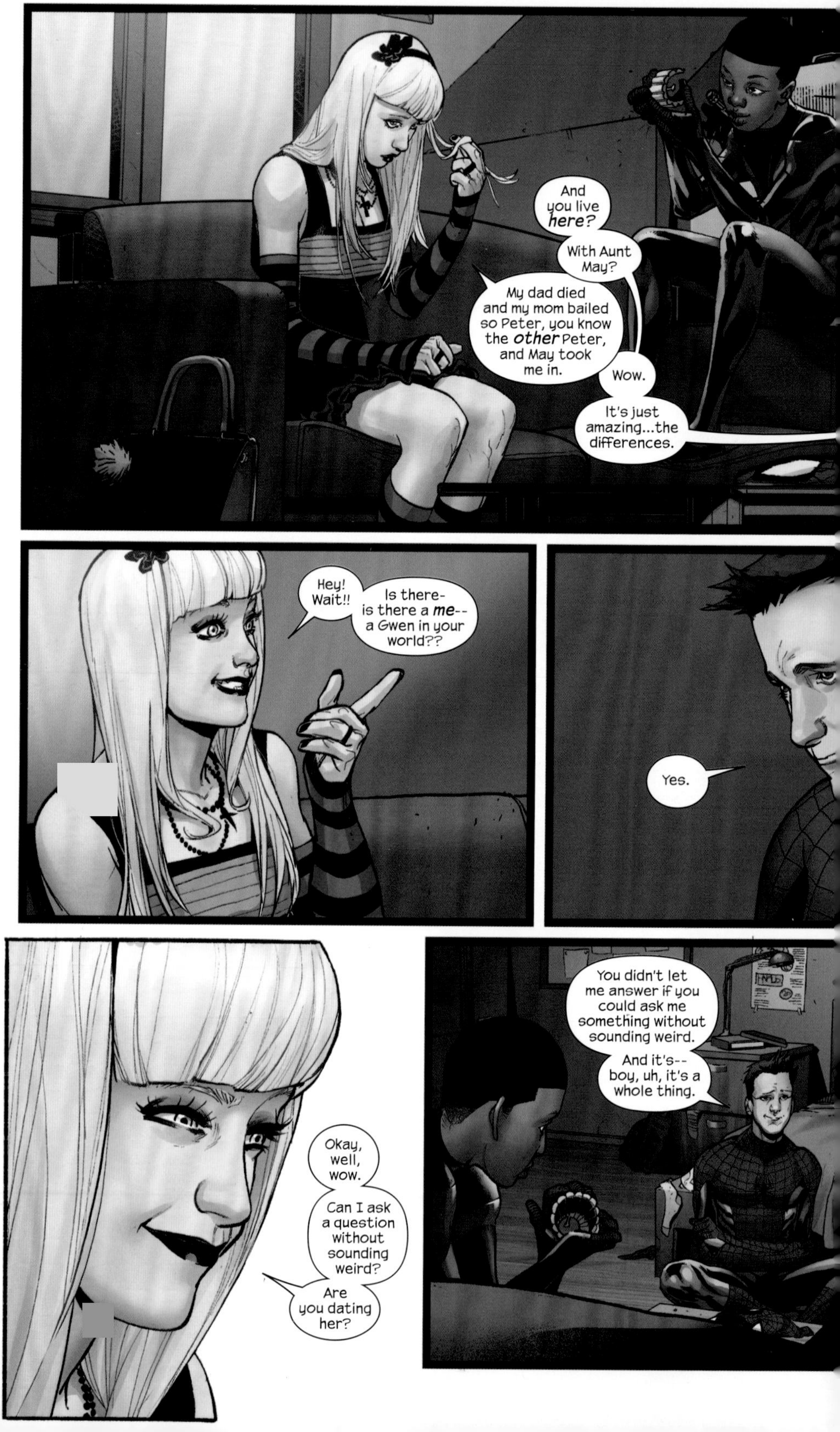
And you live *here?*
With Aunt May?
My dad died and my mom bailed so Peter, you know the *other* Peter, and May took me in.
Wow.
It's just amazing...the differences.
Hey! Wait!!
Is there- is there a *me*-- a Gwen in your world??
Yes.
Okay, well, wow.
Can I ask a question without sounding weird?
Are you dating her?
You didn't let me answer if you could ask me something without sounding weird.
And it's-- boy, uh, it's a whole thing.

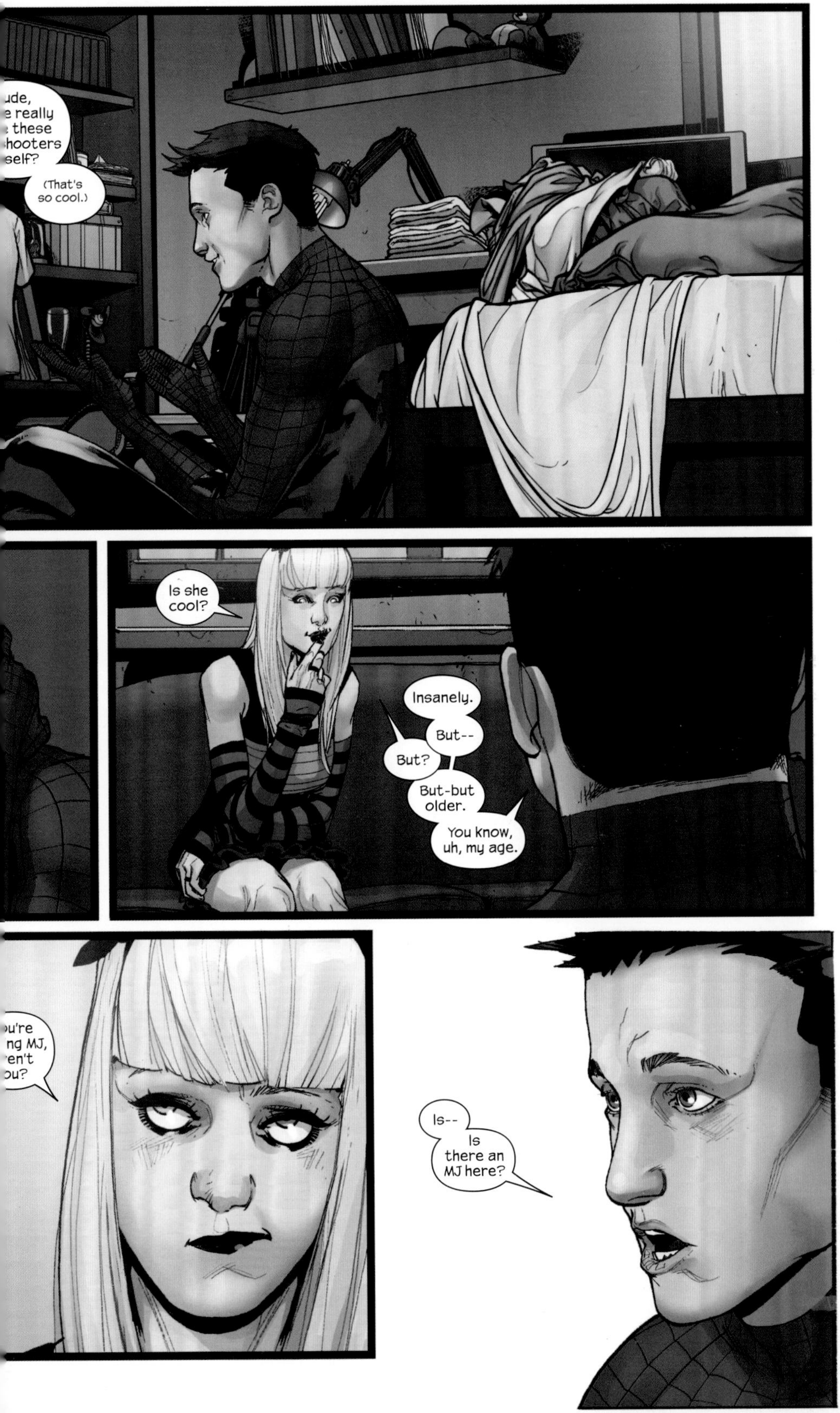
ude, e really these hooters self?
(That's so cool.)
Is she cool?
Insanely.
But--
But?
But-but older.
You know, uh, my age.
u're ng MJ, en't ou?
Is--
Is there an MJ here?

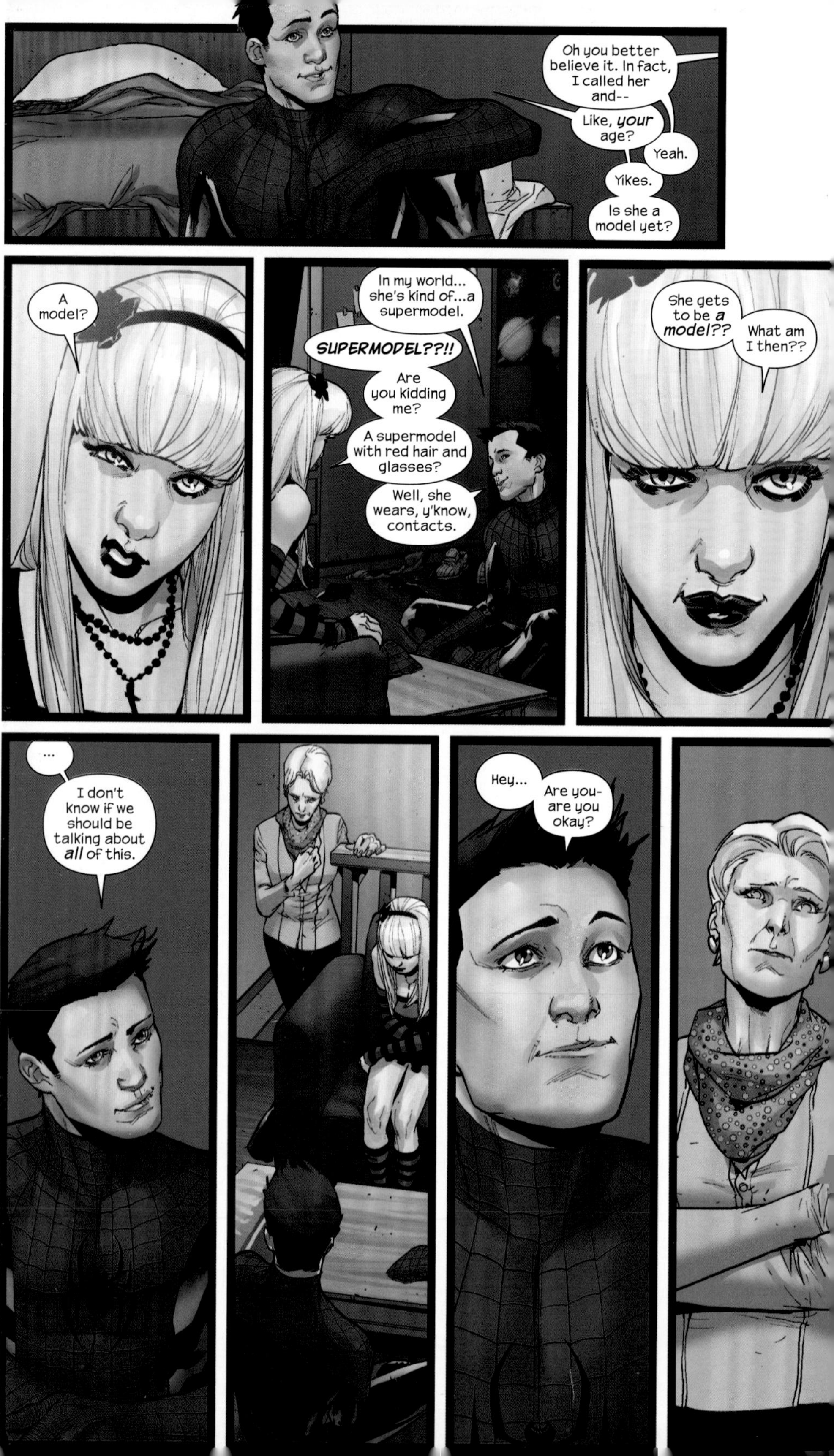
Oh you better believe it. In fact, I called her and--
Like, *your* age?
Yeah.
Yikes.
Is she a model yet?
A model?
In my world... she's kind of...a supermodel.
SUPERMODEL??!!
Are you kidding me?
A supermodel with red hair and glasses?
Well, she wears, y'know, contacts.
She gets to be *a model*??
What am I then??
...
I don't know if we should be talking about *all* of this.
Hey...
Are you- are you okay?

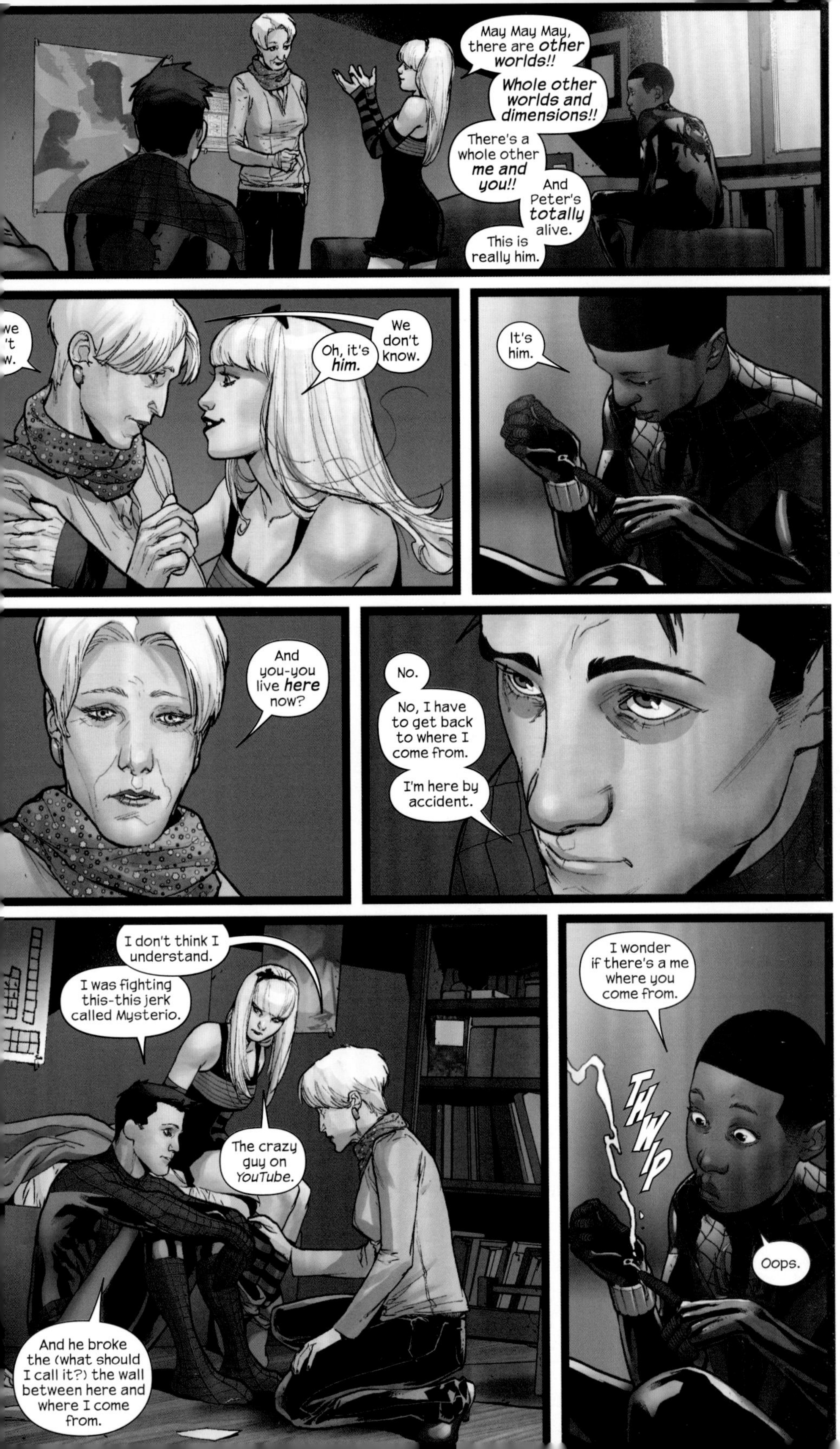

May May May, there are *other worlds!!*
Whole other worlds and dimensions!!
There's a whole other ***me and you!!***
And Peter's ***totally*** alive.
This is really him.
...we ...'t ...w.
Oh, it's ***him.***
We don't know.
It's him.
And you-you live ***here*** now?
No.
No, I have to get back to where I come from.
I'm here by accident.
I don't think I understand.
I was fighting this-this jerk called Mysterio.
The crazy guy on *YouTube.*
And he broke the (what should I call it?) the wall between here and where I come from.
I wonder if there's a me where you come from.
THWIP
Oops.

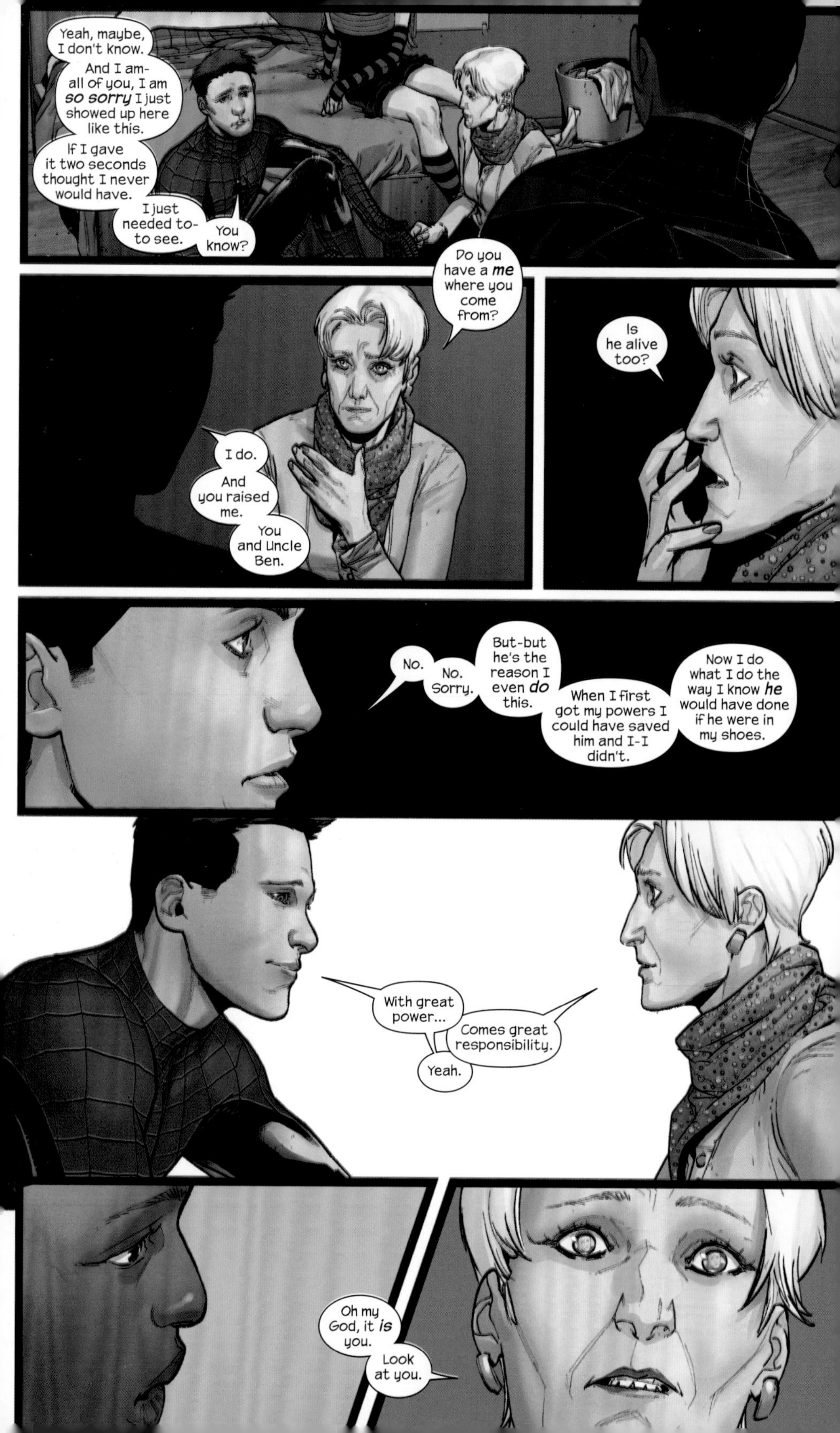
Yeah, maybe, I don't know.
And I am- all of you, I am *so sorry* I just showed up here like this.
If I gave it two seconds thought I never would have.
I just needed to- to see.
You know?
Do you have a *me* where you come from?
I do.
And you raised me.
You and Uncle Ben.
Is he alive too?
No.
No. Sorry.
But-but he's the reason I even *do* this.
When I first got my powers I could have saved him and I-I didn't.
Now I do what I do the way I know *he* would have done if he were in my shoes.
With great power...
Comes great responsibility.
Yeah.
Oh my God, it *is* you.
Look at you.

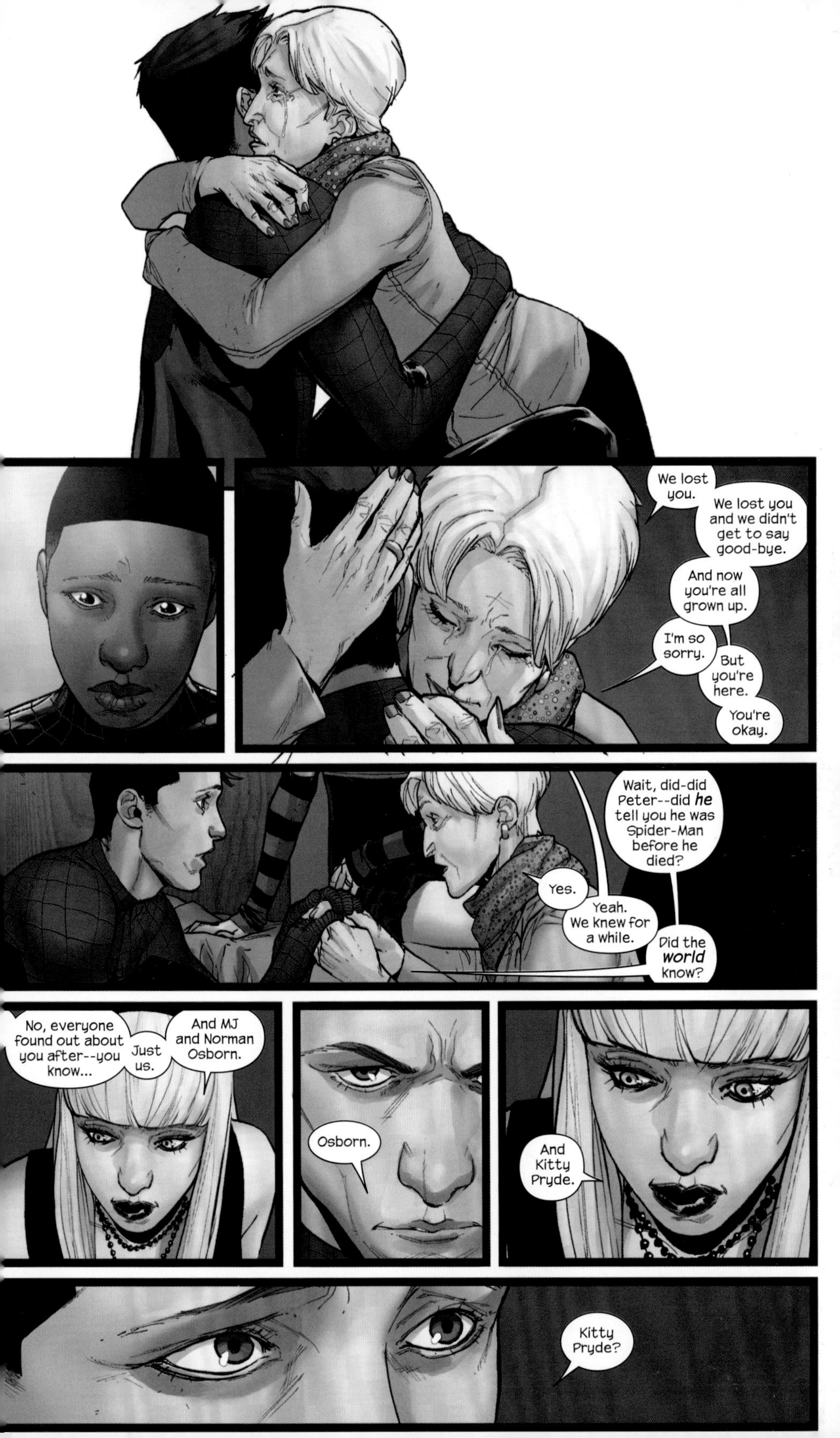
We lost you.
We lost you and we didn't get to say good-bye.
And now you're all grown up.
I'm so sorry.
But you're here.
You're okay.
Wait, did-did Peter--did *he* tell you he was Spider-Man before he died?
Yes.
Yeah. We knew for a while.
Did the *world* know?
No, everyone found out about you after--you know...
Just us.
And MJ and Norman Osborn.
Osborn.
And Kitty Pryde.
Kitty Pryde?

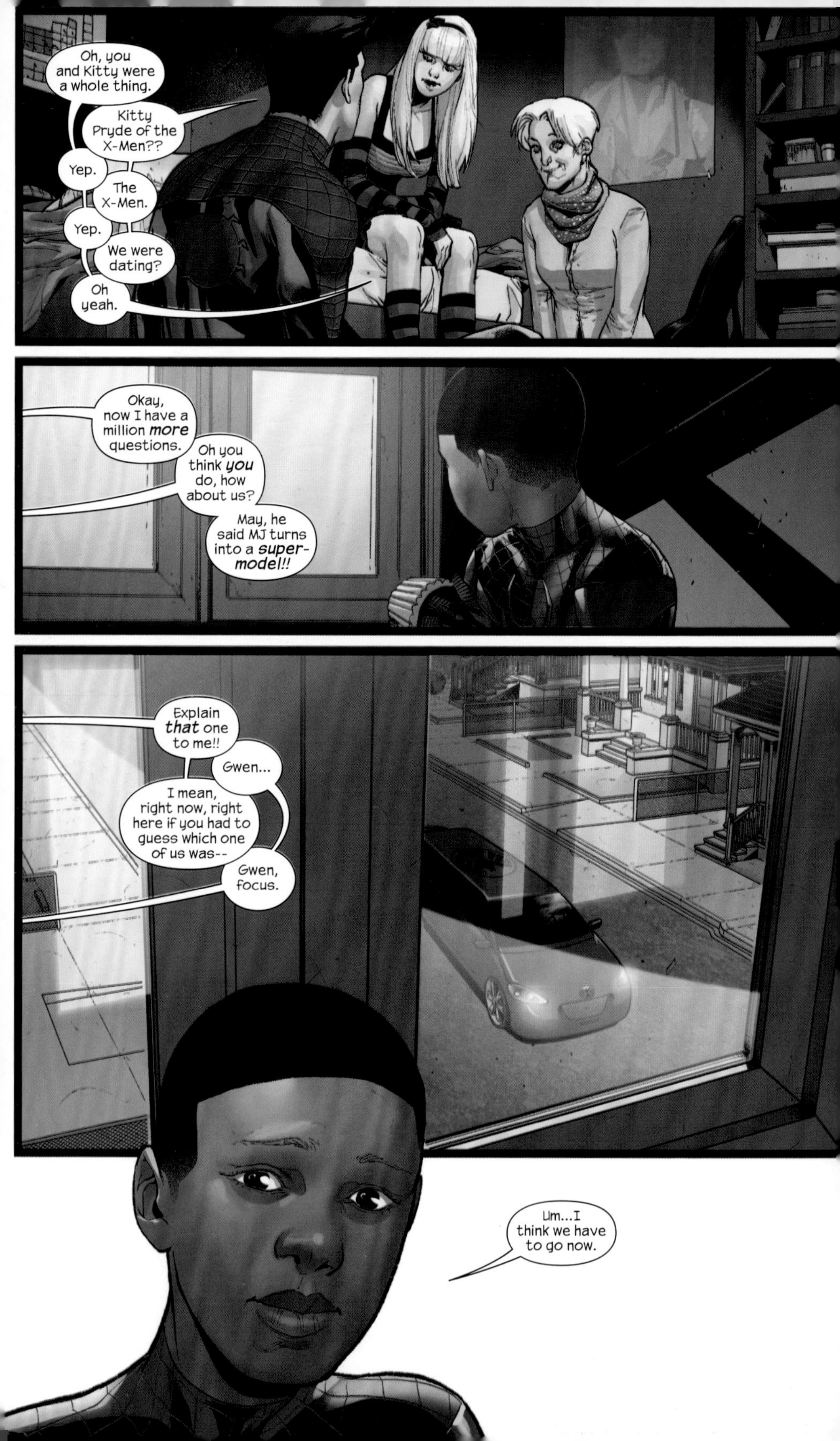
Oh, you and Kitty were a whole thing.
Kitty Pryde of the X-Men??
Yep.
The X-Men.
Yep.
We were dating?
Oh yeah.
Okay, now I have a million *more* questions.
Oh you think *you* do, how about us?
May, he said MJ turns into a *super-model*!!
Explain *that* one to me!!
Gwen...
I mean, right now, right here if you had to guess which one of us was--
Gwen, focus.
Um...I think we have to go now.

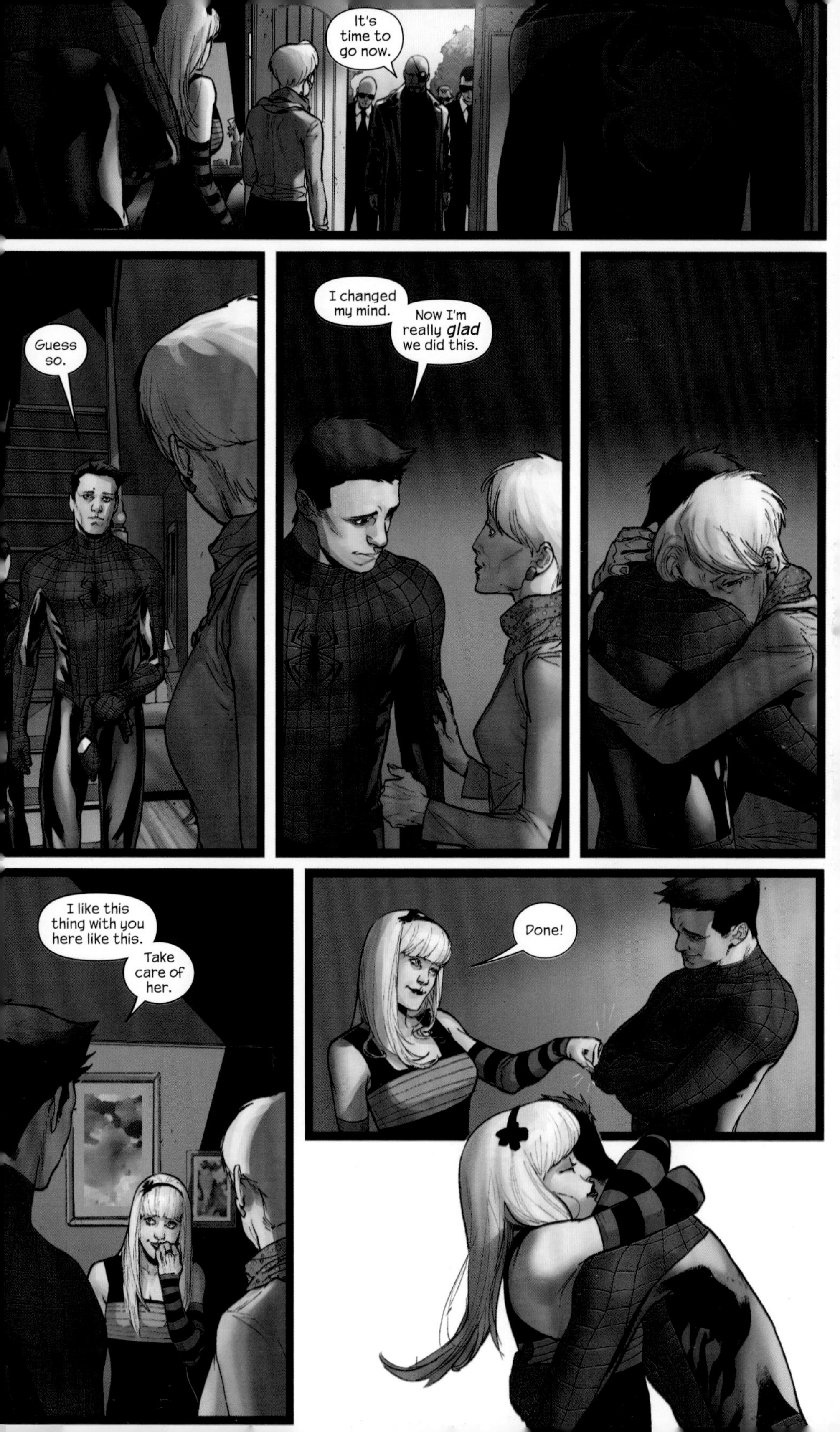
It's time to go now.
Guess so.
I changed my mind.
Now I'm really *glad* we did this.
I like this thing with you here like this.
Take care of her.
Done!

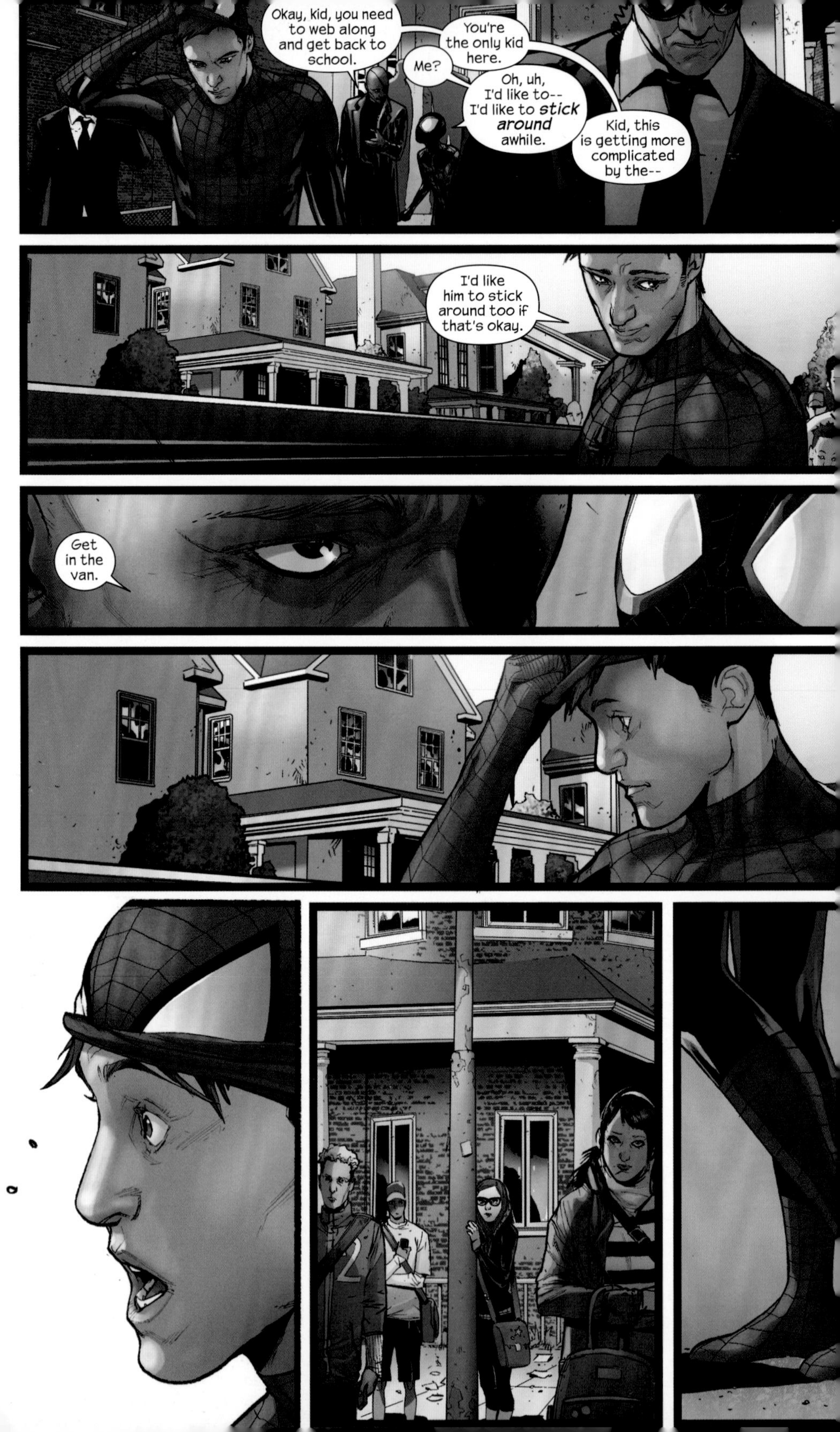
Okay, kid, you need to web along and get back to school.
You're the only kid here.
Me?
Oh, uh, I'd like to-- I'd like to *stick around* awhile.
Kid, this is getting more complicated by the--
I'd like him to stick around too if that's okay.
Get in the van.

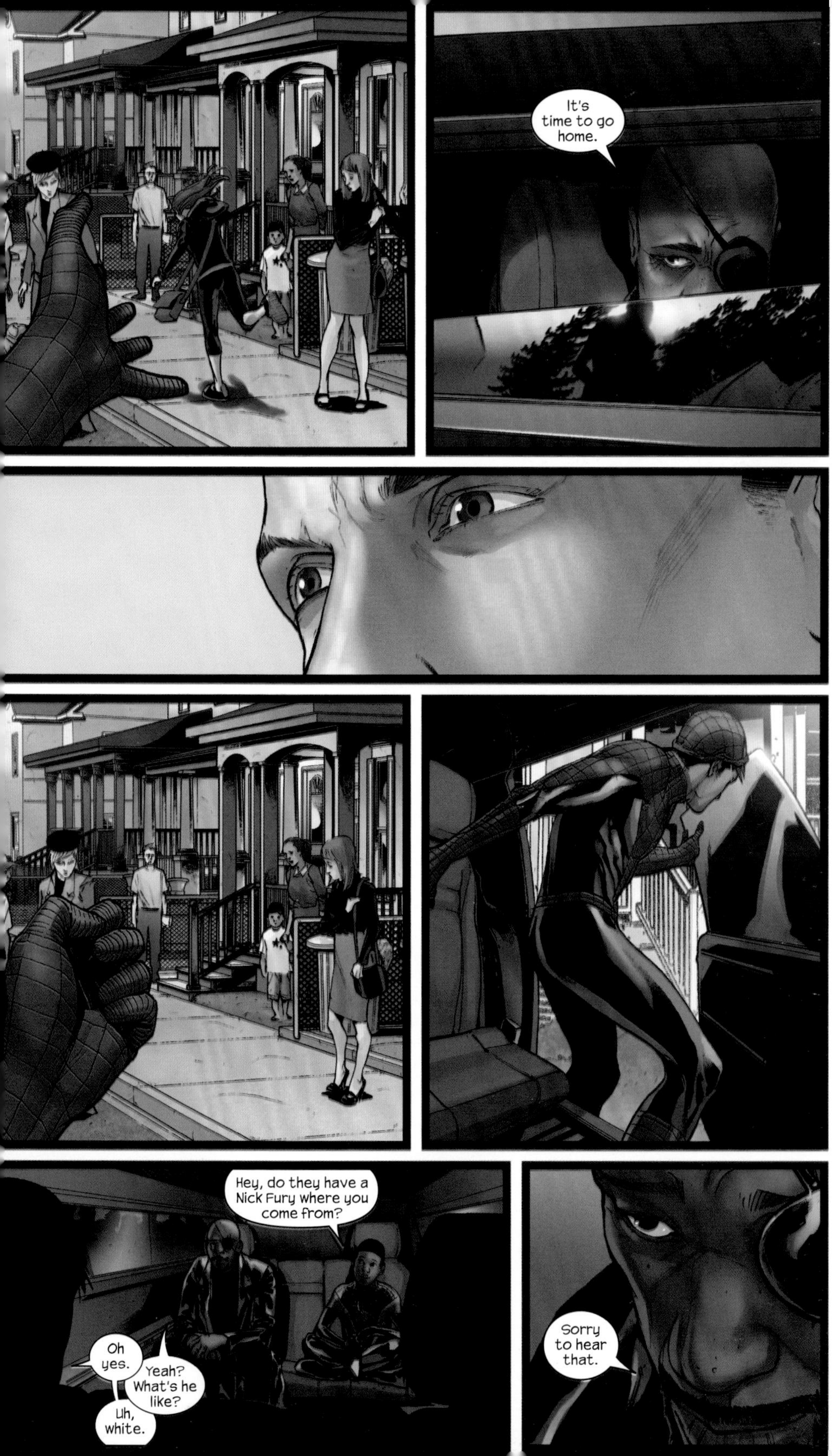
It's time to go home.
Hey, do they have a Nick Fury where you come from?
Oh yes.
Yeah? What's he like?
Uh, white.
Sorry to hear that.

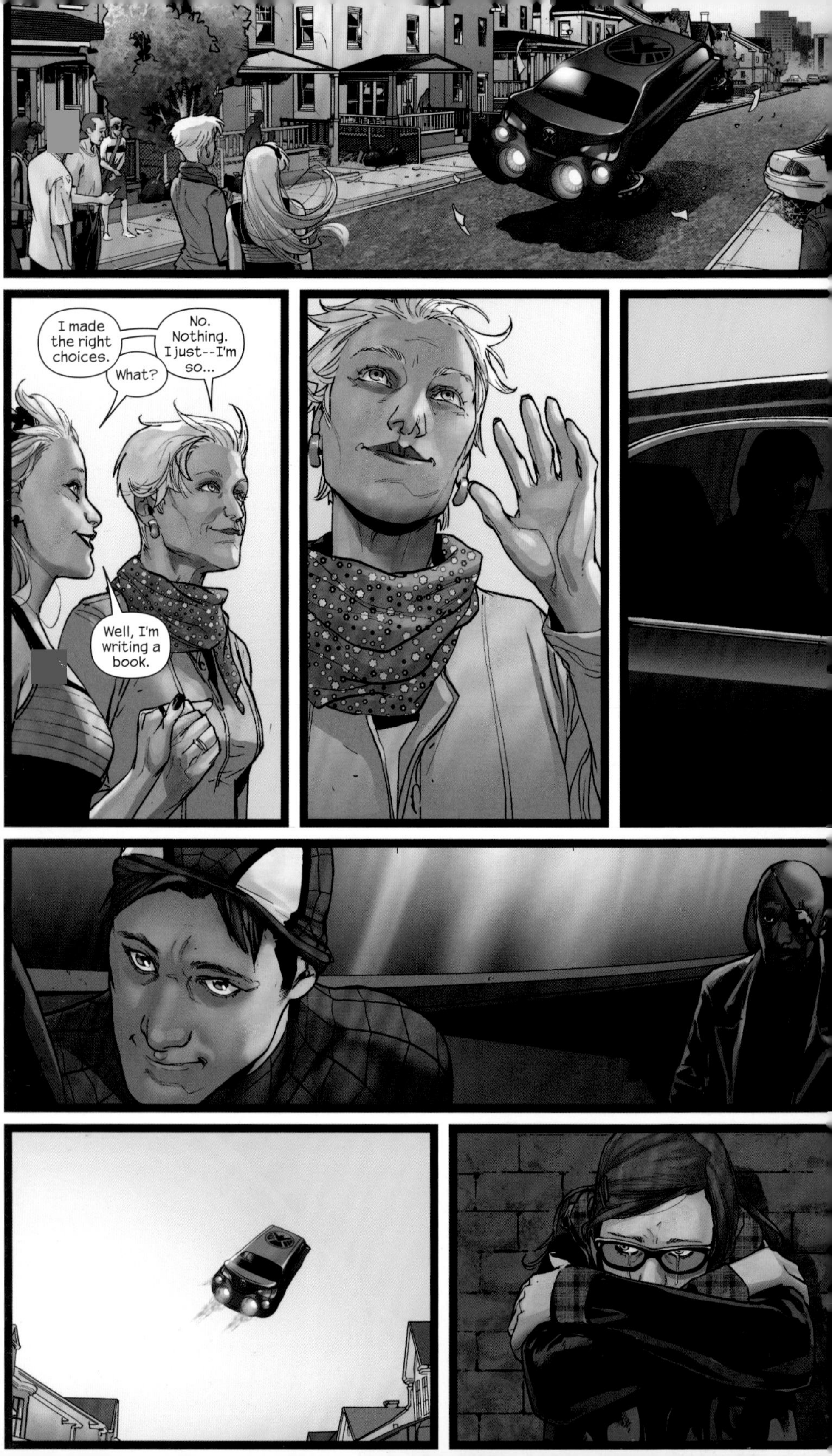

I made the right choices.
What?
No. Nothing. I just--I'm so...
Well, I'm writing a book.

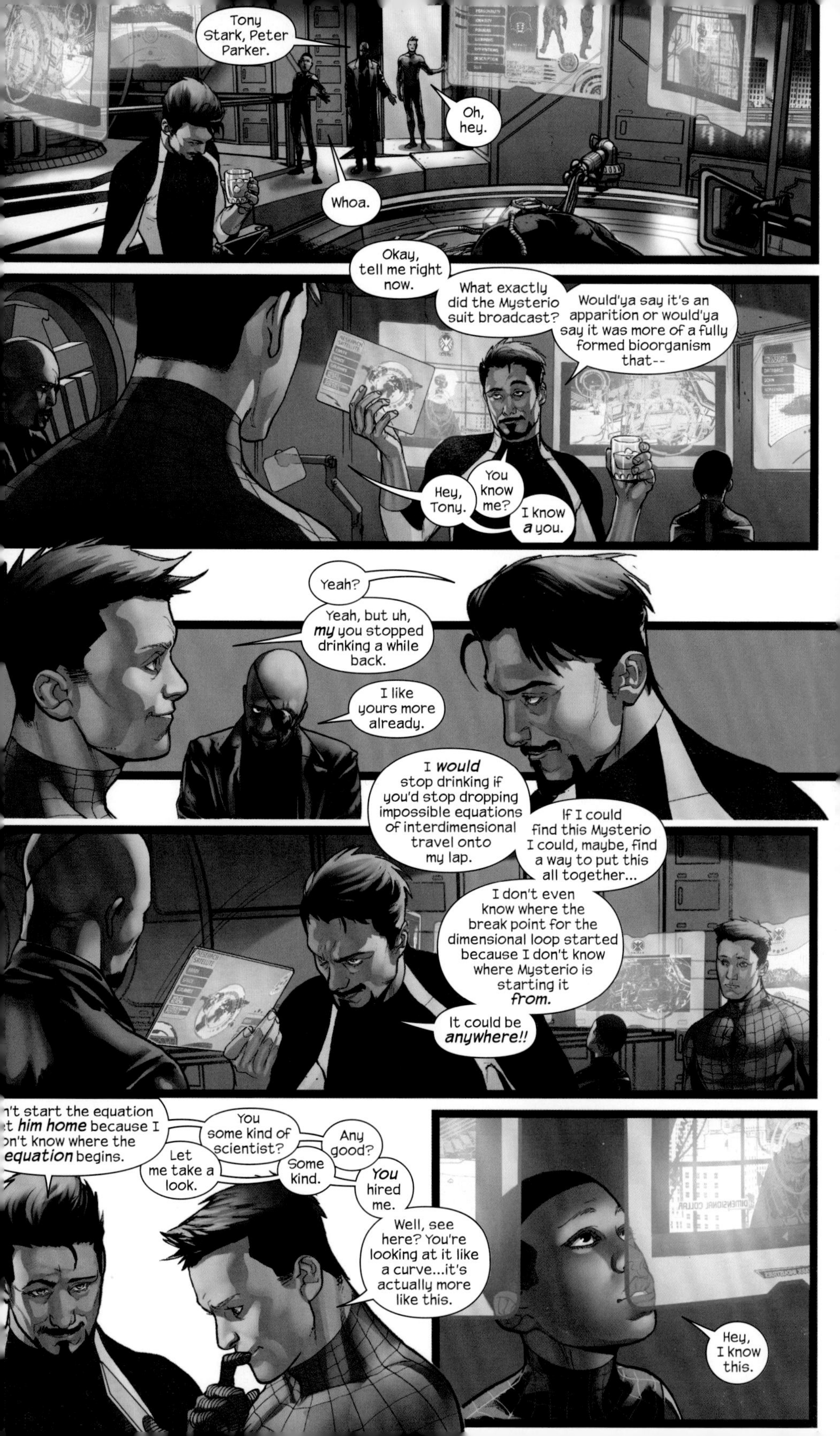
Tony Stark, Peter Parker.
Oh, hey.
Whoa.
Okay, tell me right now.
What exactly did the Mysterio suit broadcast?
Would'ya say it's an apparition or would'ya say it was more of a fully formed bioorganism that--
Hey, Tony.
You know me?
I know *a* you.
Yeah?
Yeah, but uh, *my* you stopped drinking a while back.
I like yours more already.
I *would* stop drinking if you'd stop dropping impossible equations of interdimensional travel onto my lap.
If I could find this Mysterio I could, maybe, find a way to put this all together...
I don't even know where the break point for the dimensional loop started because I don't know where Mysterio is starting it *from.*
It could be *anywhere!!*
n't start the equation t *him home* because I on't know where the *equation* begins.
You some kind of scientist?
Let me take a look.
Any good?
Some kind.
You hired me.
Well, see here? You're looking at it like a curve...it's actually more like this.
Hey, I know this.

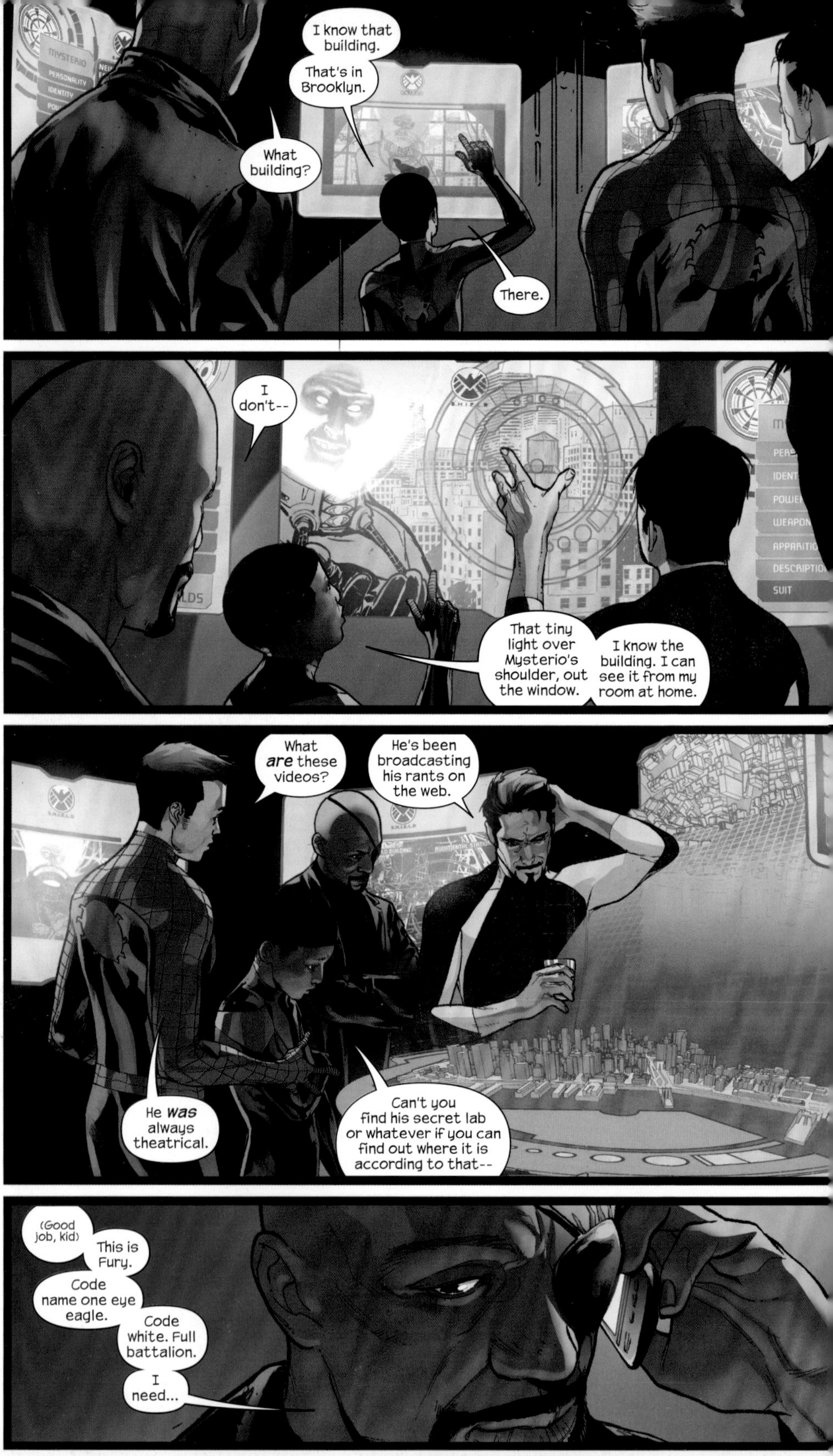

I know that building.
That's in Brooklyn.
What building?
There.
I don't--
That tiny light over Mysterio's shoulder, out the window.
I know the building. I can see it from my room at home.
What *are* these videos?
He's been broadcasting his rants on the web.
He *was* always theatrical.
Can't you find his secret lab or whatever if you can find out where it is according to that--
(Good job, kid)
This is Fury.
Code name one eye eagle.
Code white. Full battalion.
I need...

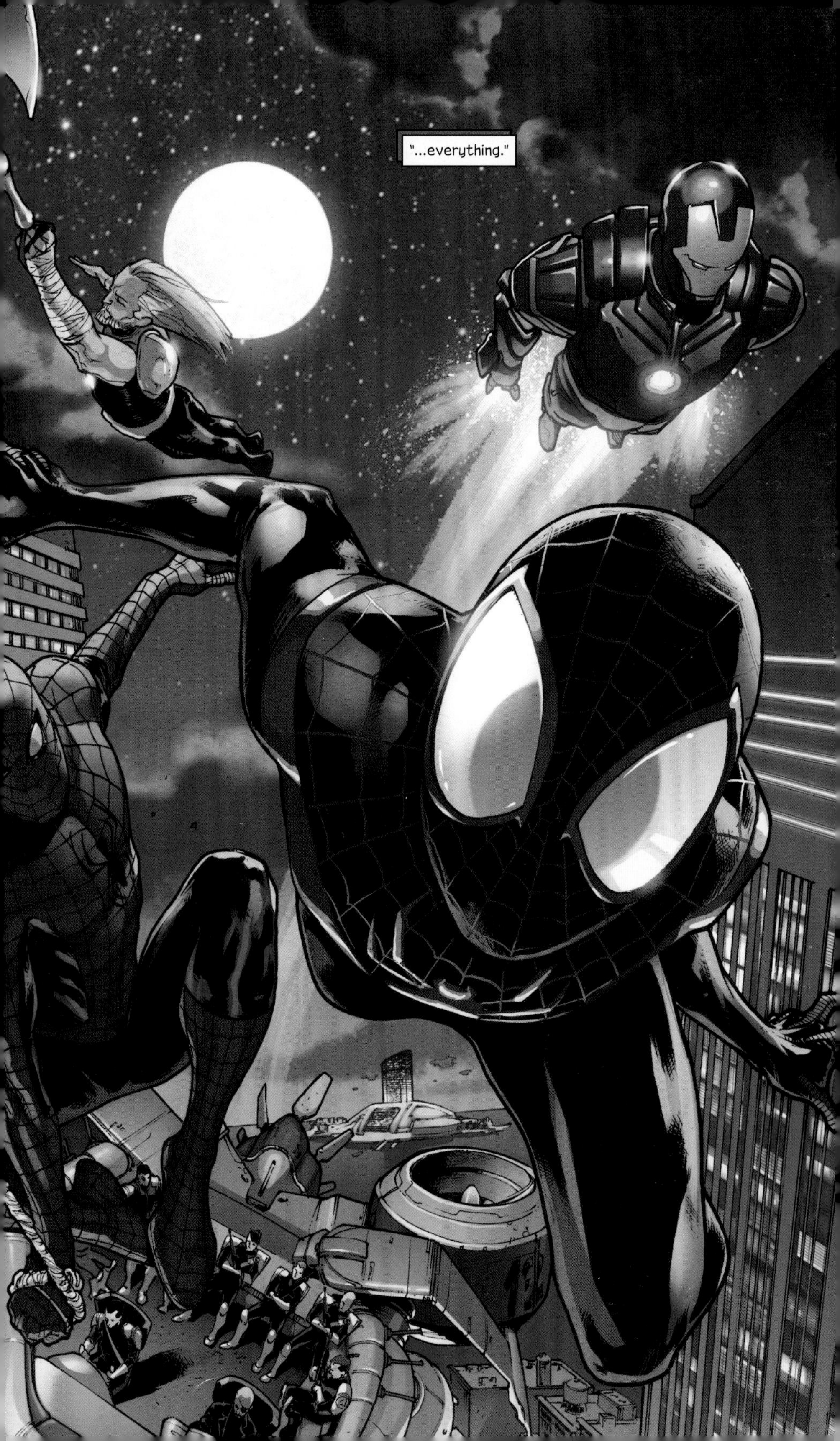
"...everything."

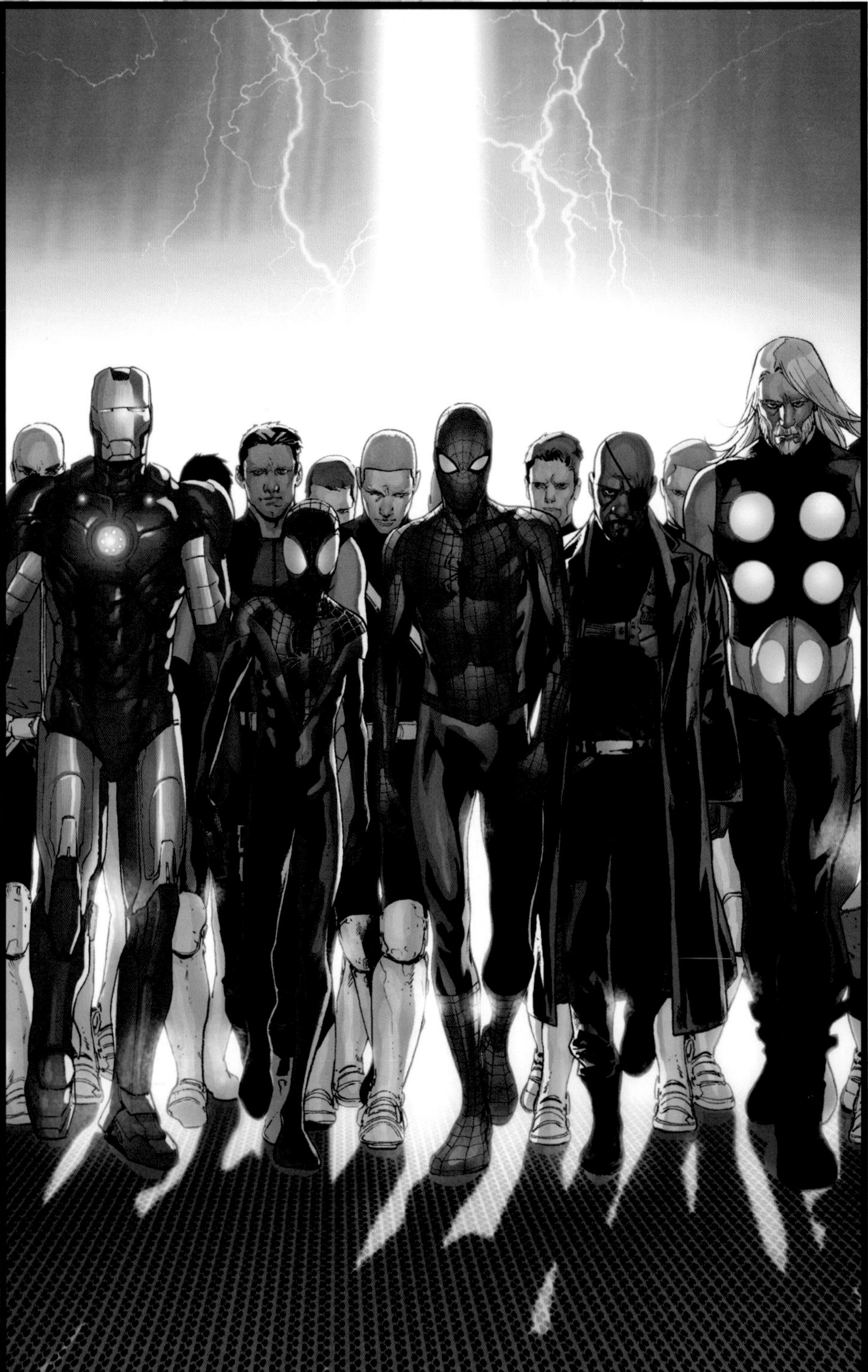

SPIDER-MEN #5 VARIANT

BY SARA PICHELLI

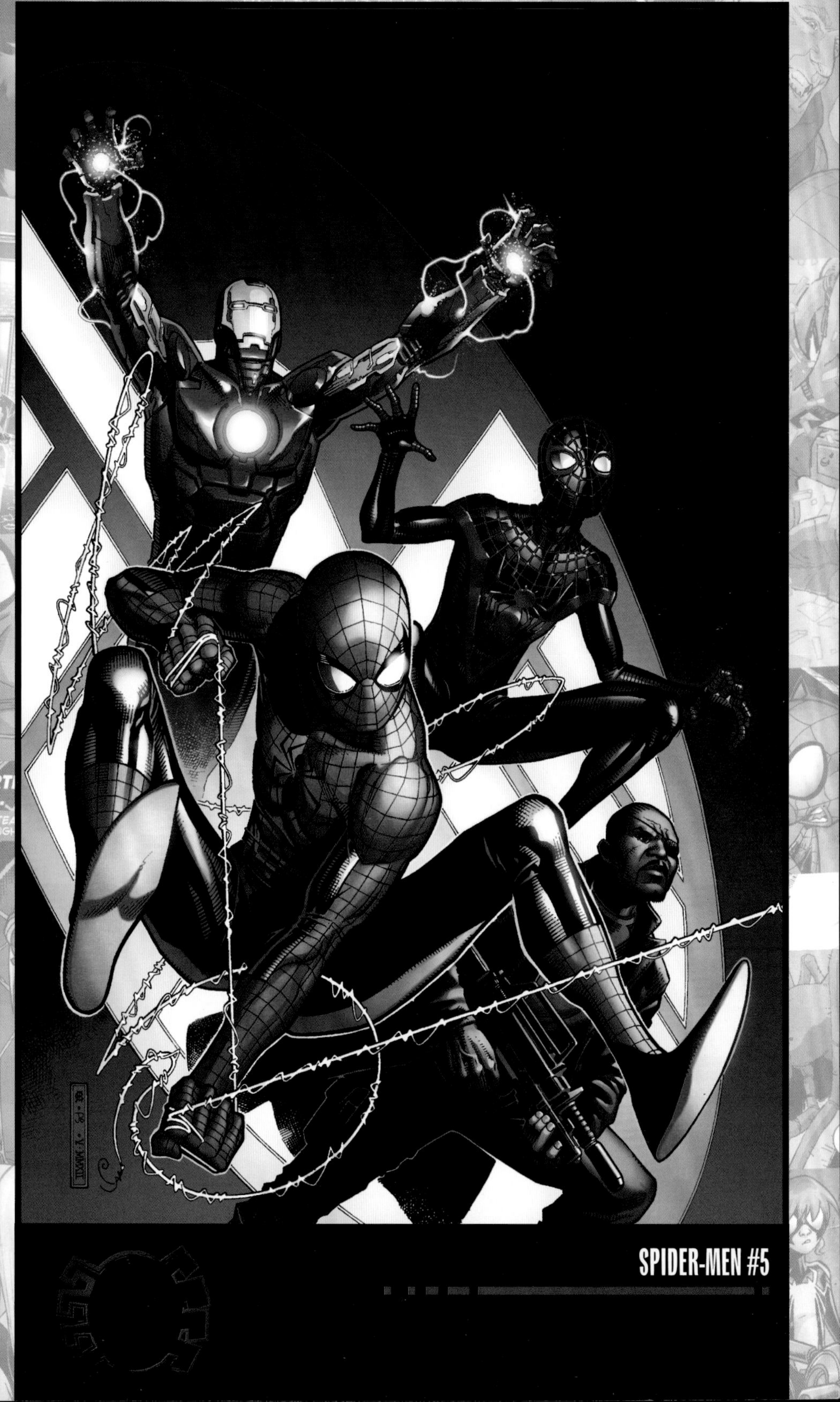

SPIDER-MEN #5

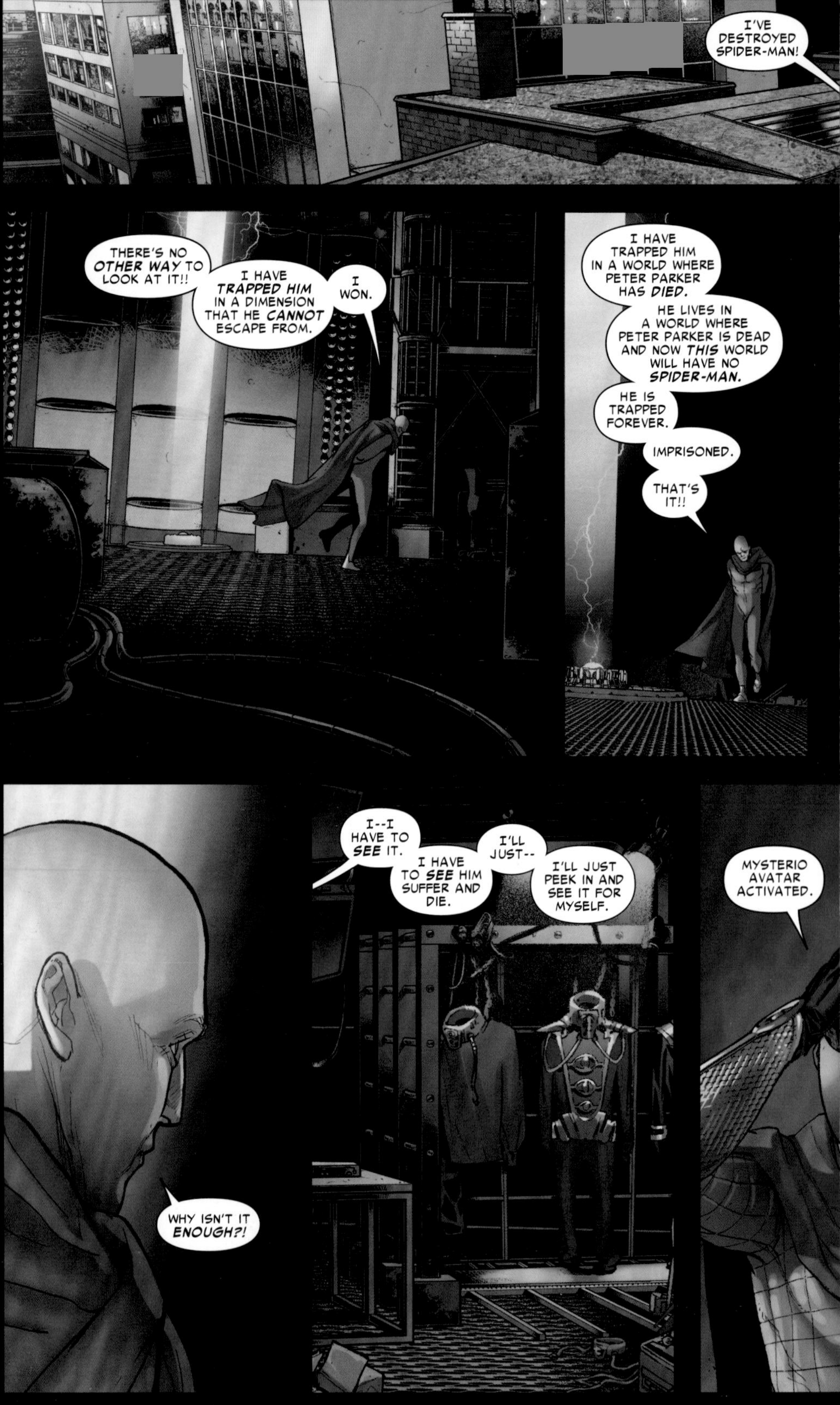
I'VE DESTROYED SPIDER-MAN!
THERE'S NO OTHER WAY TO LOOK AT IT!!
I HAVE TRAPPED HIM IN A DIMENSION THAT HE CANNOT ESCAPE FROM.
I WON.
I HAVE TRAPPED HIM IN A WORLD WHERE PETER PARKER HAS DIED.
HE LIVES IN A WORLD WHERE PETER PARKER IS DEAD AND NOW THIS WORLD WILL HAVE NO SPIDER-MAN.
HE IS TRAPPED FOREVER.
IMPRISONED.
THAT'S IT!!
WHY ISN'T IT ENOUGH?!
I--I HAVE TO SEE IT.
I HAVE TO SEE HIM SUFFER AND DIE.
I'LL JUST--
I'LL JUST PEEK IN AND SEE IT FOR MYSELF.
MYSTERIO AVATAR ACTIVATED.

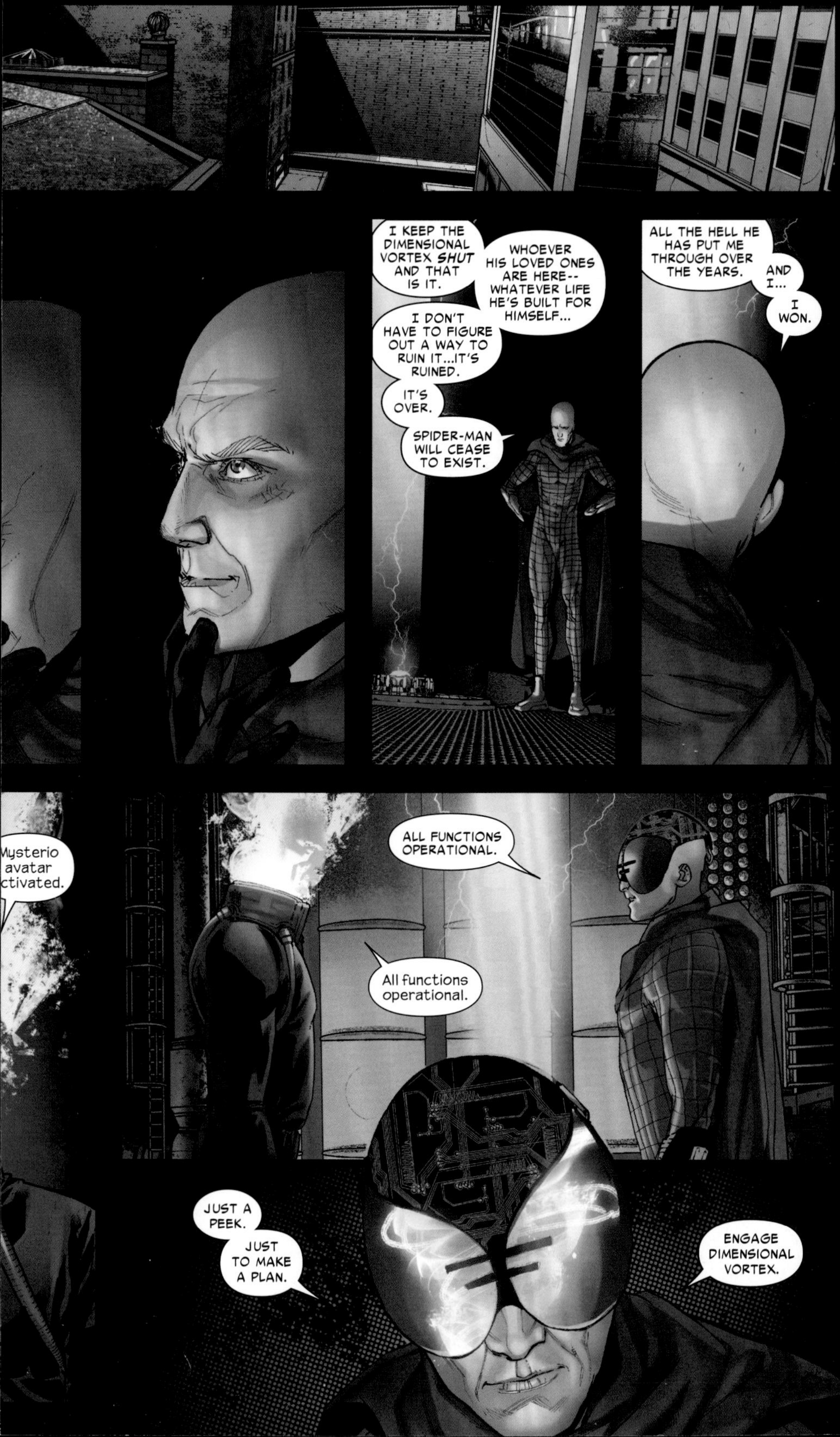

I KEEP THE DIMENSIONAL VORTEX SHUT AND THAT IS IT.
WHOEVER HIS LOVED ONES ARE HERE-- WHATEVER LIFE HE'S BUILT FOR HIMSELF...
I DON'T HAVE TO FIGURE OUT A WAY TO RUIN IT...IT'S RUINED.
IT'S OVER.
SPIDER-MAN WILL CEASE TO EXIST.
ALL THE HELL HE HAS PUT ME THROUGH OVER THE YEARS.
AND I...
I WON.
Mysterio avatar ctivated.
ALL FUNCTIONS OPERATIONAL.
All functions operational.
JUST A PEEK.
JUST TO MAKE A PLAN.
ENGAGE DIMENSIONAL VORTEX.

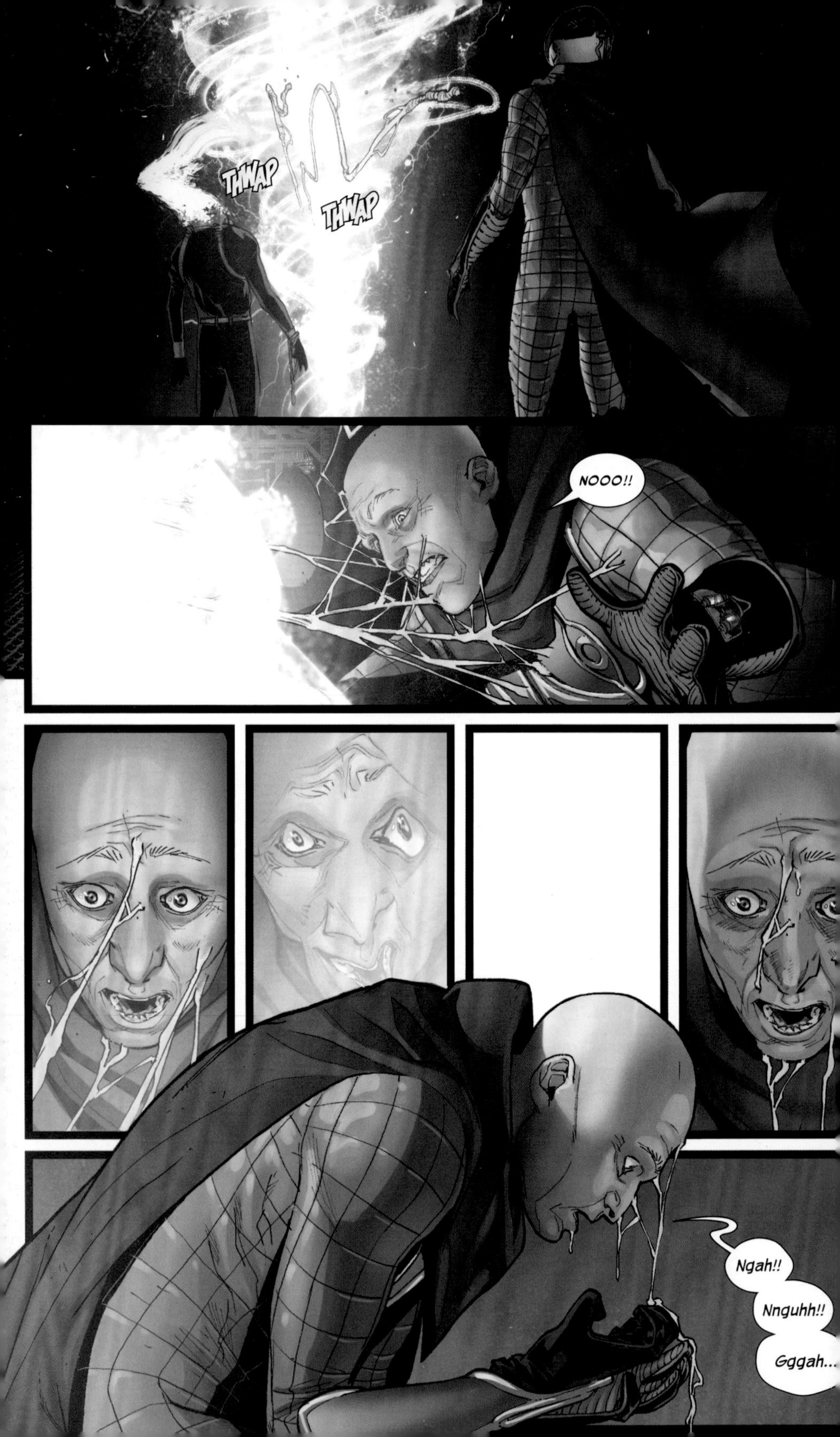
THWAP
THWAP
NOOO!!
Ngah!!
Nnguhh!!
Gggah...

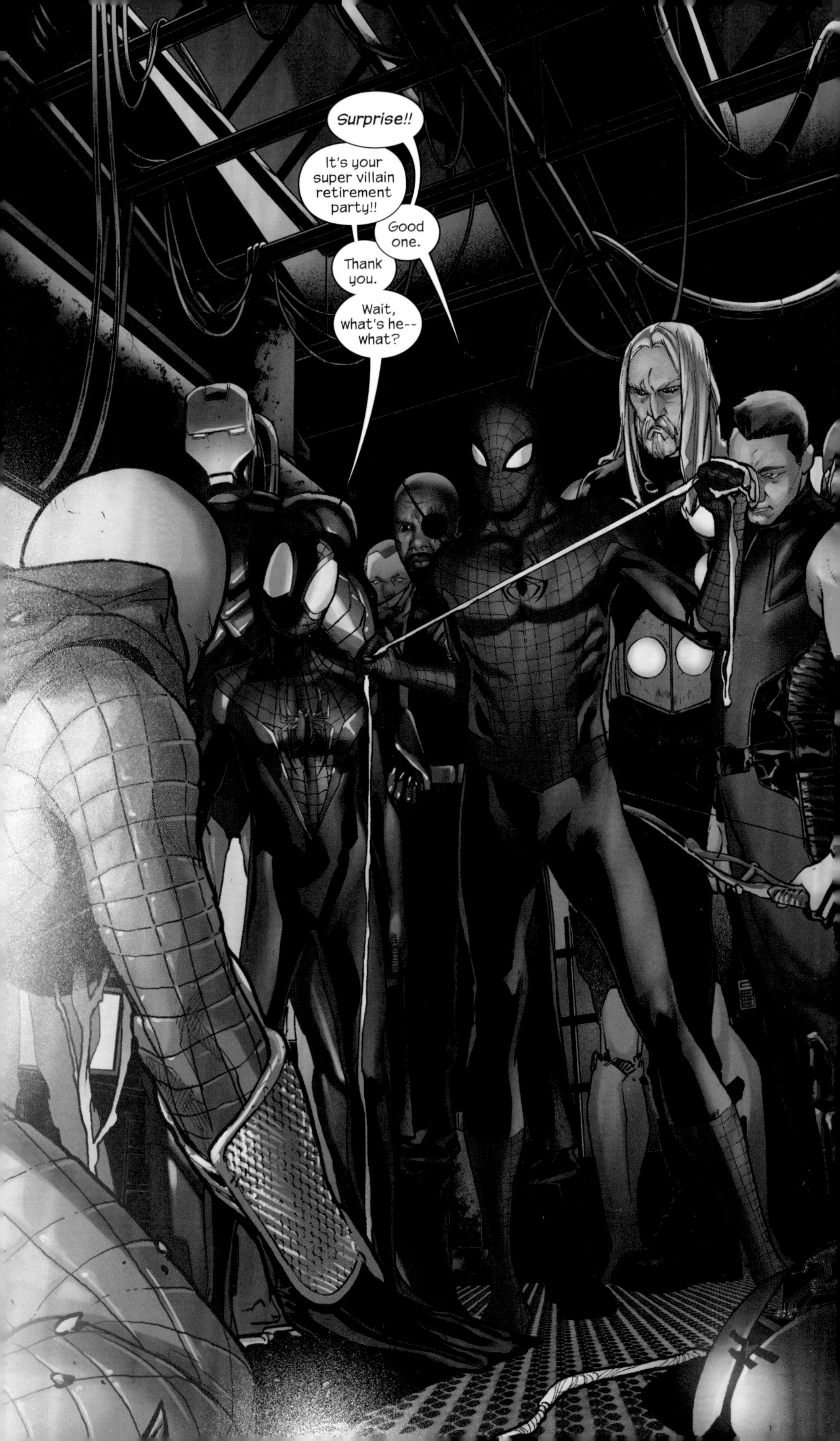
Surprise!!
It's your super villain retirement party!!
Good one.
Thank you.
Wait, what's he-- what?

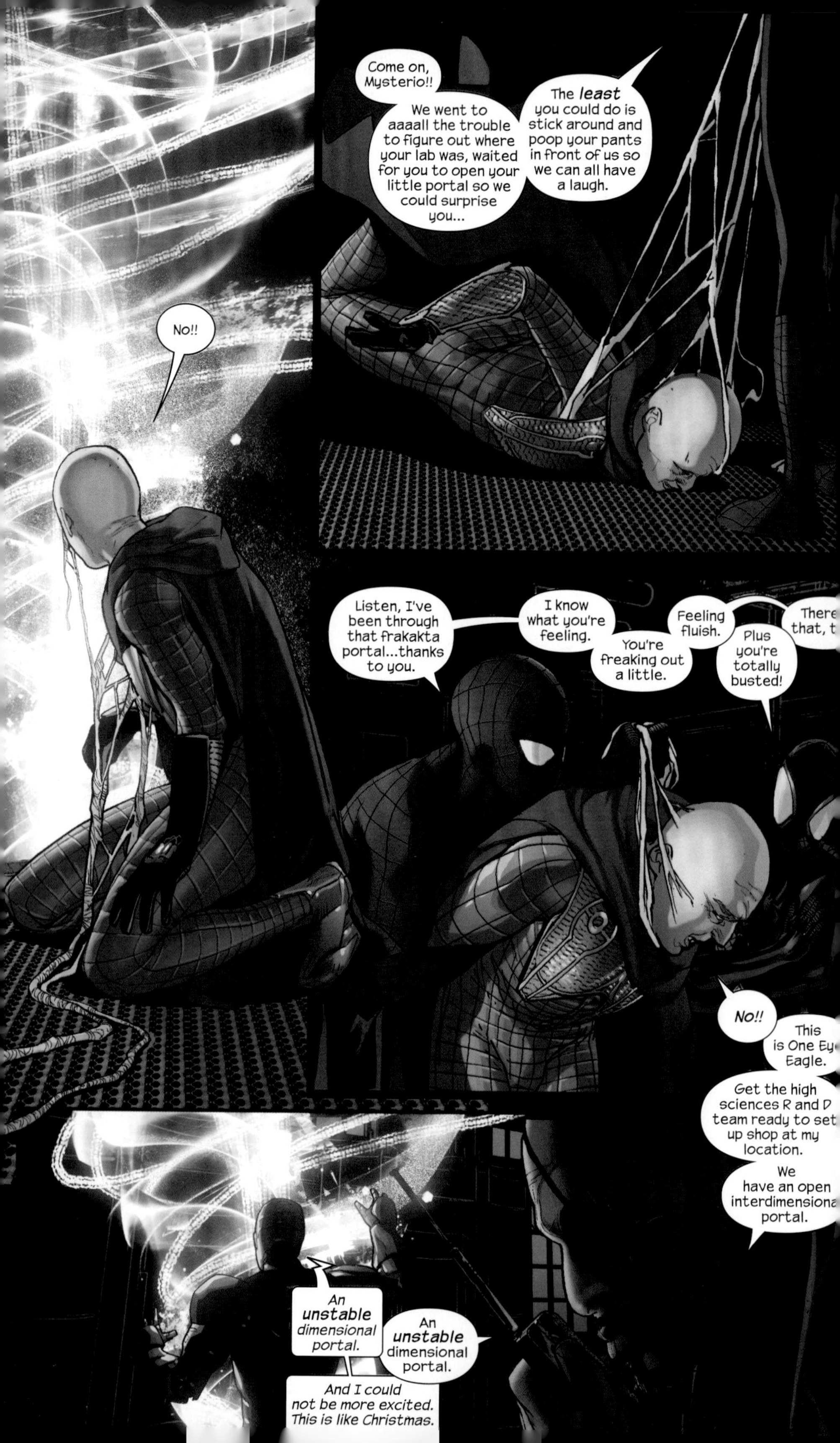

Come on, Mysterio!!
We went to aaaall the trouble to figure out where your lab was, waited for you to open your little portal so we could surprise you...
The *least* you could do is stick around and poop your pants in front of us so we can all have a laugh.
No!!
Listen, I've been through that frakakta portal...thanks to you.
I know what you're feeling.
You're freaking out a little.
Feeling fluish.
Plus you're totally busted!
No!!
This is One Ey
Eagle.
Get the high sciences R and D team ready to set up shop at my location.
We have an open interdimensiona portal.
*An **unstable** dimensional portal.*
An ***unstable*** dimensional portal.
And I could not be more excited. This is like Christmas.

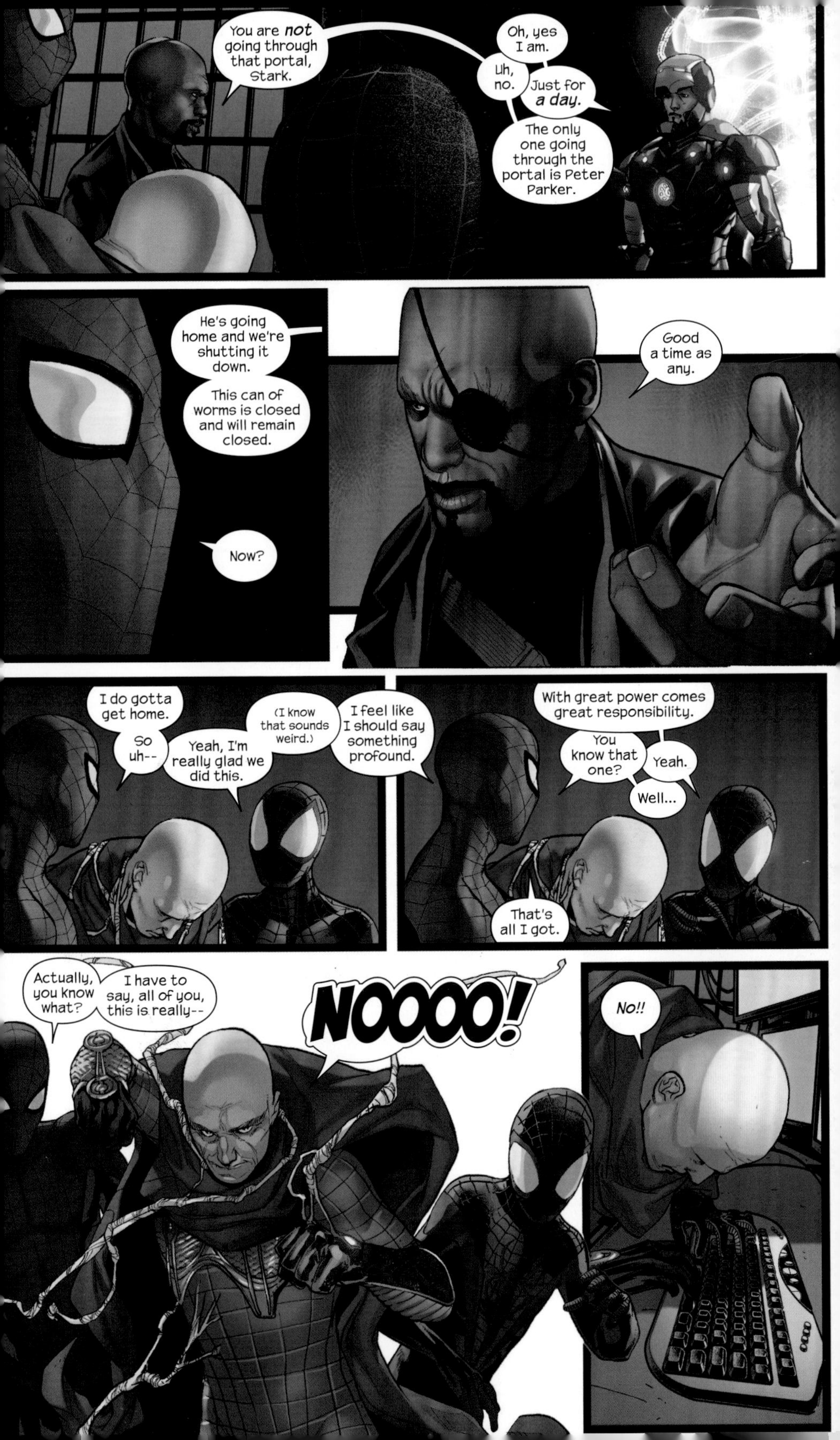
You are *not* going through that portal, Stark.
Oh, yes I am.
Uh, no.
Just for *a day.*
The only one going through the portal is Peter Parker.
He's going home and we're shutting it down.
This can of worms is closed and will remain closed.
Now?
Good a time as any.
I do gotta get home.
So uh--
Yeah, I'm really glad we did this.
(I know that sounds weird.)
I feel like I should say something profound.
With great power comes great responsibility.
You know that one?
Yeah.
Well...
That's all I got.
Actually, you know what?
I have to say, all of you, this is really--
NOOOO!
No!!

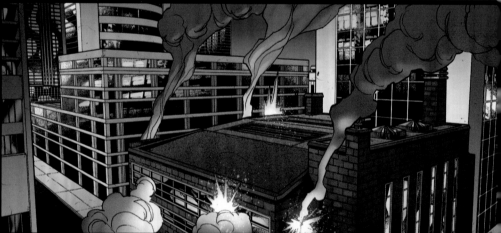

I'm ten steps *ahead* of you!!

I'm ready for anything.

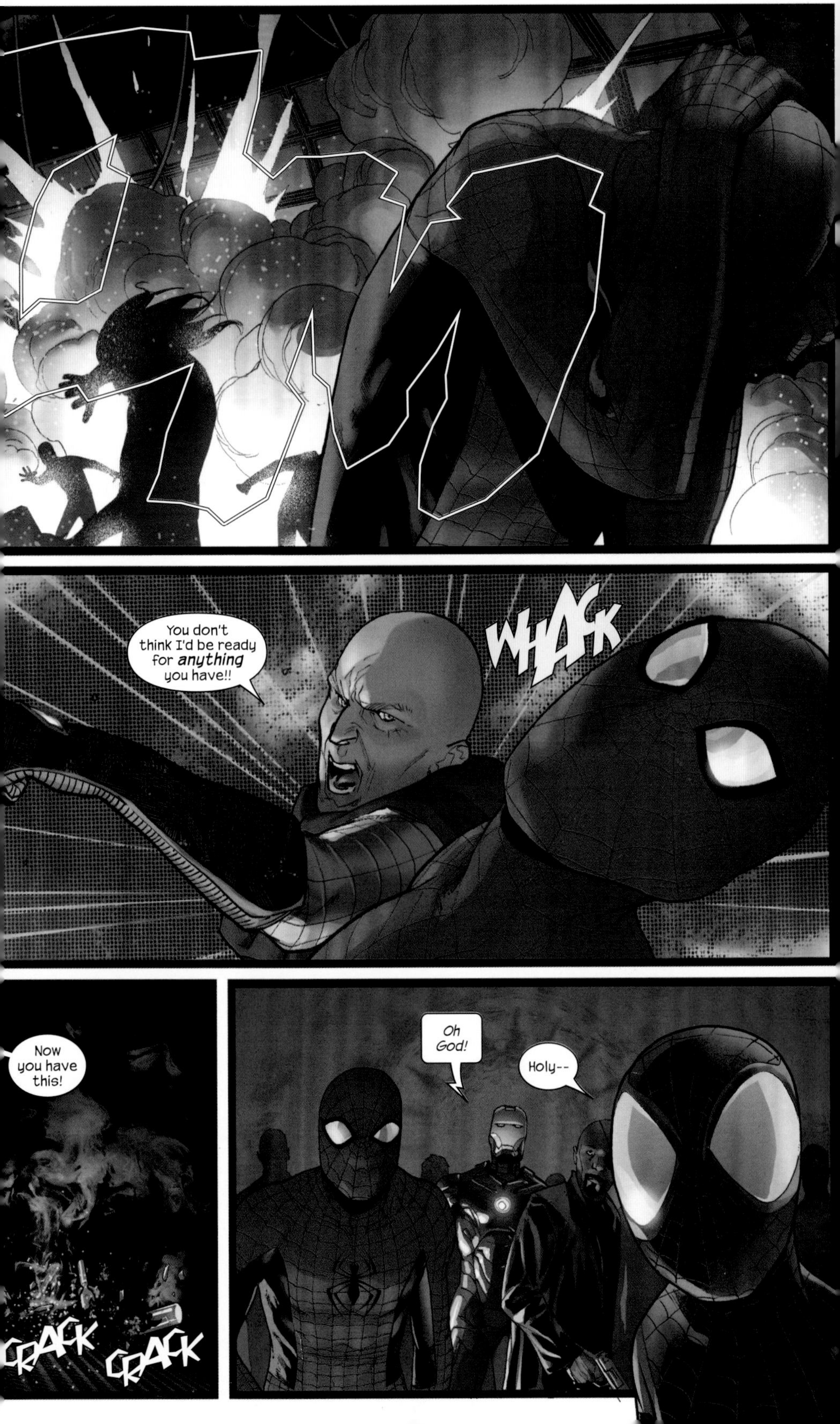
You don't think I'd be ready for *anything* you have!!
WHACK
Now you have this!
CRACK
CRACK
Oh God!
Holy--

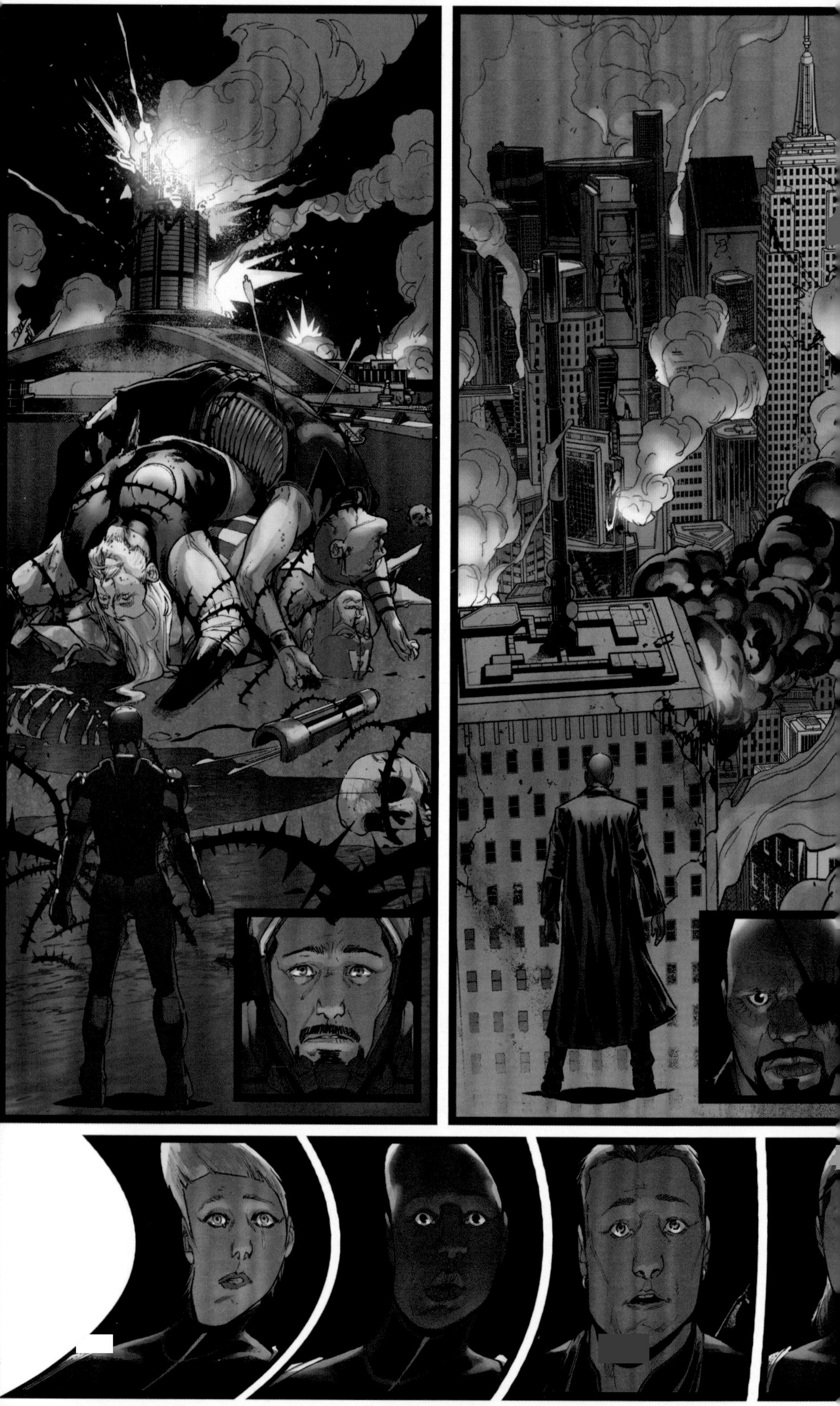

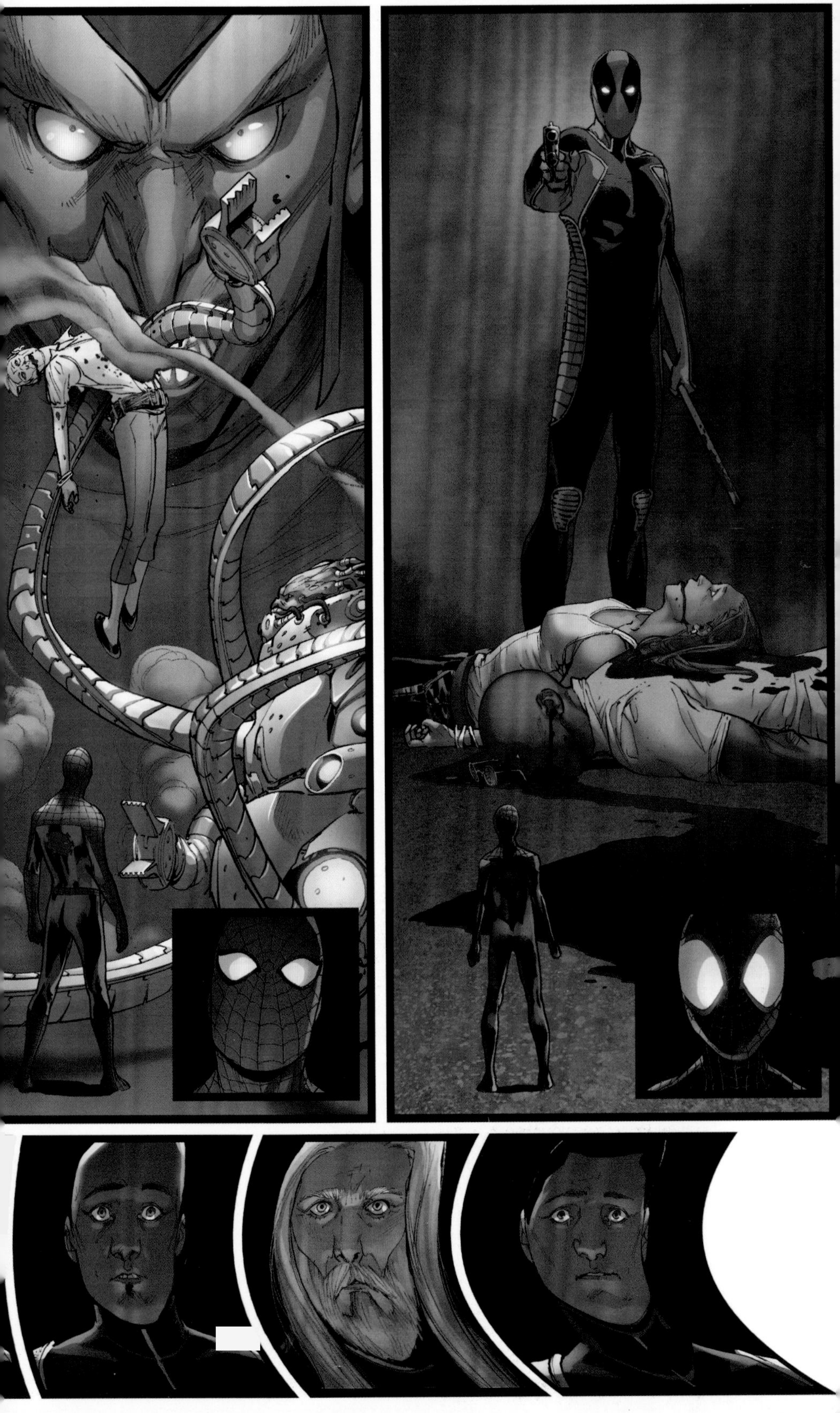

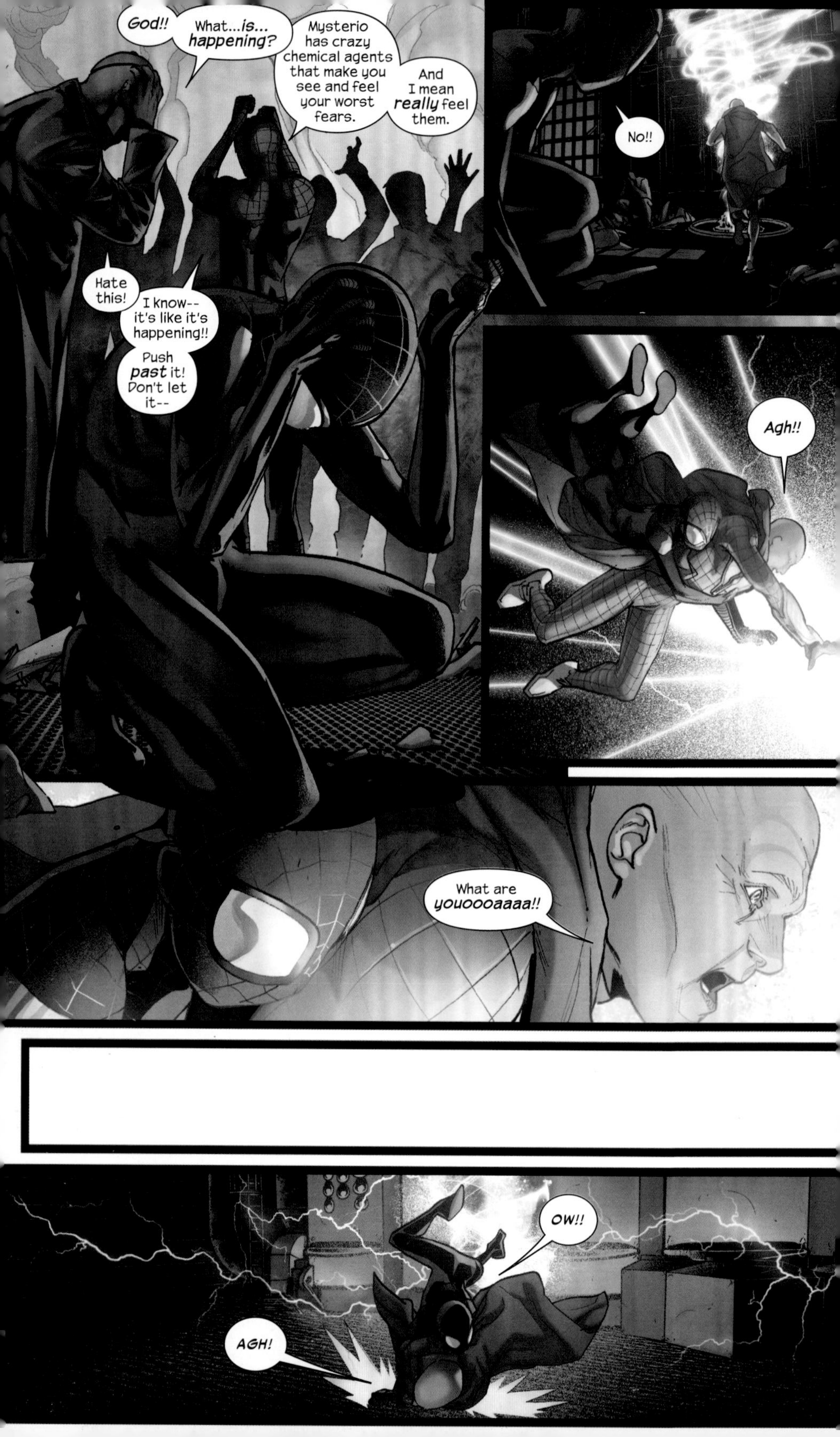
God!!
What...is... happening?
Mysterio has crazy chemical agents that make you see and feel your worst fears.
And I mean really feel them.
No!!
Hate this!
I know-- it's like it's happening!!
Push past it! Don't let it--
Agh!!
What are youoooaaaa!!
OW!!
AGH!

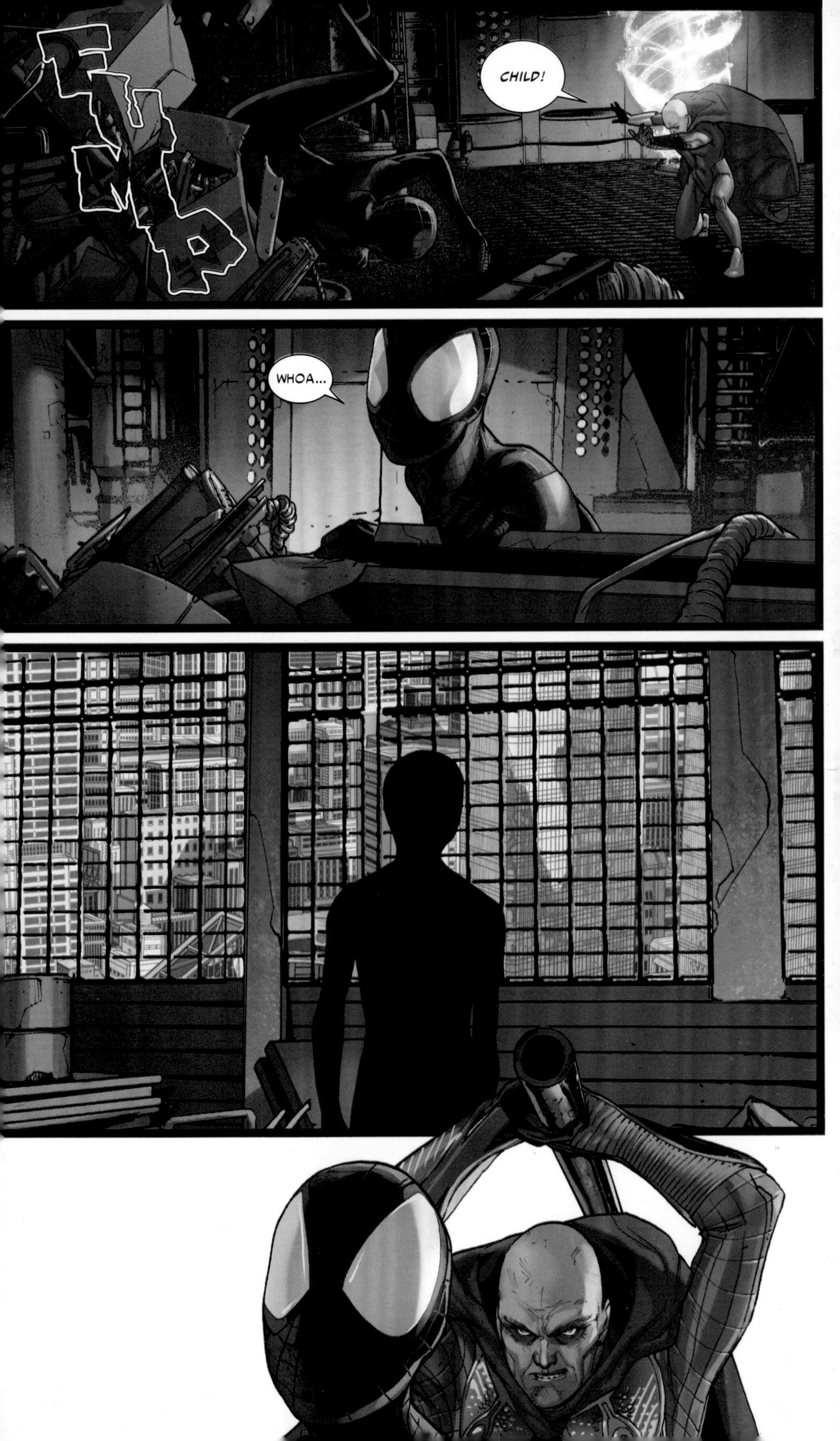
FUMP
CHILD!
WHOA...

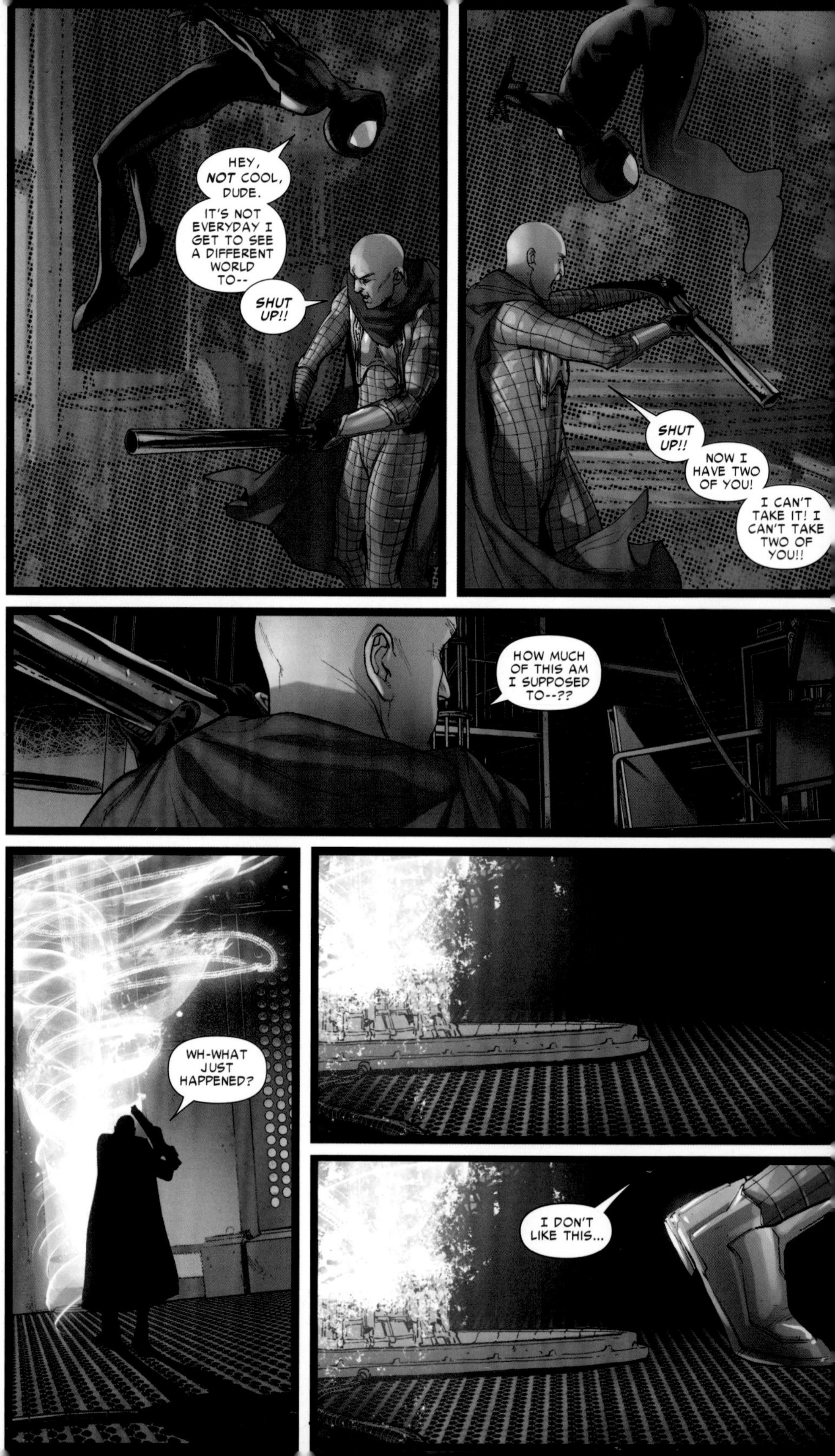
HEY, *NOT* COOL, DUDE.
IT'S NOT EVERYDAY I GET TO SEE A DIFFERENT WORLD TO--
SHUT UP!!
SHUT UP!!
NOW I HAVE TWO OF YOU!
I CAN'T TAKE IT! I CAN'T TAKE TWO OF YOU!!
HOW MUCH OF THIS AM I SUPPOSED TO--??
WH-WHAT JUST HAPPENED?
I DON'T LIKE THIS...

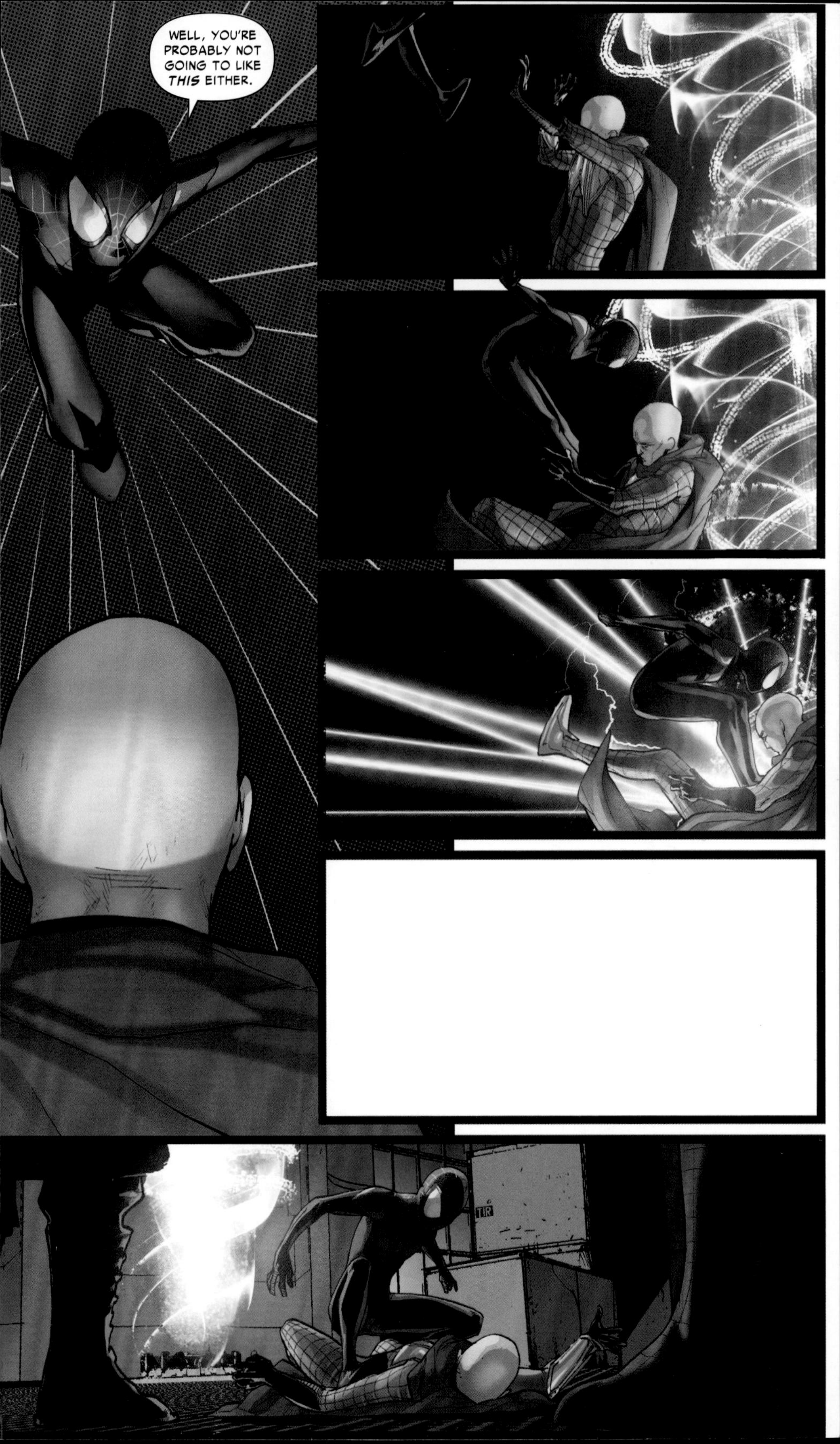
WELL, YOU'RE PROBABLY NOT GOING TO LIKE *THIS* EITHER.

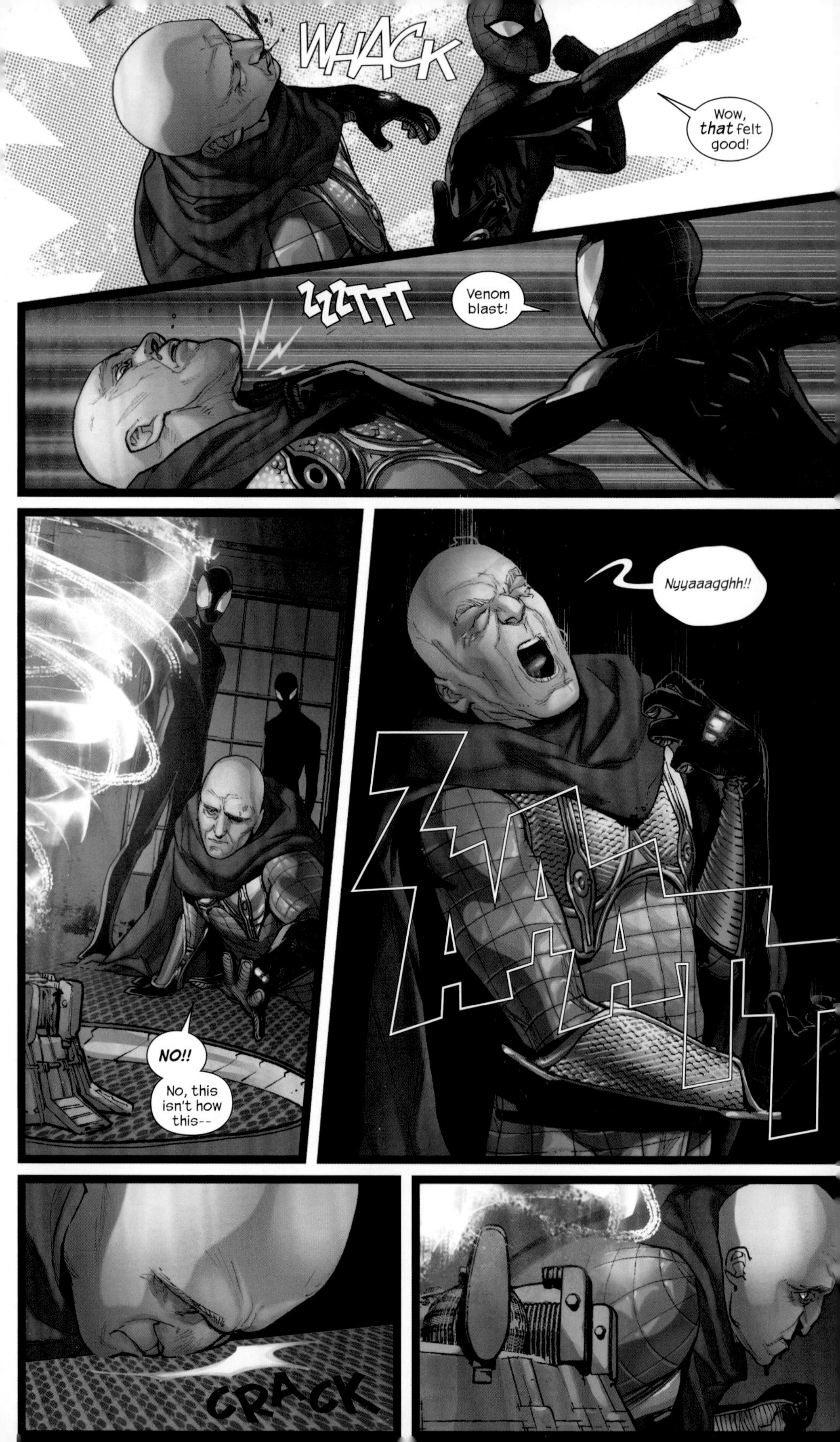
WHACK
Wow, *that* felt good!
ZZZTTT
Venom blast!
NO!!
No, this isn't how this--
Nyyaaagghh!!
ZAAAT
CRACK

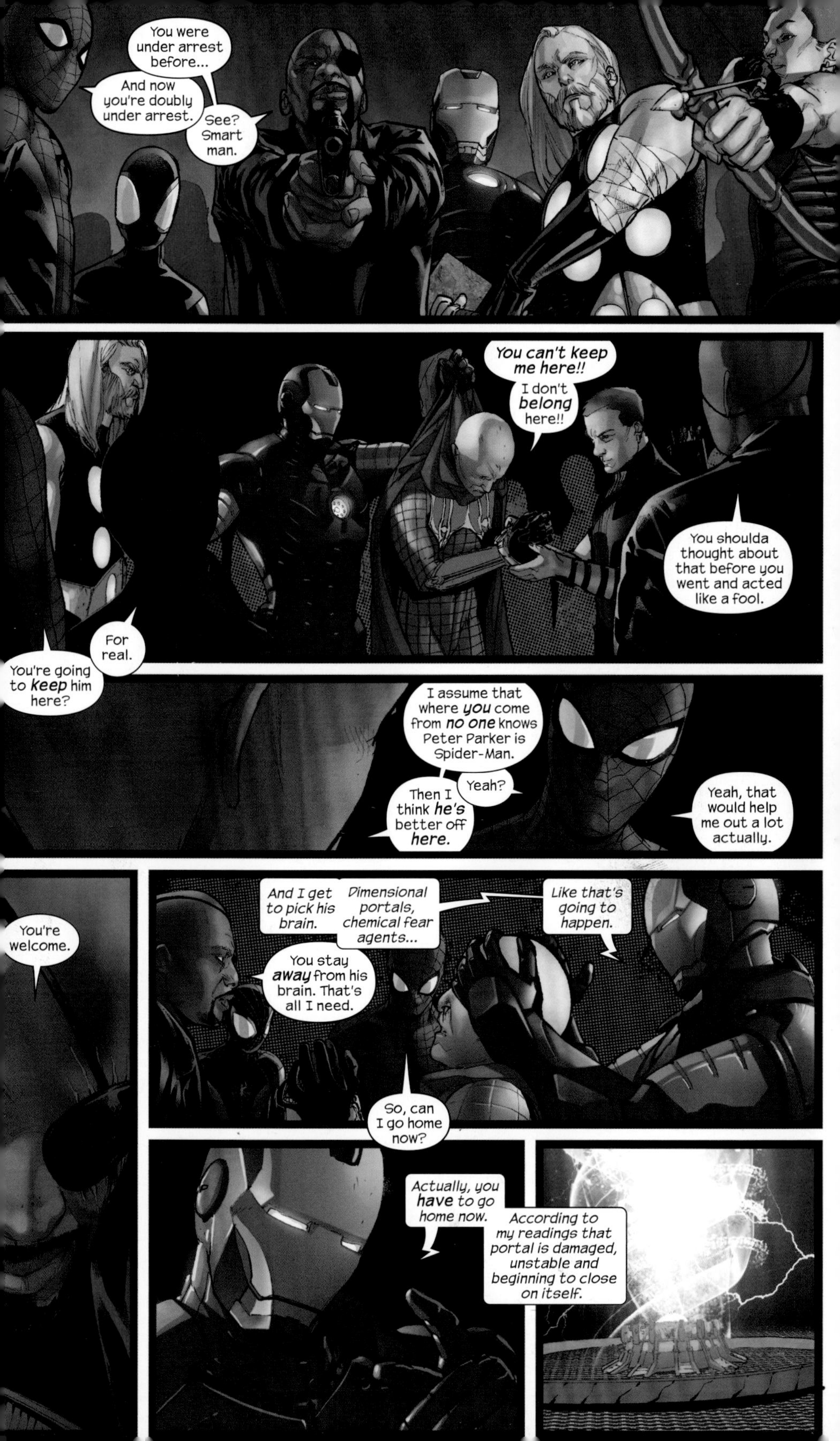

You were under arrest before...
And now you're doubly under arrest.
See? Smart man.
You can't keep me here!!
I don't *belong* here!!
You shoulda thought about that before you went and acted like a fool.
For real.
You're going to *keep* him here?
I assume that where *you* come from *no one* knows Peter Parker is Spider-Man.
Yeah?
Then I think *he's* better off *here*.
Yeah, that would help me out a lot actually.
You're welcome.
And I get to pick his brain.
Dimensional portals, chemical fear agents...
Like that's going to happen.
You stay *away* from his brain. That's all I need.
So, can I go home now?
Actually, you *have* to go home now.
According to my readings that portal is damaged, unstable and beginning to close on itself.

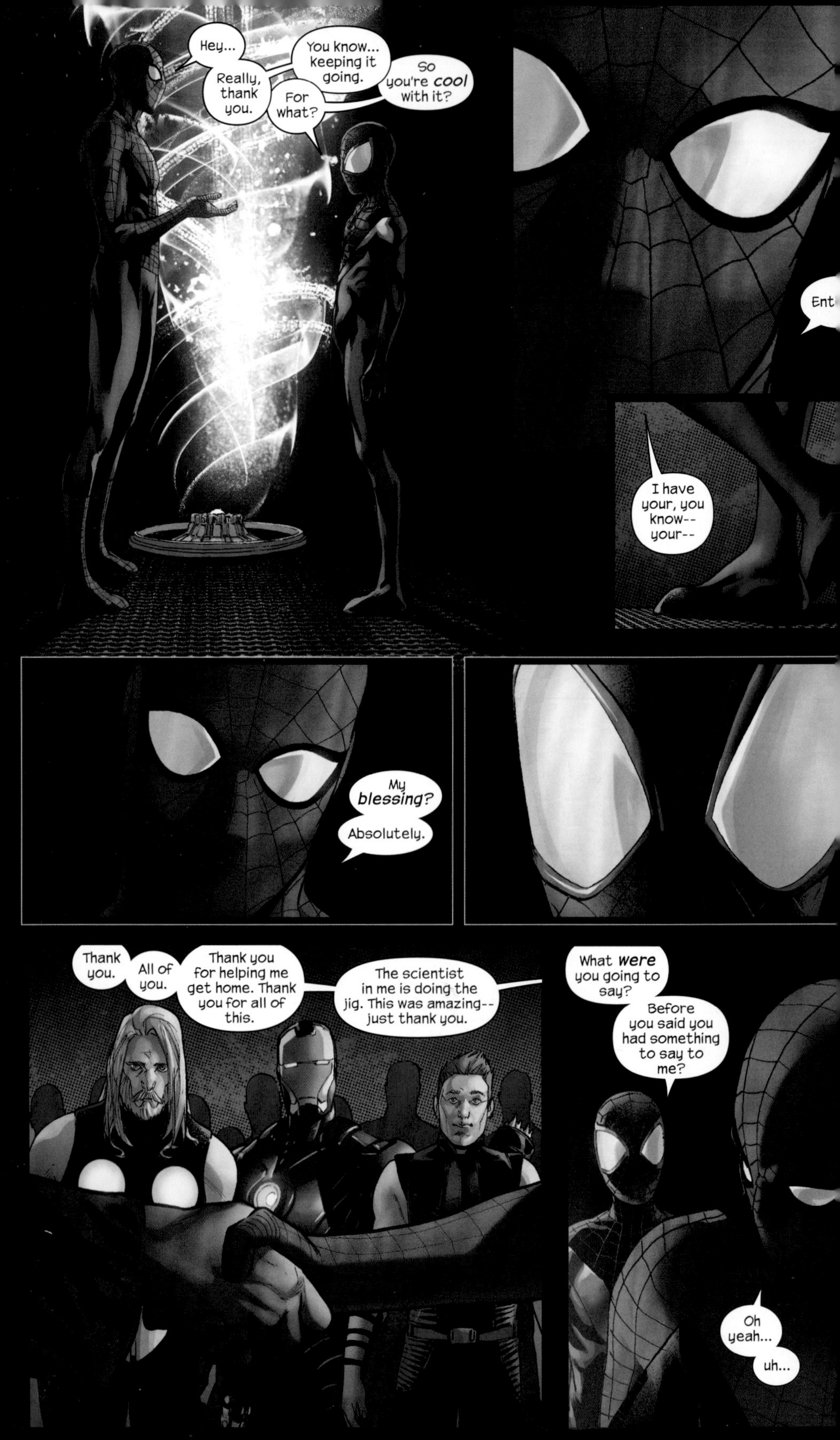

Hey...
Really, thank you.
For what?
You know... keeping it going.
So you're *cool* with it?
Ent
I have your, you know-- your--
My *blessing?*
Absolutely.
Thank you.
All of you.
Thank you for helping me get home. Thank you for all of this.
The scientist in me is doing the jig. This was amazing-- just thank you.
What *were* you going to say?
Before you said you had something to say to me?
Oh yeah...
uh...

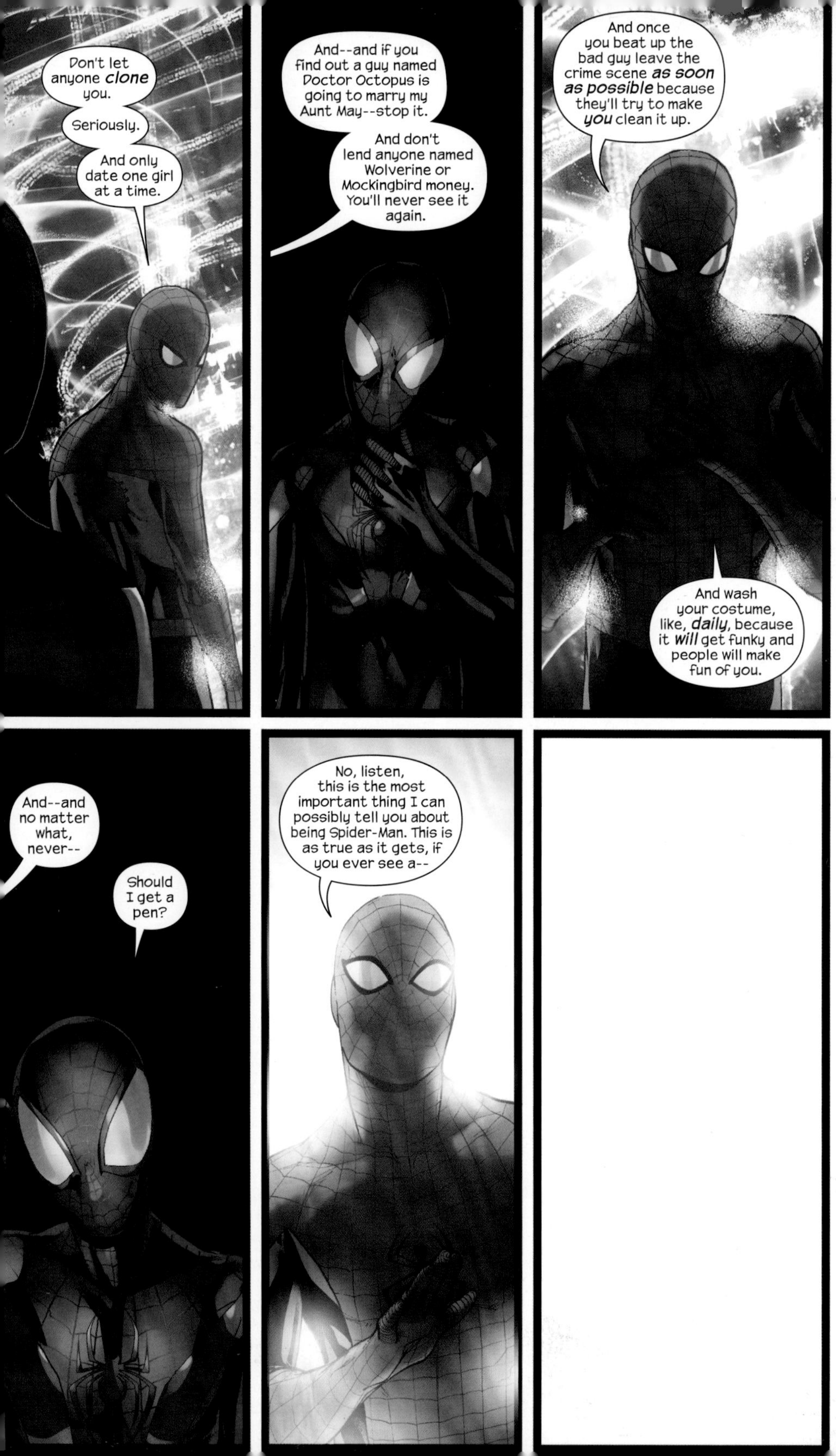
Don't let anyone clone you.
Seriously.
And only date one girl at a time.
And--and if you find out a guy named Doctor Octopus is going to marry my Aunt May--stop it.
And don't lend anyone named Wolverine or Mockingbird money. You'll never see it again.
And once you beat up the bad guy leave the crime scene as soon as possible because they'll try to make you clean it up.
And wash your costume, like, daily, because it will get funky and people will make fun of you.
And--and no matter what, never--
Should I get a pen?
No, listen, this is the most important thing I can possibly tell you about being Spider-Man. This is as true as it gets, if you ever see a--

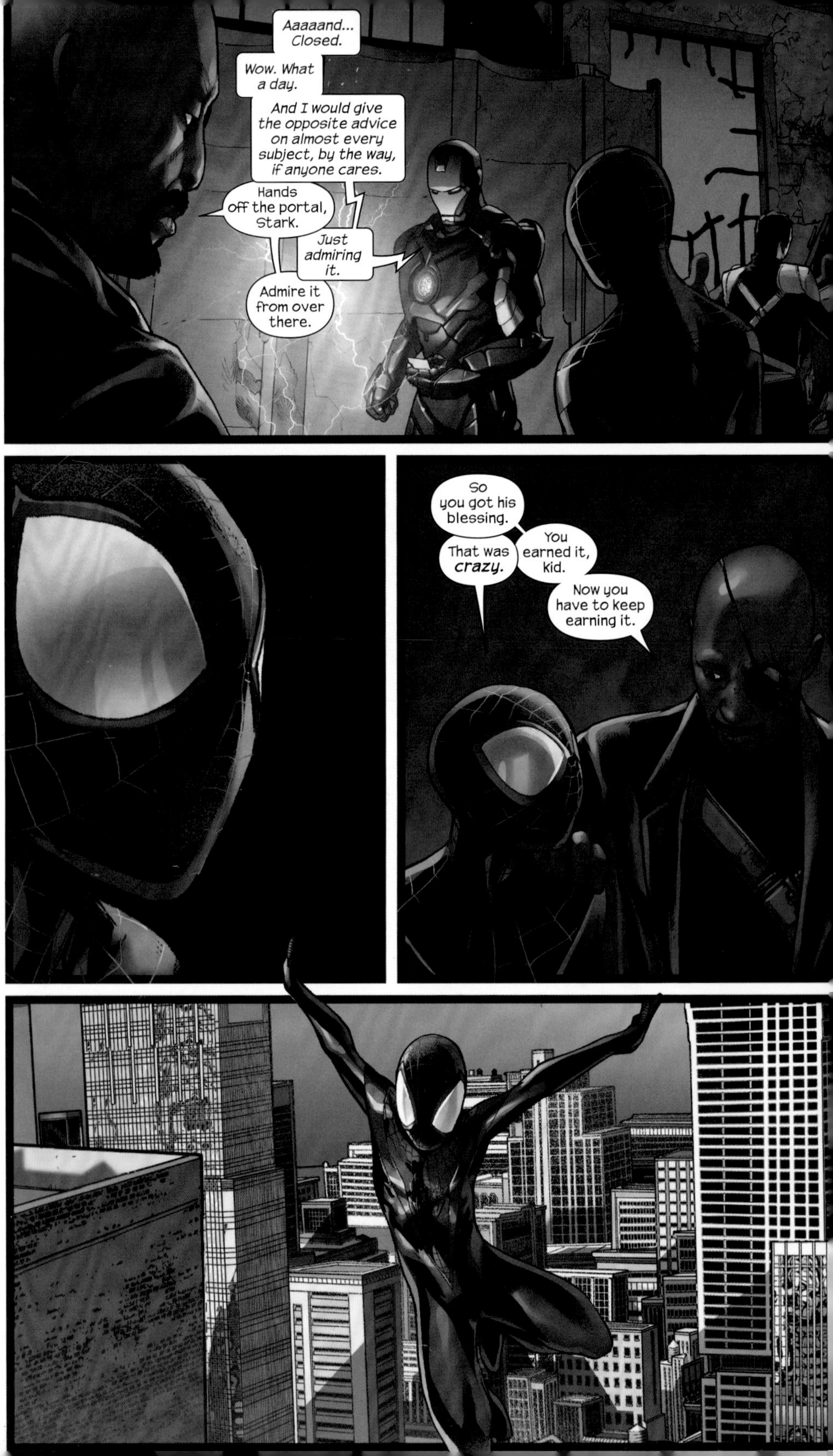
Aaaaand... Closed.
Wow. What a day.
And I would give the opposite advice on almost every subject, by the way, if anyone cares.
Hands off the portal, Stark.
Just admiring it.
Admire it from over there.
So you got his blessing.
That was *crazy.*
You earned it, kid.
Now you have to keep earning it.

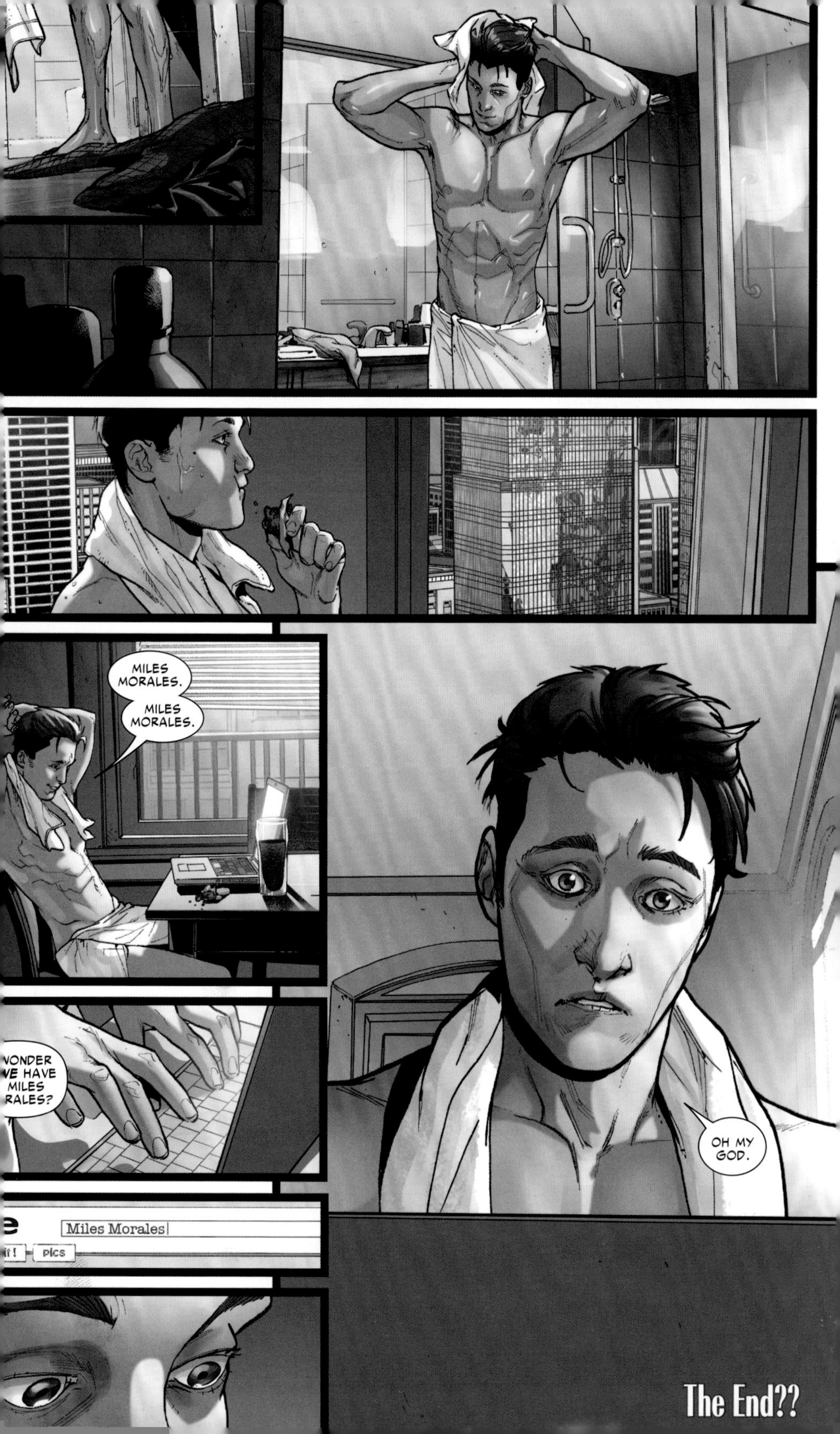

MILES MORALES.
MILES MORALES.
VONDER VE HAVE MILES RALES?
Miles Morales
PICS
OH MY GOD.
The End??

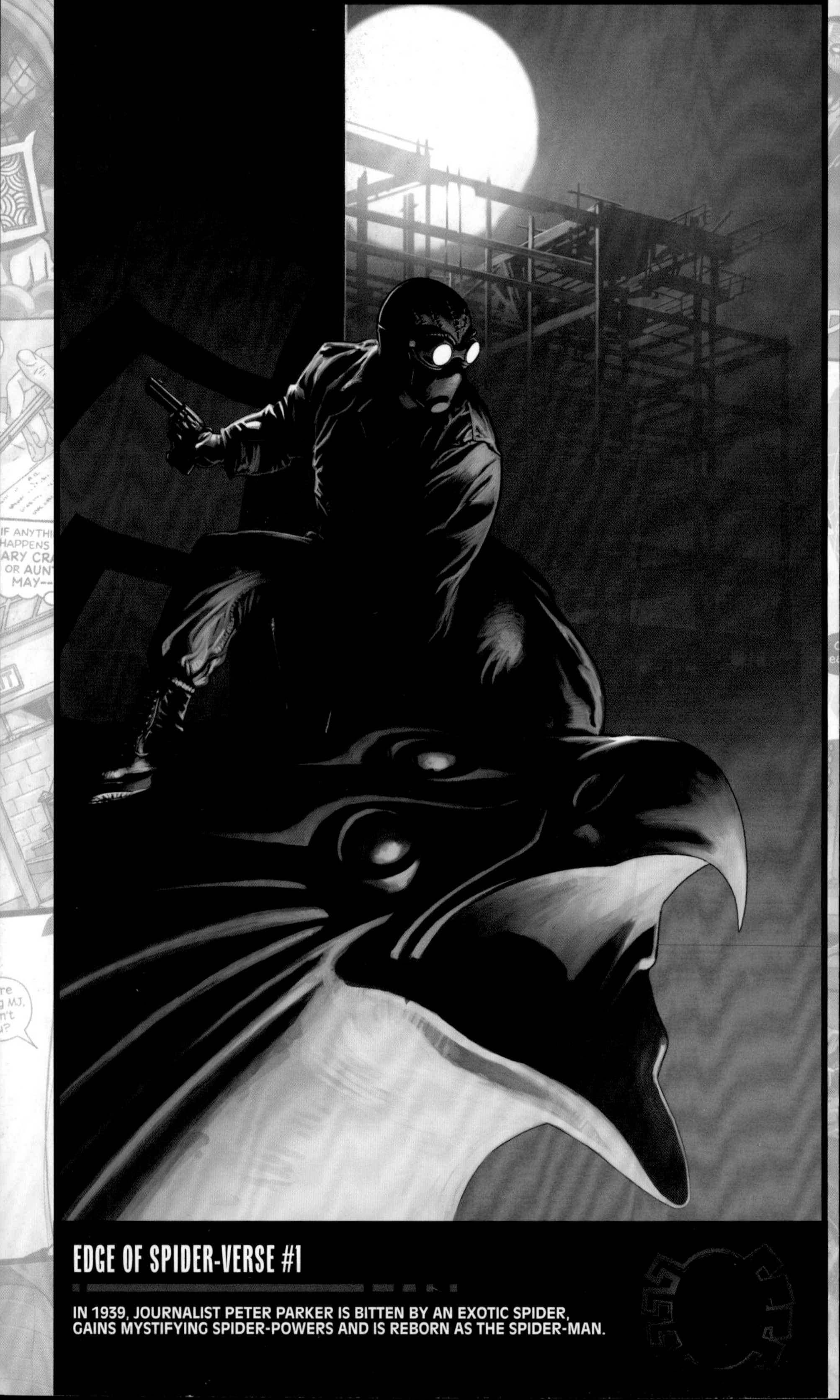

EDGE OF SPIDER-VERSE #1

IN 1939, JOURNALIST PETER PARKER IS BITTEN BY AN EXOTIC SPIDER, GAINS MYSTIFYING SPIDER-POWERS AND IS REBORN AS THE SPIDER-MAN.

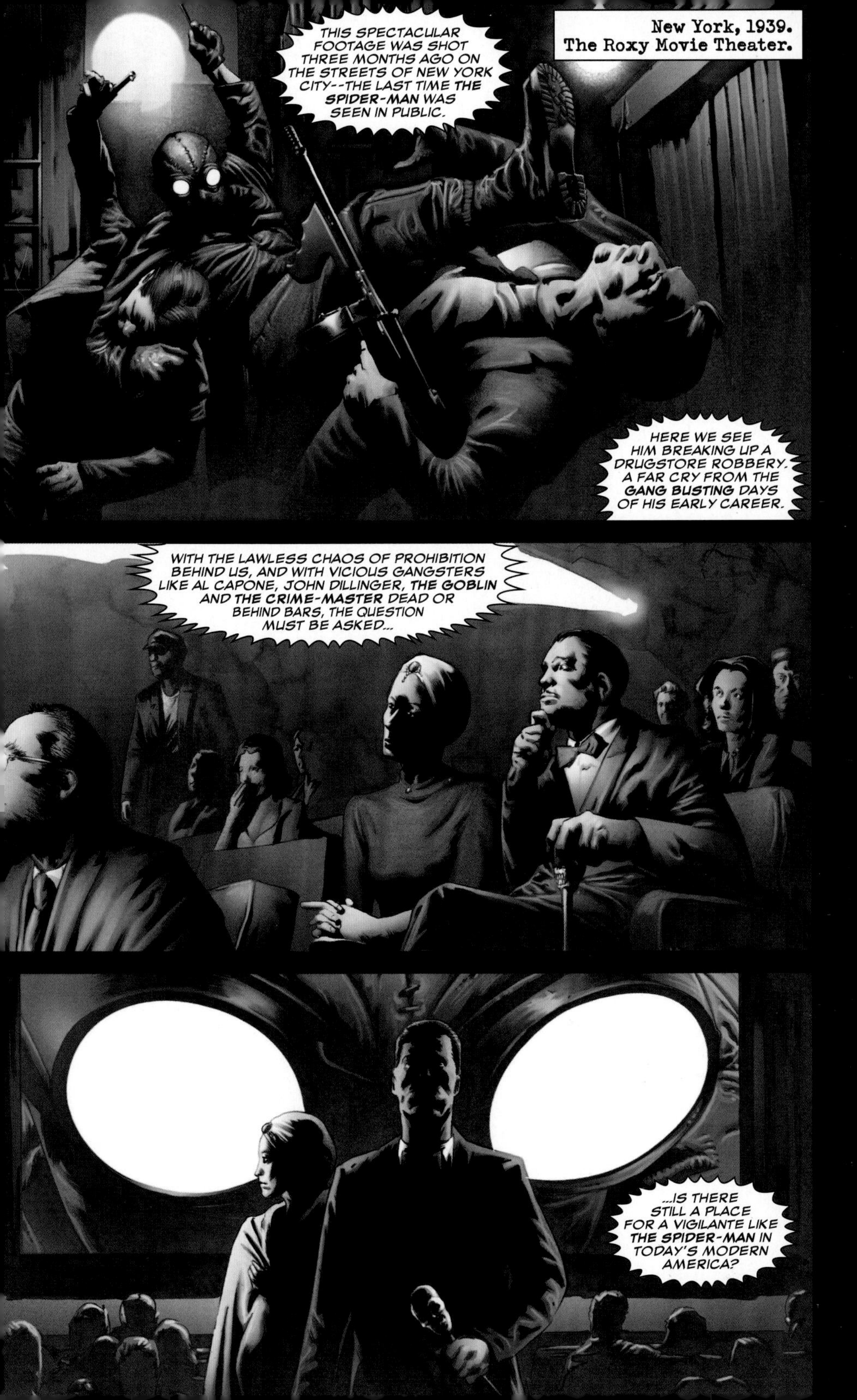
New York, 1939.
The Roxy Movie Theater.
THIS SPECTACULAR FOOTAGE WAS SHOT THREE MONTHS AGO ON THE STREETS OF NEW YORK CITY--THE LAST TIME THE SPIDER-MAN WAS SEEN IN PUBLIC.
HERE WE SEE HIM BREAKING UP A DRUGSTORE ROBBERY. A FAR CRY FROM THE GANG BUSTING DAYS OF HIS EARLY CAREER.
WITH THE LAWLESS CHAOS OF PROHIBITION BEHIND US, AND WITH VICIOUS GANGSTERS LIKE AL CAPONE, JOHN DILLINGER, THE GOBLIN AND THE CRIME-MASTER DEAD OR BEHIND BARS, THE QUESTION MUST BE ASKED...
...IS THERE STILL A PLACE FOR A VIGILANTE LIKE THE SPIDER-MAN IN TODAY'S MODERN AMERICA?

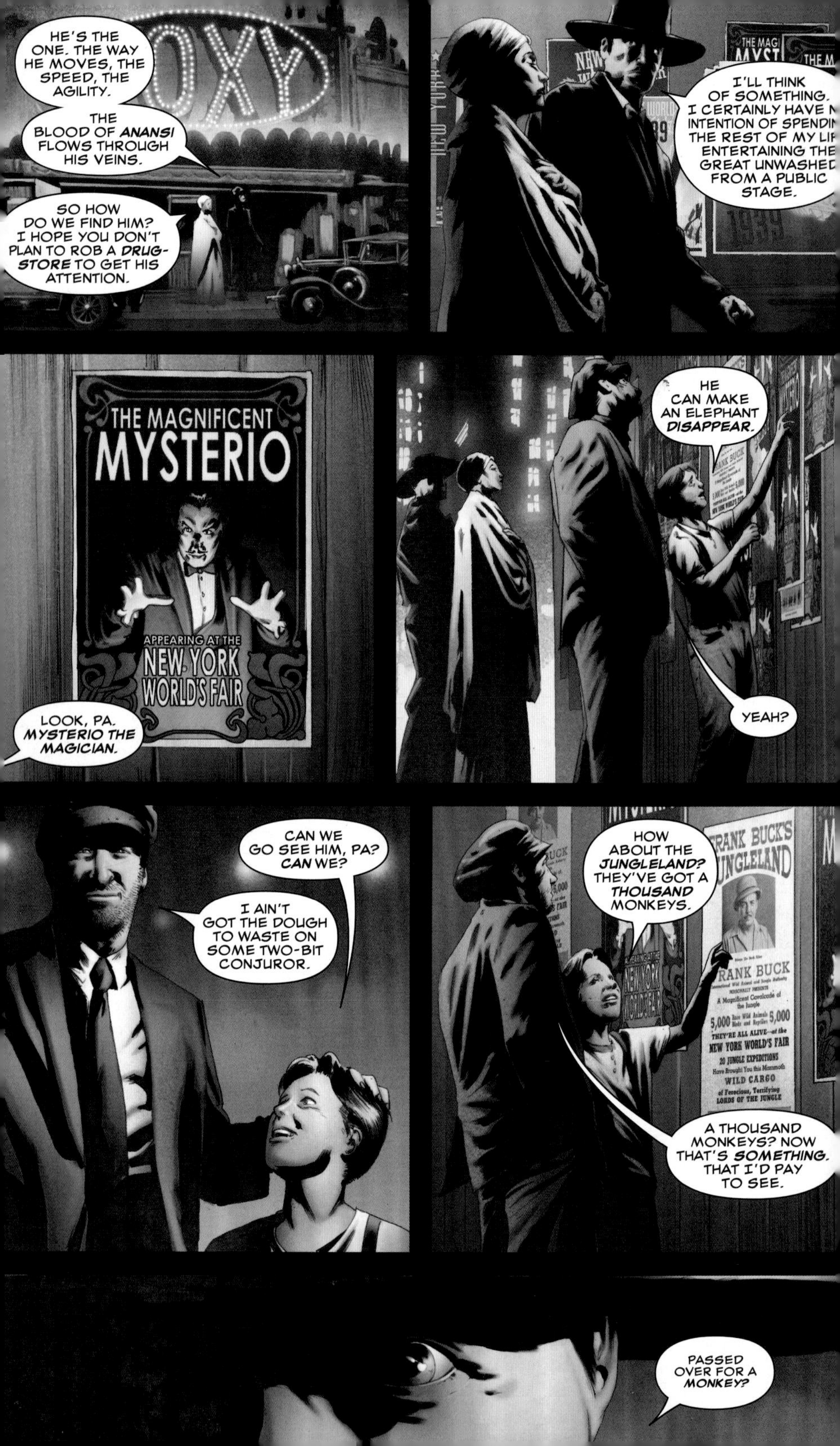
OXY
HE'S THE ONE. THE WAY HE MOVES, THE SPEED, THE AGILITY.
THE BLOOD OF *ANANSI* FLOWS THROUGH HIS VEINS.
SO HOW DO WE FIND HIM? I HOPE YOU DON'T PLAN TO ROB A *DRUG-STORE* TO GET HIS ATTENTION.
I'LL THINK OF SOMETHING. I CERTAINLY HAVE N INTENTION OF SPENDIN THE REST OF MY LIF ENTERTAINING THE GREAT UNWASHED FROM A PUBLIC STAGE.
THE MAGNIFICENT MYSTERIO
APPEARING AT THE NEW YORK WORLD'S FAIR
LOOK, PA. *MYSTERIO THE MAGICIAN.*
HE CAN MAKE AN ELEPHANT *DISAPPEAR.*
YEAH?
CAN WE GO SEE HIM, PA? *CAN* WE?
I AIN'T GOT THE DOUGH TO WASTE ON SOME TWO-BIT CONJUROR.
HOW ABOUT THE *JUNGLELAND?* THEY'VE GOT A *THOUSAND* MONKEYS.
FRANK BUCK'S JUNGLELAND
FRANK BUCK
A Magnificent Cavalcade of the Jungle
5,000 5,000
THEY'RE ALL ALIVE—at the NEW YORK WORLD'S FAIR
20 JUNGLE EXPEDITIONS
WILD CARGO
of Ferocious, Terrifying LORDS OF THE JUNGLE
A THOUSAND MONKEYS? NOW THAT'S *SOMETHING.* THAT I'D PAY TO SEE.
PASSED OVER FOR A *MONKEY?*

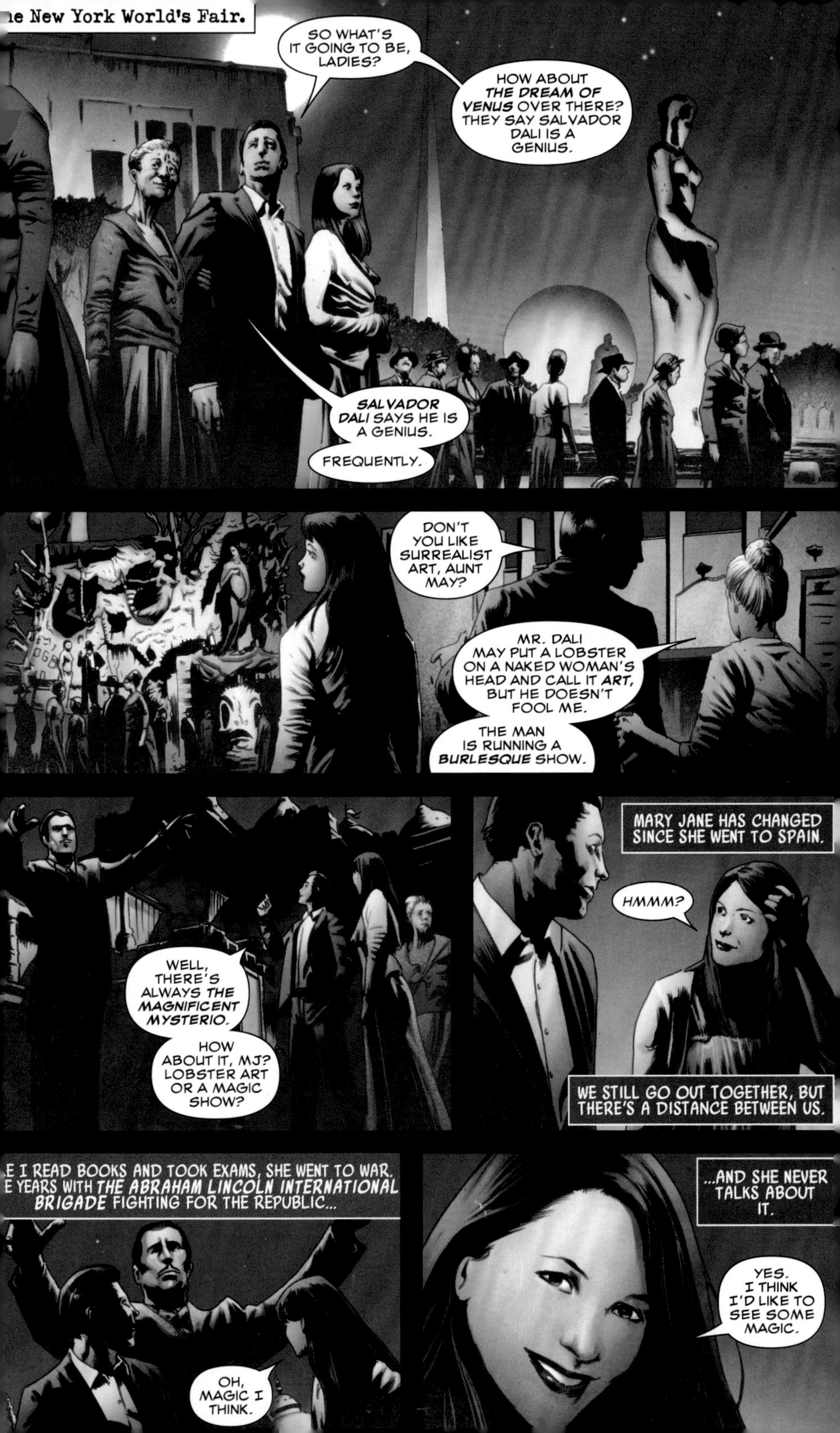
e New York World's Fair.
SO WHAT'S IT GOING TO BE, LADIES?
HOW ABOUT THE DREAM OF VENUS OVER THERE? THEY SAY SALVADOR DALI IS A GENIUS.
SALVADOR DALI SAYS HE IS A GENIUS.
FREQUENTLY.
DON'T YOU LIKE SURREALIST ART, AUNT MAY?
MR. DALI MAY PUT A LOBSTER ON A NAKED WOMAN'S HEAD AND CALL IT ART, BUT HE DOESN'T FOOL ME.
THE MAN IS RUNNING A BURLESQUE SHOW.
WELL, THERE'S ALWAYS THE MAGNIFICENT MYSTERIO.
HOW ABOUT IT, MJ? LOBSTER ART OR A MAGIC SHOW?
MARY JANE HAS CHANGED SINCE SHE WENT TO SPAIN.
HMMM?
WE STILL GO OUT TOGETHER, BUT THERE'S A DISTANCE BETWEEN US.
E I READ BOOKS AND TOOK EXAMS, SHE WENT TO WAR.
E YEARS WITH THE ABRAHAM LINCOLN INTERNATIONAL BRIGADE FIGHTING FOR THE REPUBLIC...
OH, MAGIC I THINK.
...AND SHE NEVER TALKS ABOUT IT.
YES. I THINK I'D LIKE TO SEE SOME MAGIC.

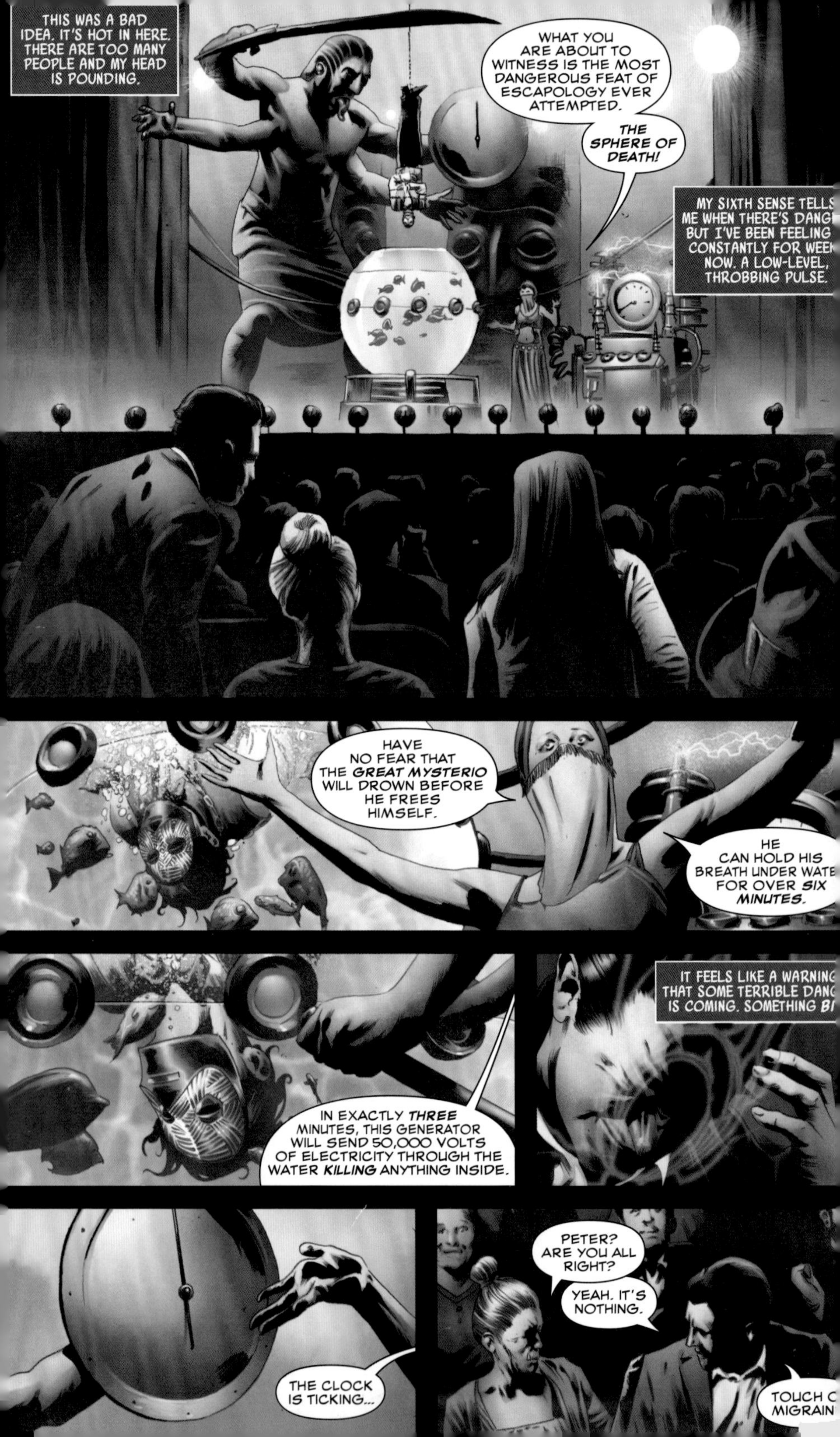
THIS WAS A BAD IDEA. IT'S HOT IN HERE. THERE ARE TOO MANY PEOPLE AND MY HEAD IS POUNDING.
WHAT YOU ARE ABOUT TO WITNESS IS THE MOST DANGEROUS FEAT OF ESCAPOLOGY EVER ATTEMPTED.
THE SPHERE OF DEATH!
MY SIXTH SENSE TELLS ME WHEN THERE'S BUT I'VE BEEN FEELING CONSTANTLY FOR NOW. A LOW-LEVEL, THROBBING PULSE.
HAVE NO FEAR THAT THE GREAT MYSTERIO WILL DROWN BEFORE HE FREES HIMSELF.
HE CAN HOLD HIS BREATH UNDER FOR OVER SIX MINUTES.
IN EXACTLY THREE MINUTES, THIS GENERATOR WILL SEND 50,000 VOLTS OF ELECTRICITY THROUGH THE WATER KILLING ANYTHING INSIDE.
IT FEELS LIKE A WARNING THAT SOME TERRIBLE IS COMING. SOMETHING
THE CLOCK IS TICKING...
PETER? ARE YOU ALL RIGHT?
YEAH. IT'S NOTHING.
TOUCH

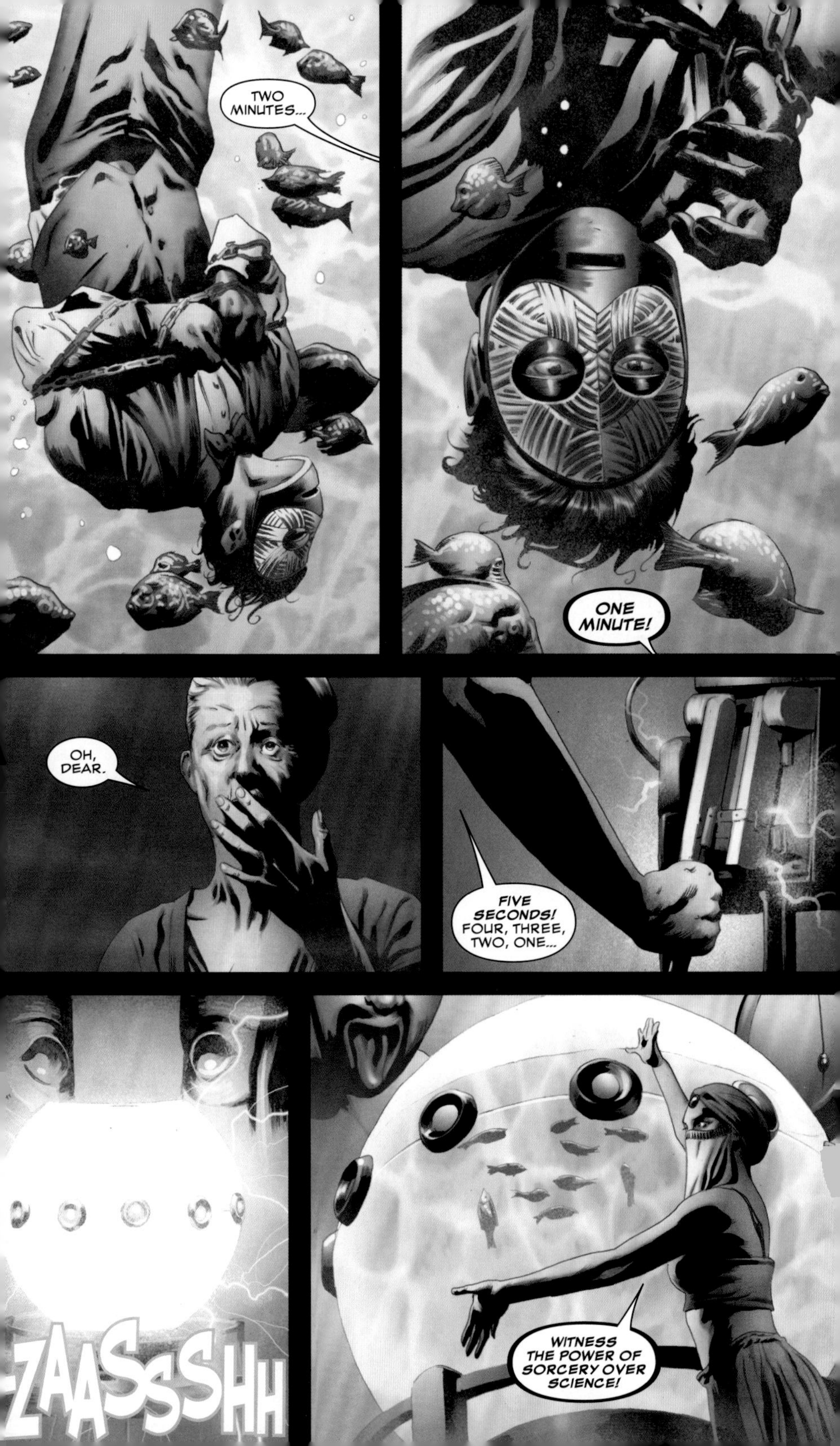
TWO MINUTES...
ONE MINUTE!
OH, DEAR.
FIVE SECONDS! FOUR, THREE, TWO, ONE...
ZAASSSHH
WITNESS THE POWER OF SORCERY OVER SCIENCE!

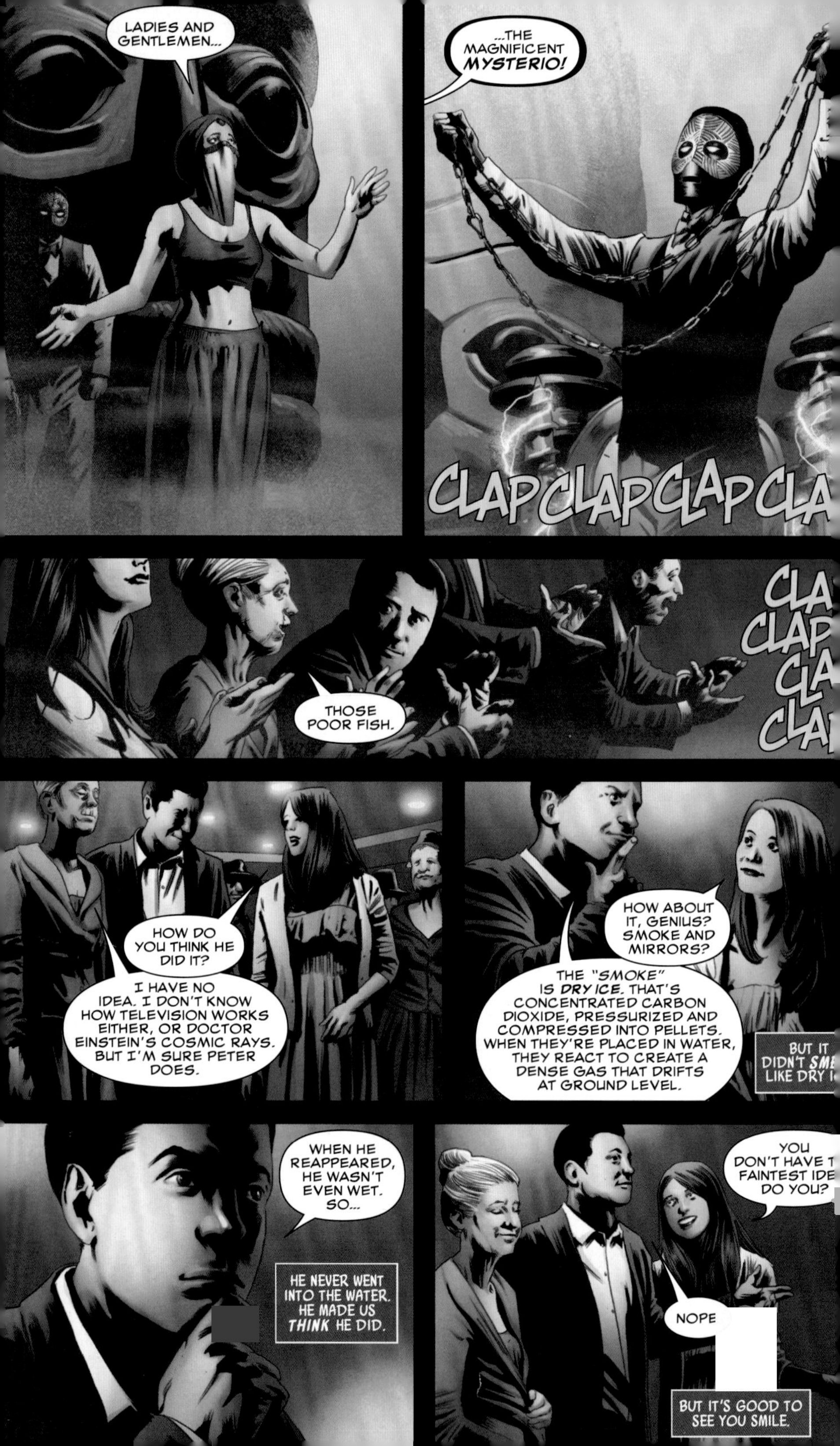
LADIES AND GENTLEMEN...
...THE MAGNIFICENT MYSTERIO!
CLAP CLAP CLAP CLA
CLA CLAP CLA CLA
THOSE POOR FISH.
HOW DO YOU THINK HE DID IT?
I HAVE NO IDEA. I DON'T KNOW HOW TELEVISION WORKS EITHER, OR DOCTOR EINSTEIN'S COSMIC RAYS. BUT I'M SURE PETER DOES.
HOW ABOUT IT, GENIUS? SMOKE AND MIRRORS?
THE "SMOKE" IS DRY ICE. THAT'S CONCENTRATED CARBON DIOXIDE, PRESSURIZED AND COMPRESSED INTO PELLETS. WHEN THEY'RE PLACED IN WATER, THEY REACT TO CREATE A DENSE GAS THAT DRIFTS AT GROUND LEVEL.
BUT IT DIDN'T SME LIKE DRY I
WHEN HE REAPPEARED, HE WASN'T EVEN WET. SO...
HE NEVER WENT INTO THE WATER. HE MADE US THINK HE DID.
YOU DON'T HAVE T FAINTEST IDE DO YOU?
NOPE
BUT IT'S GOOD TO SEE YOU SMILE.

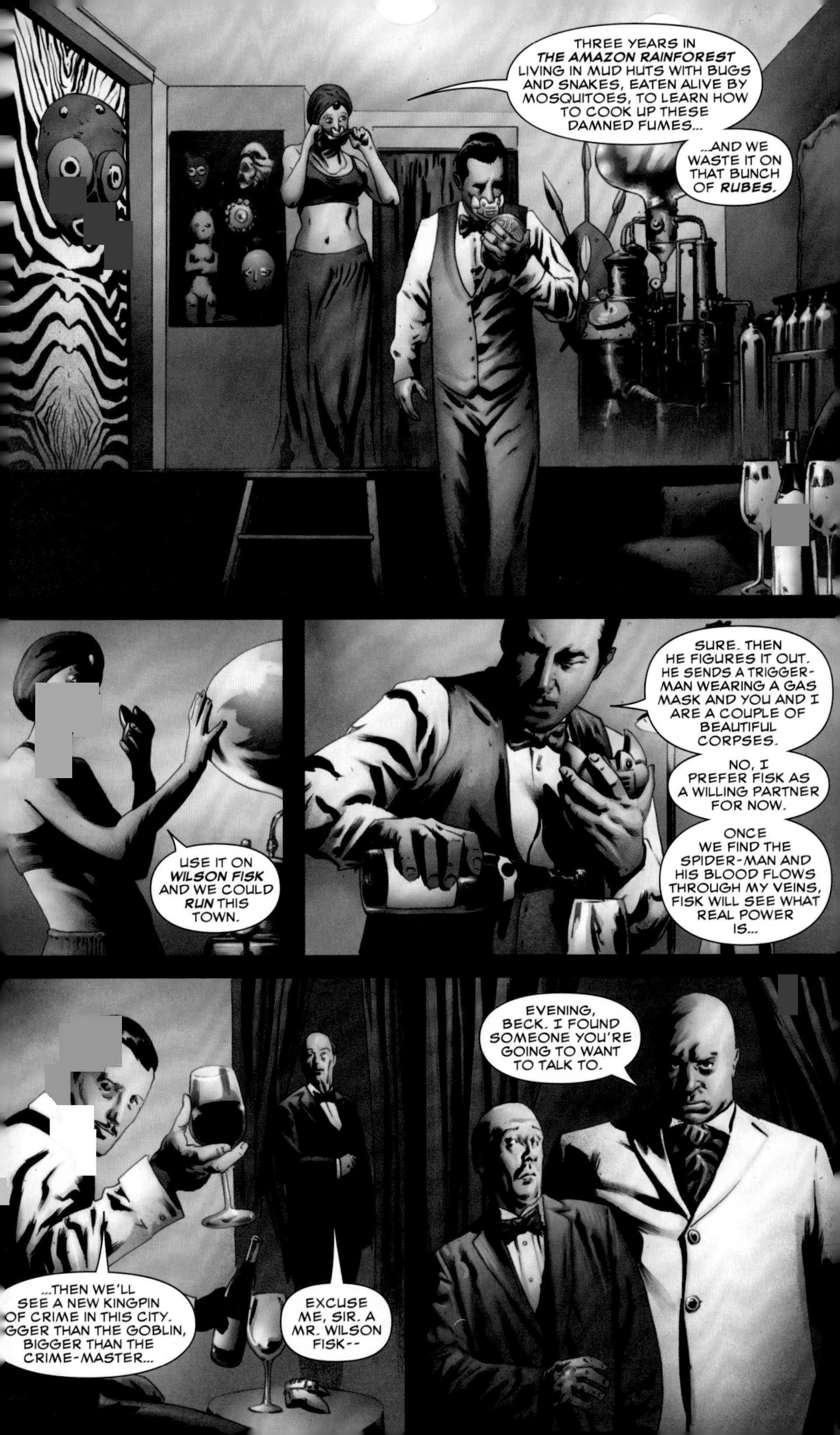
THREE YEARS IN THE AMAZON RAINFOREST LIVING IN MUD HUTS WITH BUGS AND SNAKES, EATEN ALIVE BY MOSQUITOES, TO LEARN HOW TO COOK UP THESE DAMNED FUMES...
...AND WE WASTE IT ON THAT BUNCH OF RUBES.
USE IT ON WILSON FISK AND WE COULD RUN THIS TOWN.
SURE. THEN HE FIGURES IT OUT. HE SENDS A TRIGGER-MAN WEARING A GAS MASK AND YOU AND I ARE A COUPLE OF BEAUTIFUL CORPSES.
NO, I PREFER FISK AS A WILLING PARTNER FOR NOW.
ONCE WE FIND THE SPIDER-MAN AND HIS BLOOD FLOWS THROUGH MY VEINS, FISK WILL SEE WHAT REAL POWER IS...
...THEN WE'LL SEE A NEW KINGPIN OF CRIME IN THIS CITY. GGER THAN THE GOBLIN, BIGGER THAN THE CRIME-MASTER...
EXCUSE ME, SIR. A MR. WILSON FISK--
EVENING, BECK. I FOUND SOMEONE YOU'RE GOING TO WANT TO TALK TO.

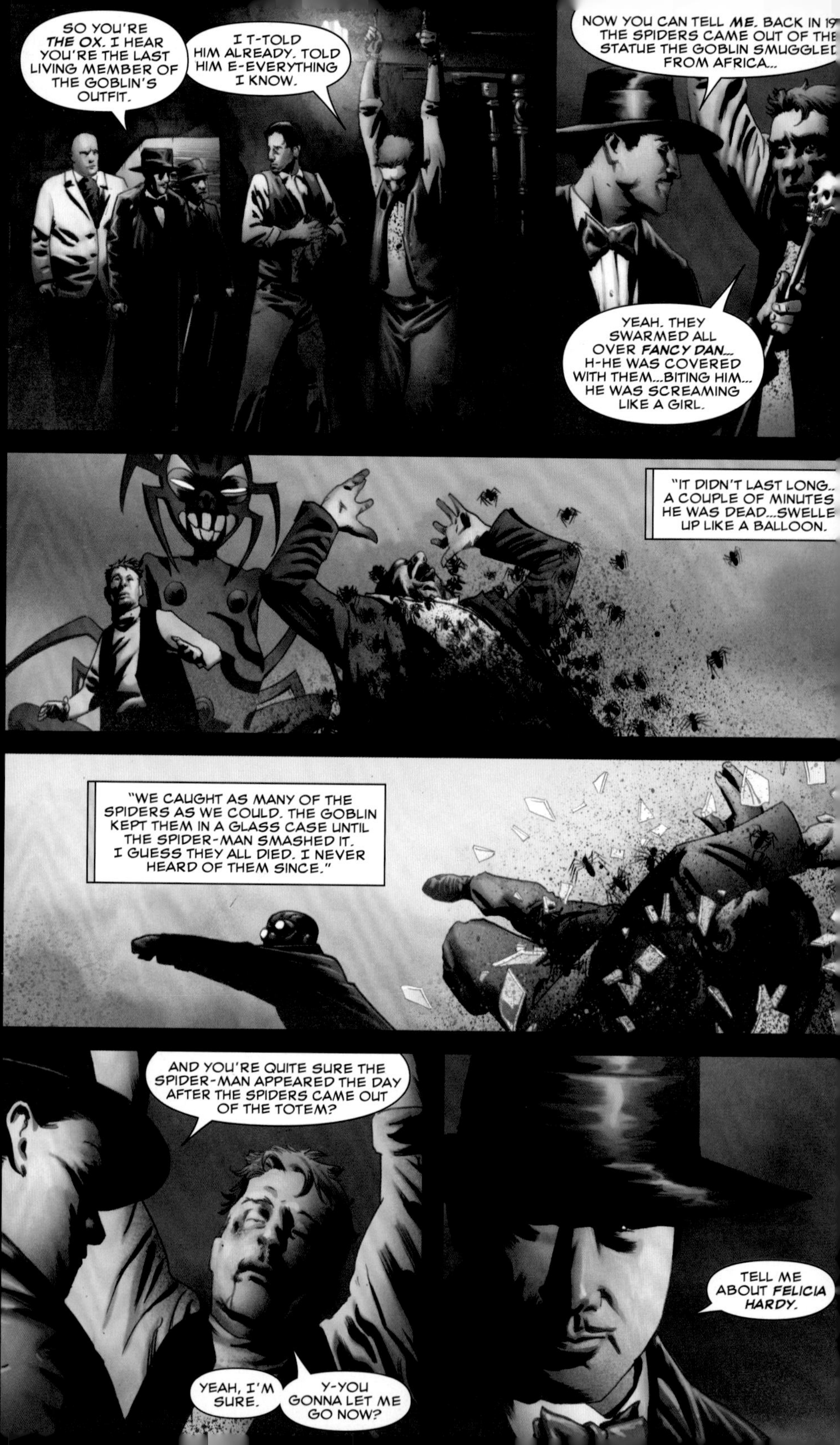
SO YOU'RE THE OX. I HEAR YOU'RE THE LAST LIVING MEMBER OF THE GOBLIN'S OUTFIT.
I T-TOLD HIM ALREADY. TOLD HIM E-EVERYTHING I KNOW.
NOW YOU CAN TELL ME. BACK IN 19 THE SPIDERS CAME OUT OF THE STATUE THE GOBLIN SMUGGLED FROM AFRICA...
YEAH. THEY SWARMED ALL OVER FANCY DAN... H-HE WAS COVERED WITH THEM...BITING HIM... HE WAS SCREAMING LIKE A GIRL.
"IT DIDN'T LAST LONG.. A COUPLE OF MINUTES HE WAS DEAD...SWELLE UP LIKE A BALLOON.
"WE CAUGHT AS MANY OF THE SPIDERS AS WE COULD. THE GOBLIN KEPT THEM IN A GLASS CASE UNTIL THE SPIDER-MAN SMASHED IT. I GUESS THEY ALL DIED. I NEVER HEARD OF THEM SINCE."
AND YOU'RE QUITE SURE THE SPIDER-MAN APPEARED THE DAY AFTER THE SPIDERS CAME OUT OF THE TOTEM?
YEAH, I'M SURE.
Y-YOU GONNA LET ME GO NOW?
TELL ME ABOUT FELICIA HARDY.

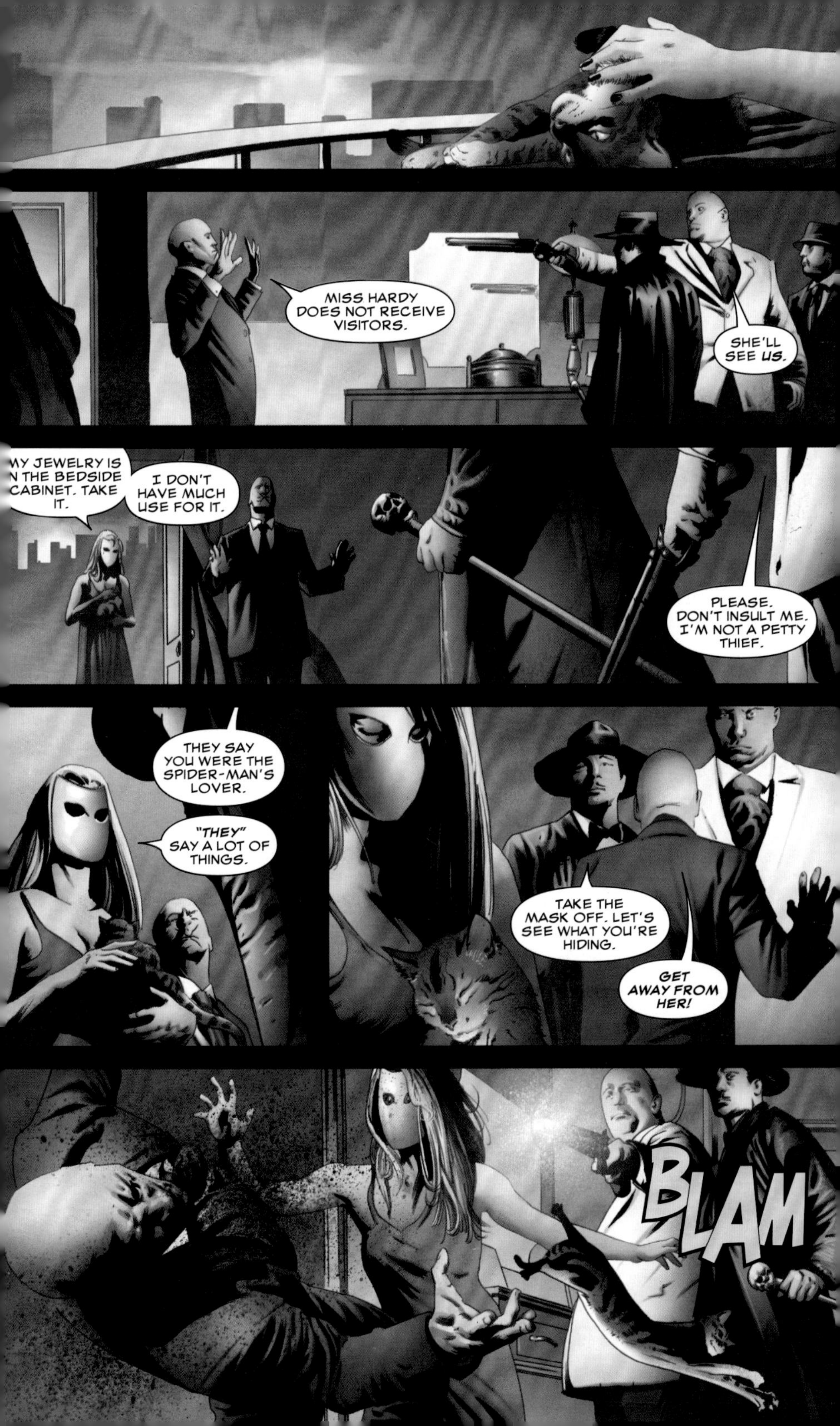
MISS HARDY DOES NOT RECEIVE VISITORS.
SHE'LL SEE *US*.
MY JEWELRY IS N THE BEDSIDE CABINET. TAKE IT.
I DON'T HAVE MUCH USE FOR IT.
PLEASE. DON'T INSULT ME. I'M NOT A PETTY THIEF.
THEY SAY YOU WERE THE SPIDER-MAN'S LOVER.
"THEY" SAY A LOT OF THINGS.
TAKE THE MASK OFF. LET'S SEE WHAT YOU'RE HIDING.
GET AWAY FROM HER!
BLAM

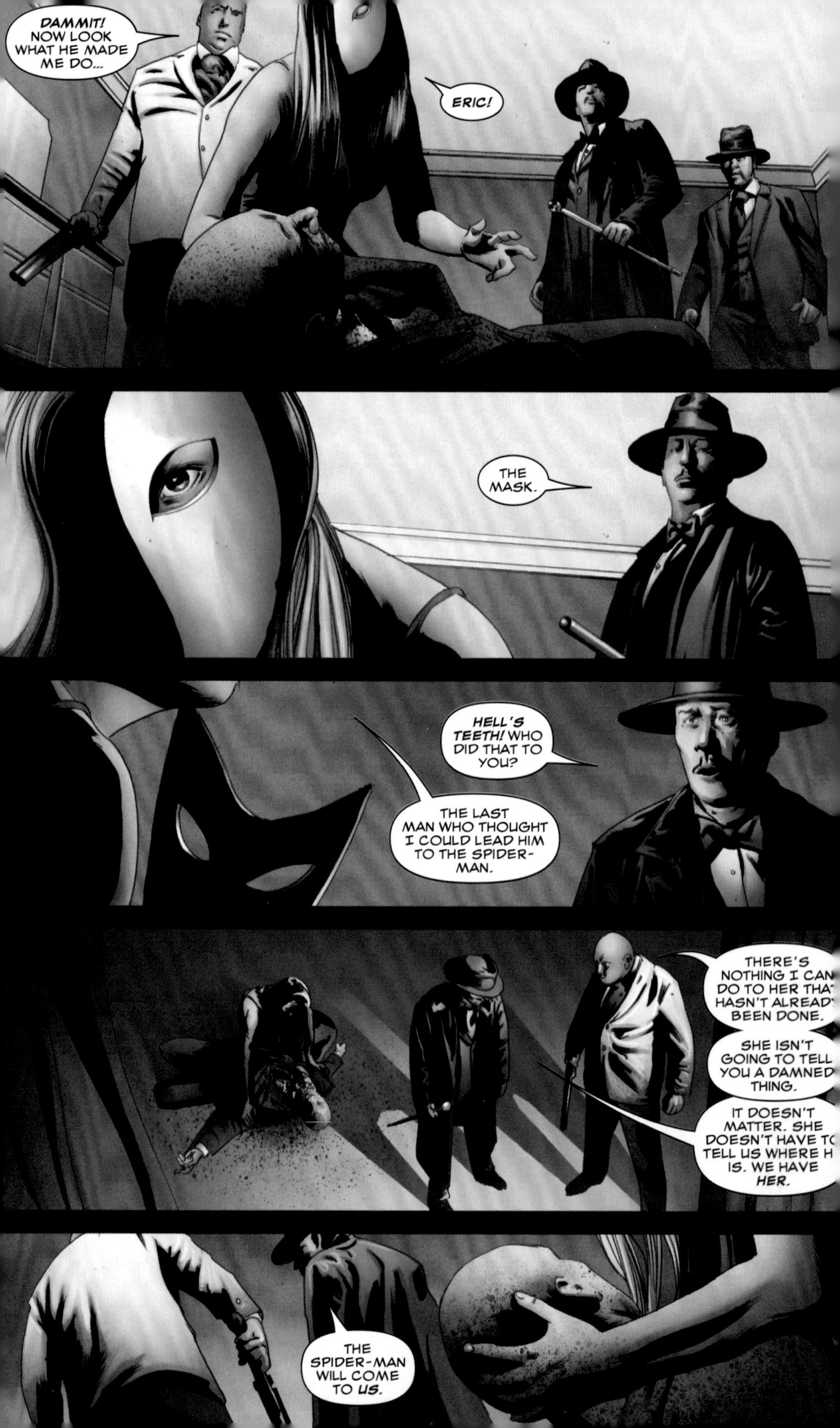
DAMMIT! NOW LOOK WHAT HE MADE ME DO...
ERIC!
THE MASK.
HELL'S TEETH! WHO DID THAT TO YOU?
THE LAST MAN WHO THOUGHT I COULD LEAD HIM TO THE SPIDER-MAN.
THERE'S NOTHING I CAN DO TO HER THAT HASN'T ALREADY BEEN DONE.
SHE ISN'T GOING TO TELL YOU A DAMNED THING.
IT DOESN'T MATTER. SHE DOESN'T HAVE TO TELL US WHERE HE IS. WE HAVE HER.
THE SPIDER-MAN WILL COME TO US.

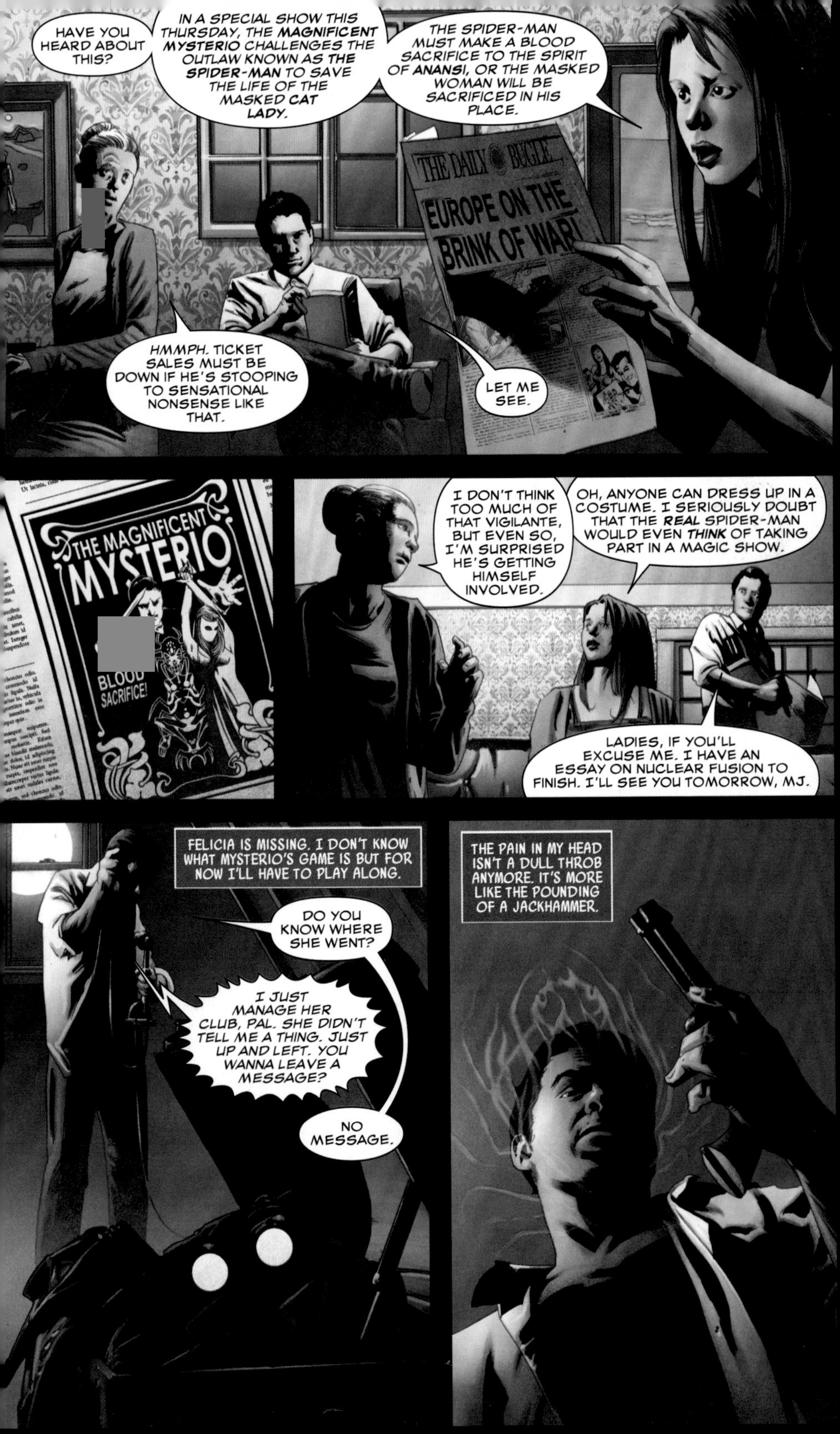
HAVE YOU HEARD ABOUT THIS?
IN A SPECIAL SHOW THIS THURSDAY, THE MAGNIFICENT MYSTERIO CHALLENGES THE OUTLAW KNOWN AS THE SPIDER-MAN TO SAVE THE LIFE OF THE MASKED CAT LADY.
THE SPIDER-MAN MUST MAKE A BLOOD SACRIFICE TO THE SPIRIT OF ANANSI, OR THE MASKED WOMAN WILL BE SACRIFICED IN HIS PLACE.
THE DAILY BUGLE
EUROPE ON THE BRINK OF WAR!
HMMPH. TICKET SALES MUST BE DOWN IF HE'S STOOPING TO SENSATIONAL NONSENSE LIKE THAT.
LET ME SEE.
THE MAGNIFICENT MYSTERIO
BLOOD SACRIFICE!
I DON'T THINK TOO MUCH OF THAT VIGILANTE, BUT EVEN SO, I'M SURPRISED HE'S GETTING HIMSELF INVOLVED.
OH, ANYONE CAN DRESS UP IN A COSTUME. I SERIOUSLY DOUBT THAT THE REAL SPIDER-MAN WOULD EVEN THINK OF TAKING PART IN A MAGIC SHOW.
LADIES, IF YOU'LL EXCUSE ME. I HAVE AN ESSAY ON NUCLEAR FUSION TO FINISH. I'LL SEE YOU TOMORROW, MJ.
FELICIA IS MISSING. I DON'T KNOW WHAT MYSTERIO'S GAME IS BUT FOR NOW I'LL HAVE TO PLAY ALONG.
DO YOU KNOW WHERE SHE WENT?
I JUST MANAGE HER CLUB, PAL. SHE DIDN'T TELL ME A THING. JUST UP AND LEFT. YOU WANNA LEAVE A MESSAGE?
NO MESSAGE.
THE PAIN IN MY HEAD ISN'T A DULL THROB ANYMORE. IT'S MORE LIKE THE POUNDING OF A JACKHAMMER.

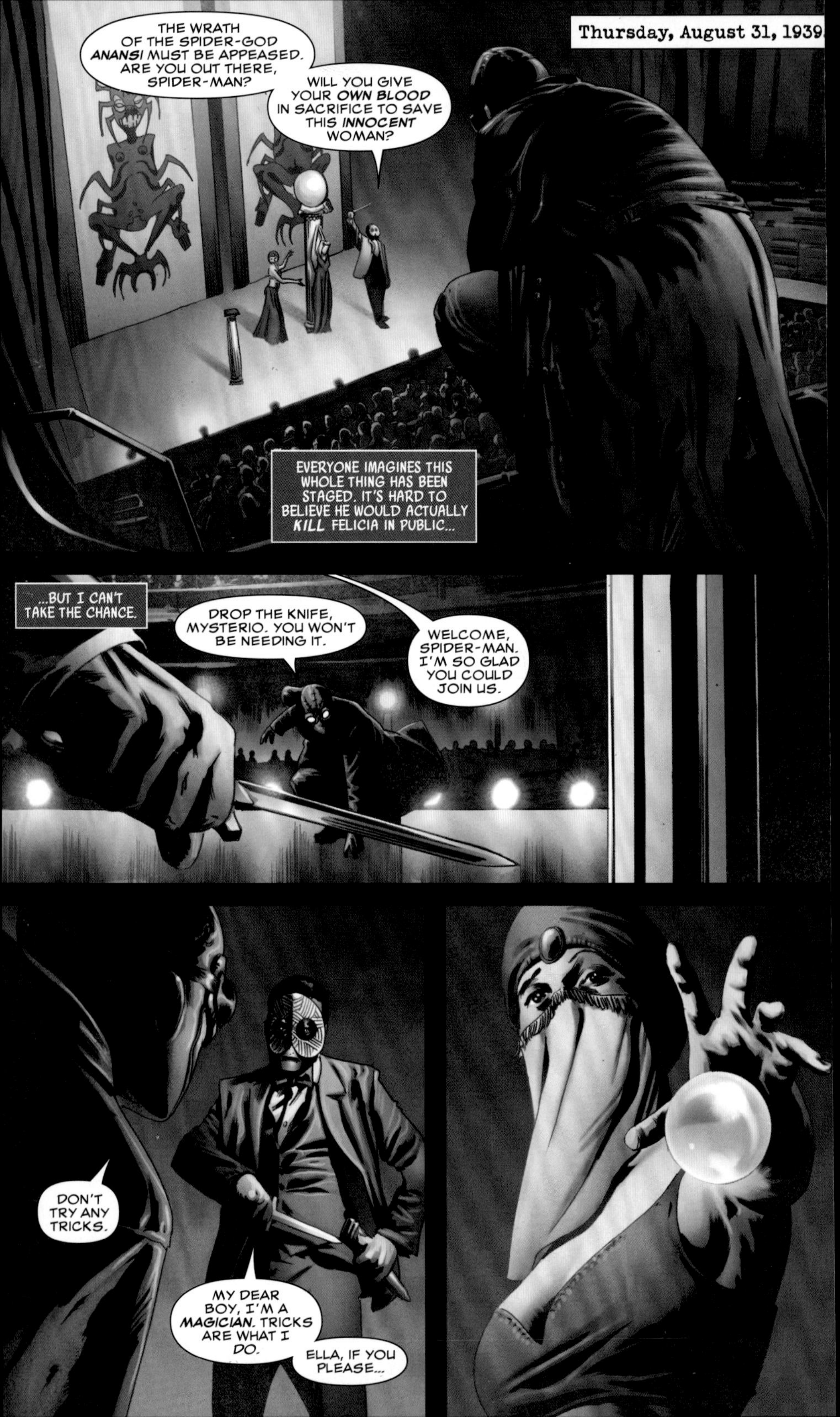
Thursday, August 31, 1939.
THE WRATH OF THE SPIDER-GOD ANANSI MUST BE APPEASED. ARE YOU OUT THERE, SPIDER-MAN?
WILL YOU GIVE YOUR OWN BLOOD IN SACRIFICE TO SAVE THIS INNOCENT WOMAN?
EVERYONE IMAGINES THIS WHOLE THING HAS BEEN STAGED. IT'S HARD TO BELIEVE HE WOULD ACTUALLY KILL FELICIA IN PUBLIC...
...BUT I CAN'T TAKE THE CHANCE.
DROP THE KNIFE, MYSTERIO. YOU WON'T BE NEEDING IT.
WELCOME, SPIDER-MAN. I'M SO GLAD YOU COULD JOIN US.
DON'T TRY ANY TRICKS.
MY DEAR BOY, I'M A MAGICIAN. TRICKS ARE WHAT I DO.
ELLA, IF YOU PLEASE...

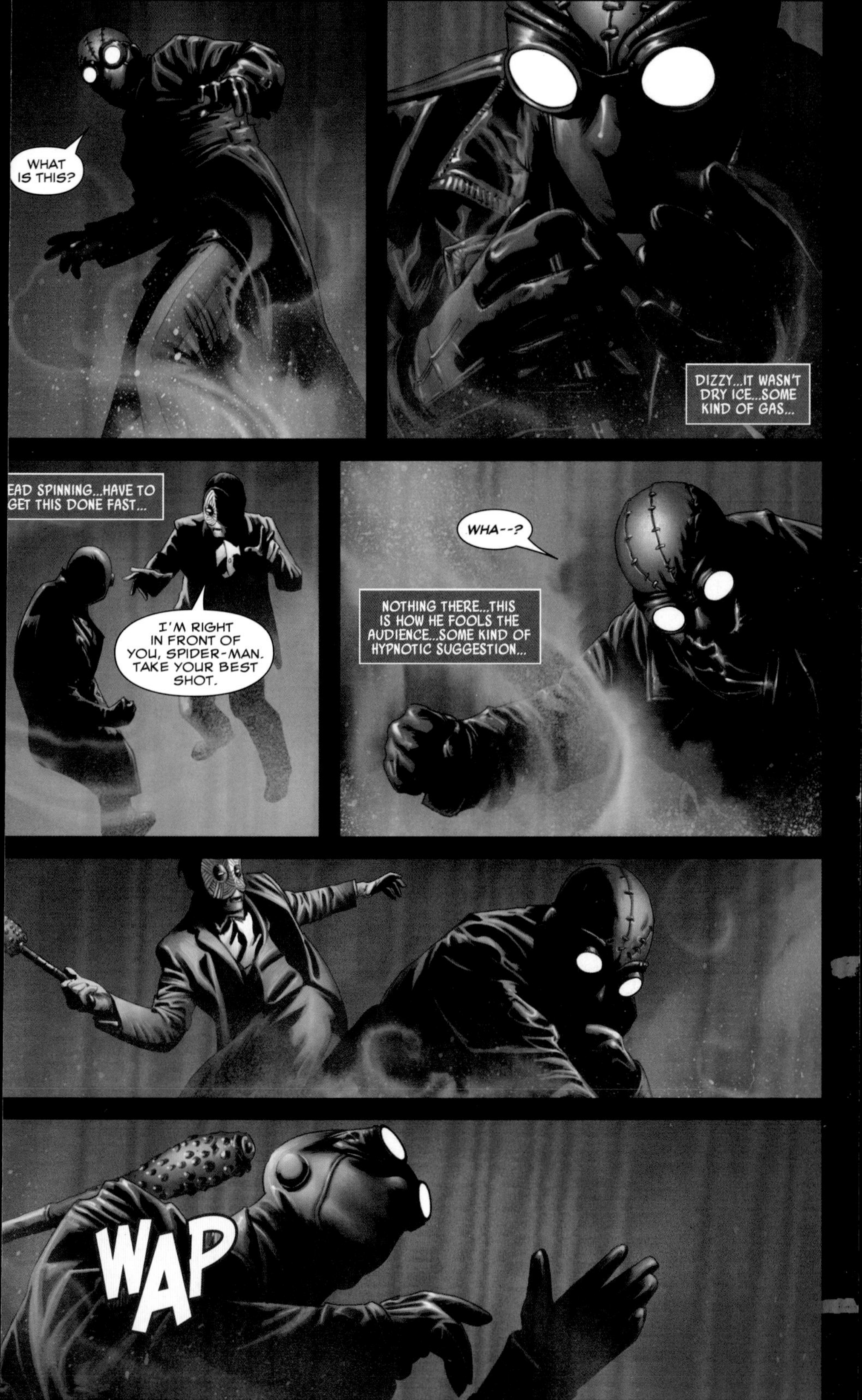
WHAT IS THIS?
DIZZY...IT WASN'T DRY ICE...SOME KIND OF GAS...
EAD SPINNING...HAVE TO GET THIS DONE FAST...
I'M RIGHT IN FRONT OF YOU, SPIDER-MAN. TAKE YOUR BEST SHOT.
WHA--?
NOTHING THERE...THIS IS HOW HE FOOLS THE AUDIENCE...SOME KIND OF HYPNOTIC SUGGESTION...
WAP

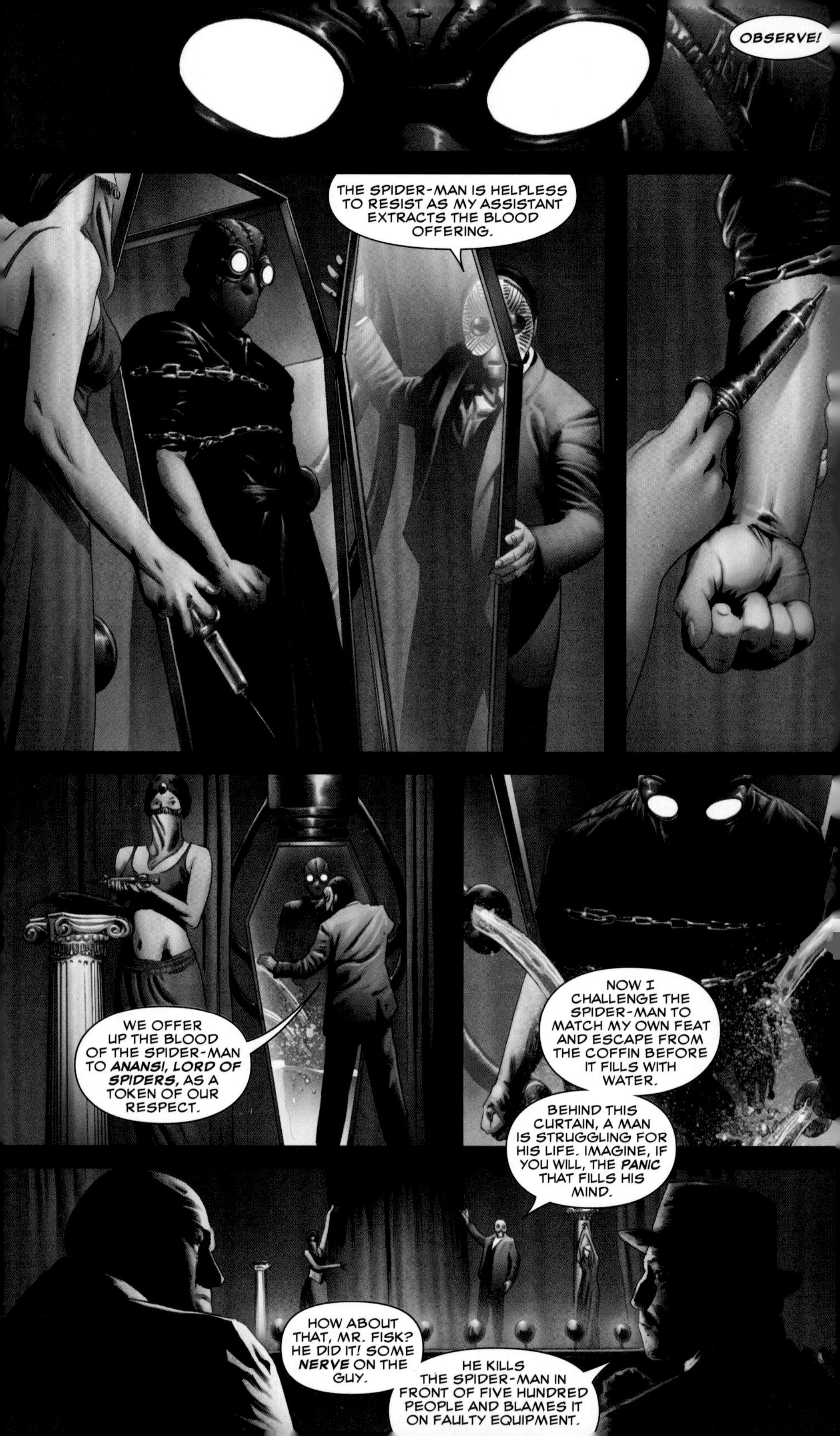
OBSERVE!
THE SPIDER-MAN IS HELPLESS TO RESIST AS MY ASSISTANT EXTRACTS THE BLOOD OFFERING.
WE OFFER UP THE BLOOD OF THE SPIDER-MAN TO ANANSI, LORD OF SPIDERS, AS A TOKEN OF OUR RESPECT.
NOW I CHALLENGE THE SPIDER-MAN TO MATCH MY OWN FEAT AND ESCAPE FROM THE COFFIN BEFORE IT FILLS WITH WATER.
BEHIND THIS CURTAIN, A MAN IS STRUGGLING FOR HIS LIFE. IMAGINE, IF YOU WILL, THE PANIC THAT FILLS HIS MIND.
HOW ABOUT THAT, MR. FISK? HE DID IT! SOME NERVE ON THE GUY.
HE KILLS THE SPIDER-MAN IN FRONT OF FIVE HUNDRED PEOPLE AND BLAMES IT ON FAULTY EQUIPMENT.

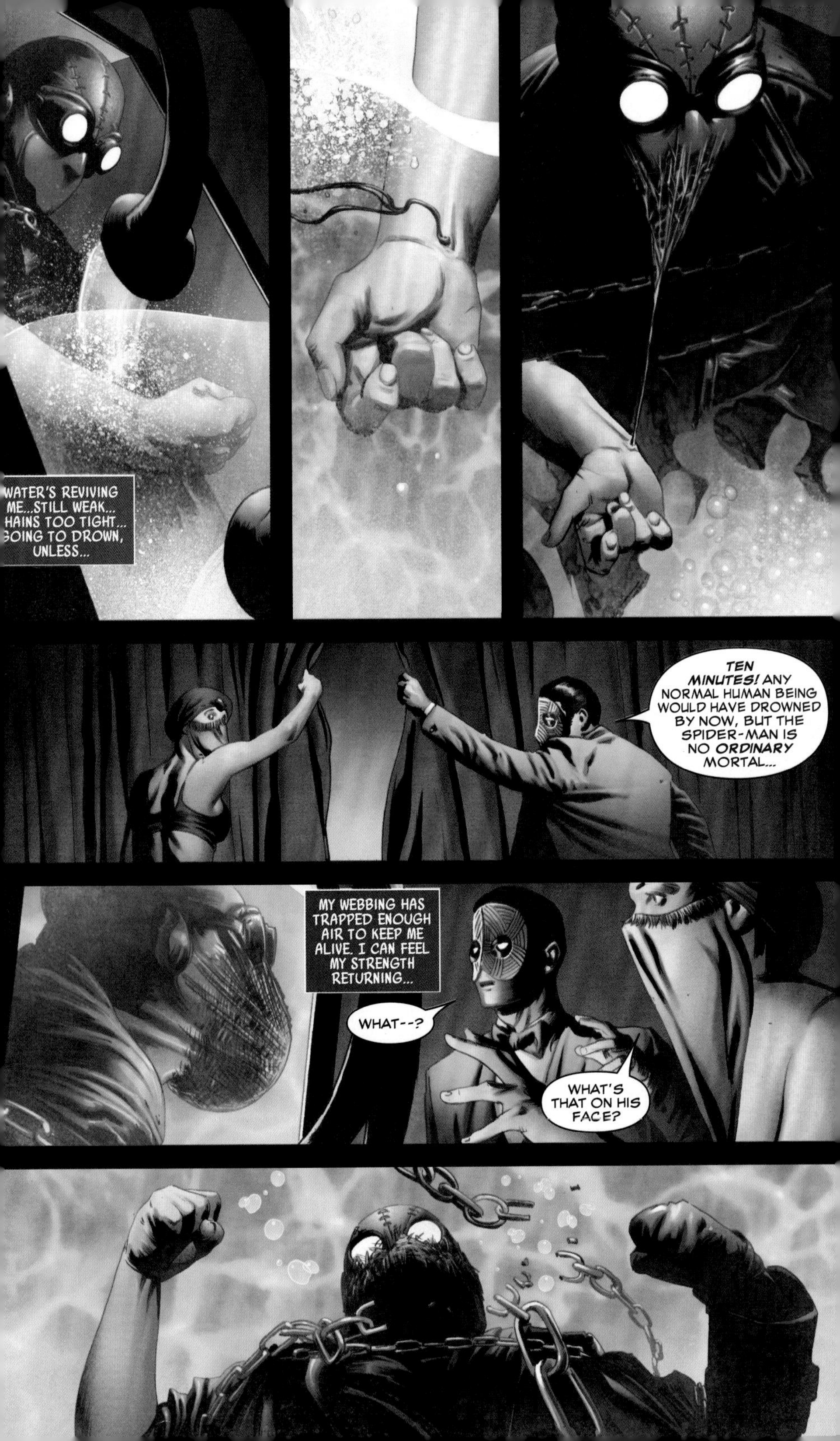
WATER'S REVIVING ME...STILL WEAK... HAINS TOO TIGHT... GOING TO DROWN, UNLESS...
TEN MINUTES! ANY NORMAL HUMAN BEING WOULD HAVE DROWNED BY NOW, BUT THE SPIDER-MAN IS NO ORDINARY MORTAL...
MY WEBBING HAS TRAPPED ENOUGH AIR TO KEEP ME ALIVE. I CAN FEEL MY STRENGTH RETURNING...
WHAT--?
WHAT'S THAT ON HIS FACE?

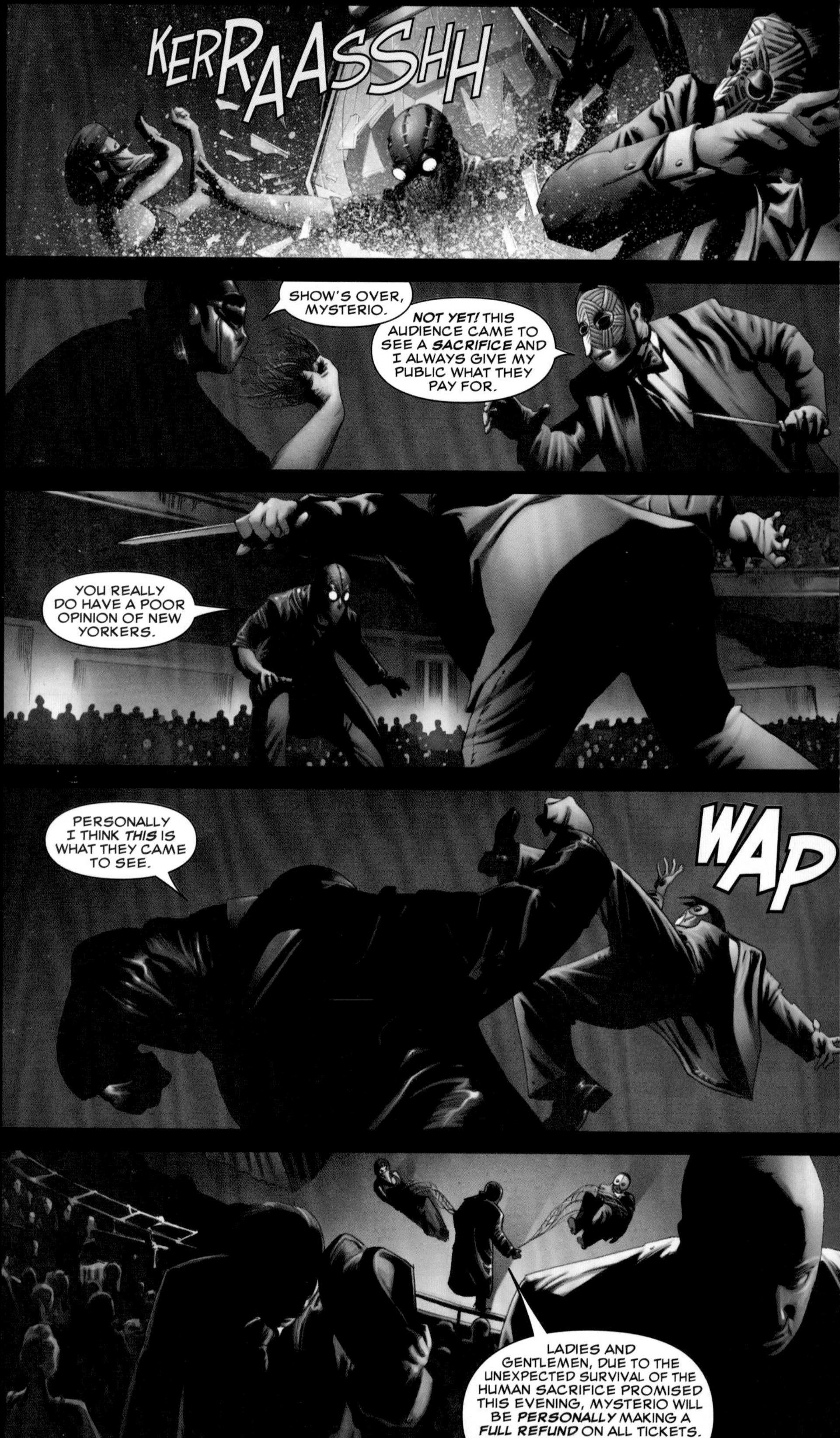
KERRAASSHH
SHOW'S OVER, MYSTERIO.
NOT YET! THIS AUDIENCE CAME TO SEE A SACRIFICE AND I ALWAYS GIVE MY PUBLIC WHAT THEY PAY FOR.
YOU REALLY DO HAVE A POOR OPINION OF NEW YORKERS.
PERSONALLY I THINK THIS IS WHAT THEY CAME TO SEE.
WAP
LADIES AND GENTLEMEN, DUE TO THE UNEXPECTED SURVIVAL OF THE HUMAN SACRIFICE PROMISED THIS EVENING, MYSTERIO WILL BE PERSONALLY MAKING A FULL REFUND ON ALL TICKETS.

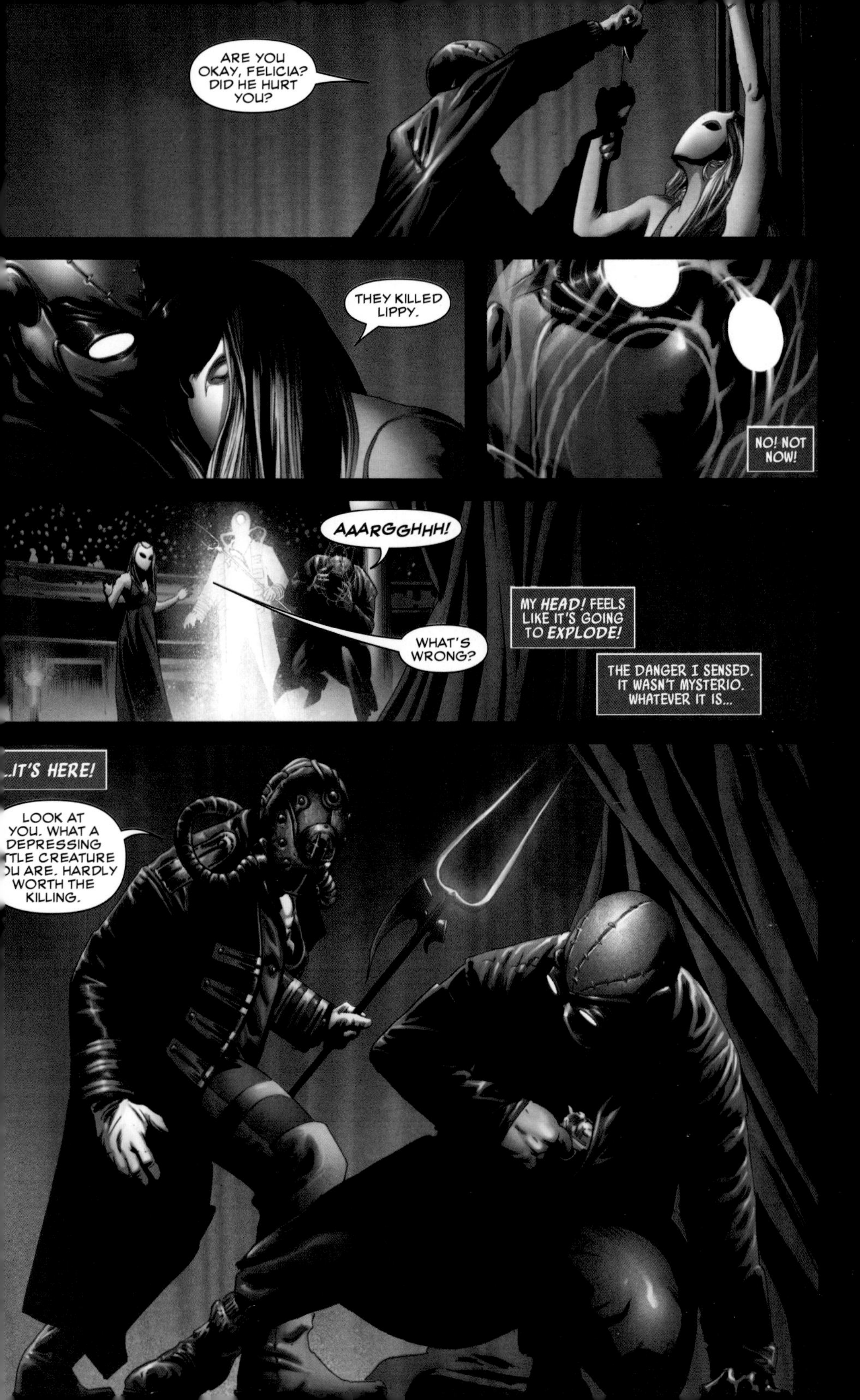
ARE YOU OKAY, FELICIA? DID HE HURT YOU?
THEY KILLED LIPPY.
NO! NOT NOW!
AAARGGHHH!
WHAT'S WRONG?
MY HEAD! FEELS LIKE IT'S GOING TO EXPLODE!
THE DANGER I SENSED. IT WASN'T MYSTERIO. WHATEVER IT IS...
..IT'S HERE!
LOOK AT YOU. WHAT A DEPRESSING ...TTLE CREATURE ...U ARE. HARDLY WORTH THE KILLING.

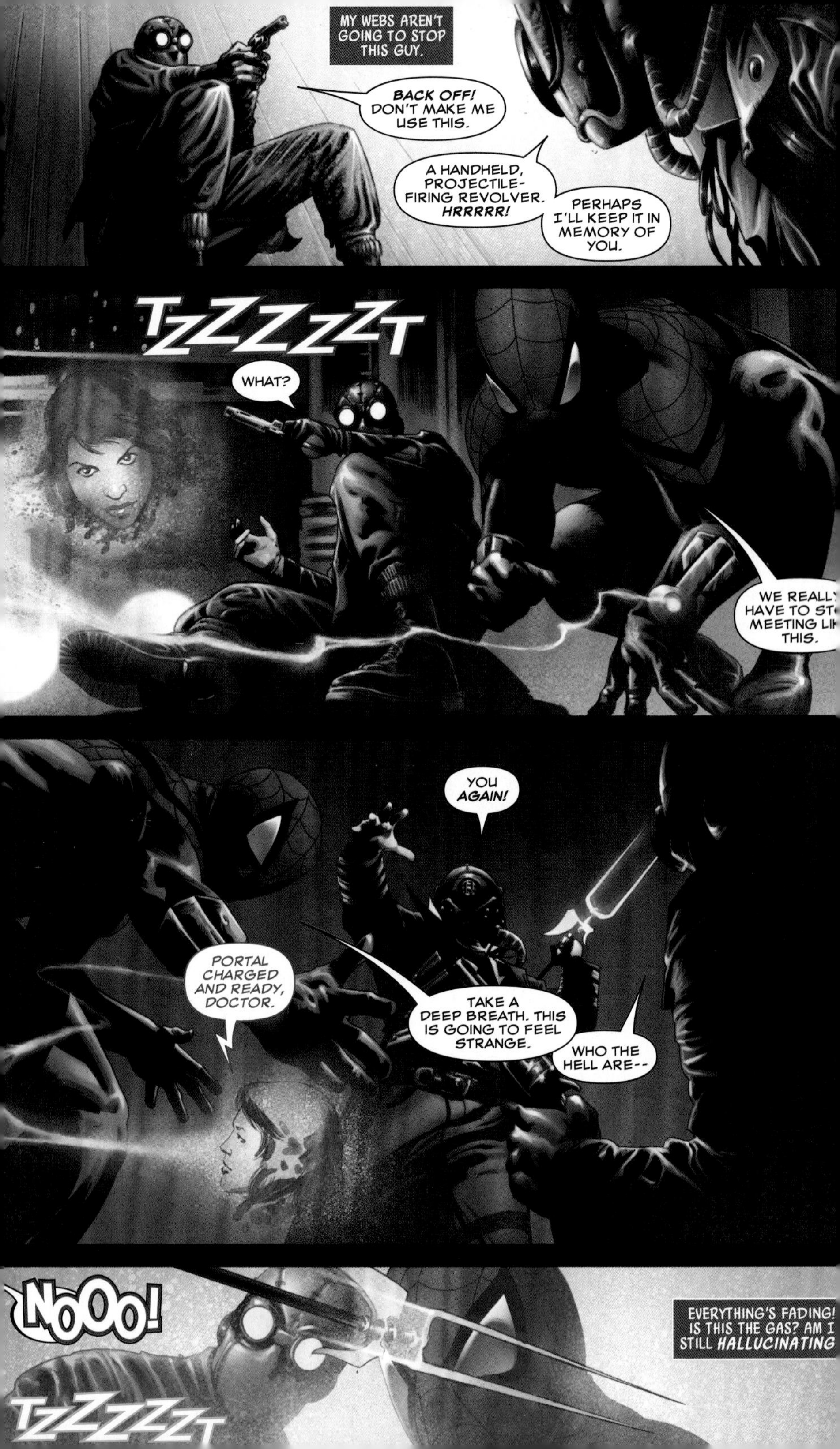
MY WEBS AREN'T GOING TO STOP THIS GUY.
BACK OFF! DON'T MAKE ME USE THIS.
A HANDHELD, PROJECTILE-FIRING REVOLVER. HRRRRR!
PERHAPS I'LL KEEP IT IN MEMORY OF YOU.
TZZZZZZT
WHAT?
WE REALLY HAVE TO ST MEETING LI THIS.
YOU AGAIN!
PORTAL CHARGED AND READY, DOCTOR.
TAKE A DEEP BREATH. THIS IS GOING TO FEEL STRANGE.
WHO THE HELL ARE--
NOOOO!
EVERYTHING'S FADING! IS THIS THE GAS? AM I STILL HALLUCINATING
TZZZZZT

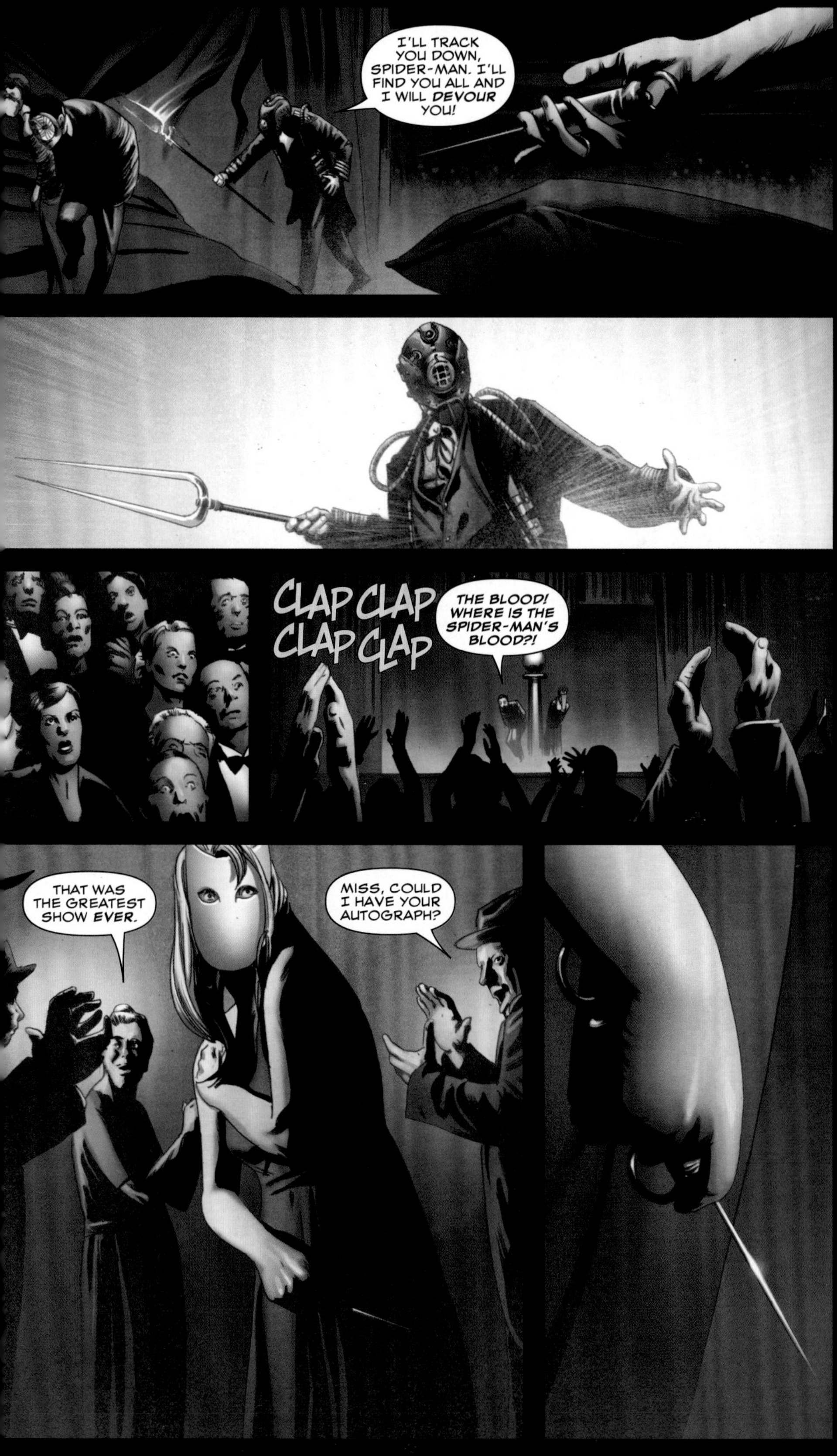
I'LL TRACK YOU DOWN, SPIDER-MAN. I'LL FIND YOU ALL AND I WILL DEVOUR YOU!
CLAP CLAP CLAP CLAP
THE BLOOD! WHERE IS THE SPIDER-MAN'S BLOOD?!
THAT WAS THE GREATEST SHOW EVER.
MISS, COULD I HAVE YOUR AUTOGRAPH?

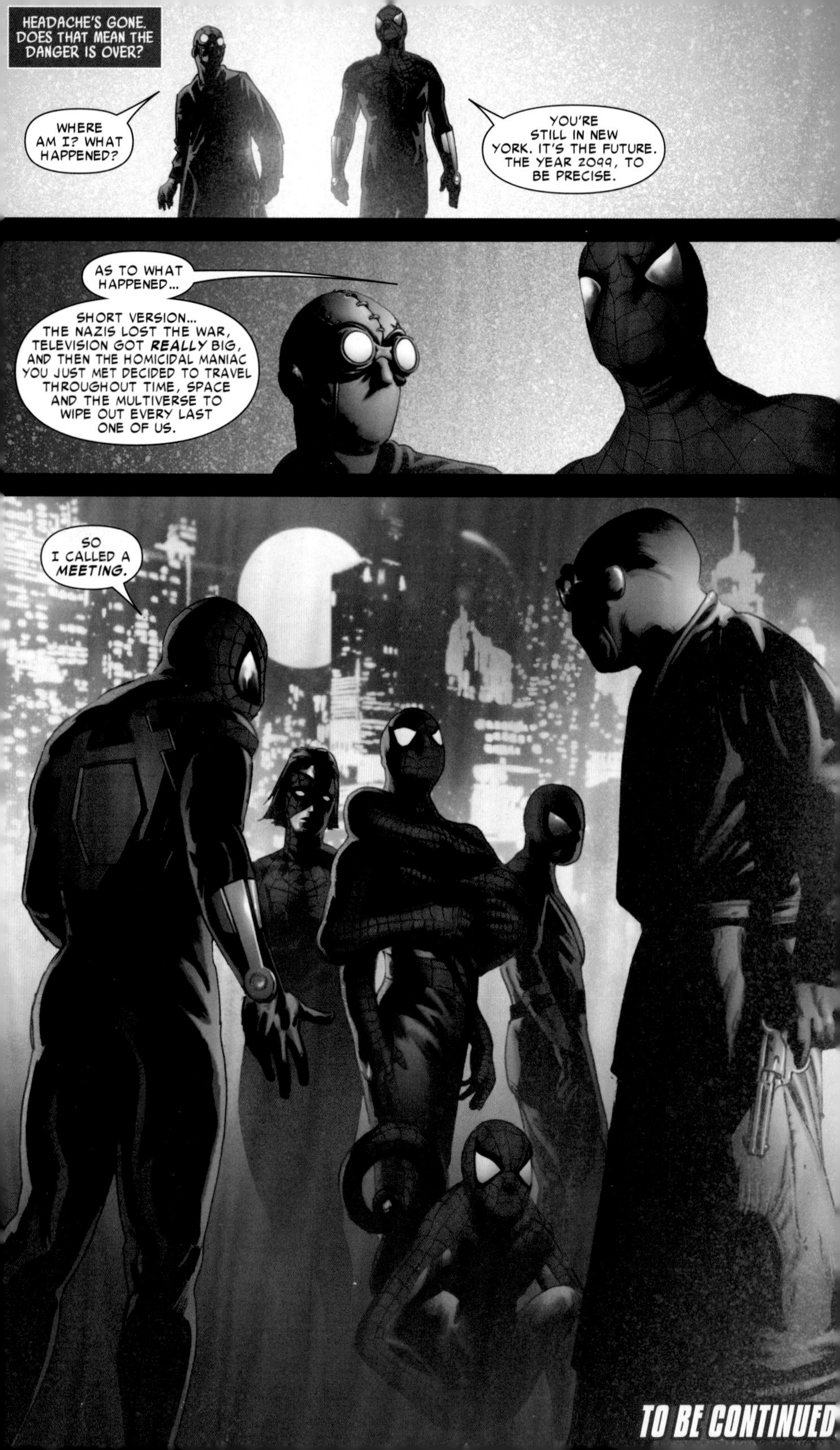
HEADACHE'S GONE. DOES THAT MEAN THE DANGER IS OVER?
WHERE AM I? WHAT HAPPENED?
YOU'RE STILL IN NEW YORK. IT'S THE FUTURE. THE YEAR 2099, TO BE PRECISE.
AS TO WHAT HAPPENED...
SHORT VERSION... THE NAZIS LOST THE WAR, TELEVISION GOT *REALLY* BIG, AND THEN THE HOMICIDAL MANIAC YOU JUST MET DECIDED TO TRAVEL THROUGHOUT TIME, SPACE AND THE MULTIVERSE TO WIPE OUT EVERY LAST ONE OF US.
SO I CALLED A *MEETING.*
TO BE CONTINUED

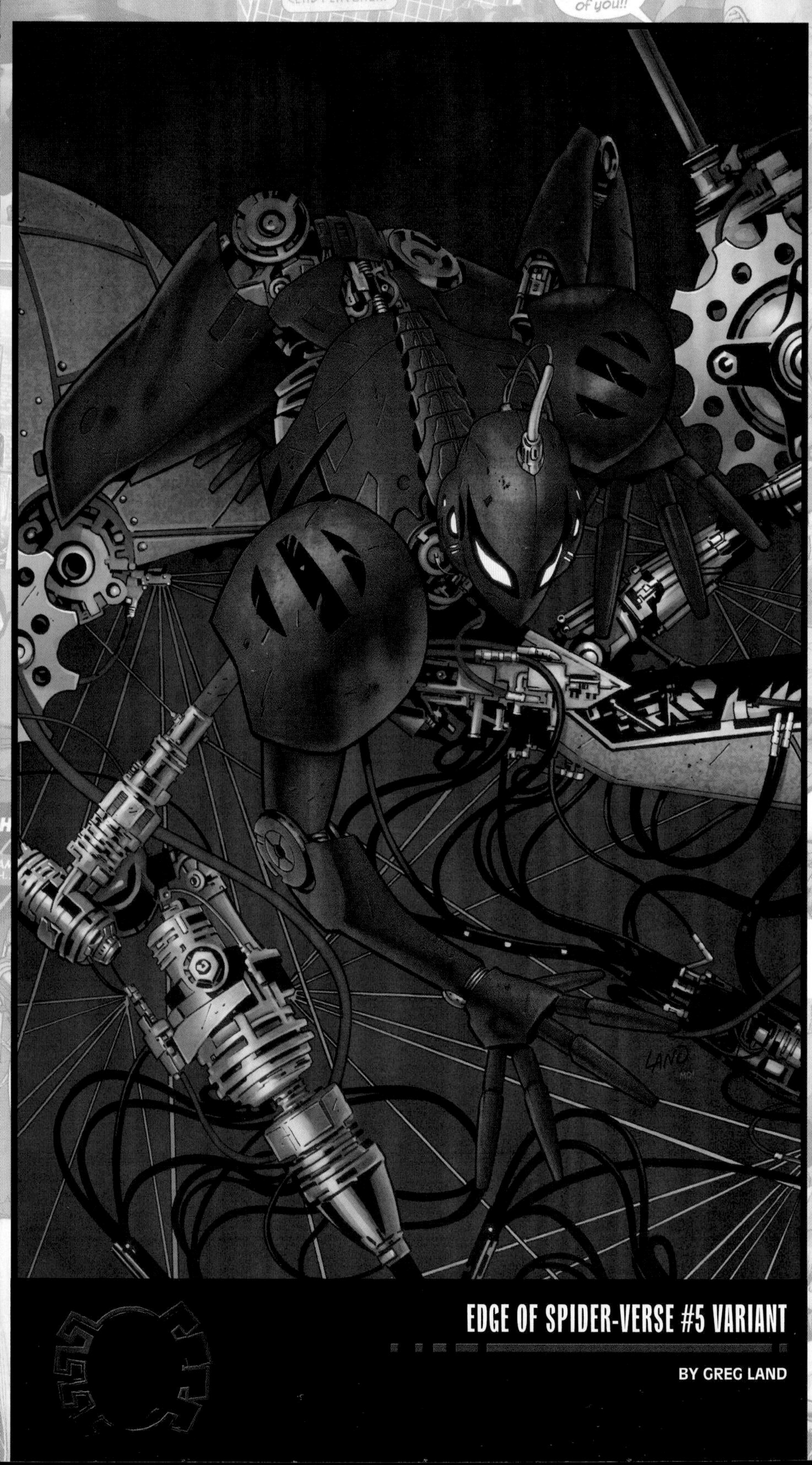

EDGE OF SPIDER-VERSE #5 VARIANT

BY GREG LAND

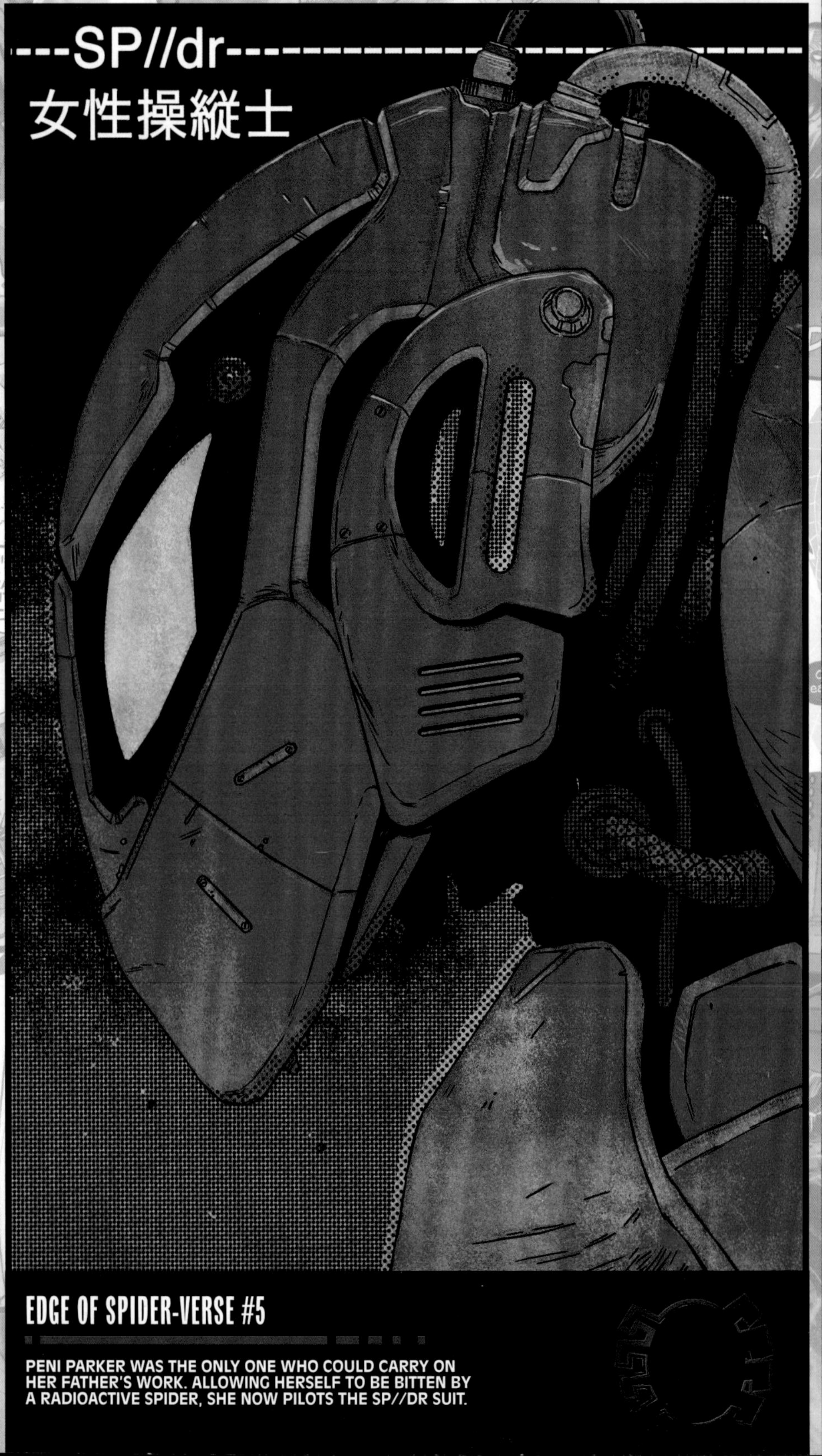
---SP//dr---
女性操縦士

EDGE OF SPIDER-VERSE #5

PENI PARKER WAS THE ONLY ONE WHO COULD CARRY ON HER FATHER'S WORK. ALLOWING HERSELF TO BE BITTEN BY A RADIOACTIVE SPIDER, SHE NOW PILOTS THE SP//DR SUIT.

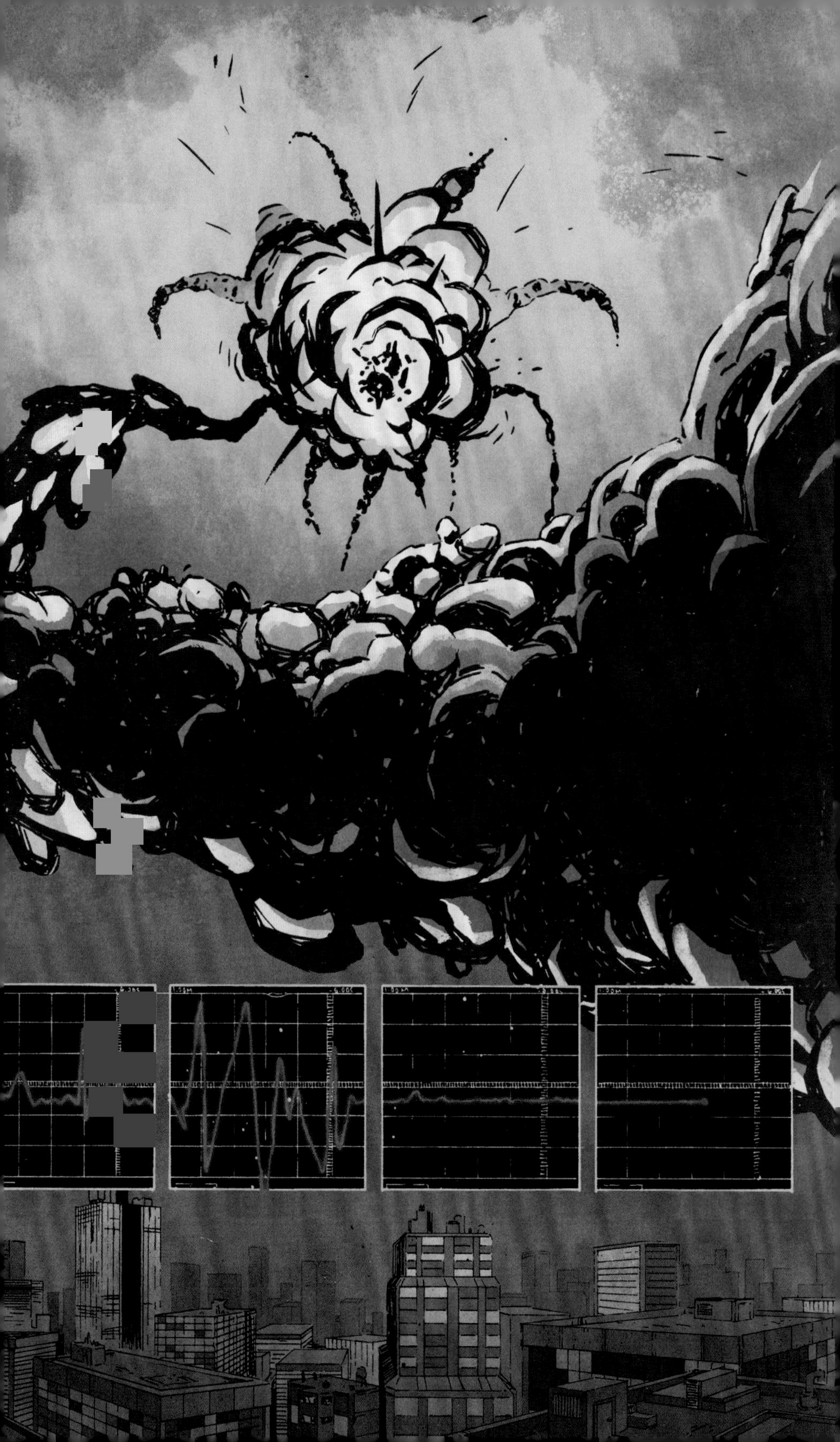

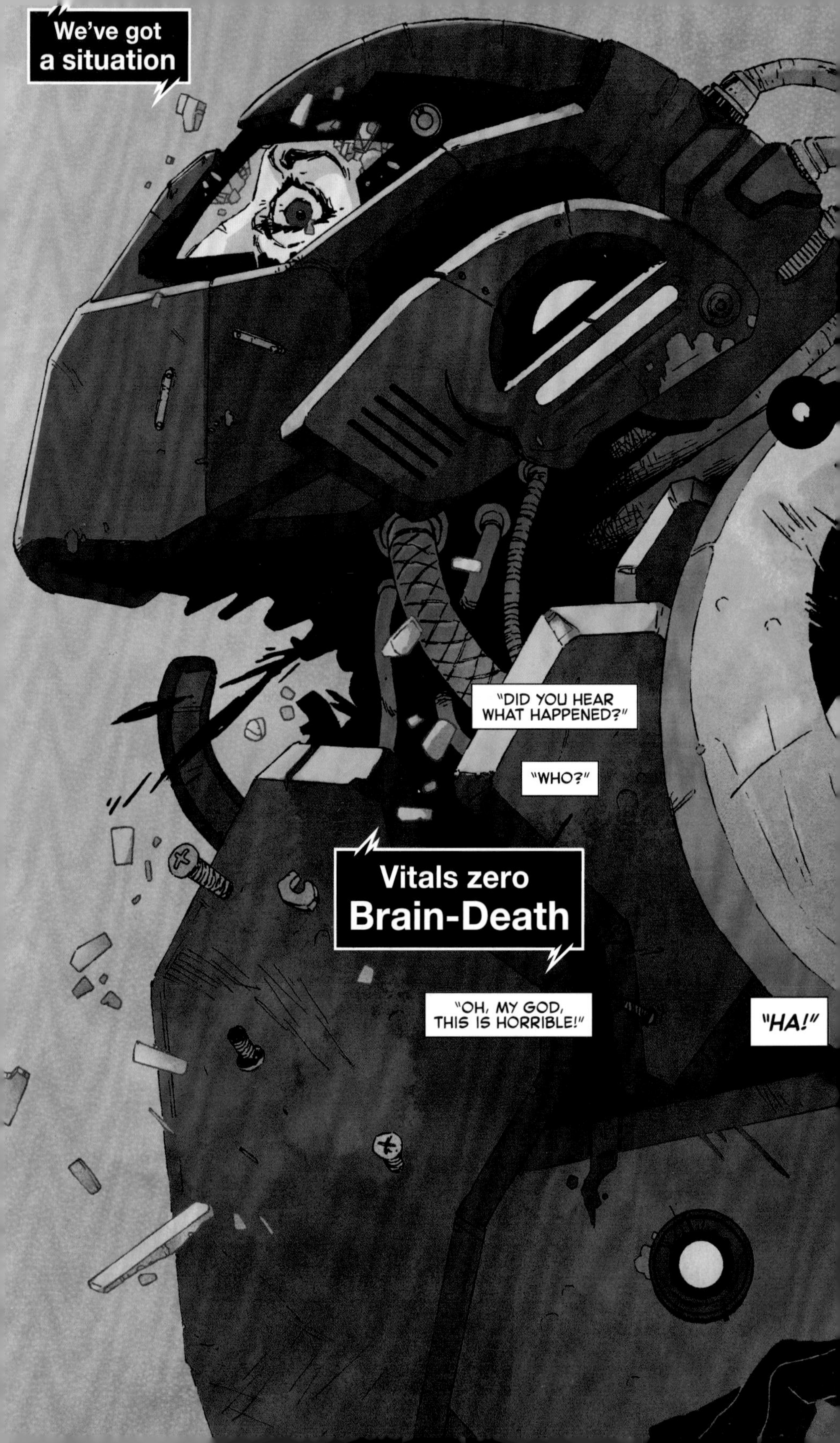
We've got a situation
"DID YOU HEAR WHAT HAPPENED?"
"WHO?"
Vitals zero Brain-Death
"OH, MY GOD, THIS IS HORRIBLE!"
"HA!"

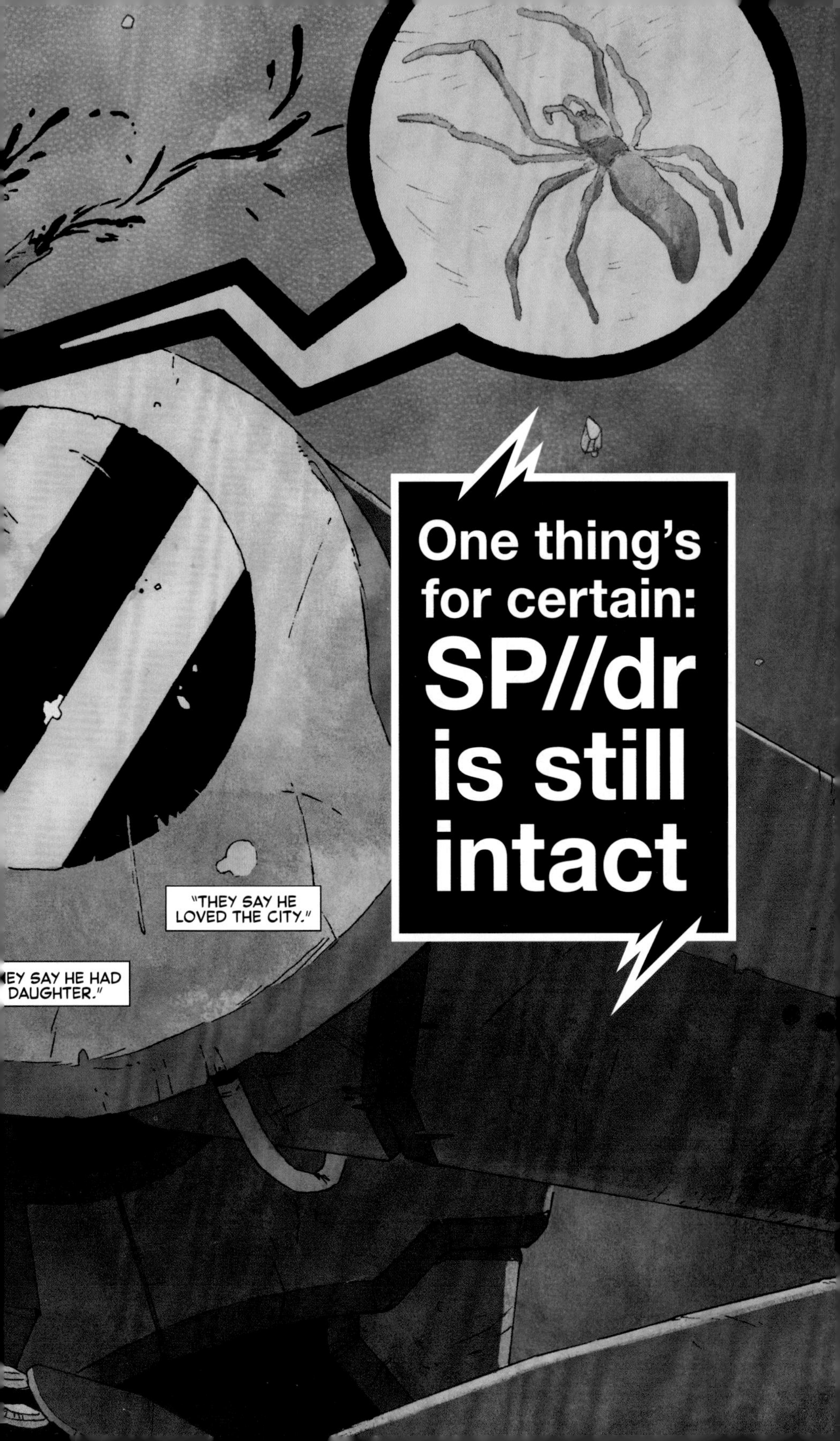

"THEY SAY HE LOVED THE CITY."
EY SAY HE HAD DAUGHTER."
One thing's for certain: SP//dr is still intact

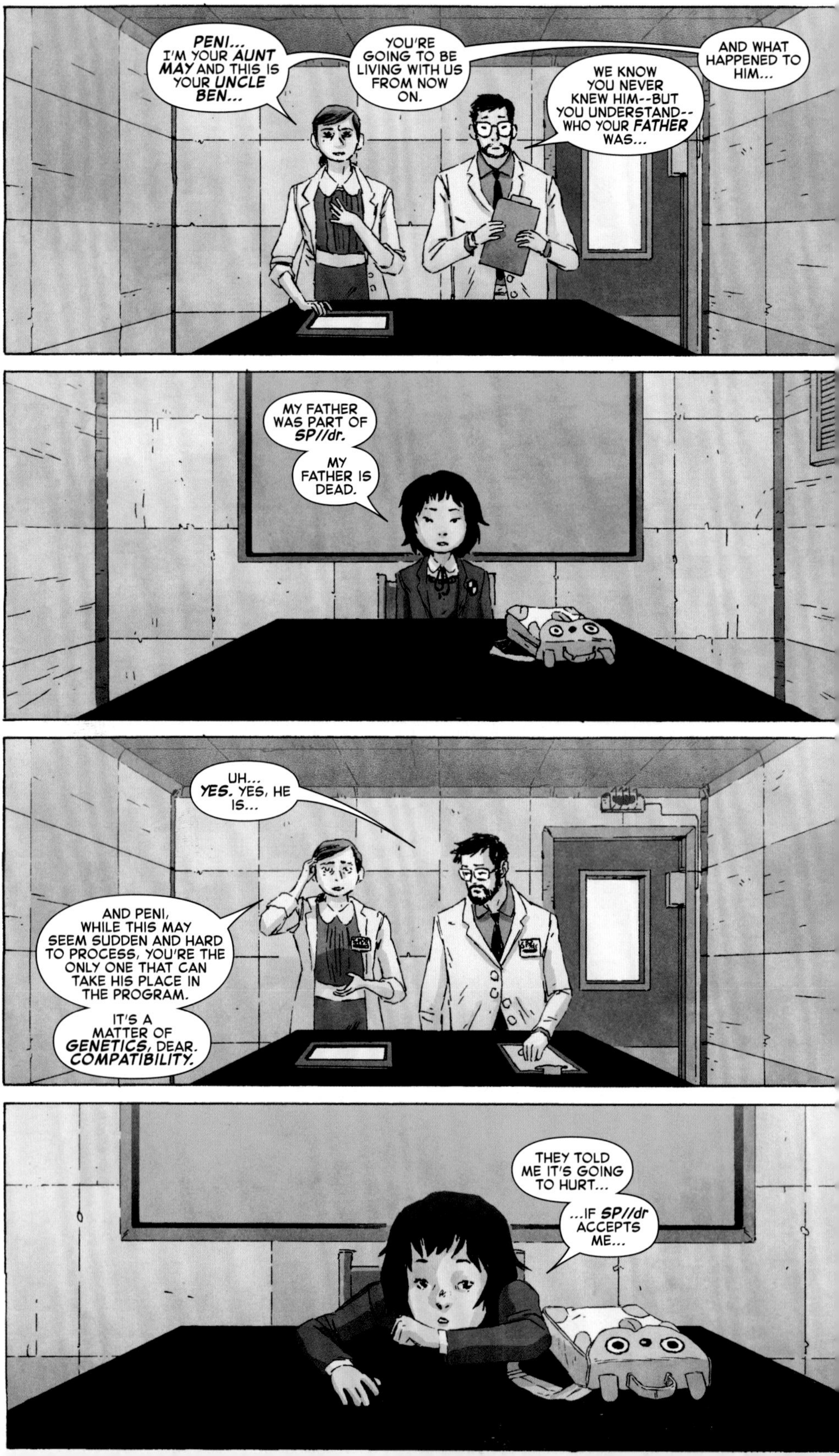
PENI... I'M YOUR AUNT MAY AND THIS IS YOUR UNCLE BEN...
YOU'RE GOING TO BE LIVING WITH US FROM NOW ON.
WE KNOW YOU NEVER KNEW HIM--BUT YOU UNDERSTAND--WHO YOUR FATHER WAS...
AND WHAT HAPPENED TO HIM...
MY FATHER WAS PART OF SP//dr.
MY FATHER IS DEAD.
UH... YES. YES, HE IS...
AND PENI, WHILE THIS MAY SEEM SUDDEN AND HARD TO PROCESS, YOU'RE THE ONLY ONE THAT CAN TAKE HIS PLACE IN THE PROGRAM.
IT'S A MATTER OF GENETICS, DEAR. COMPATIBILITY.
THEY TOLD ME IT'S GOING TO HURT...
...IF SP//dr ACCEPTS ME...

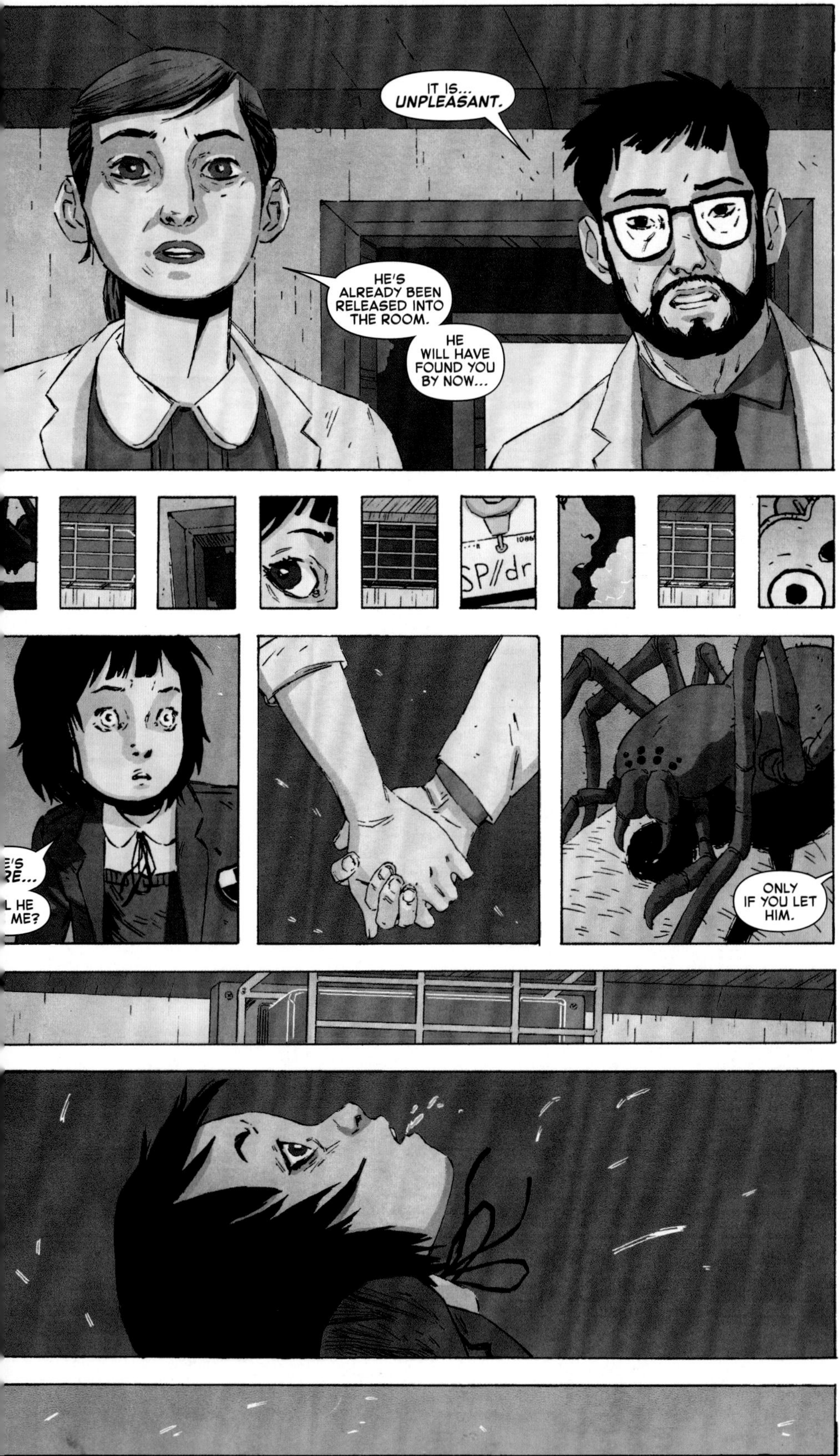
IT IS... UNPLEASANT.
HE'S ALREADY BEEN RELEASED INTO THE ROOM.
HE WILL HAVE FOUND YOU BY NOW...
SP//dr
E'S RE...
L HE ME?
ONLY IF YOU LET HIM.

Five Years Later...

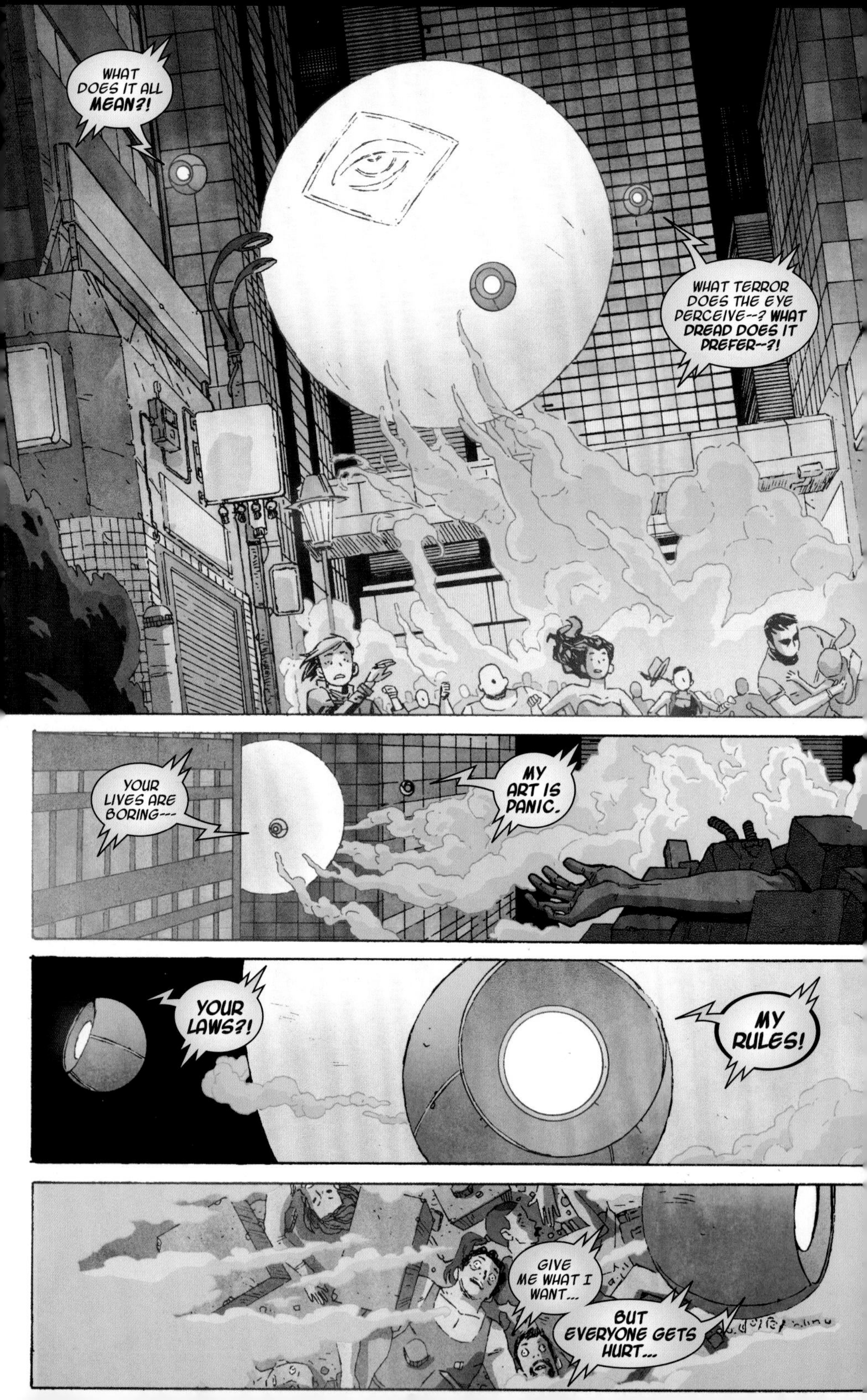

WHAT DOES IT ALL MEAN?!
WHAT TERROR DOES THE EYE PERCEIVE--? WHAT DREAD DOES IT PREFER--?!
YOUR LIVES ARE BORING---
MY ART IS PANIC.
YOUR LAWS?!
MY RULES!
GIVE ME WHAT I WANT...
BUT EVERYONE GETS HURT...

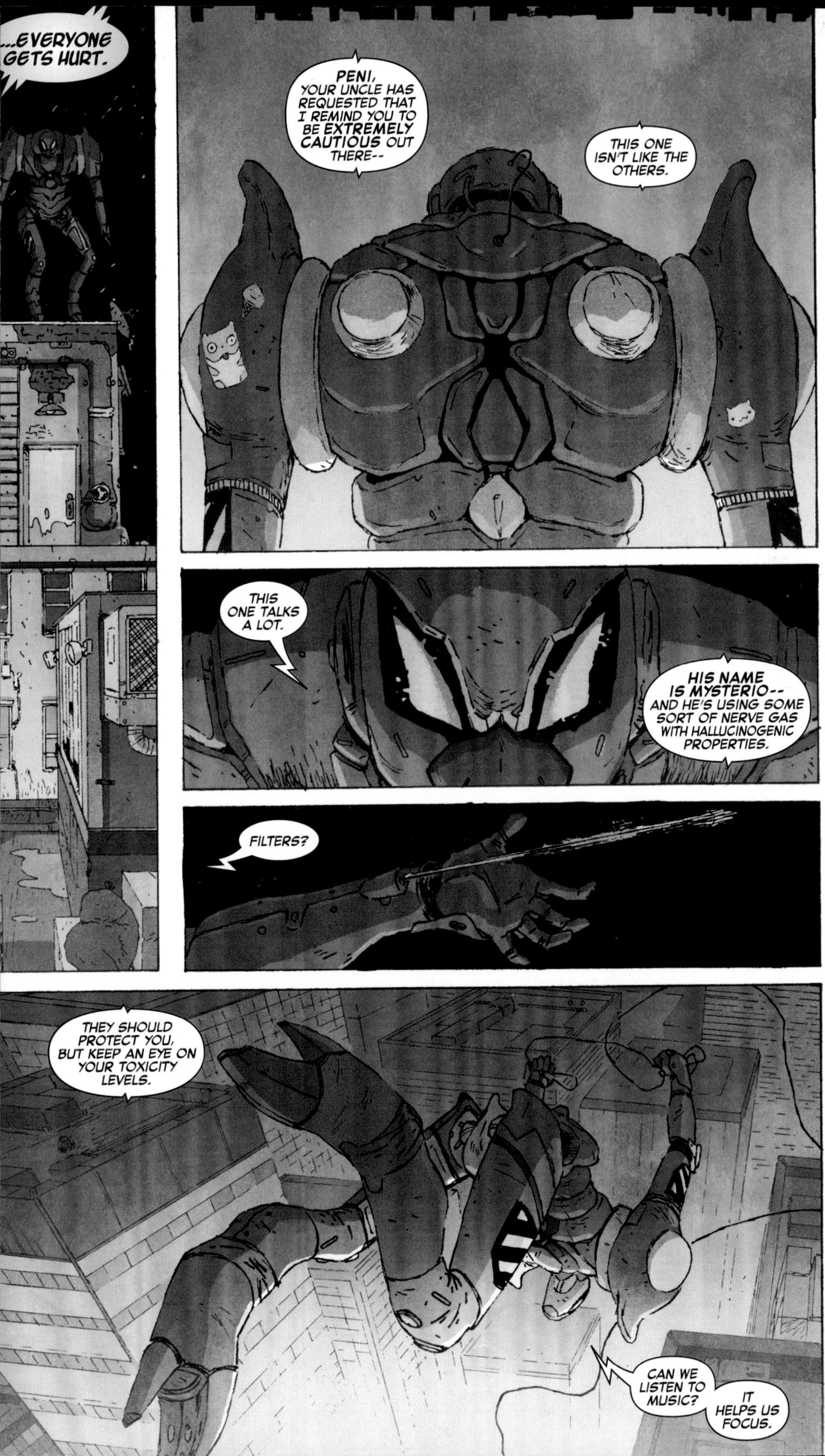
...EVERYONE GETS HURT.
PENI, YOUR UNCLE HAS REQUESTED THAT I REMIND YOU TO BE EXTREMELY CAUTIOUS OUT THERE--
THIS ONE ISN'T LIKE THE OTHERS.
THIS ONE TALKS A LOT.
HIS NAME IS MYSTERIO-- AND HE'S USING SOME SORT OF NERVE GAS WITH HALLUCINOGENIC PROPERTIES.
FILTERS?
THEY SHOULD PROTECT YOU, BUT KEEP AN EYE ON YOUR TOXICITY LEVELS.
CAN WE LISTEN TO MUSIC?
IT HELPS US FOCUS.

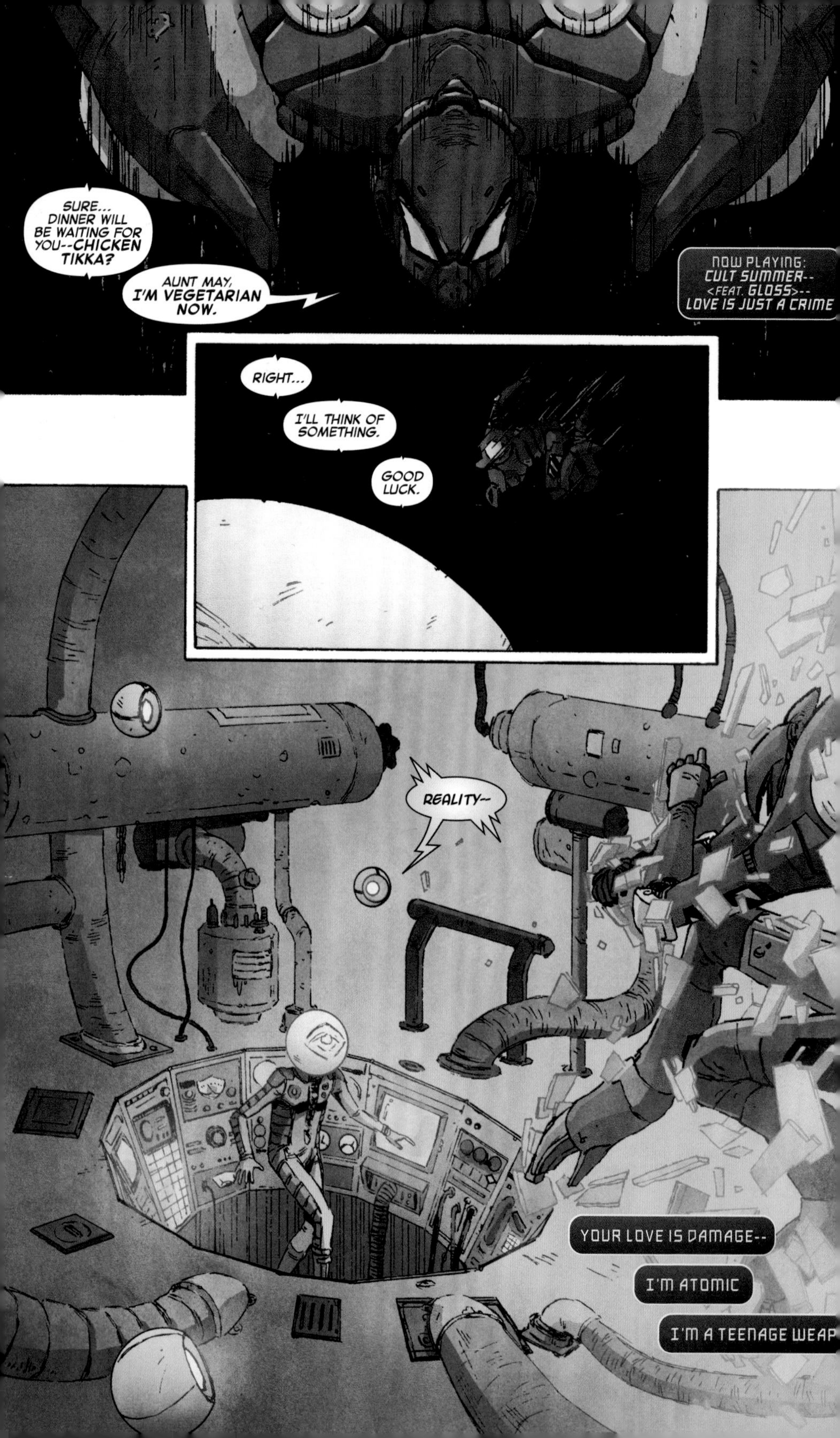
SURE... DINNER WILL BE WAITING FOR YOU--CHICKEN TIKKA?
AUNT MAY, I'M VEGETARIAN NOW.
NOW PLAYING: CULT SUMMER-- <FEAT. GLOSS>-- LOVE IS JUST A CRIME
RIGHT...
I'LL THINK OF SOMETHING.
GOOD LUCK.
REALITY--
YOUR LOVE IS DAMAGE--
I'M ATOMIC
I'M A TEENAGE WEAP

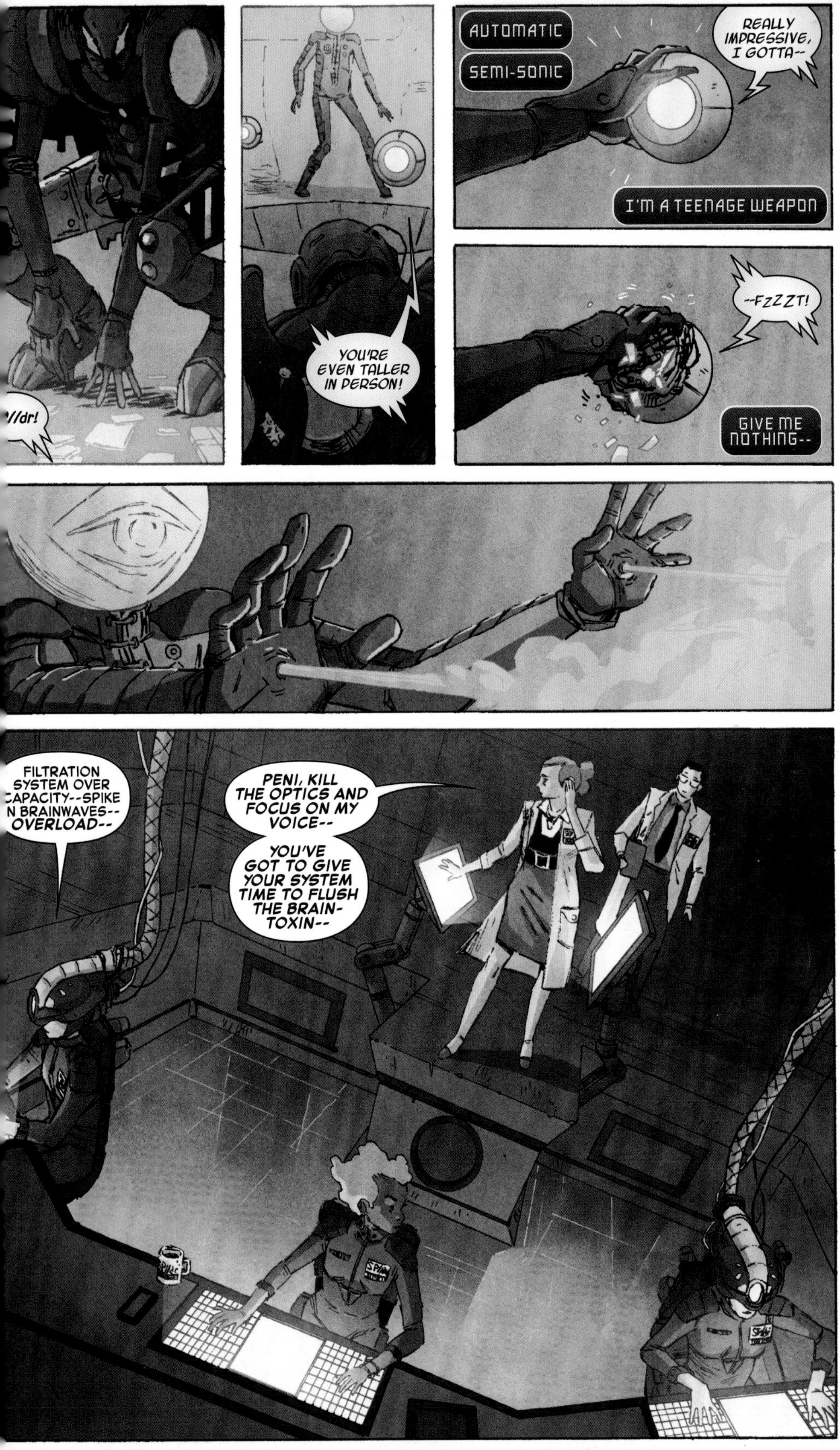

//dr!
YOU'RE EVEN TALLER IN PERSON!
AUTOMATIC
SEMI-SONIC
REALLY IMPRESSIVE, I GOTTA--
I'M A TEENAGE WEAPON
--FZZZT!
GIVE ME NOTHING--
FILTRATION SYSTEM OVER CAPACITY--SPIKE N BRAINWAVES--OVERLOAD--
PENI, KILL THE OPTICS AND FOCUS ON MY VOICE--
YOU'VE GOT TO GIVE YOUR SYSTEM TIME TO FLUSH THE BRAIN-TOXIN--

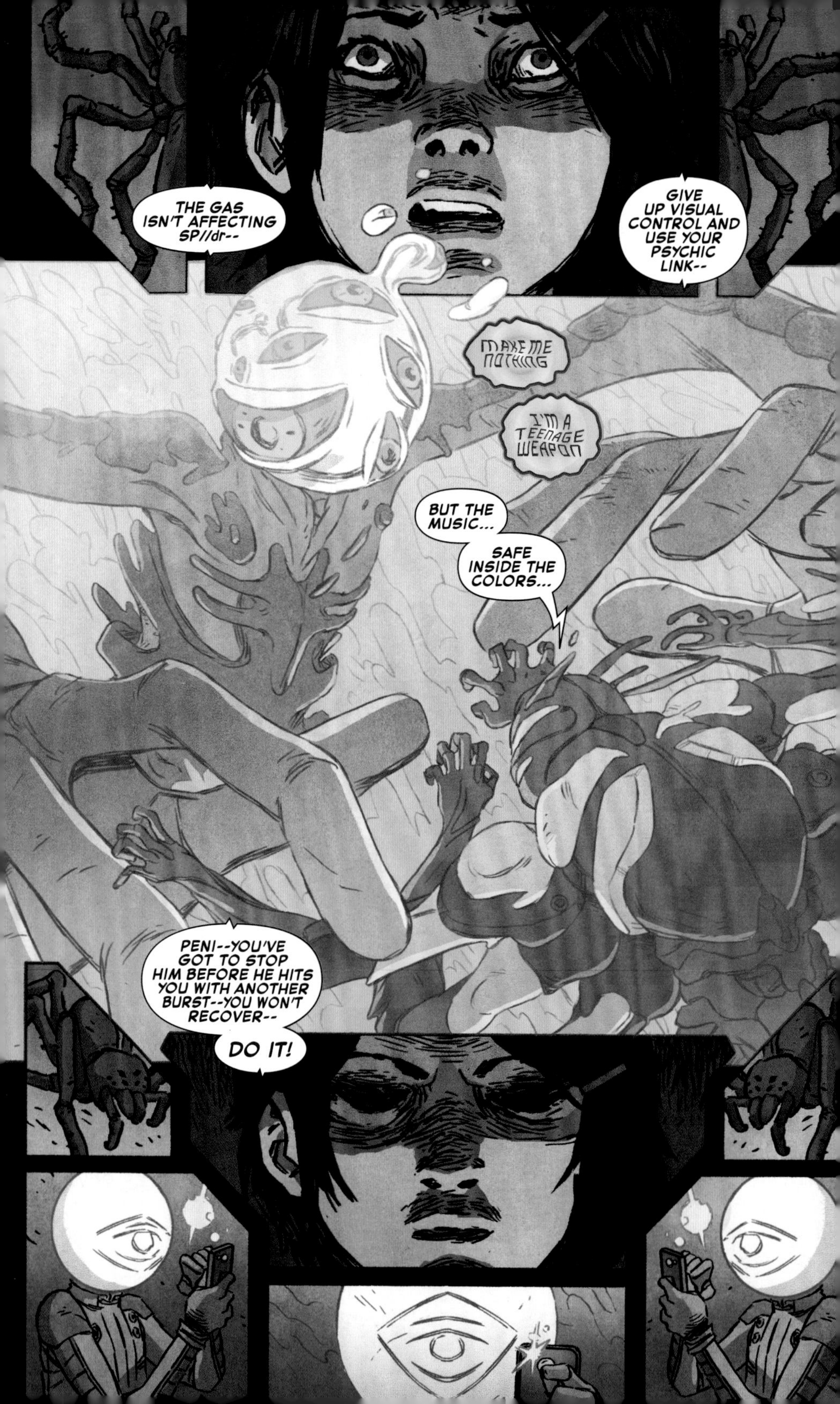
THE GAS ISN'T AFFECTING SP//dr--
GIVE UP VISUAL CONTROL AND USE YOUR PSYCHIC LINK--
MAKE ME NOTHING
I'M A TEENAGE WEAPON
BUT THE MUSIC...
SAFE INSIDE THE COLORS...
PENI--YOU'VE GOT TO STOP HIM BEFORE HE HITS YOU WITH ANOTHER BURST--YOU WON'T RECOVER--
DO IT!

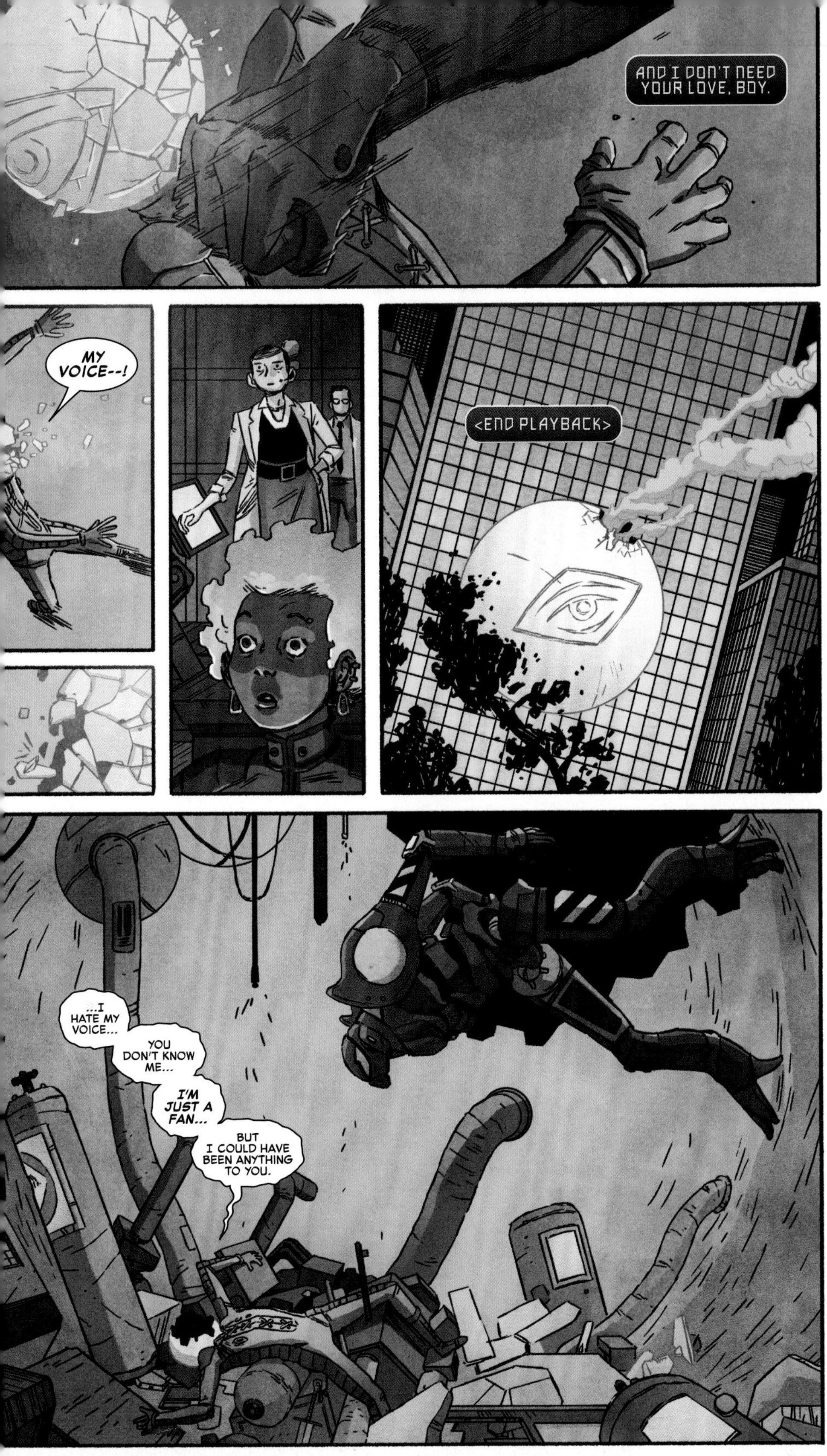
AND I DON'T NEED YOUR LOVE, BOY.
MY VOICE--!
<END PLAYBACK>
...I HATE MY VOICE...
YOU DON'T KNOW ME...
I'M JUST A FAN...
BUT I COULD HAVE BEEN ANYTHING TO YOU.

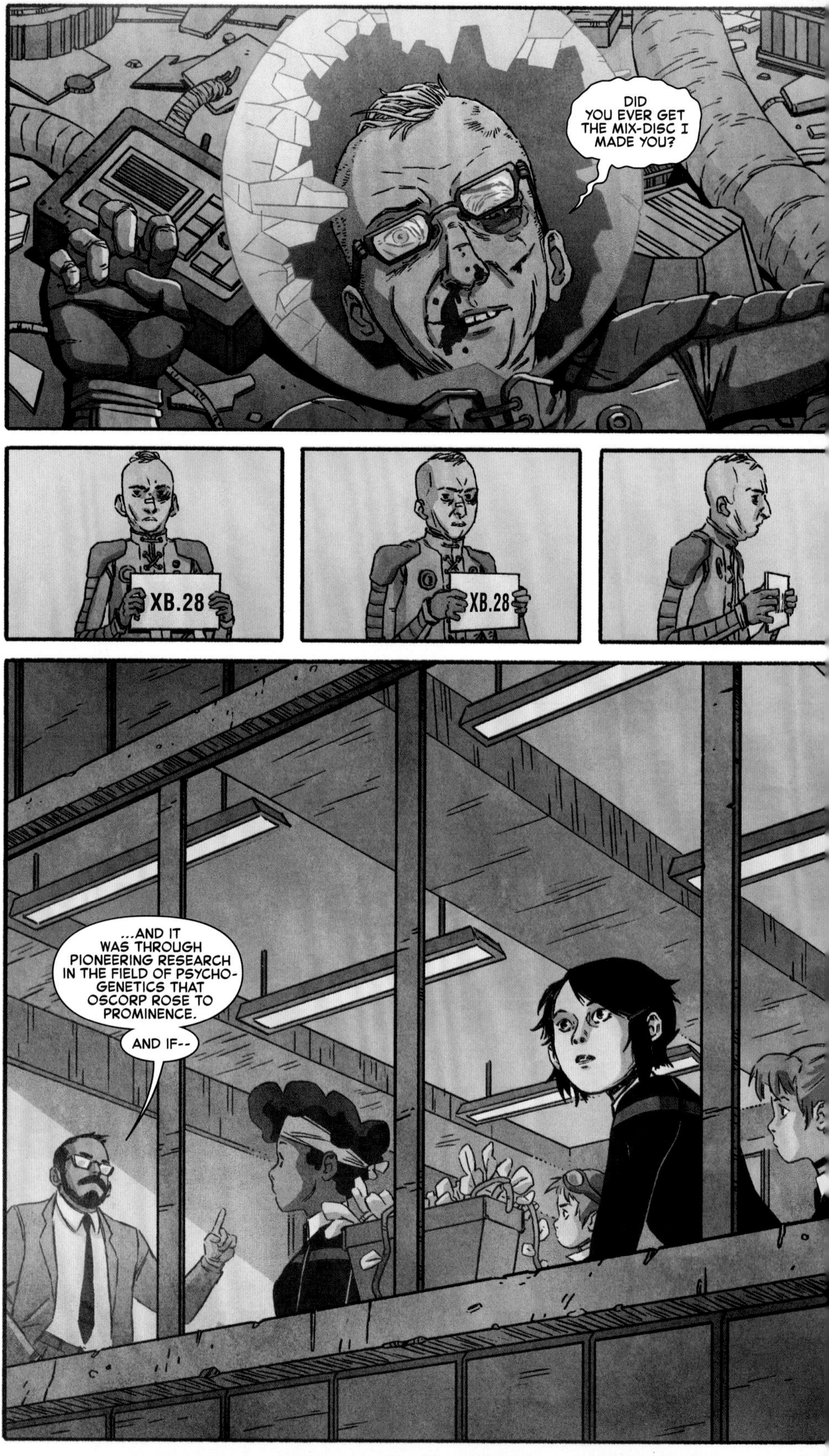
DID YOU EVER GET THE MIX-DISC I MADE YOU?
XB.28
XB.28
...AND IT WAS THROUGH PIONEERING RESEARCH IN THE FIELD OF PSYCHO-GENETICS THAT OSCORP ROSE TO PROMINENCE.
AND IF--

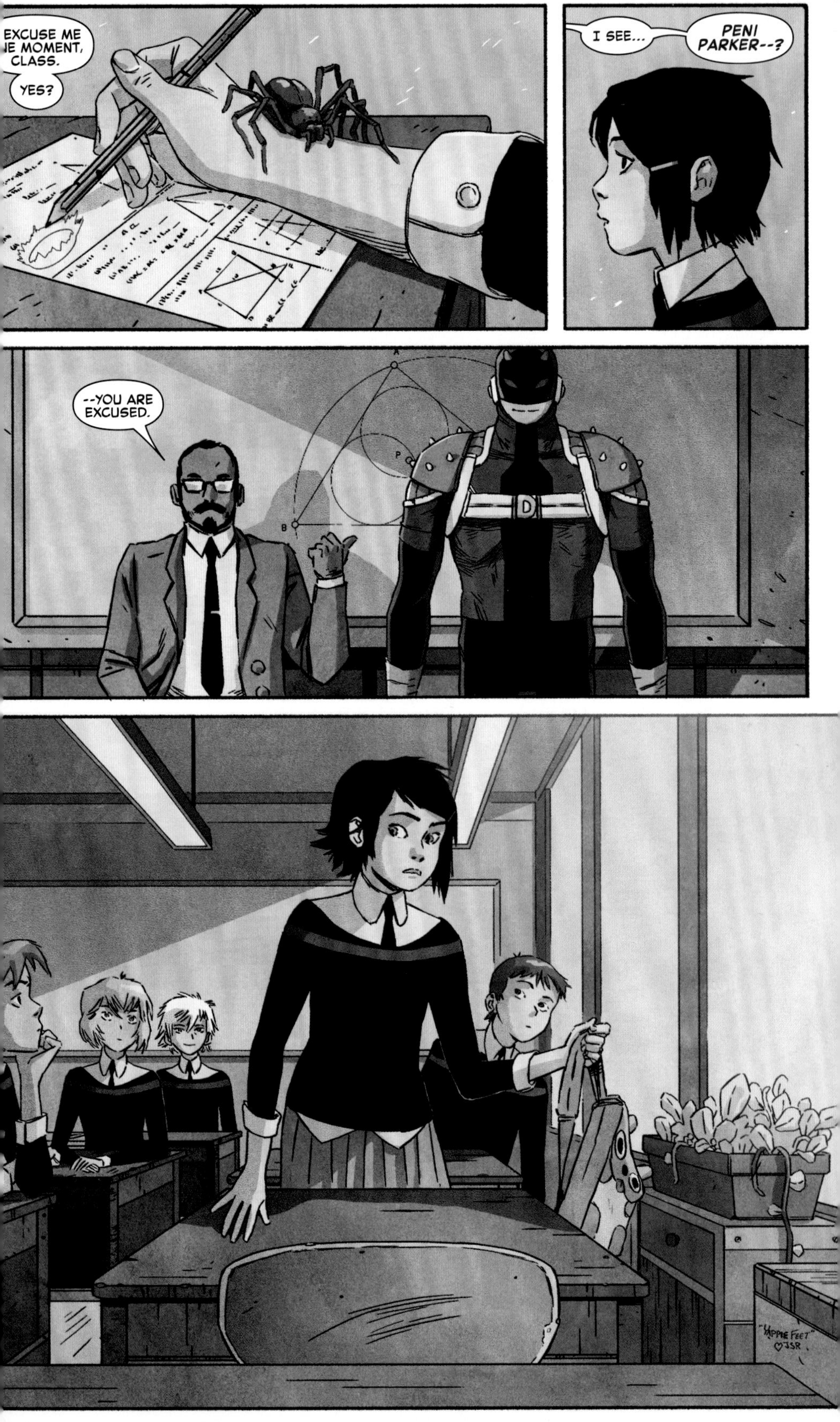

EXCUSE ME NE MOMENT, CLASS.
YES?
I SEE...
PENI PARKER--?
--YOU ARE EXCUSED.
"YAPPIE FEET" ♡JSR

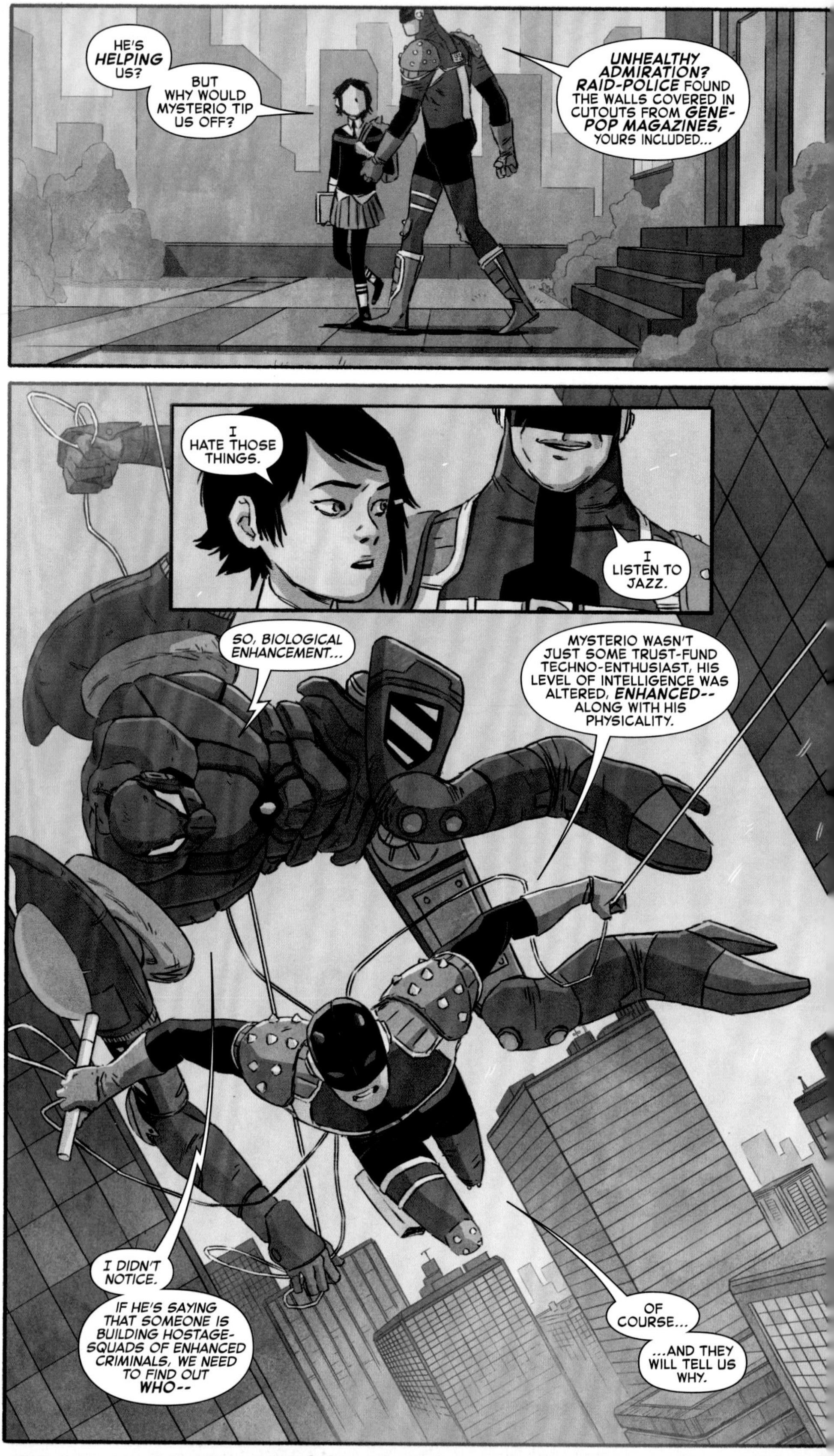

HE'S HELPING US?
BUT WHY WOULD MYSTERIO TIP US OFF?
UNHEALTHY ADMIRATION? RAID-POLICE FOUND THE WALLS COVERED IN CUTOUTS FROM GENE-POP MAGAZINES, YOURS INCLUDED...
I HATE THOSE THINGS.
I LISTEN TO JAZZ.
SO, BIOLOGICAL ENHANCEMENT...
MYSTERIO WASN'T JUST SOME TRUST-FUND TECHNO-ENTHUSIAST, HIS LEVEL OF INTELLIGENCE WAS ALTERED, ENHANCED--ALONG WITH HIS PHYSICALITY.
I DIDN'T NOTICE.
IF HE'S SAYING THAT SOMEONE IS BUILDING HOSTAGE-SQUADS OF ENHANCED CRIMINALS, WE NEED TO FIND OUT WHO--
OF COURSE...
...AND THEY WILL TELL US WHY.

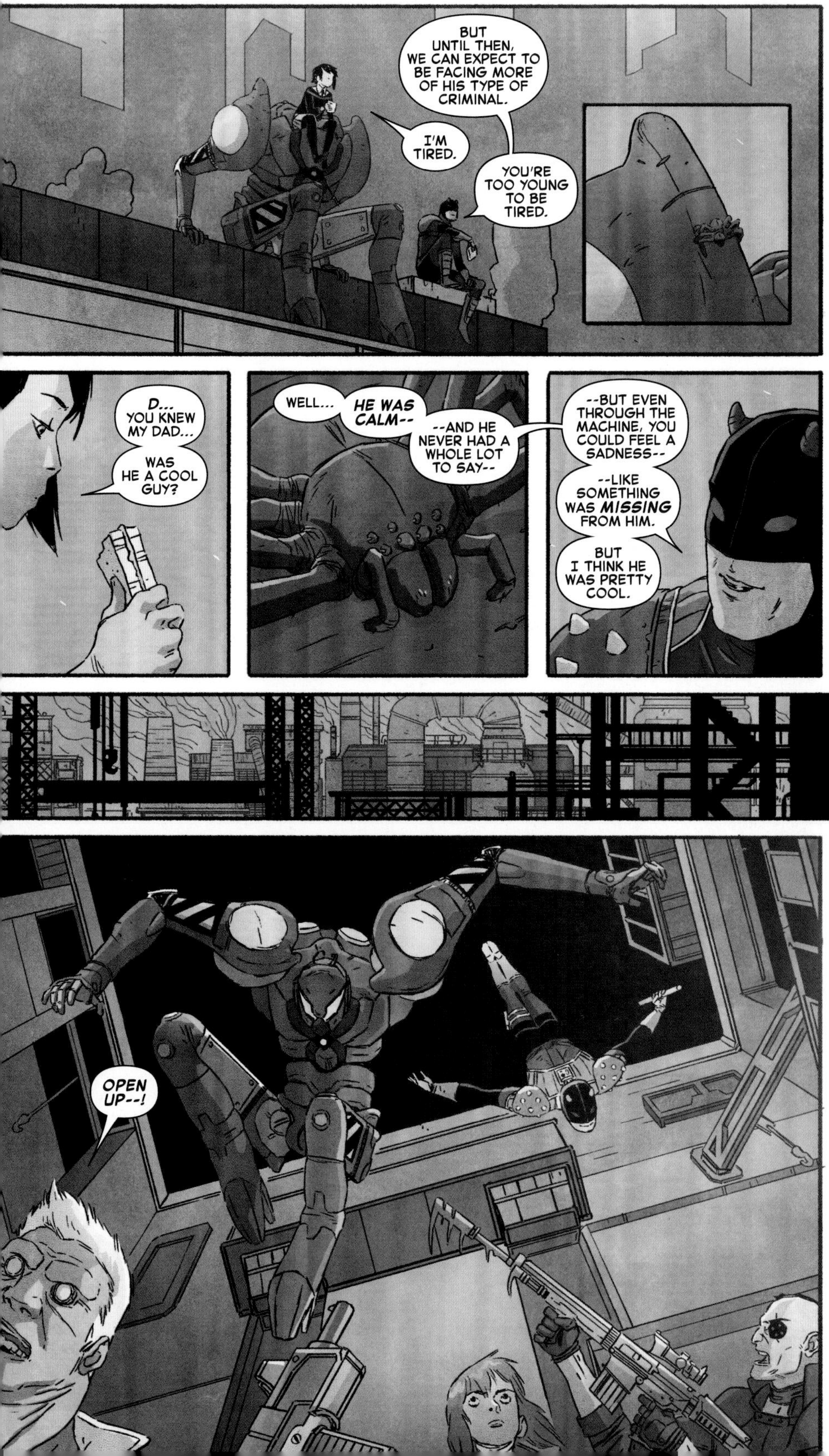
BUT UNTIL THEN, WE CAN EXPECT TO BE FACING MORE OF HIS TYPE OF CRIMINAL.
I'M TIRED.
YOU'RE TOO YOUNG TO BE TIRED.
D... YOU KNEW MY DAD...
WAS HE A COOL GUY?
WELL... HE WAS CALM--
--AND HE NEVER HAD A WHOLE LOT TO SAY--
--BUT EVEN THROUGH THE MACHINE, YOU COULD FEEL A SADNESS--
--LIKE SOMETHING WAS MISSING FROM HIM.
BUT I THINK HE WAS PRETTY COOL.
OPEN UP--!

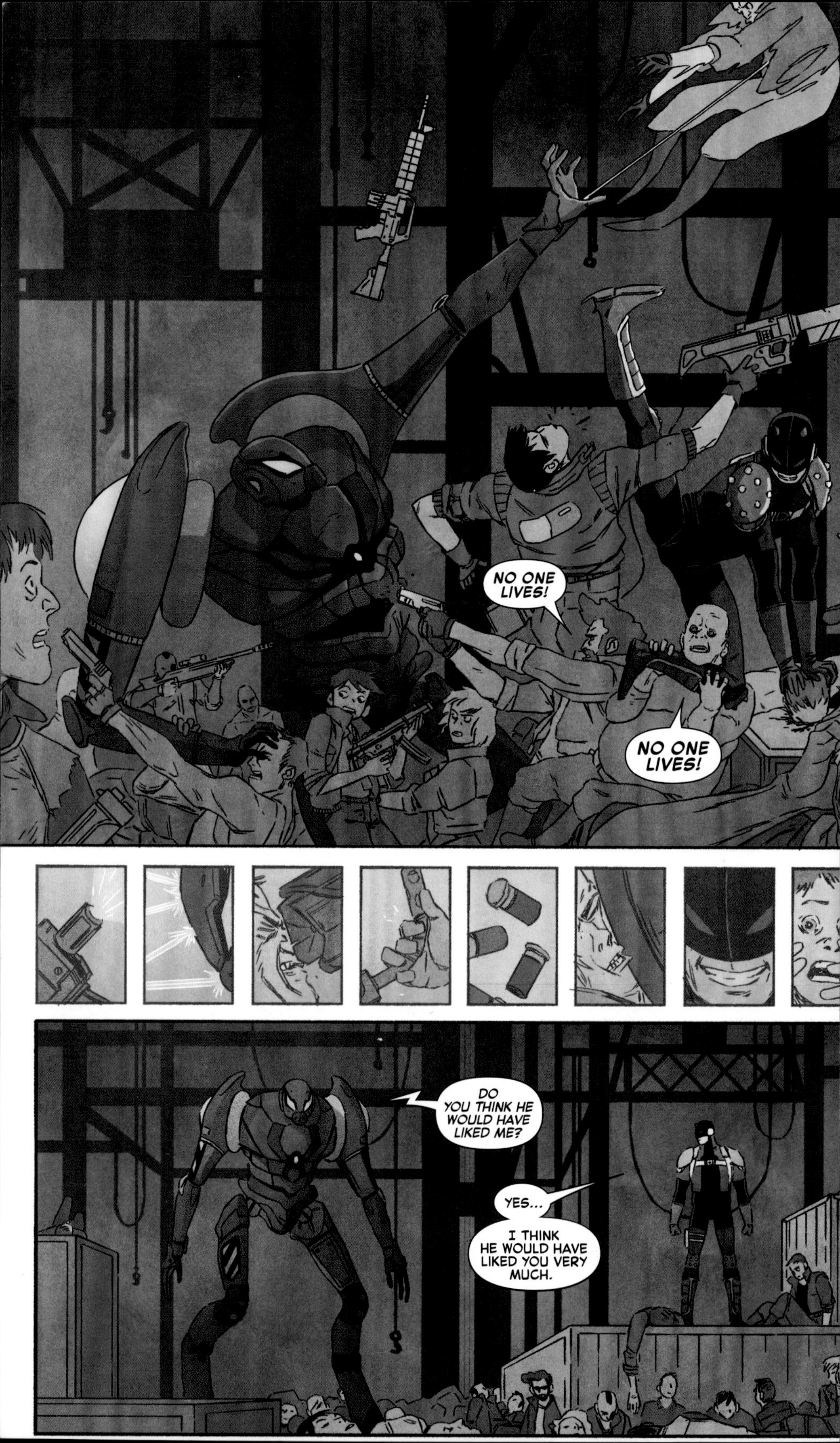
NO ONE LIVES!
NO ONE LIVES!
DO YOU THINK HE WOULD HAVE LIKED ME?
YES...
I THINK HE WOULD HAVE LIKED YOU VERY MUCH.

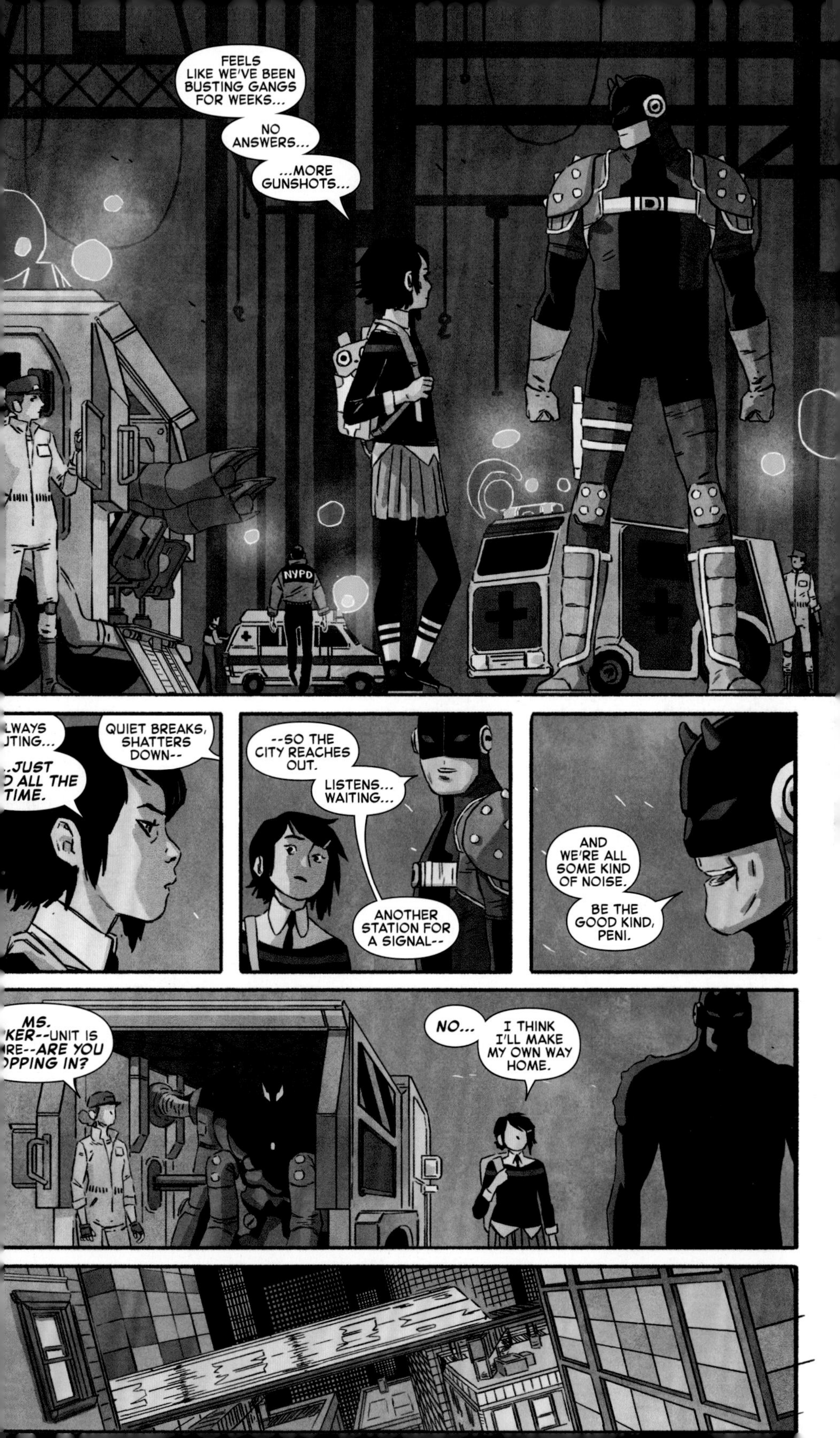
FEELS LIKE WE'VE BEEN BUSTING GANGS FOR WEEKS...
NO ANSWERS...
...MORE GUNSHOTS...
LWAYS
UTING...
..JUST
ALL THE TIME.
QUIET BREAKS, SHATTERS DOWN--
--SO THE CITY REACHES OUT.
LISTENS... WAITING...
ANOTHER STATION FOR A SIGNAL--
AND WE'RE ALL SOME KIND OF NOISE.
BE THE GOOD KIND, PENI.
MS.
KER--UNIT IS
RE--ARE YOU
PPING IN?
NO...
I THINK I'LL MAKE MY OWN WAY HOME.

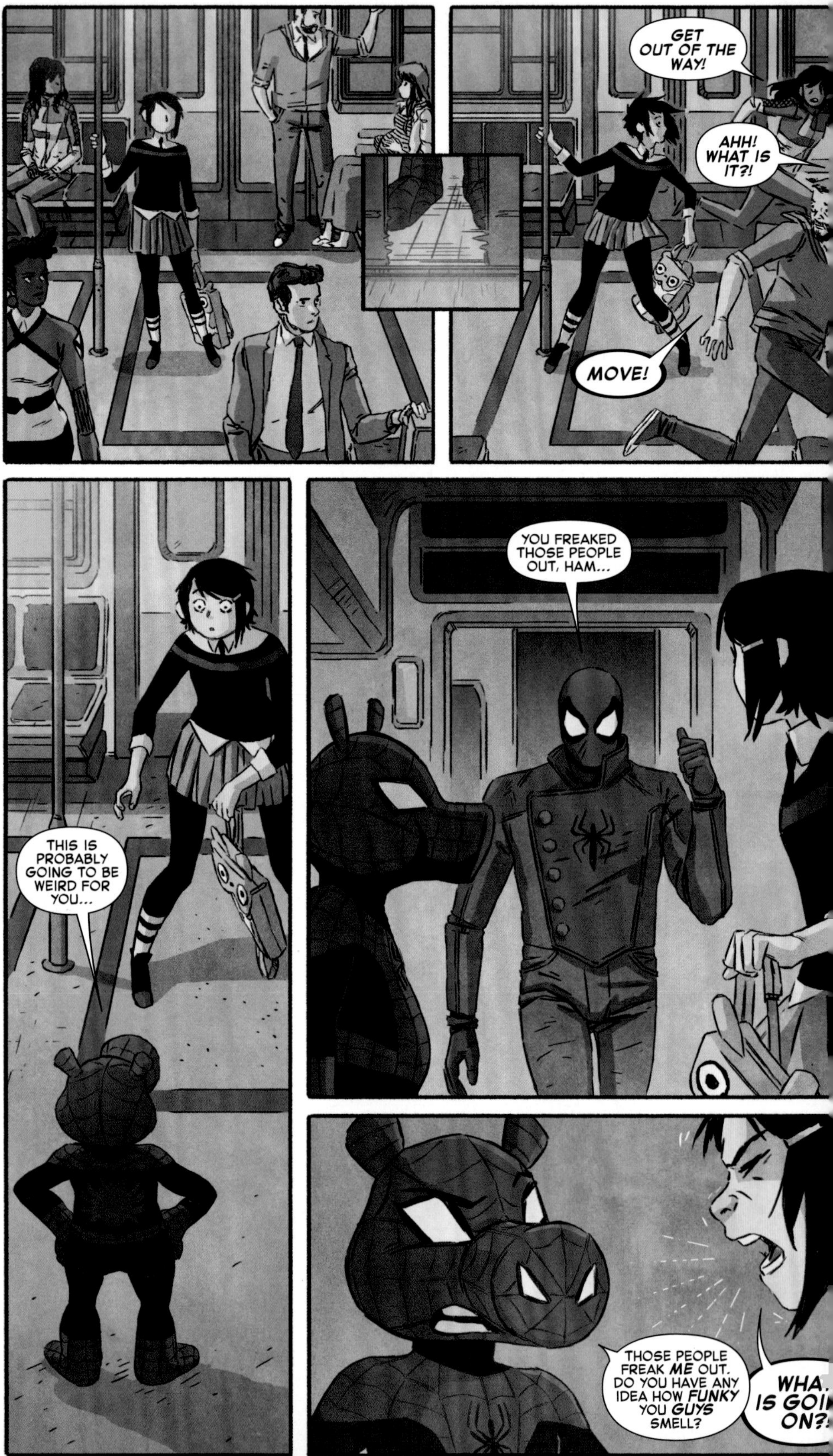
GET OUT OF THE WAY!
AHH! WHAT IS IT?!
MOVE!
THIS IS PROBABLY GOING TO BE WEIRD FOR YOU...
YOU FREAKED THOSE PEOPLE OUT, HAM...
THOSE PEOPLE FREAK ME OUT. DO YOU HAVE ANY IDEA HOW FUNKY YOU GUYS SMELL?

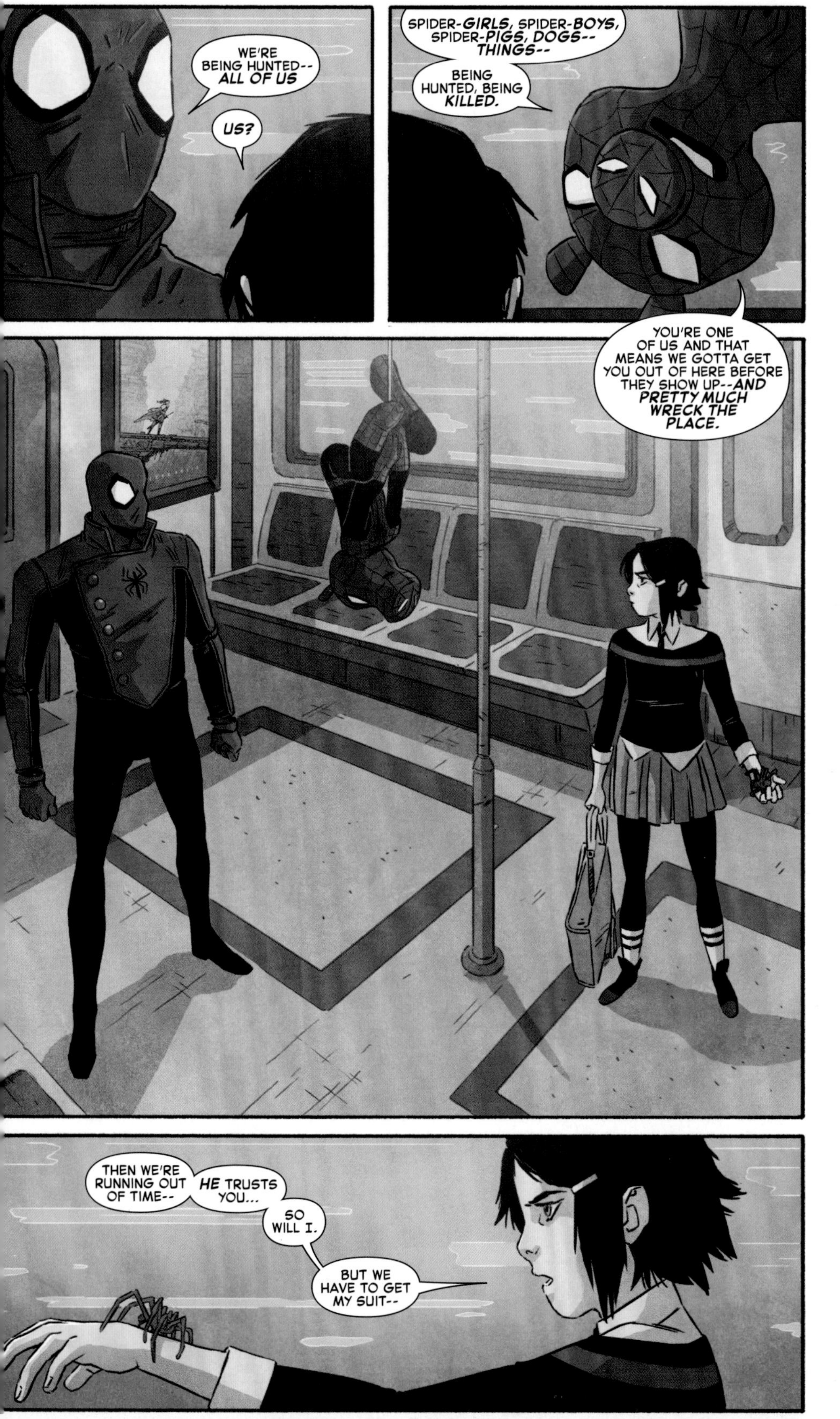
WE'RE BEING HUNTED-- ALL OF US
US?
SPIDER-GIRLS, SPIDER-BOYS, SPIDER-PIGS, DOGS-- THINGS--
BEING HUNTED, BEING KILLED.
YOU'RE ONE OF US AND THAT MEANS WE GOTTA GET YOU OUT OF HERE BEFORE THEY SHOW UP--AND PRETTY MUCH WRECK THE PLACE.
THEN WE'RE RUNNING OUT OF TIME--
HE TRUSTS YOU...
SO WILL I.
BUT WE HAVE TO GET MY SUIT--

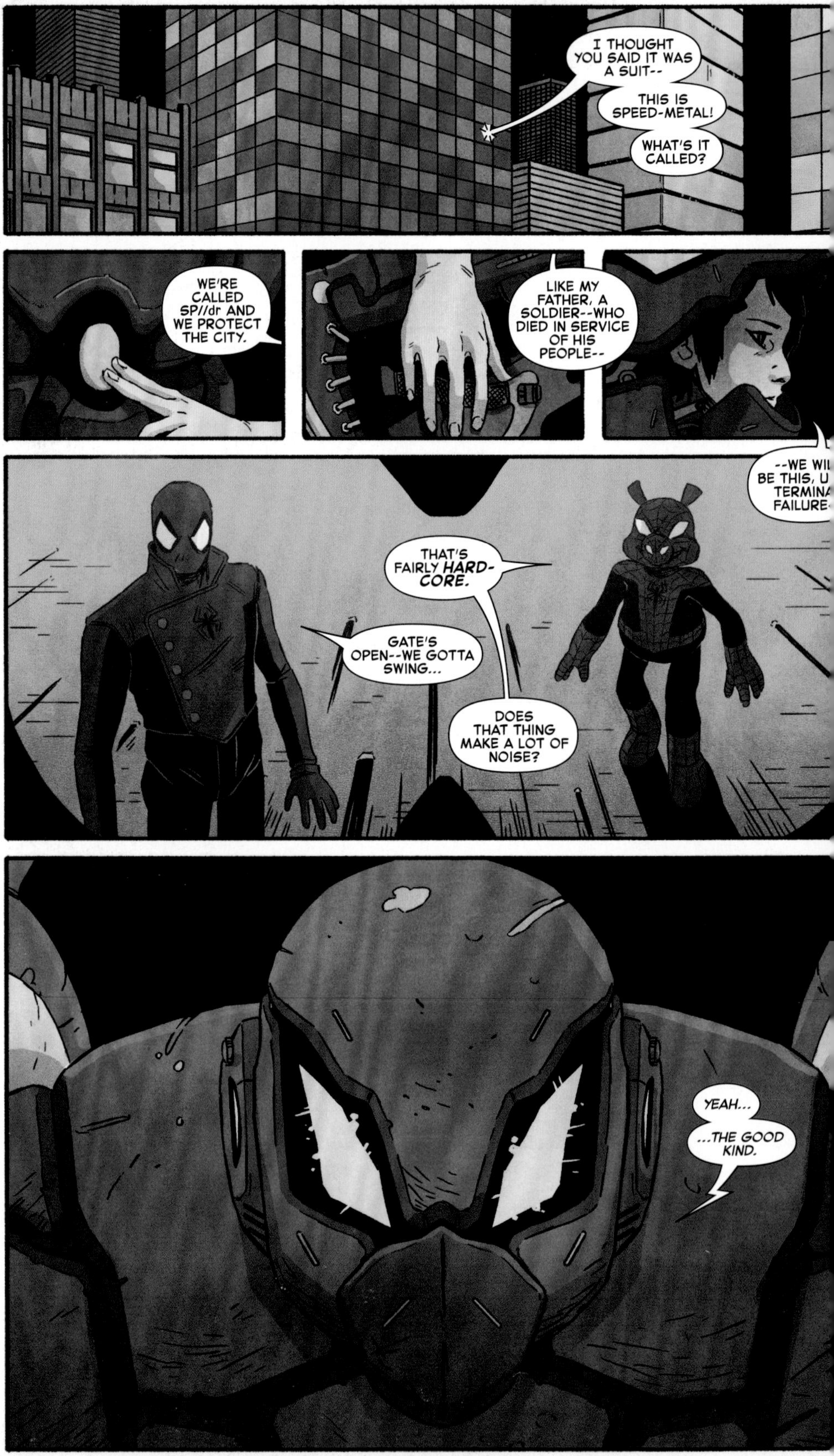
I THOUGHT YOU SAID IT WAS A SUIT--
THIS IS SPEED-METAL!
WHAT'S IT CALLED?
WE'RE CALLED SP//dr AND WE PROTECT THE CITY.
LIKE MY FATHER, A SOLDIER--WHO DIED IN SERVICE OF HIS PEOPLE--
THAT'S FAIRLY ***HARD-CORE.***
GATE'S OPEN--WE GOTTA SWING...
DOES THAT THING MAKE A LOT OF NOISE?
YEAH...
...THE GOOD KIND.

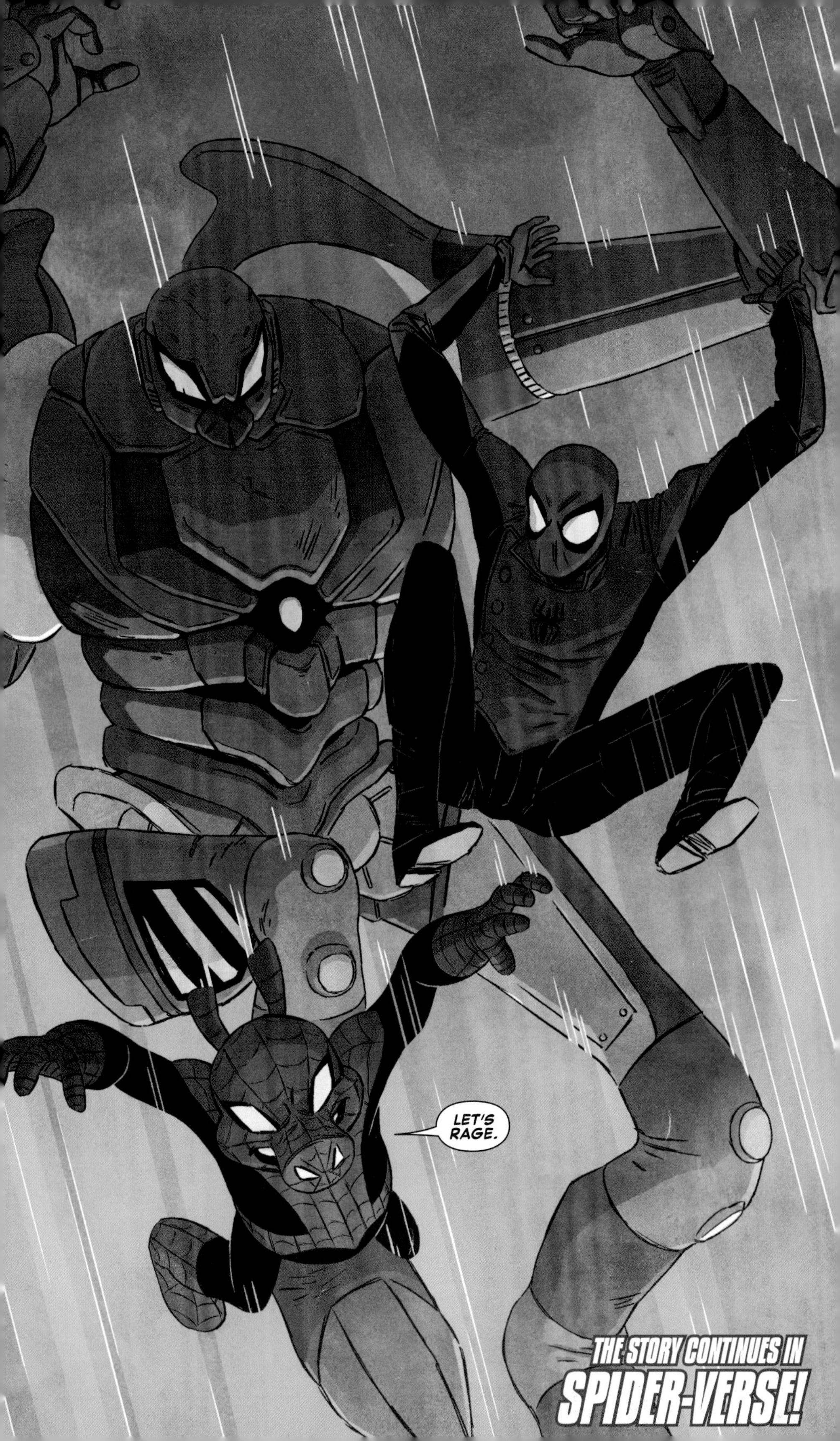
LET'S RAGE.
THE STORY CONTINUES IN
SPIDER-VERSE!

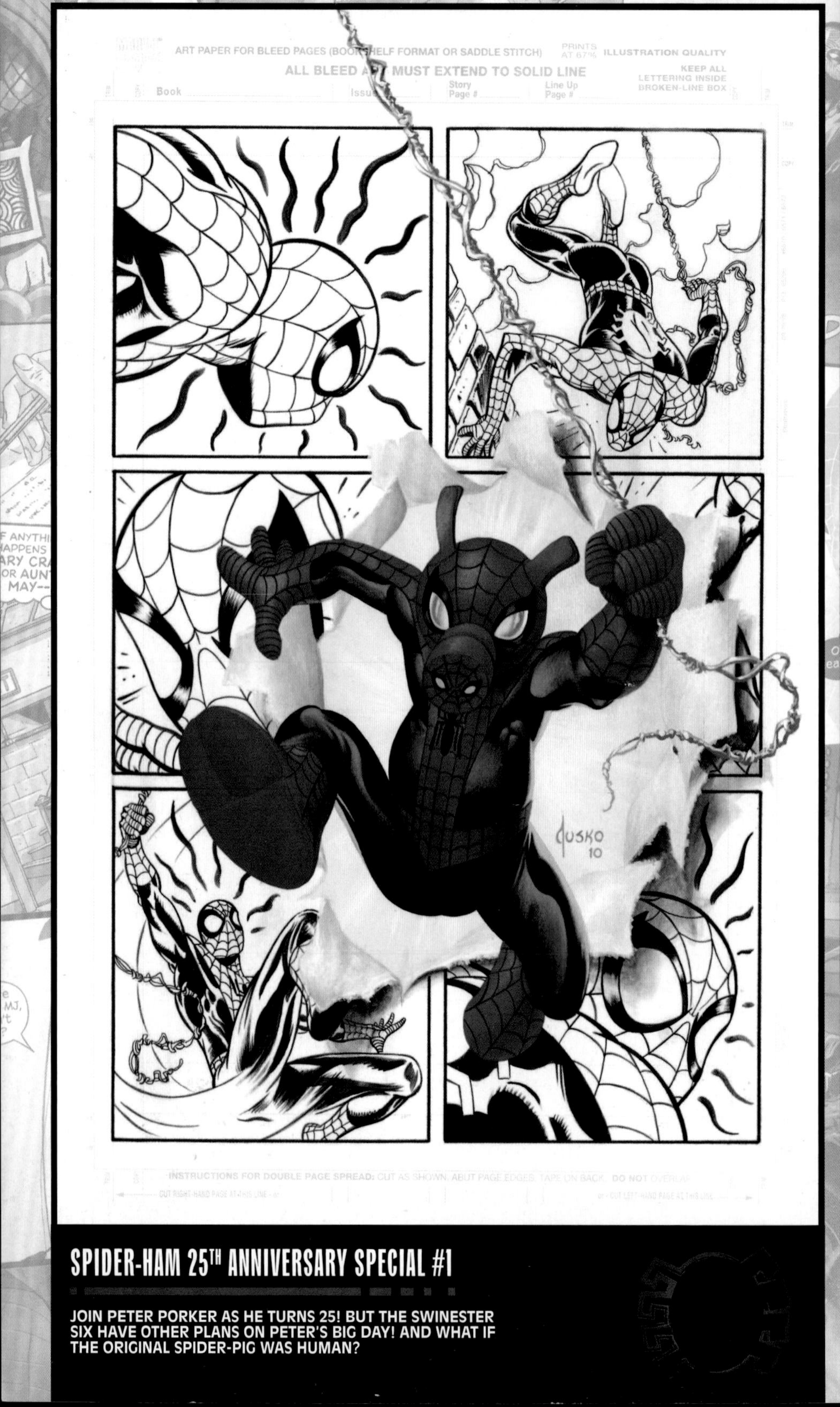
ART PAPER FOR BLEED PAGES (BOOKSHELF FORMAT OR SADDLE STITCH)
PRINTS AT 67%
ILLUSTRATION QUALITY
KEEP ALL LETTERING INSIDE BROKEN-LINE BOX
Book
Story Page #
Line Up Page #
JUSKO 10

SPIDER-HAM 25TH ANNIVERSARY SPECIAL #1

JOIN PETER PORKER AS HE TURNS 25! BUT THE SWINESTER SIX HAVE OTHER PLANS ON PETER'S BIG DAY! AND WHAT IF THE ORIGINAL SPIDER-PIG WAS HUMAN?

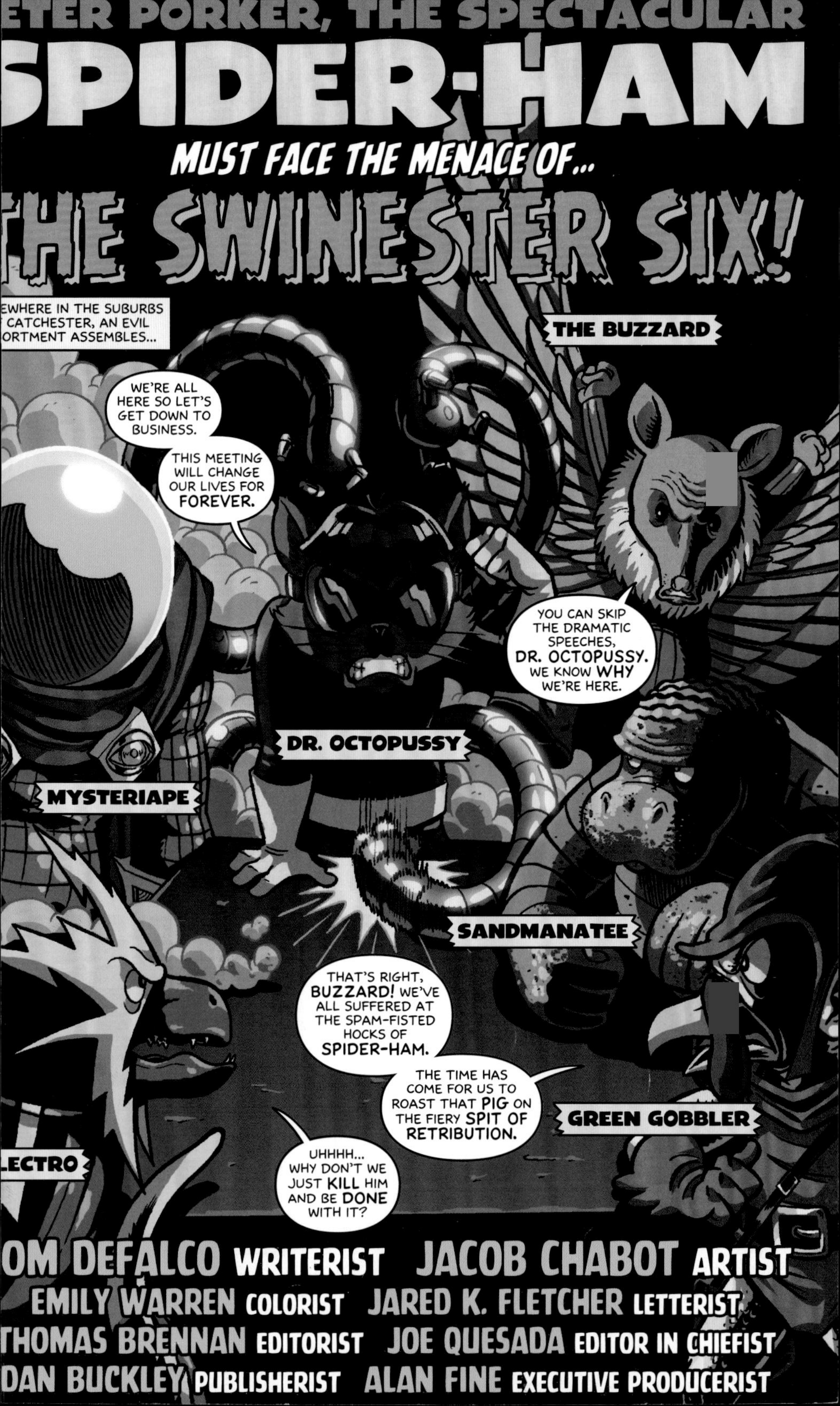
ETER PORKER, THE SPECTACULAR
SPIDER-HAM
MUST FACE THE MENACE OF...
THE SWINESTER SIX!
EWHERE IN THE SUBURBS CATCHESTER, AN EVIL ORTMENT ASSEMBLES...
THE BUZZARD
WE'RE ALL HERE SO LET'S GET DOWN TO BUSINESS.
THIS MEETING WILL CHANGE OUR LIVES FOR FOREVER.
YOU CAN SKIP THE DRAMATIC SPEECHES, DR. OCTOPUSSY. WE KNOW WHY WE'RE HERE.
DR. OCTOPUSSY
MYSTERIAPE
SANDMANATEE
THAT'S RIGHT, BUZZARD! WE'VE ALL SUFFERED AT THE SPAM-FISTED HOCKS OF SPIDER-HAM.
THE TIME HAS COME FOR US TO ROAST THAT PIG ON THE FIERY SPIT OF RETRIBUTION.
GREEN GOBBLER
LECTRO
UHHHH... WHY DON'T WE JUST KILL HIM AND BE DONE WITH IT?
OM DEFALCO WRITERIST JACOB CHABOT ARTIST
EMILY WARREN COLORIST JARED K. FLETCHER LETTERIST
THOMAS BRENNAN EDITORIST JOE QUESADA EDITOR IN CHIEFIST
DAN BUCKLEY PUBLISHERIST ALAN FINE EXECUTIVE PRODUCERIST

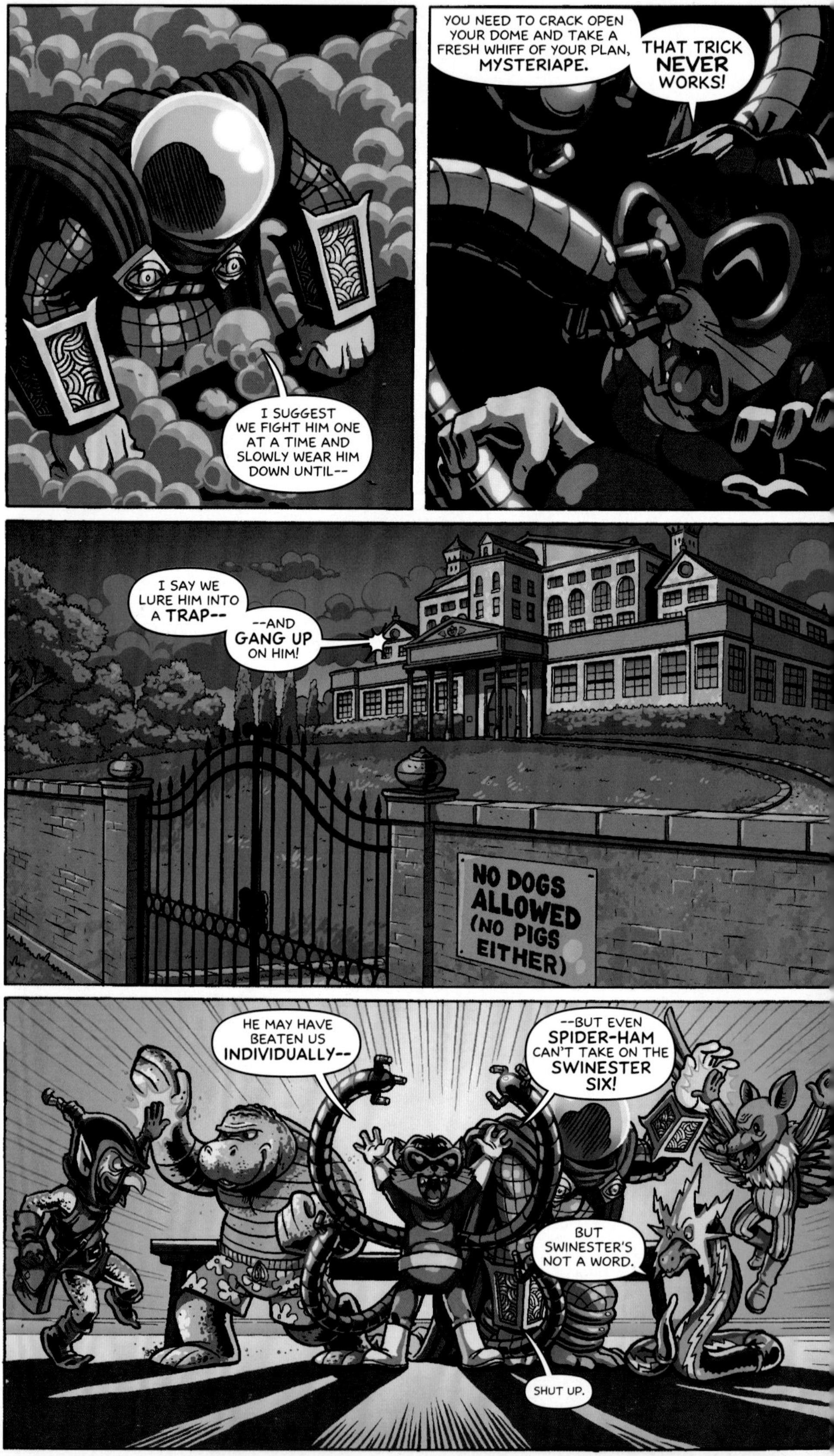
I SUGGEST WE FIGHT HIM ONE AT A TIME AND SLOWLY WEAR HIM DOWN UNTIL--
YOU NEED TO CRACK OPEN YOUR DOME AND TAKE A FRESH WHIFF OF YOUR PLAN, MYSTERIAPE.
THAT TRICK NEVER WORKS!
I SAY WE LURE HIM INTO A TRAP--
--AND GANG UP ON HIM!
NO DOGS ALLOWED (NO PIGS EITHER)
HE MAY HAVE BEATEN US INDIVIDUALLY--
--BUT EVEN SPIDER-HAM CAN'T TAKE ON THE SWINESTER SIX!
BUT SWINESTER'S NOT A WORD.
SHUT UP.

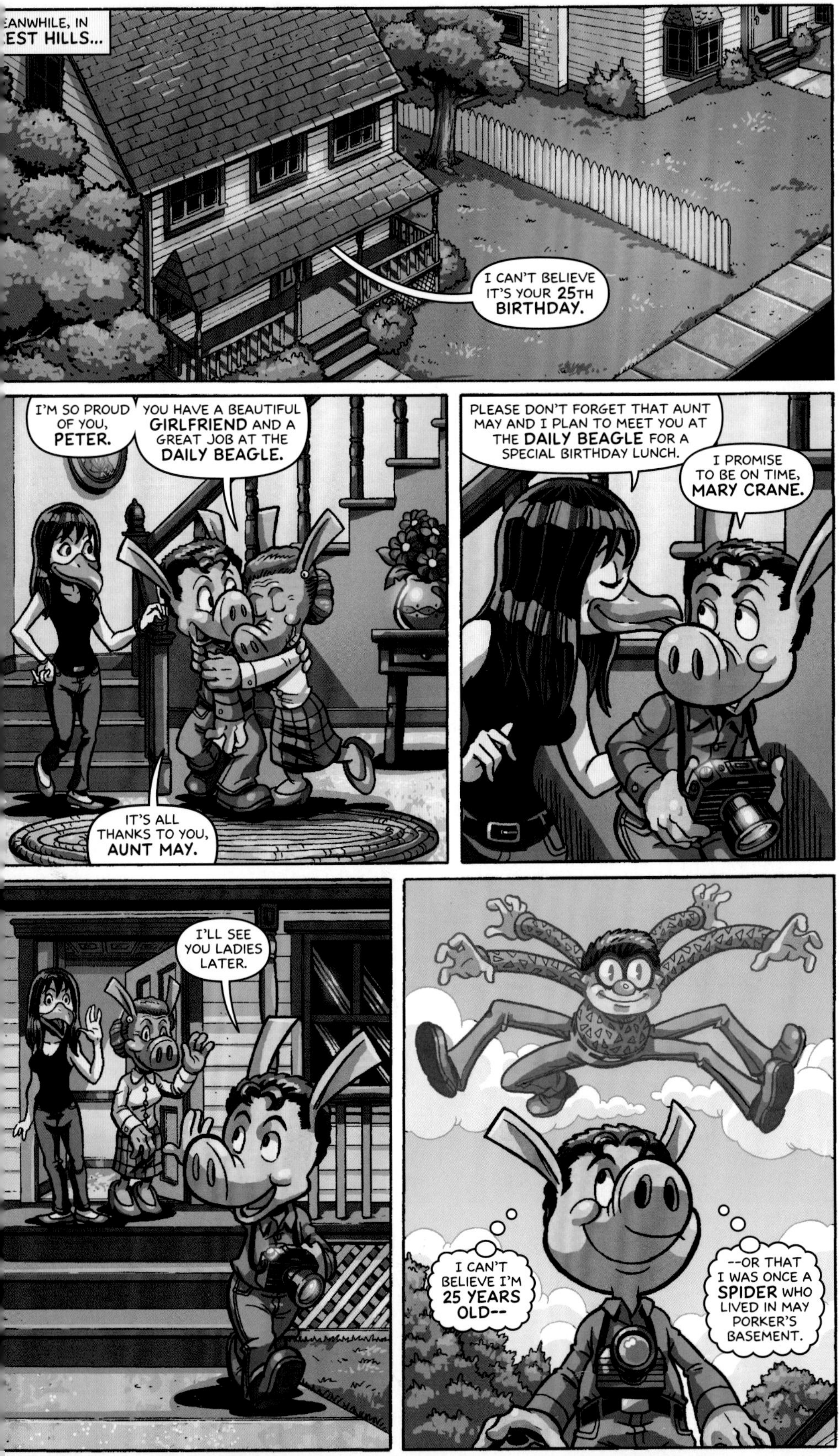

EANWHILE, IN
EST HILLS...
I CAN'T BELIEVE IT'S YOUR 25TH BIRTHDAY.
I'M SO PROUD OF YOU, PETER.
YOU HAVE A BEAUTIFUL GIRLFRIEND AND A GREAT JOB AT THE DAILY BEAGLE.
IT'S ALL THANKS TO YOU, AUNT MAY.
PLEASE DON'T FORGET THAT AUNT MAY AND I PLAN TO MEET YOU AT THE DAILY BEAGLE FOR A SPECIAL BIRTHDAY LUNCH.
I PROMISE TO BE ON TIME, MARY CRANE.
I'LL SEE YOU LADIES LATER.
I CAN'T BELIEVE I'M 25 YEARS OLD--
--OR THAT I WAS ONCE A SPIDER WHO LIVED IN MAY PORKER'S BASEMENT.

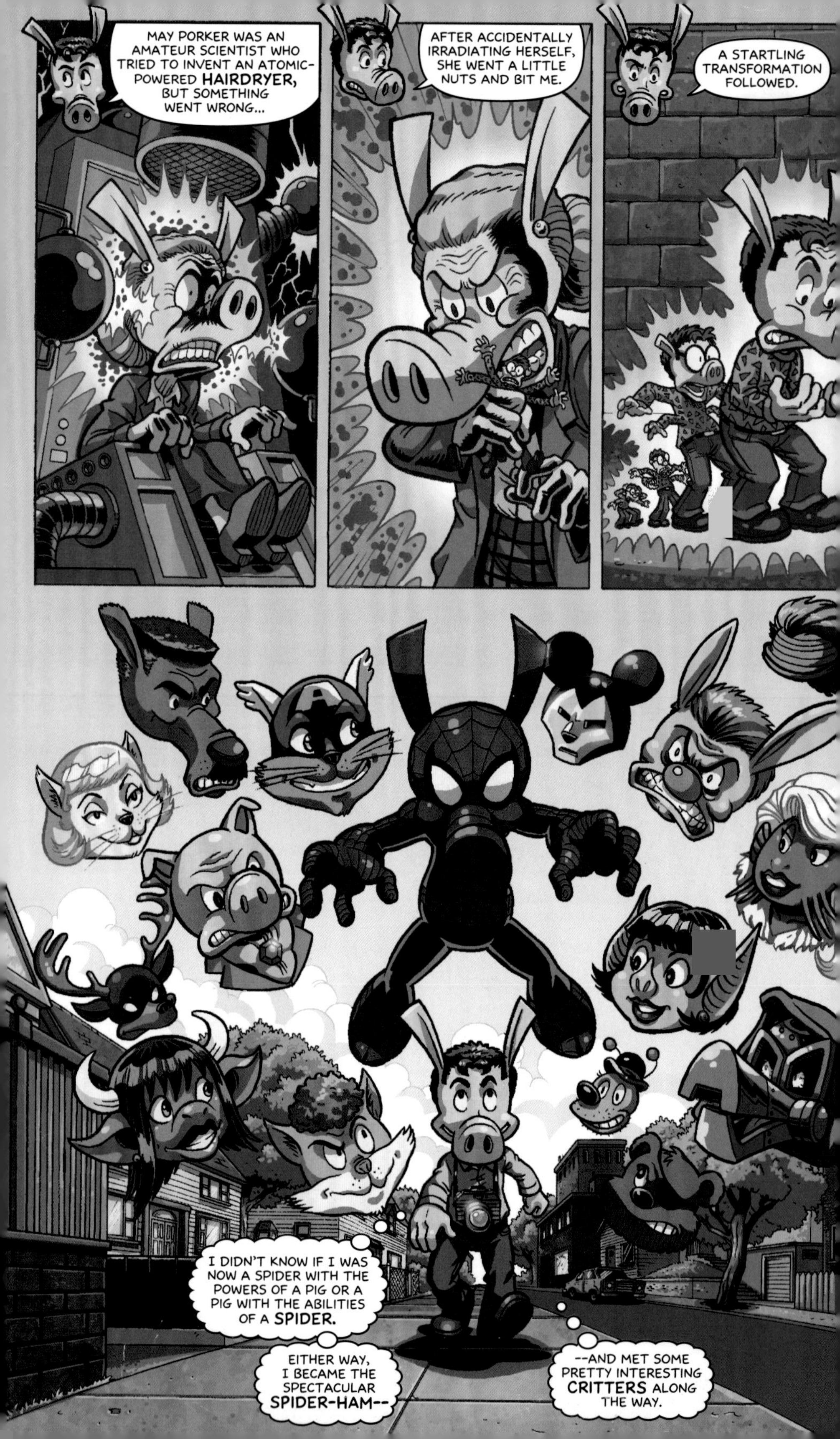
MAY PORKER WAS AN AMATEUR SCIENTIST WHO TRIED TO INVENT AN ATOMIC-POWERED **HAIRDRYER,** BUT SOMETHING WENT WRONG...
AFTER ACCIDENTALLY IRRADIATING HERSELF, SHE WENT A LITTLE NUTS AND BIT ME.
A STARTLING TRANSFORMATION FOLLOWED.
I DIDN'T KNOW IF I WAS NOW A SPIDER WITH THE POWERS OF A PIG OR A PIG WITH THE ABILITIES OF A **SPIDER.**
EITHER WAY, I BECAME THE SPECTACULAR **SPIDER-HAM--**
--AND MET SOME PRETTY INTERESTING **CRITTERS** ALONG THE WAY.

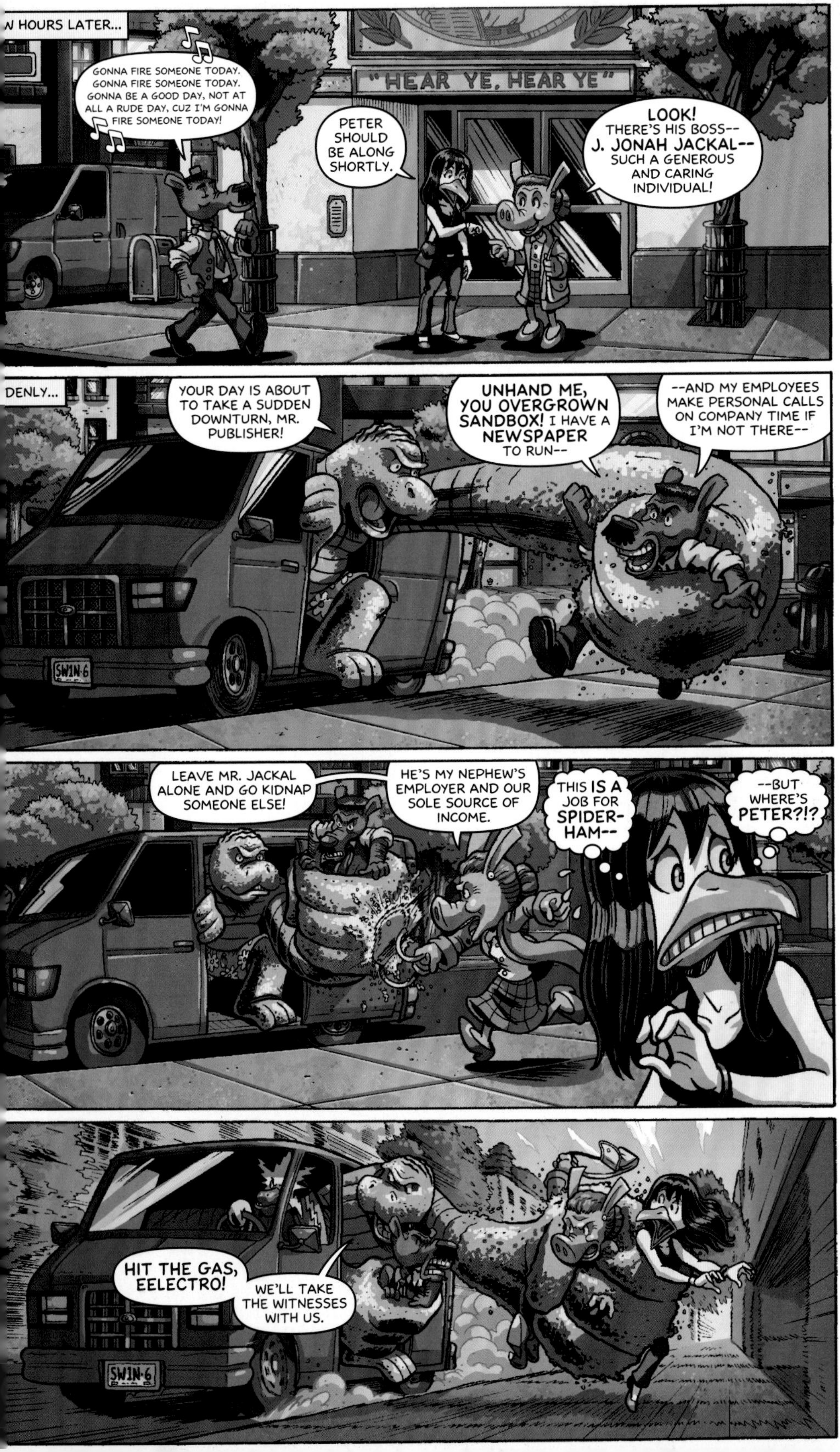

W HOURS LATER...
GONNA FIRE SOMEONE TODAY. GONNA FIRE SOMEONE TODAY. GONNA BE A GOOD DAY, NOT AT ALL A RUDE DAY, CUZ I'M GONNA FIRE SOMEONE TODAY!
"HEAR YE, HEAR YE"
PETER SHOULD BE ALONG SHORTLY.
LOOK! THERE'S HIS BOSS-- J. JONAH JACKAL-- SUCH A GENEROUS AND CARING INDIVIDUAL!
DENLY...
YOUR DAY IS ABOUT TO TAKE A SUDDEN DOWNTURN, MR. PUBLISHER!
UNHAND ME, YOU OVERGROWN SANDBOX! I HAVE A NEWSPAPER TO RUN--
--AND MY EMPLOYEES MAKE PERSONAL CALLS ON COMPANY TIME IF I'M NOT THERE--
SW1N-6
LEAVE MR. JACKAL ALONE AND GO KIDNAP SOMEONE ELSE!
HE'S MY NEPHEW'S EMPLOYER AND OUR SOLE SOURCE OF INCOME.
THIS IS A JOB FOR SPIDER-HAM--
--BUT WHERE'S PETER?!?
HIT THE GAS, EELECTRO!
WE'LL TAKE THE WITNESSES WITH US.
SW1N-6

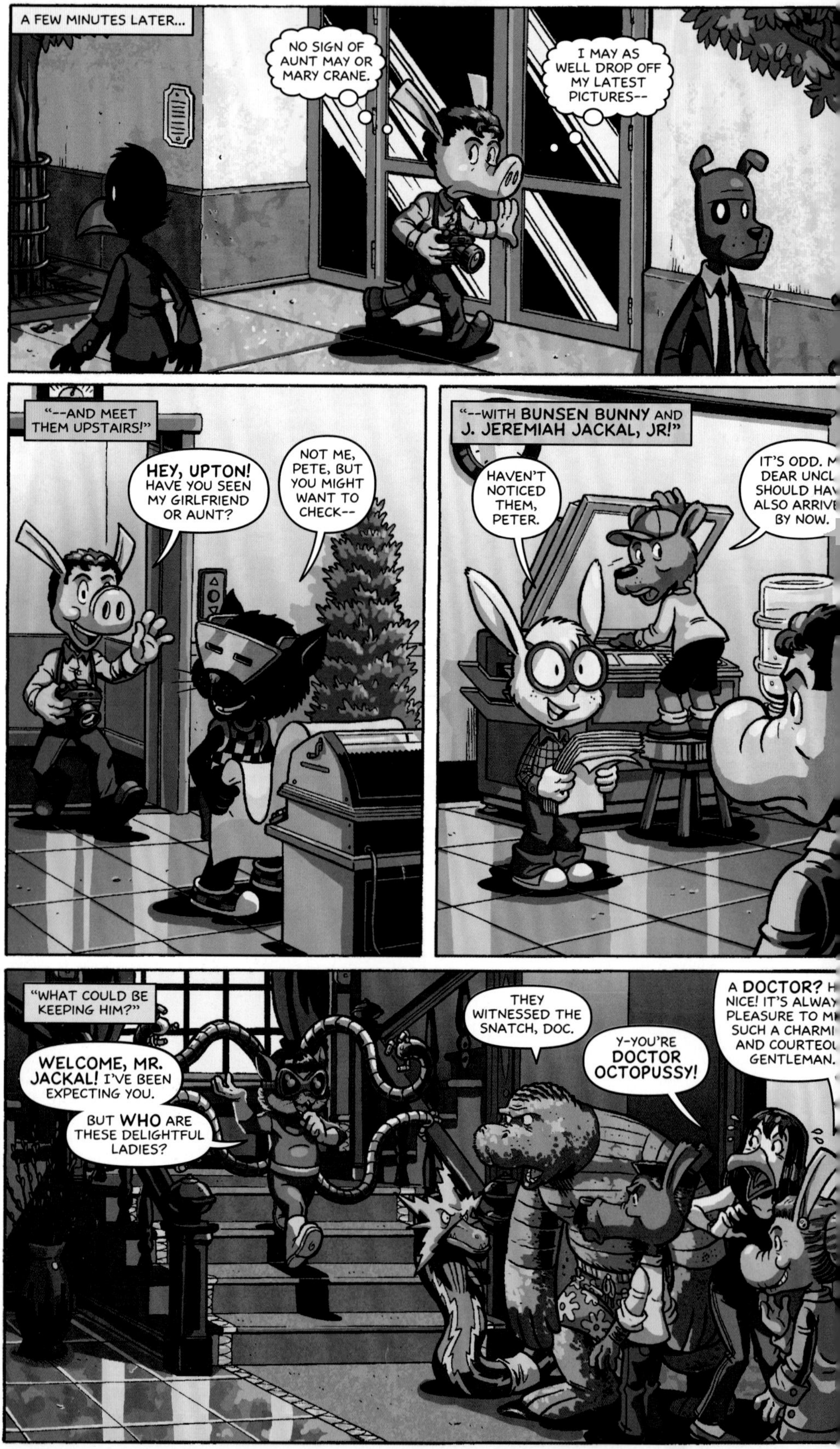
A FEW MINUTES LATER...
NO SIGN OF AUNT MAY OR MARY CRANE.
I MAY AS WELL DROP OFF MY LATEST PICTURES--
"--AND MEET THEM UPSTAIRS!"
HEY, UPTON! HAVE YOU SEEN MY GIRLFRIEND OR AUNT?
NOT ME, PETE, BUT YOU MIGHT WANT TO CHECK--
"--WITH BUNSEN BUNNY AND J. JEREMIAH JACKAL, JR!"
HAVEN'T NOTICED THEM, PETER.
IT'S ODD.
DEAR UNCL
SHOULD HA
ALSO ARRIV
BY NOW.
"WHAT COULD BE KEEPING HIM?"
WELCOME, MR. JACKAL! I'VE BEEN EXPECTING YOU.
BUT WHO ARE THESE DELIGHTFUL LADIES?
THEY WITNESSED THE SNATCH, DOC.
Y-YOU'RE DOCTOR OCTOPUSSY!
A DOCTOR?
NICE! IT'S ALWA
PLEASURE TO M
SUCH A CHARM
AND COURTEO
GENTLEMAN.

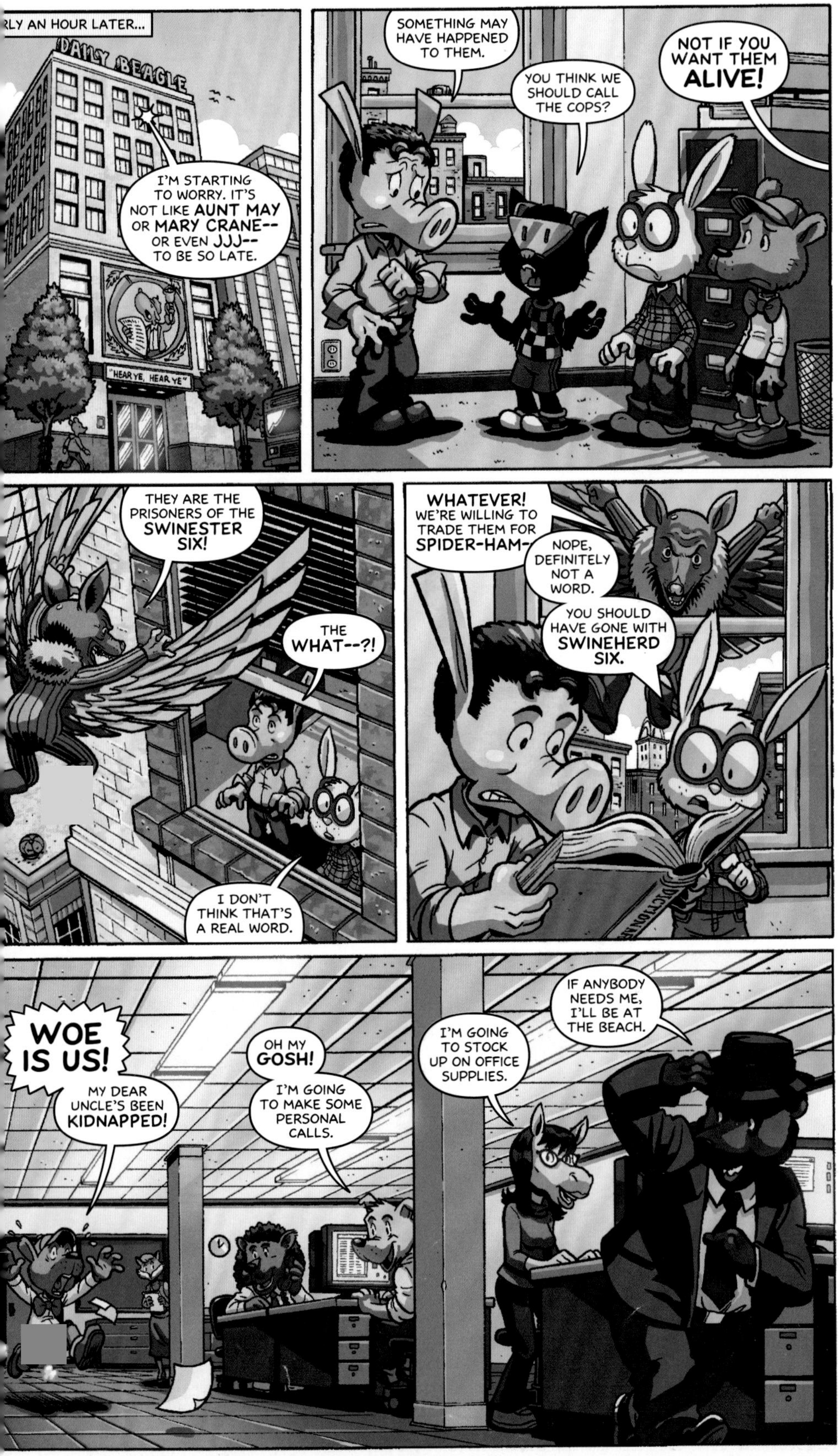
RLY AN HOUR LATER...
DAILY BEAGLE
I'M STARTING TO WORRY. IT'S NOT LIKE AUNT MAY OR MARY CRANE-- OR EVEN JJJ-- TO BE SO LATE.
"HEAR YE, HEAR YE"
SOMETHING MAY HAVE HAPPENED TO THEM.
YOU THINK WE SHOULD CALL THE COPS?
NOT IF YOU WANT THEM ALIVE!
THEY ARE THE PRISONERS OF THE SWINESTER SIX!
THE WHAT--?!
I DON'T THINK THAT'S A REAL WORD.
WHATEVER! WE'RE WILLING TO TRADE THEM FOR SPIDER-HAM--
NOPE, DEFINITELY NOT A WORD.
YOU SHOULD HAVE GONE WITH SWINEHERD SIX.
WOE IS US!
MY DEAR UNCLE'S BEEN KIDNAPPED!
OH MY GOSH!
I'M GOING TO MAKE SOME PERSONAL CALLS.
I'M GOING TO STOCK UP ON OFFICE SUPPLIES.
IF ANYBODY NEEDS ME, I'LL BE AT THE BEACH.

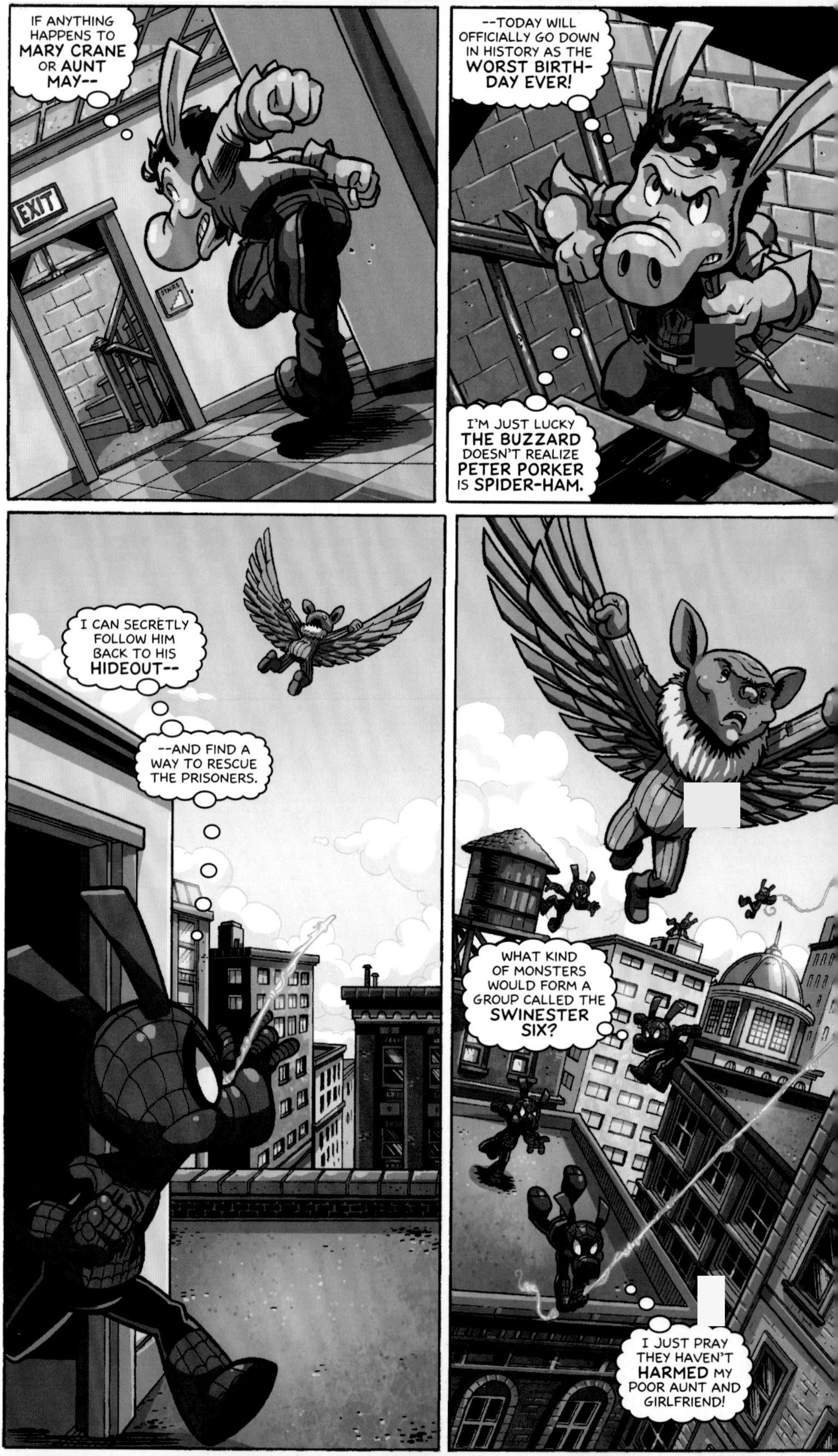
IF ANYTHING HAPPENS TO MARY CRANE OR AUNT MAY--
--TODAY WILL OFFICIALLY GO DOWN IN HISTORY AS THE WORST BIRTH-DAY EVER!
I'M JUST LUCKY THE BUZZARD DOESN'T REALIZE PETER PORKER IS SPIDER-HAM.
EXIT
I CAN SECRETLY FOLLOW HIM BACK TO HIS HIDEOUT--
--AND FIND A WAY TO RESCUE THE PRISONERS.
WHAT KIND OF MONSTERS WOULD FORM A GROUP CALLED THE SWINESTER SIX?
I JUST PRAY THEY HAVEN'T HARMED MY POOR AUNT AND GIRLFRIEND!

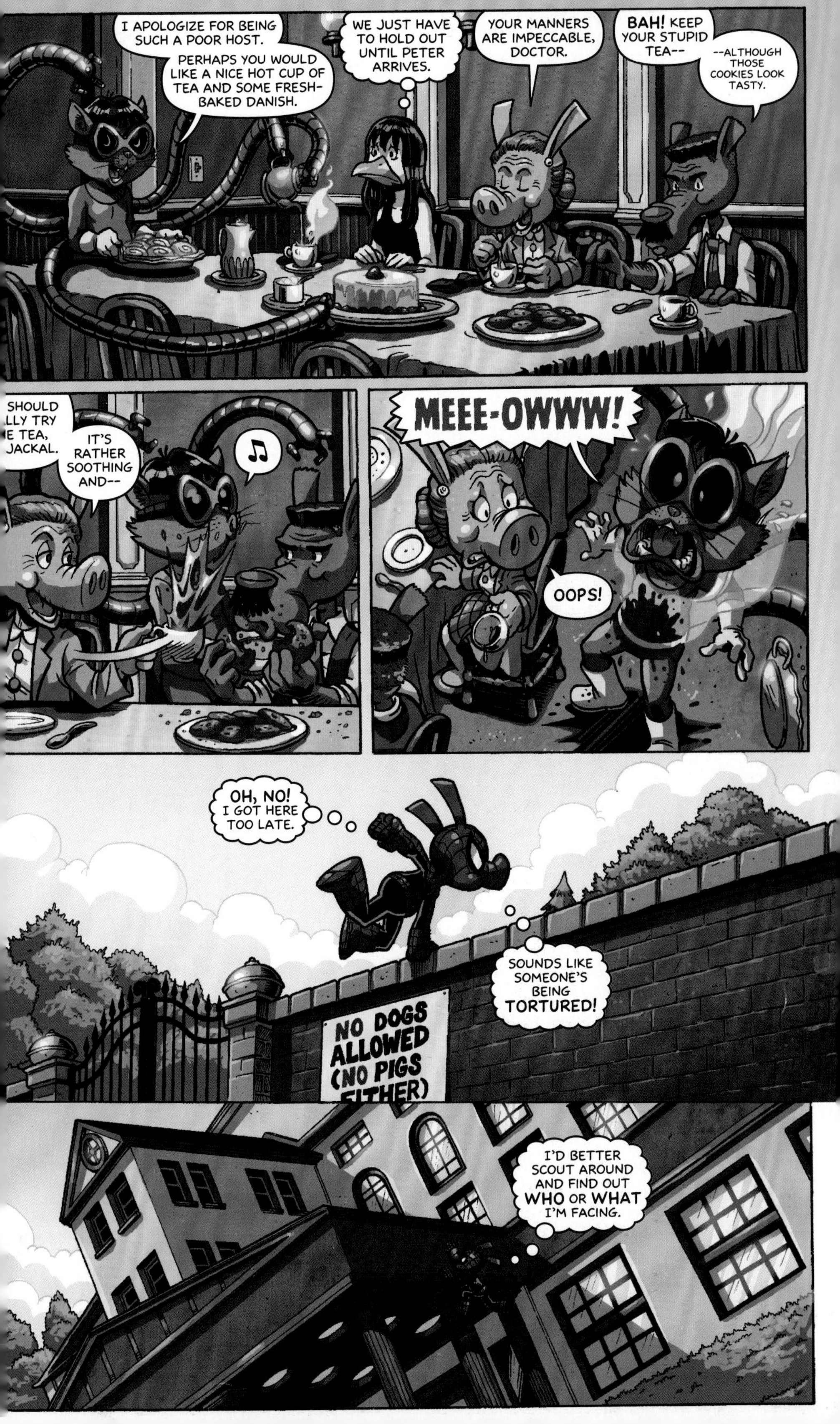
I APOLOGIZE FOR BEING SUCH A POOR HOST.
PERHAPS YOU WOULD LIKE A NICE HOT CUP OF TEA AND SOME FRESH-BAKED DANISH.
WE JUST HAVE TO HOLD OUT UNTIL PETER ARRIVES.
YOUR MANNERS ARE IMPECCABLE, DOCTOR.
BAH! KEEP YOUR STUPID TEA--
--ALTHOUGH THOSE COOKIES LOOK TASTY.
SHOULD
LLY TRY
E TEA,
JACKAL.
IT'S RATHER SOOTHING AND--
MEEE-OWWW!
OOPS!
OH, NO! I GOT HERE TOO LATE.
SOUNDS LIKE SOMEONE'S BEING TORTURED!
NO DOGS ALLOWED (NO PIGS EITHER)
I'D BETTER SCOUT AROUND AND FIND OUT WHO OR WHAT I'M FACING.

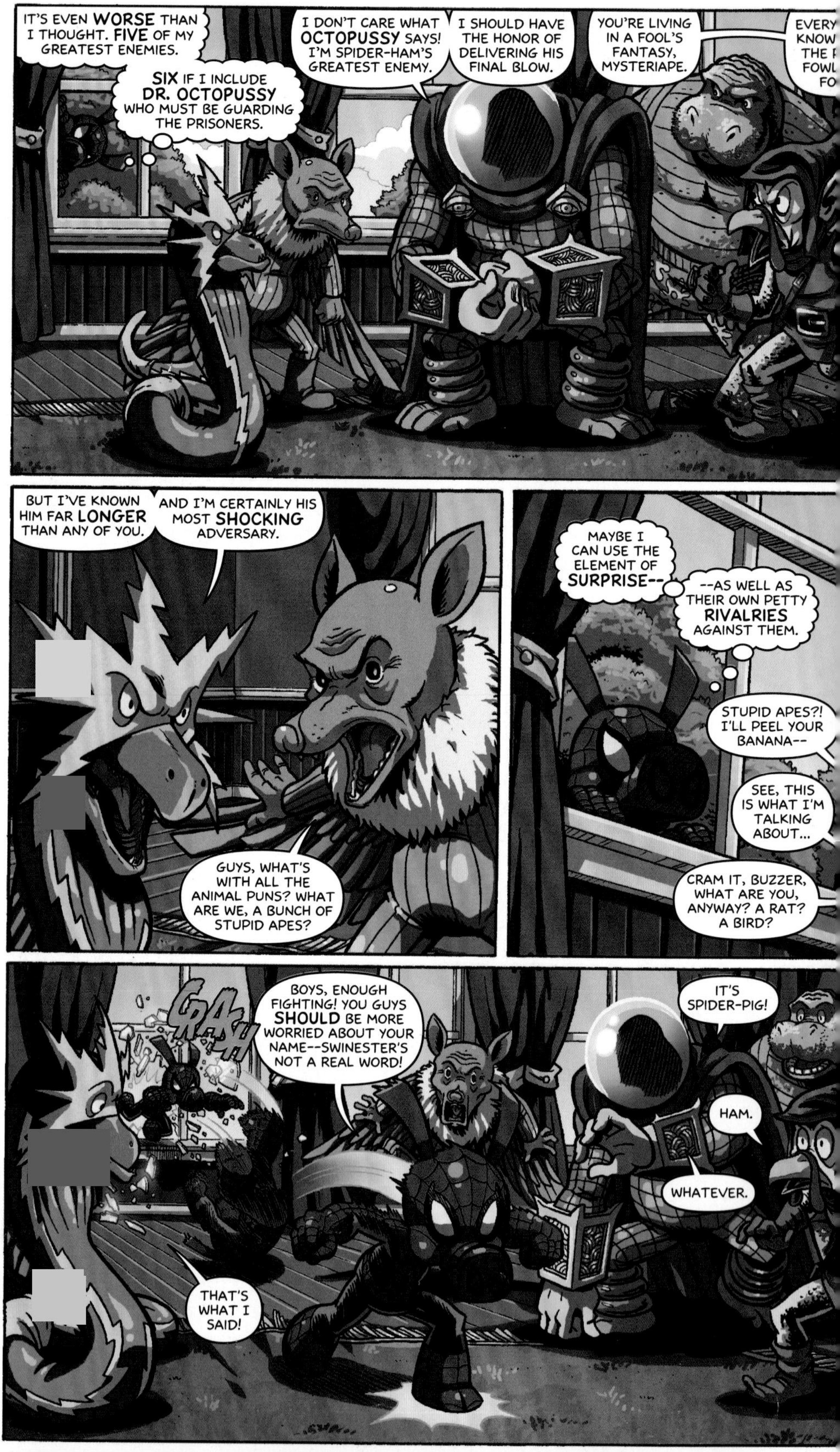
IT'S EVEN WORSE THAN I THOUGHT. FIVE OF MY GREATEST ENEMIES.
SIX IF I INCLUDE DR. OCTOPUSSY WHO MUST BE GUARDING THE PRISONERS.
I DON'T CARE WHAT OCTOPUSSY SAYS! I'M SPIDER-HAM'S GREATEST ENEMY.
I SHOULD HAVE THE HONOR OF DELIVERING HIS FINAL BLOW.
YOU'RE LIVING IN A FOOL'S FANTASY, MYSTERIAPE.
BUT I'VE KNOWN HIM FAR LONGER THAN ANY OF YOU.
AND I'M CERTAINLY HIS MOST SHOCKING ADVERSARY.
GUYS, WHAT'S WITH ALL THE ANIMAL PUNS? WHAT ARE WE, A BUNCH OF STUPID APES?
MAYBE I CAN USE THE ELEMENT OF SURPRISE--
--AS WELL AS THEIR OWN PETTY RIVALRIES AGAINST THEM.
STUPID APES?! I'LL PEEL YOUR BANANA--
SEE, THIS IS WHAT I'M TALKING ABOUT...
CRAM IT, BUZZER, WHAT ARE YOU, ANYWAY? A RAT? A BIRD?
CRASH
BOYS, ENOUGH FIGHTING! YOU GUYS SHOULD BE MORE WORRIED ABOUT YOUR NAME--SWINESTER'S NOT A REAL WORD!
IT'S SPIDER-PIG!
HAM.
WHATEVER.
THAT'S WHAT I SAID!

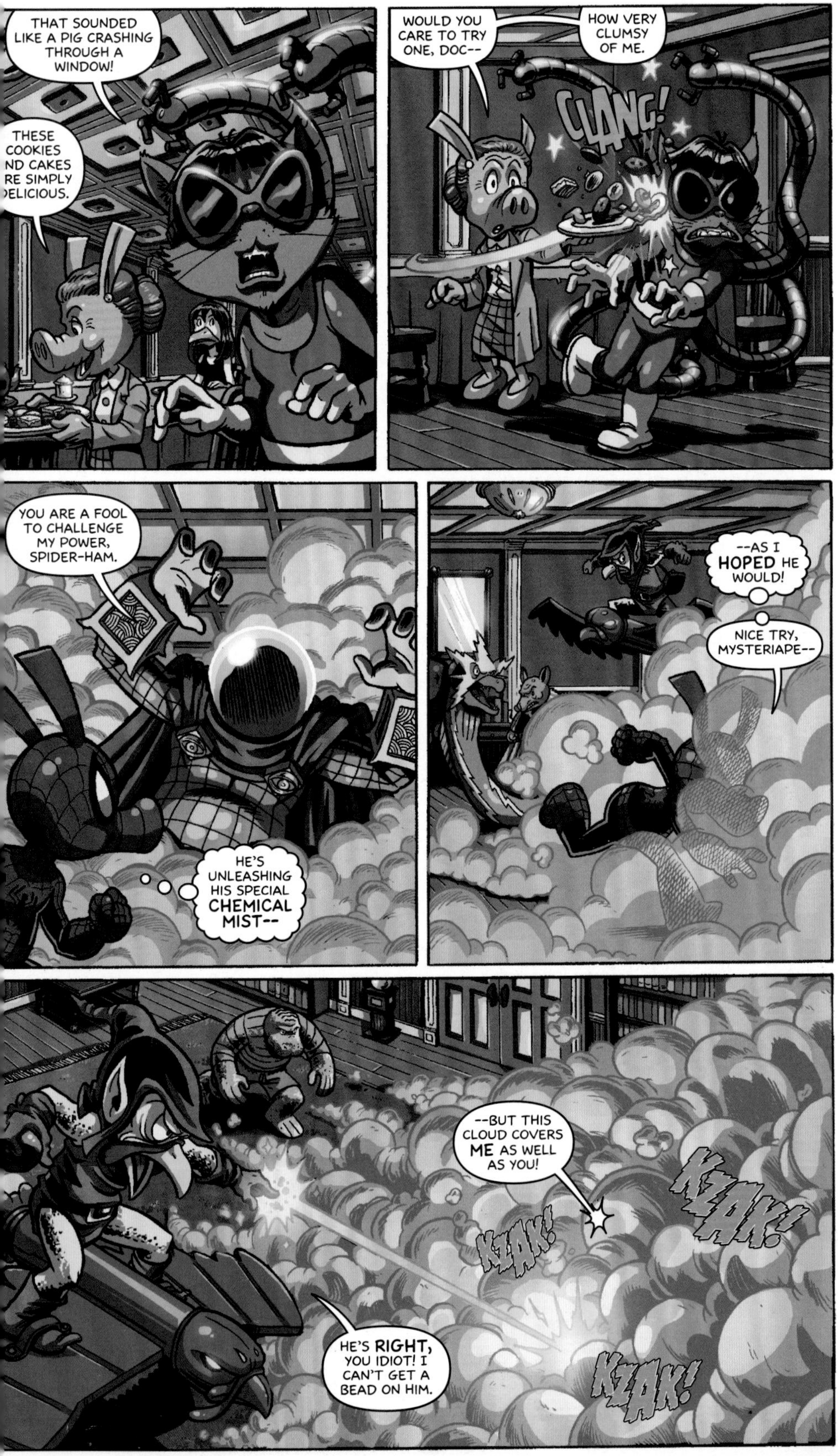
THAT SOUNDED LIKE A PIG CRASHING THROUGH A WINDOW!
THESE COOKIES ND CAKES RE SIMPLY ELICIOUS.
WOULD YOU CARE TO TRY ONE, DOC--
HOW VERY CLUMSY OF ME.
CLANG!
YOU ARE A FOOL TO CHALLENGE MY POWER, SPIDER-HAM.
HE'S UNLEASHING HIS SPECIAL CHEMICAL MIST--
--AS I HOPED HE WOULD!
NICE TRY, MYSTERIAPE--
--BUT THIS CLOUD COVERS ME AS WELL AS YOU!
KZAK!
KZAK!
HE'S RIGHT, YOU IDIOT! I CAN'T GET A BEAD ON HIM.
KZAK!

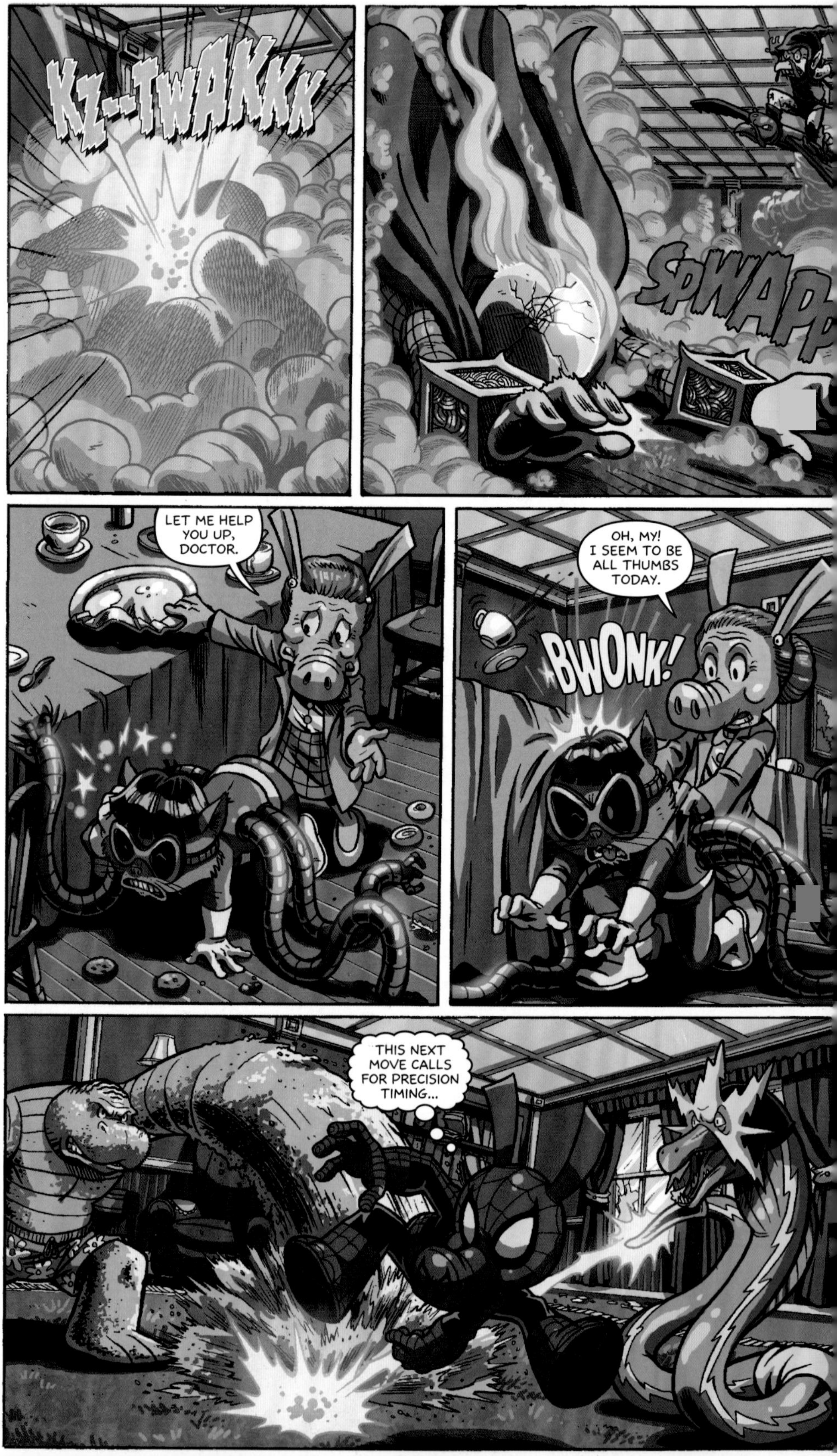
KZ--TWAKKK
SPWAPP
LET ME HELP YOU UP, DOCTOR.
OH, MY! I SEEM TO BE ALL THUMBS TODAY.
BWONK!
THIS NEXT MOVE CALLS FOR PRECISION TIMING...

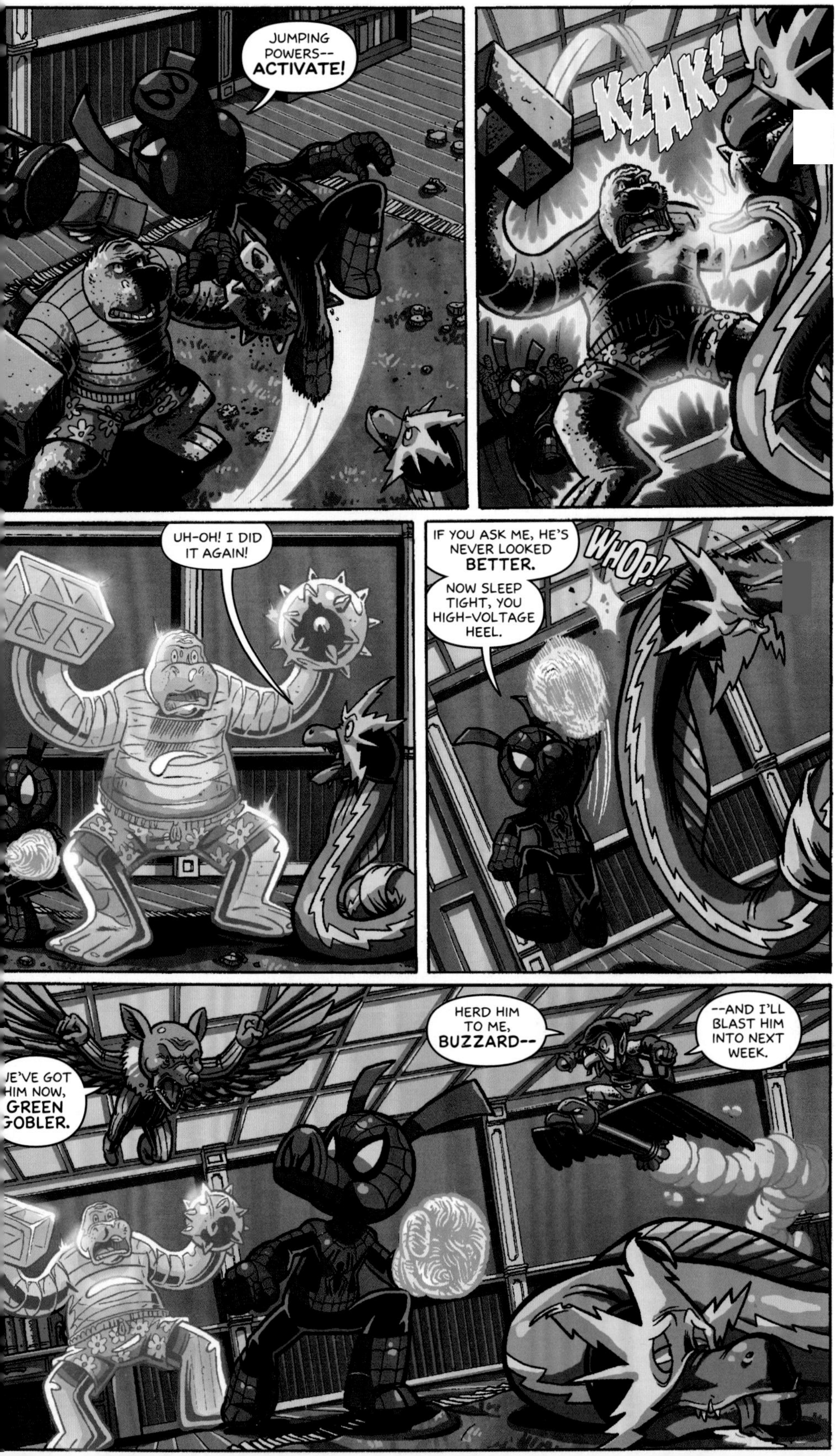
JUMPING POWERS-- ACTIVATE!
KZAK!
UH-OH! I DID IT AGAIN!
IF YOU ASK ME, HE'S NEVER LOOKED BETTER.
NOW SLEEP TIGHT, YOU HIGH-VOLTAGE HEEL.
WHOP!
E'VE GOT HIM NOW, GREEN GOBLER.
HERD HIM TO ME, BUZZARD--
--AND I'LL BLAST HIM INTO NEXT WEEK.

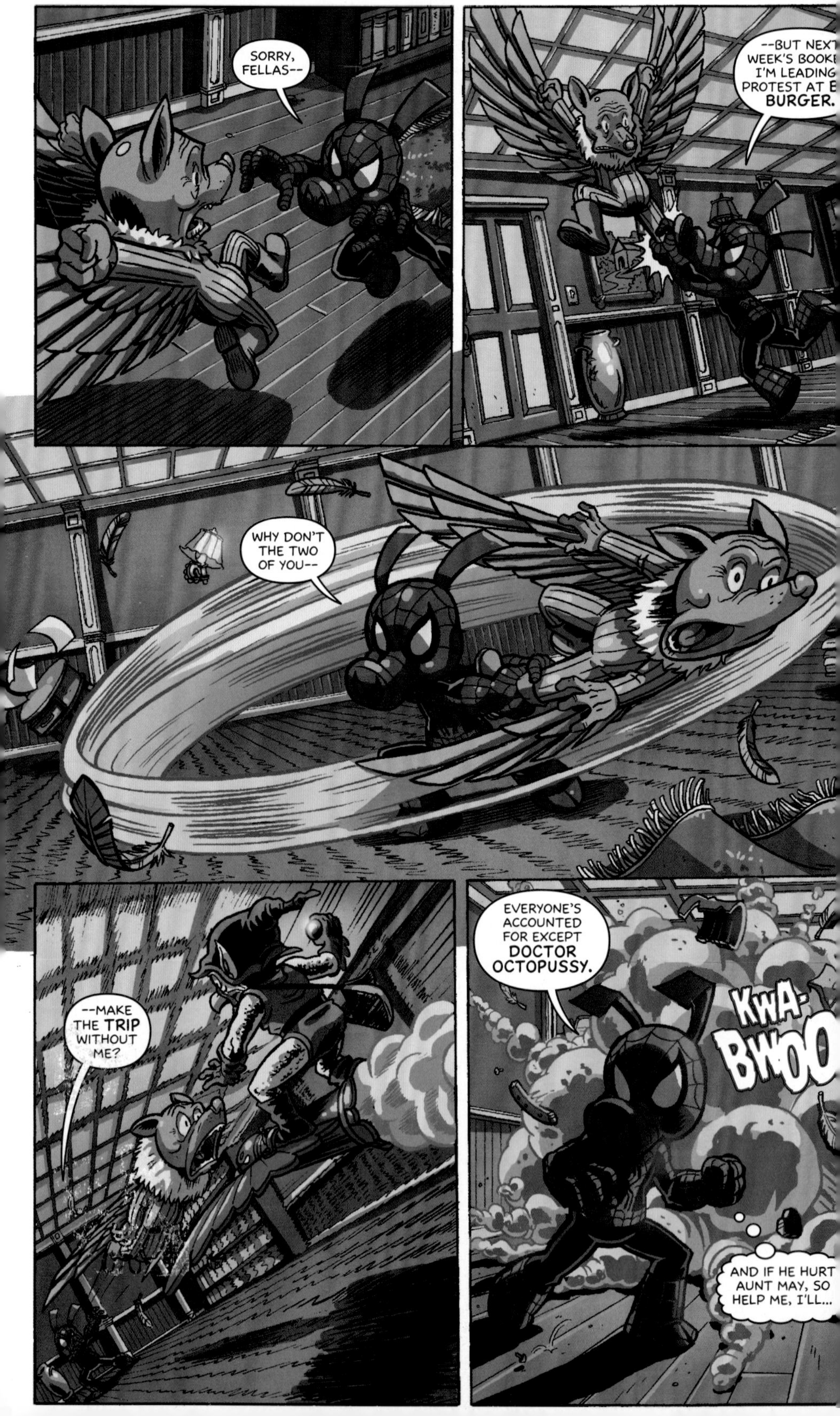
SORRY, FELLAS--
--BUT NEXT WEEK'S BOOKE
I'M LEADING PROTEST AT B
BURGER.
WHY DON'T THE TWO OF YOU--
--MAKE THE TRIP WITHOUT ME?
EVERYONE'S ACCOUNTED FOR EXCEPT DOCTOR OCTOPUSSY.
KWA-BWOO
AND IF HE HURT AUNT MAY, SO HELP ME, I'LL...

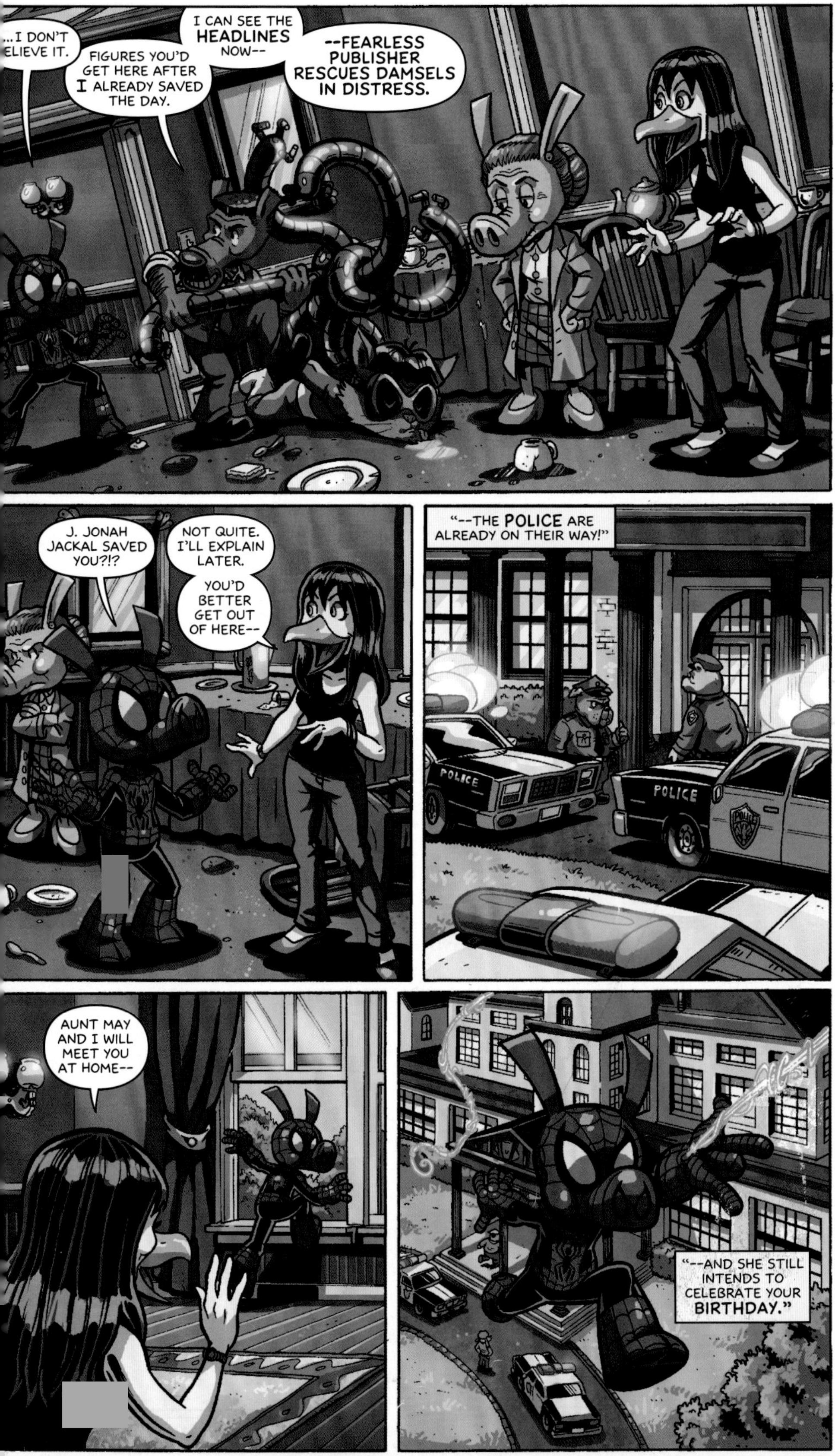
...I DON'T ELIEVE IT.
I CAN SEE THE HEADLINES NOW--
FIGURES YOU'D GET HERE AFTER I ALREADY SAVED THE DAY.
--FEARLESS PUBLISHER RESCUES DAMSELS IN DISTRESS.
J. JONAH JACKAL SAVED YOU?!?
NOT QUITE. I'LL EXPLAIN LATER.
YOU'D BETTER GET OUT OF HERE--
"--THE POLICE ARE ALREADY ON THEIR WAY!"
POLICE
POLICE
AUNT MAY AND I WILL MEET YOU AT HOME--
"--AND SHE STILL INTENDS TO CELEBRATE YOUR BIRTHDAY."

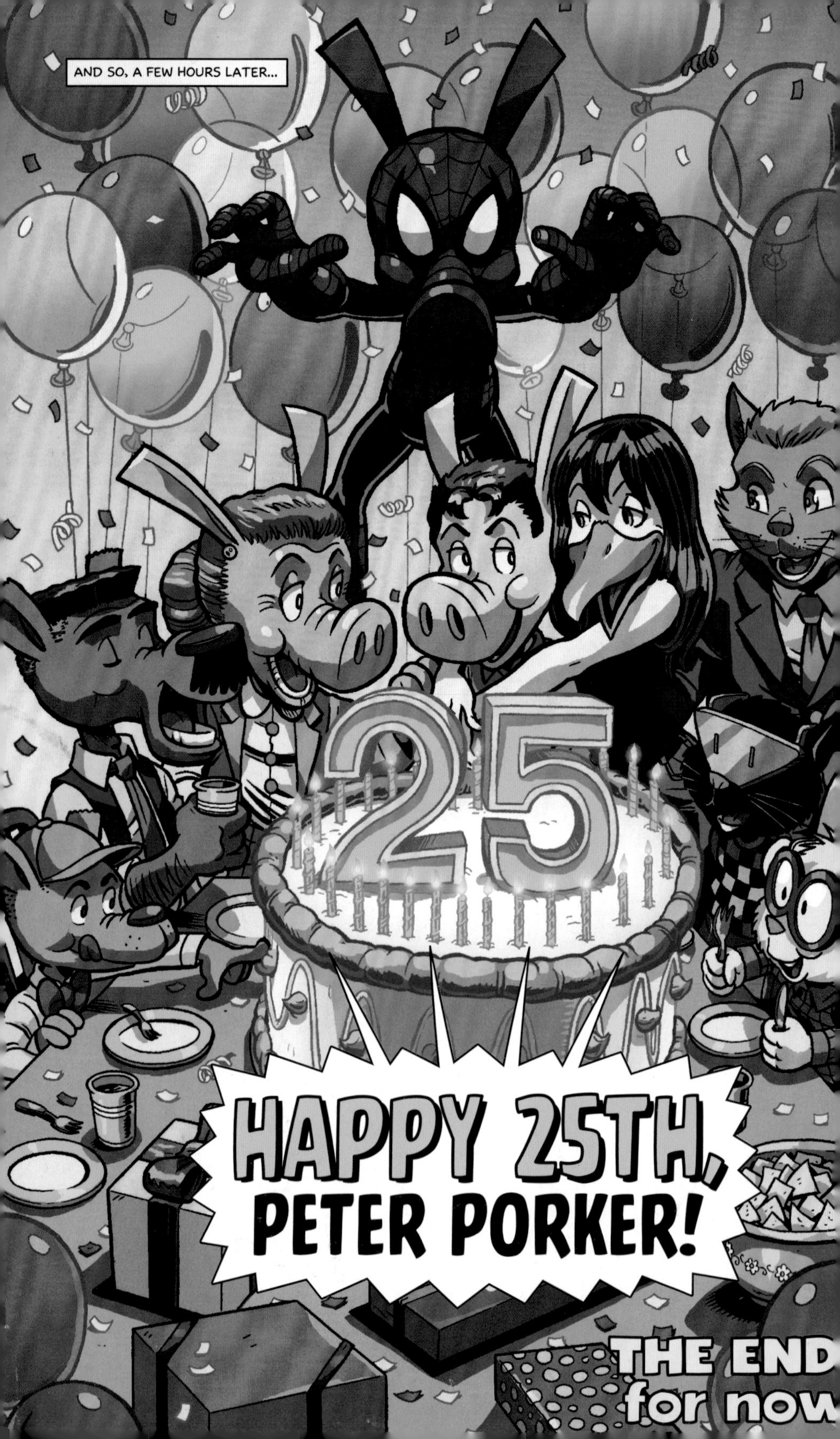

AND SO, A FEW HOURS LATER...
HAPPY 25TH, PETER PORKER!
THE END for now

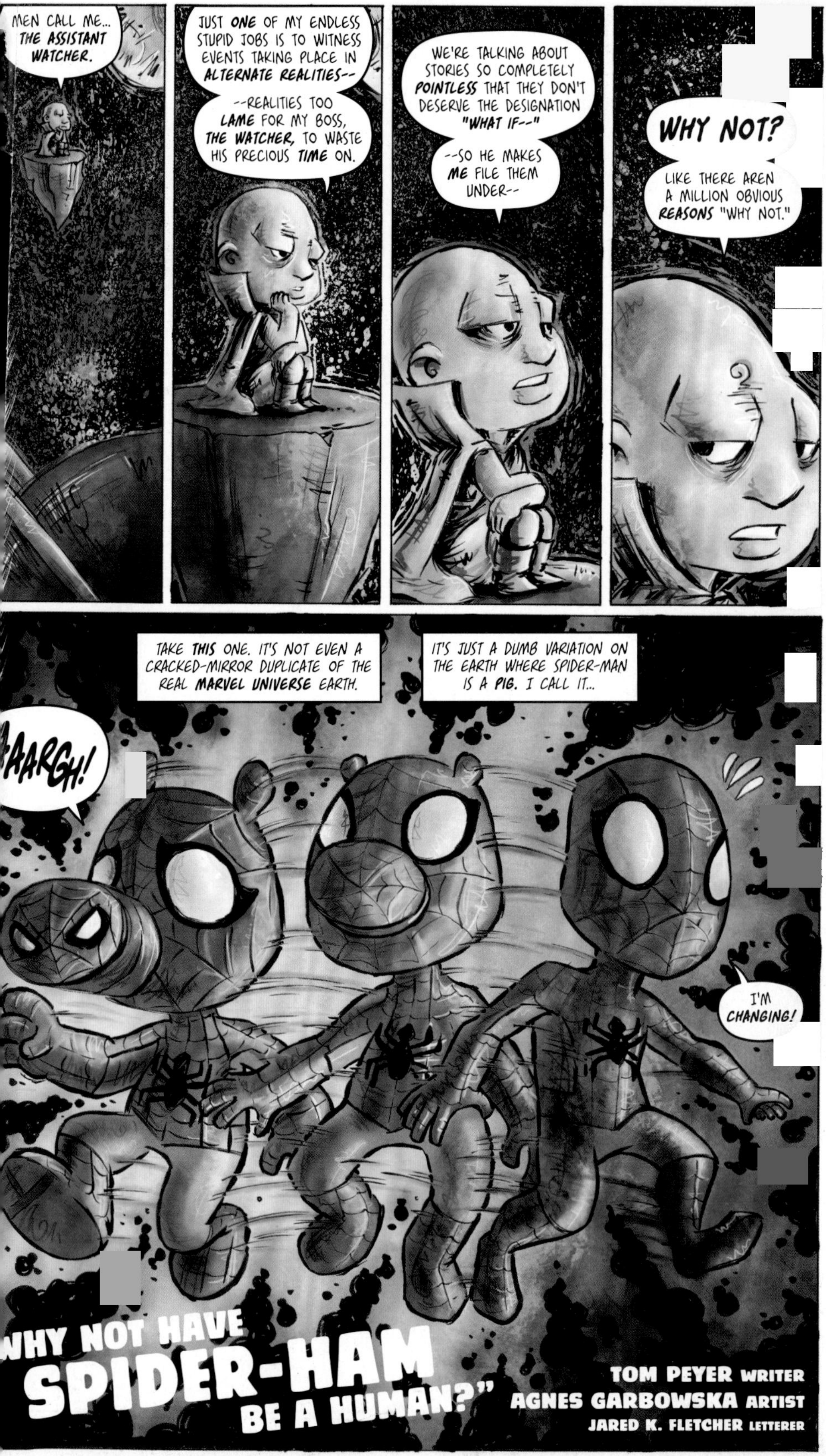
MEN CALL ME... THE ASSISTANT WATCHER.
JUST ONE OF MY ENDLESS STUPID JOBS IS TO WITNESS EVENTS TAKING PLACE IN ALTERNATE REALITIES--
--REALITIES TOO LAME FOR MY BOSS, THE WATCHER, TO WASTE HIS PRECIOUS TIME ON.
WE'RE TALKING ABOUT STORIES SO COMPLETELY POINTLESS THAT THEY DON'T DESERVE THE DESIGNATION "WHAT IF--"
--SO HE MAKES ME FILE THEM UNDER--
WHY NOT?
LIKE THERE AREN A MILLION OBVIOUS REASONS "WHY NOT."
TAKE THIS ONE. IT'S NOT EVEN A CRACKED-MIRROR DUPLICATE OF THE REAL MARVEL UNIVERSE EARTH.
IT'S JUST A DUMB VARIATION ON THE EARTH WHERE SPIDER-MAN IS A PIG. I CALL IT...
AARGH!
I'M CHANGING!
"WHY NOT HAVE SPIDER-HAM BE A HUMAN?"
TOM PEYER WRITER
AGNES GARBOWSKA ARTIST
JARED K. FLETCHER LETTERER

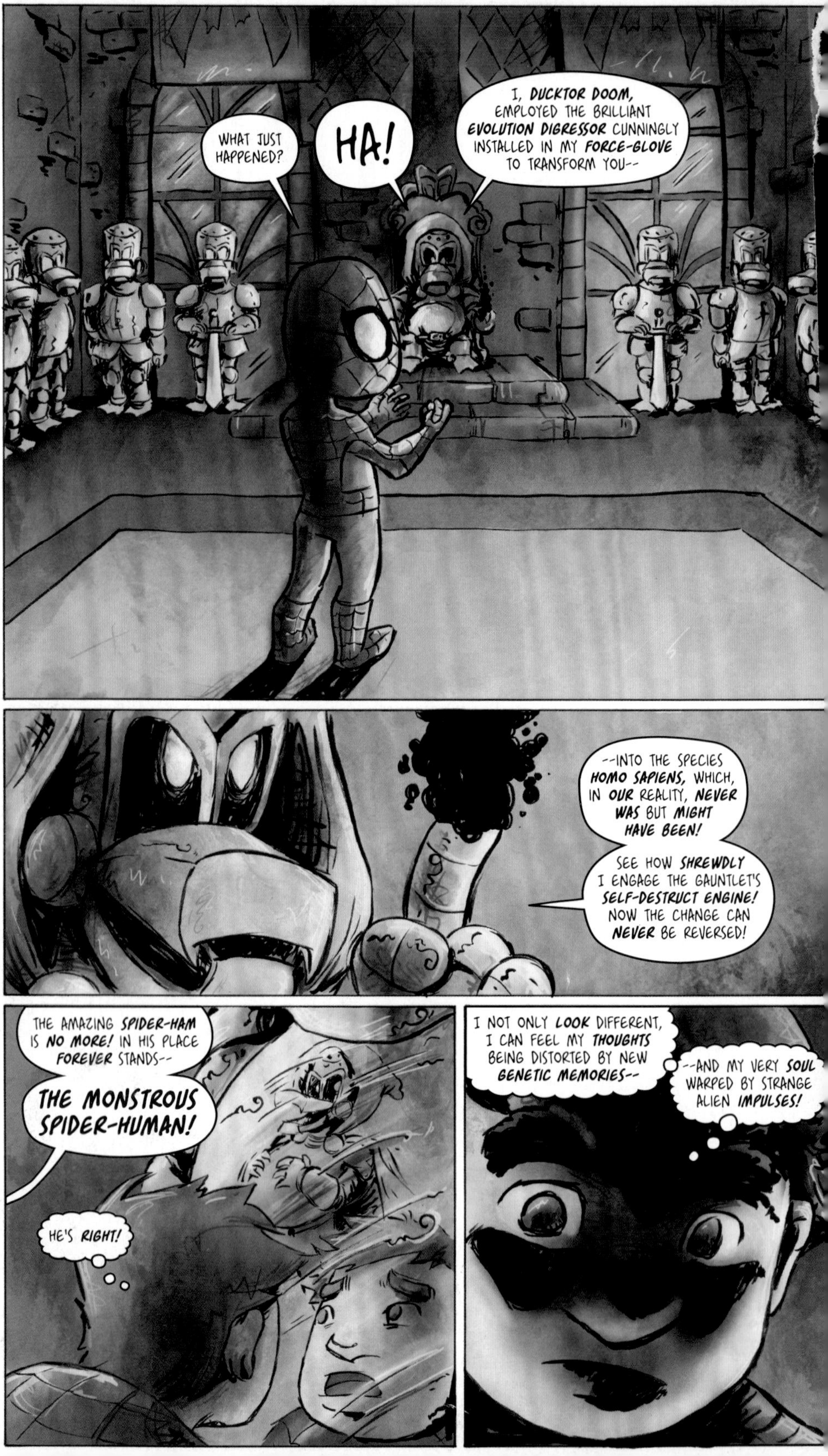
WHAT JUST HAPPENED?
HA!
I, DUCKTOR DOOM, EMPLOYED THE BRILLIANT EVOLUTION DIGRESSOR CUNNINGLY INSTALLED IN MY FORCE-GLOVE TO TRANSFORM YOU--
--INTO THE SPECIES HOMO SAPIENS, WHICH, IN OUR REALITY, NEVER WAS BUT MIGHT HAVE BEEN!
SEE HOW SHREWDLY I ENGAGE THE GAUNTLET'S SELF-DESTRUCT ENGINE! NOW THE CHANGE CAN NEVER BE REVERSED!
THE AMAZING SPIDER-HAM IS NO MORE! IN HIS PLACE FOREVER STANDS--
THE MONSTROUS SPIDER-HUMAN!
HE'S RIGHT!
I NOT ONLY LOOK DIFFERENT, I CAN FEEL MY THOUGHTS BEING DISTORTED BY NEW GENETIC MEMORIES--
--AND MY VERY SOUL WARPED BY STRANGE ALIEN IMPULSES!

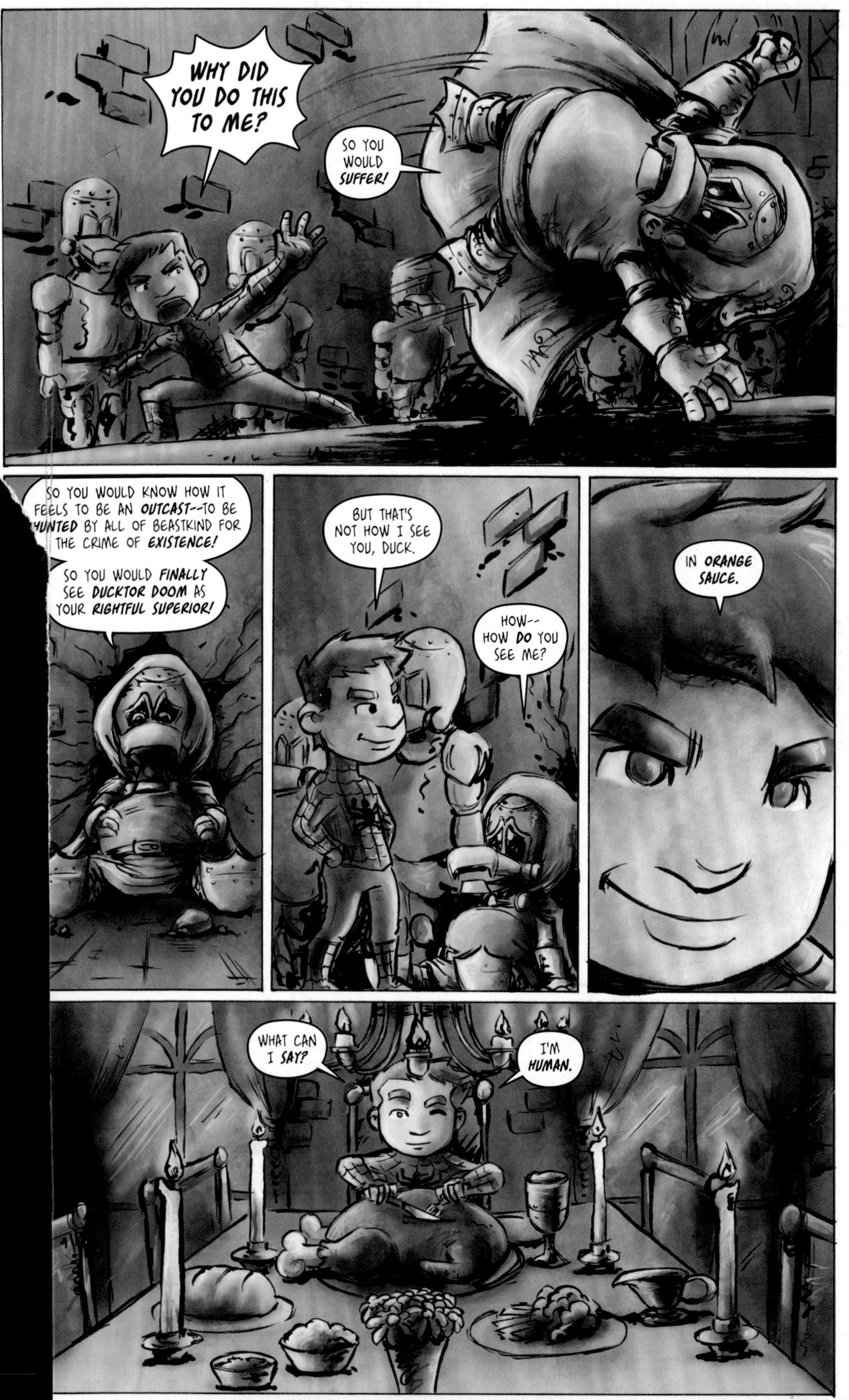
WHY DID YOU DO THIS TO ME?
SO YOU WOULD SUFFER!
SO YOU WOULD KNOW HOW IT FEELS TO BE AN OUTCAST--TO BE HUNTED BY ALL OF BEASTKIND FOR THE CRIME OF EXISTENCE!
SO YOU WOULD FINALLY SEE DUCKTOR DOOM AS YOUR RIGHTFUL SUPERIOR!
BUT THAT'S NOT HOW I SEE YOU, DUCK.
HOW--HOW DO YOU SEE ME?
IN ORANGE SAUCE.
WHAT CAN I SAY?
I'M HUMAN.

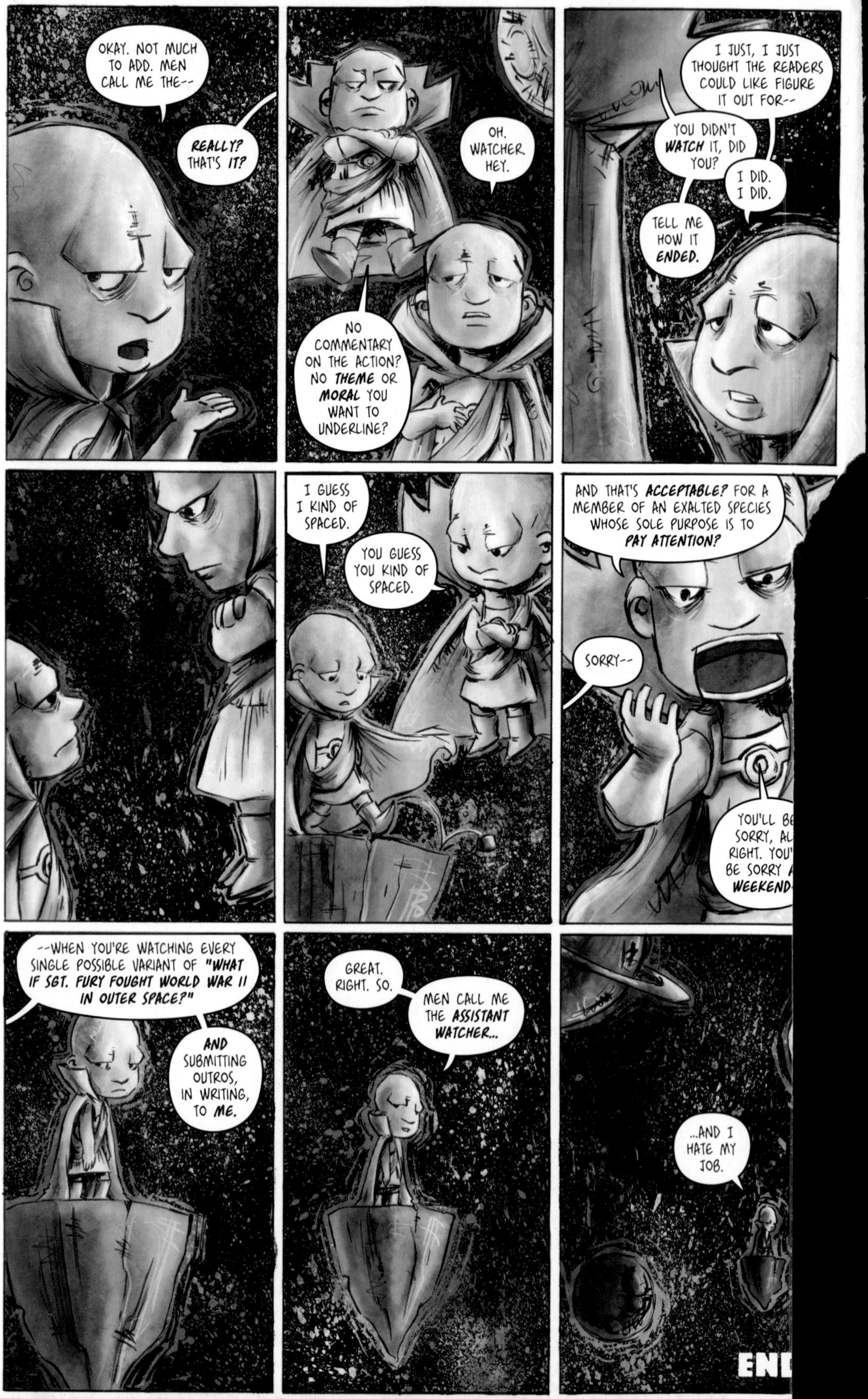
OKAY. NOT MUCH TO ADD. MEN CALL ME THE--
REALLY? THAT'S IT?
OH. WATCHER HEY.
NO COMMENTARY ON THE ACTION? NO THEME OR MORAL YOU WANT TO UNDERLINE?
I JUST, I JUST THOUGHT THE READERS COULD LIKE FIGURE IT OUT FOR--
YOU DIDN'T WATCH IT, DID YOU?
I DID. I DID.
TELL ME HOW IT ENDED.
I GUESS I KIND OF SPACED.
YOU GUESS YOU KIND OF SPACED.
AND THAT'S ACCEPTABLE? FOR A MEMBER OF AN EXALTED SPECIES WHOSE SOLE PURPOSE IS TO PAY ATTENTION?
SORRY--
--WHEN YOU'RE WATCHING EVERY SINGLE POSSIBLE VARIANT OF "WHAT IF SGT. FURY FOUGHT WORLD WAR II IN OUTER SPACE?"
AND SUBMITTING OUTROS, IN WRITING, TO ME.
GREAT. RIGHT. SO.
MEN CALL ME THE ASSISTANT WATCHER...
...AND I HATE MY JOB.